SERVANTS OF THE SANDS, PART II

Leona Wisoker

Breathing Life into Great Books

ReAnimus Press
1100 Johnson Road #16-143
Golden, CO 80402
www.ReAnimus.com

Cover by Aaron Miller

ISBN-13: 9798713519278

Second ReAnimus Press print edition: February, 2021

2102170932
10 9 8 7 6 5 4 3 2 1

This book is for my family: those related by blood and those to whom I am heart-bound. I could not have made it through this journey to date without your support and love.

You know who you are.

Thank you.

Acknowledgements

What is there left to say that I haven't already said in the acknowledgements for the first four books? I'm surrounded by an absolutely amazing community of friends and family. I've learned so much from writing this series: about myself, about the real world, about the craft of writing, about the business of writing and self-promotion. I'm deeply indebted to everyone who's taken a moment to help along the way. There really are far too many people to list here!

That being said, there are three new people I need to thank this time around: L. M. Kate JohnsTon, who reviewed a lengthy excerpt as a sensitivity reader and caught a handful of egregiously foolish mistakes. Malcolm Gin, who has also read some of my work with an eye to pointing out unseen bias. Kat Tanaka Okopnik, whose discussions proved excellent at making me rethink many underlying assumptions. They were not the only people to help, but made the greatest contribution overall. I'm not arrogant enough to think I got everything "right," but any remaining missteps are entirely my own fault and not the result of poor teachers.

I will, as always, point out my wonderful husband, Earl Harris, without whom I absolutely would not have made it this far in so many respects. In addition, over the two years of my frequent travels dealing with my mother's decline, during which much of this book was written, Russell Schroeder and Patrick Winch were equally sturdy supports (and excellent drinking buddies!).

This is the first book in the series that was not edited by Barbara Friend Ish; as much as we both would have loved that, circumstances intervened on multiple levels. Instead, the editor for Servants of the Sands was Edward Morris, a ferociously intelligent gent who beat me about the head and shoulders about adding details and yanking out passive wording alongside my overly beloved em-dashes and semicolons. The book is much, much better for his input.

Last but not least, I owe a deep bow of gratitude to my publisher, Andrew Burt of ReAnimus Press, who gave this series a new home when the original publisher folded. Andrew has been incredibly patient and understanding in spite of the manuscript delivery taking *cough years cough* a bit longer than expected.

Thank you, everyone. Thank you so very, very, very much, for so many, many moments. I hope the book proves worth the wait!

Foreword

Once intended as a three book story, Children of the Desert has sprawled a bit. In part, each book has grown as my grasp of adding detail and complexity of plot has improved; in part, they've expanded because of the need to wrap up plot points from previous volumes.

In Secrets of the Sands, a fairly standard adventure story, a young street thief (Idisio) finds out that he's more important than he ever dreamed of being, and a young noblewoman (Alyea) finds out that she's less important than she thought. Ancient creatures (ha'reye) stir from slumber, raising their heads to take note of a world drastically changed from their last visit to human time. In the deep background, multiple factions (Aerthraim, teyanain, Kingdom, Sessin, Darden, F'Heing, Toscin, and more) are plotting to advance their interests. Deiq, a ha'ra'ha (half human, half ha'rethe), interferes with matters mainly from malicious amusement, and misses the hooks being gently set as he plays with human lives. Alyea's quest for power becomes more about helping others than protecting herself, and she nearly dies in the process. Idisio is forced to revise everything he thinks he knows about himself, and steps up to a visibility he really doesn't want.

Their path takes them from the northern city of Bright Bay to the deep southern Scratha Fortress, where Alyea, who had intended to take charge of the deserted territory in the name of the nothern king, is faced with a very angry Cafad Scratha, who is not in the least willing to cede his claim. Deiq intervenes again, and matters are uneasily settled, with Cafad committing to restart his Family (something he's been avoiding for a long time) and Alyea and Idisio under Deiq's wing to keep them safe as they figure out what to do next.

At the time of writing *Secrets*, I didn't have the skill to show many small moments as clearly as I would have liked. Looking back, I wish I'd been able to show the deviousness of the teyanain, not just their ruthlessness; I wish I'd been able to show why Alyea was so completely biddable in her innocent ambition, rather than pressing for the answers she later learns to demand up front. I wish I'd been able to show that Deiq had repressed so much of his memory, at the time of their first encounter, that he was a completely different person than even fifty years previously, and to hint at how incredibly fortunate that was for all concerned.

But done is done, and after all, that book is written from the point of view of two characters who are completely unaware of what they've walked into.

At the end of *Secrets*, Alyea and Idisio both have a beginning grasp on an entirely diferent sort of power than what they set out to have. They're now People Of Significant Interest, and there's no going back.

In *Guardians of the Desert*, the cast expands, offering more experienced views on the developing situation. Deiq starts off the story with the irritable realization that he's basically promised to help Alyea for an indefinite length of time, which is a colossal waste of his energy; but the aforementioned repressed memories remain locked away, and so he dismisses his annoyance and keeps mentoring Alyea. He also completely fails to point out the danger his tentative allies have put themselves in by restarting Scratha Fortress. He traipses off with Alyea and Idisio, leaving the foolish Cafad Scratha and his household to fend for themselves. Whether he actually allows himself to think about the scope of what he's abandoning is an open question at this point. He's so very good at lying to himself, after all, and those hooks set in the previous book are starting to tug ever so gently.

Alyea and Deiq trade off viewpoints in *Guardians*, the former showing a growing understanding of complexities and the latter a growing awareness of how much he's blocked out of his memory over the years. They run afoul of teyanain plotting, not for the first nor last time, and Deiq is tricked into a nearly intolerable political subordination to Alyea. Returning to Bright Bay, Alyea, Deiq, and Idisio walk straight into more drastic threats: a mad ha'ra'ha is rampaging through the city, searching for something unknown, and a mad human is out for revenge against Alyea. The resulting tangle winds up with Idisio kidnapped, Deiq seriously wounded, Alyea near death, and the appearance of a new face: Tank, a young man with a complicated past and a great deal of raw, largely untrained psychic power. He heals Alyea where Deiq fails, which triggers Deiq into a mixture of intense jealousy and despair. Alyea, in turn, has to bring Deiq back from the edge of destroying himself, and their bond deepens further, even as Deiq's memories start returning and his personality begins to revert to a considerably harsher tone.

In *Bells of the Kingdom*, a fair part of the story overlaps with the beginning of *Guardians*. I felt that the opening situation, a tricky political meeting, was pivotal enough to later events that a thorough examination here would avoid a lot of explanation down the road. Some readers have expressed annoyance at having to read the same events twice over, although through different points of view. Today, I would probably have shortened the overlap considerably or skipped it. At the time, it was a technique I'd always wanted to try, and so I did.

Bells is the most complicated book of the series, in my opinion, with a great deal of emotion, action, and multiple character perspectives packed into a relatively short tale. The mad ha'ra'ha from *Guardians* gets to tell her story, as do a northern priest, Idisio, and Tank. It's not a gentle book. It contains a hefty amount of sexualized violence and abuse by way of obstacles to overcome. It's intended to be a dark book, a stomach punch, and it's also designed to be easy to skip if a reader can't tolerate that sort of tension. I did my best to add enough explanation to the following two books to support stepping around this one.

I will never again write a book like *Bells*. It was hideously hard to write. I cried and felt nauseous throughout most of the process. I never want to get that dark ever again, but it was a side of the story, an angle of the politics, that is so essential to later plot points that it couldn't be avoided or lightened.

Ha'reye are not nice creatures. Ha'ra'hain are not nice creatures. Humans are not nice creatures. That's the underpinning of the entire series, really, and it becomes starkly evident from this point on. No amount of salvation curve can erase the damage done along the way.

In *Fires of the Desert*, the story returns to Deiq, Tank, and Alyea, with a new character added: Eredion of Sessin Family, an aging statesman who's done good in the service of evil and evil in the service of good for so many years that he's having trouble telling the difference these days. Deiq is once more attacked, then abducted to parts unknown. Alyea sets off to rescue him, turning her local political responsibilities over to Eredion. Once more, the teyanain wind up being a central part of both abduction and rescue; there's been a political split amongst them for the first time in centuries. The hooks set into Deiq, back in the first book, get yanked on hard this time. He winds up marrying Alyea in a ceremony far more powerful than he anticipated, which drains away (he thinks at the time) the bulk of his abilities for an unknown length of time.

The ceremony also burns away the last of the mist Deiq's been keeping over his memories, and he sees just how deep the hole he's flung himself into is, and what needs to be done to fix an array of mistakes—including his choice to walk away from Scratha Fortress. Even convinced that he's dangerously crippled, he chooses to leave Alyea behind and heads south at best speed, hoping to be in time to stop a disaster.

In *Servants of the Sands* ... well, you'll have to keep reading to find out, now, won't you?

Servants was the first book I wrote without the guidance of Barbara Friend Ish. It's also a book in which I attempted to gather up the many loose threads from the previous four. I discovered, after initial publication, that I had missed several, despite the excellent guidance of my new editor. One reason for republishing this is that the missing bits have been bothering me so badly that I can't move on without fixing them.

I am a perfectionist, so I see various mistakes I made in this book that I cannot fix because they are too deeply ingrained in the story to change. The one I regret the most involves the trope I fell into regarding Seg, Cafad's closest advisor, a black man with pale blue eyes. I did not know enough, when I wrote the book initially, to avoid that trope; all I can do is promise to never do that again, and hope the reader forgives me this time around.

All substantive changes are in the second volume, including an entirely new ending epilogue chapter that closes out Idisio's story far more satisfactorily. I am extremely grateful to Andrew Burt of ReAnimus Press, for supporting my desire to make the book better both in content and appearance. I dearly hope you, my wonderful readers, like the changes as much as I do.

It's been a long journey from that first page of *Secrets of the Sands*, and I've learned so much along the way. I'm not done with these characters, nor this setting. How long it will take me to get the next book out is impossible to predict. But with this burden off my mind, I'll proceed with more confidence and energy. There's little quite as draining to me as the hovering, anxious surety that I've not done my very best. I'm proud of all of my writing, even the terrible stuff, because each story is markedly better than the previous. And what else can a writer really ask for from life?

On to the story, then. Teth-kavit, and remember: never play a game of chabi with a teyanin.

They *cheat*.

Royal Library Map no. 123: The Southlands and Southern Kingdom

TWO: LIFE IN THE DARK

Chapter 1

The whimsically-named *Wild Eyes* shuddered as it crested another wind-frothed wave. The bitter cold pulled extra creakiness from her thick timbers and added more snap to the flapping of the sails.

Or perhaps it was all Deiq's imagination. The sailors around him, wrapped up in motley layers of cloth right down to the fingernails, seemed completely unconcerned about the violent noises ratcheting into Deiq's sensitive ears. They worked their way along the wind-ropes to their stations and duties with the speed of long practice, laughing in the lulls and tossing fragments of songs back and forth.

Deiq, meanwhile, hung over the rail—downwind, lee, whatever the hells they called it these days—and heaved acid from an empty stomach. His trembling hands were locked onto the rail with a fierceness just shy of splintering the wood as he shivered more from comprehensive disorientation than from chill.

He couldn't feel the ground. Couldn't feel the world around him. Couldn't tell which way was east. He had no sense of time: had he been standing at the rail for moments, hours, days?

It wasn't the first time the fit had come on him. He remembered that much. It wouldn't be the last, either. He hated traveling over water. And from Sandlaen to Agyaer, over the deep waters, was far, far worse than a simple coast hopper would have been.

Should have gone with Teilo after all—underwater would be easier—

Except that he hadn't gone with Teilo because—because—

The tey-b'stibik. I didn't think I'd be able to shift form reliably. I was afraid of drowning.

Drowning, at the moment, seemed preferable to this endless, inside-out agony. And Teilo maybe could have kept him alive long enough, in a crisis, to get him to the surface. Why hadn't he thought of that?

Maybe she could have. But I'm not at all sure that she would *have...* Humans were far too unpredictable, and Teilo, with her centuries of training under the ha'reye of the Jungles, was infinitely more so.

He knew perfectly well that she'd argued for his recall more than once over the years, although she'd stopped short of explaining to the Jungles *why* she was increasingly anxious as to his stability. And he'd always managed to convince his kin that Teilo was overreacting... which had led to her being reprimanded...

Oh, yes, she had multiple reasons to hate him. Best to not put his life in her hands.

Someone slapped him on the back, a large, friendly hand. "Eh, there, Estah," a familiar voice said. "Here, then, have a drink."

A metal flask pressed against Deiq's shoulder. Deeply tempted to tell the human to go away and leave him to die in peace, Deiq somehow made himself loosen one hand of his death-grip on the rail and reached out to take the offered flask.

I remember this. I've done this before. It works.

The chill liquor burned like frozen fire on the way down, exploding in his stomach in a way that should have made everything ten times worse—but for some bizarre reason, instantly cooled his disoriented nausea to a vague background queasiness instead.

The human reclaimed the flask, slapped Deiq on the back once more, and went away about his duties, whistling cheerfully.

"Thank you," Deiq muttered, wiping a hand over his mouth and then his eyes, blinking hard to focus. Belatedly, he remembered—and added—the human's name, "Pinin."

"You ready to get back to work yet, then, Estah, or did you feel like playing with the rail a bit more?" someone else called out sardonically. It took a moment more for Deiq's mind to assign *first mate* to the voice. He searched for a name to match the title, without success. "Ain't done with that mending yet, are you? Go on, then, get moving!"

Deiq drew in a steadying breath and straightened. The sea had calmed considerably. Quite possibly it had never been as bad as the fit had made it seem. He could never entirely trust his perceptions at those times.

At least his control hadn't yet broken. He'd never lost himself so far as to hurt anyone. Hardnosed practicality always won that battle, not kindness. Stranded alone on a ship this large, he'd have no option but to chance the open water.

As he turned and waved at the first mate, he plastered a faintly stupid, genial smile on his face. The man shook his head, rolled his eyes, and moved on without further harassment. Deiq returned to his perch on a coil of rope and collected the scattered bundle of needlework he'd tossed aside in his frenzied dash for the rail. It took some work to untangle the mess and resume the tedious stitching.

I could kill every single one of these humans in the space of one of their breaths. Four of their heartbeats. They'd never see it coming.

His gaze tracked back to the rail, and settled on a husky, fair-haired young man standing, apparently idle, looking out to sea.

Then again, maybe they would.

The young man turned and met Deiq's stare equably. Most humans, Deiq had noticed, shied away from meeting Pinin's gaze. Understandable, in a way, since Pinin's left eye tracked several degrees off from his right, and the flesh around it was noticeably swollen and scabby. Deiq had seen worse deformities over the years, so he'd never flinched.

Pinin raised his metal flask in a friendly gesture, took a swig, then tucked the flask away and went back to staring out at the water. He was—at least as far as the crew knew—the ship's 'listener,' as humans currently called those with a marginal ability to hear or sense the presence of ha'reye and ha'ra'hain.

He'd seen past Deiq's friendly-foolish persona of 'Estah' at their first meeting, of course. There had been a mutually tense moment, when their gazes locked, filled with a rapid measuring and weighing of decisions. Then Pinin simply nodded and accepted the introduction without raising an alarm.

Their first conversation, two days out to sea, had been more troubling. Deiq had taken advantage of a quiet time in both weather and work duties to stand beside Pinin at the rail.

"What are you hearing, listener?" he said without—much— irony.

"Nothing," Pinin said. "Yet. What are you hearing... ha'inn?"

Deiq tilted his head to one side, listening: nothing within miles in any direction, although the faint sense of a lesser ha'ra'ha came from far to the northeast. Not close enough to trouble this ship, however, so he shrugged and said, amiably mimicking Pinin's delivery, "Nothing. Yet."

Pinin nodded, not taking his gaze from the water. "There's something out there that I can't quite place." He swept his arm out in an uncertain, wide gesture—in a different direction than the lesser ha'ra'ha Deiq had sensed. Ropy, puckered scars laced along both of Pinin's arms from wrist to shoulder—yet another visual aberration that tended to make humans intensely uncomfortable. "It's too far away in both distance and time for me to hear it properly yet, but I can feel it in my bones and joints, like a bad change in the weather—only not the same at all."

He glanced sideways at Deiq, one eyebrow raised, as though to see whether Deiq understood. Deiq drew a sharp breath, then said, "You're not just a listener, then. You're a seer."

Pinin smiled and dipped his head in a shallow nod. "Don't tell the crew," he said. "They're a bit skittish about such things. But it makes no sense to try hiding it from you."

"How far ahead do you see? How clearly?" Deiq carefully allowed interest, not alarm, into his tone.

Pinin's right shoulder moved in a faint shrug. "It's not so important. I'm better at listening." Something about his crooked smile as he said the last sentence hinted he'd heard past the pretense.

Deiq kept his tone mild and amiable to avoid conveying any sense of threat as he answered. "It's still impressive that you're taking the risk. I've never met a seer willing to cross the open waters."

Inwardly, Deiq cursed the luck. A listener would have been one thing, but a seer—he wouldn't be able to draw from the crew after all. Seers had an unfortunate tendency to go berserk when they sensed a ha'ra'ha feeding, and the Wild Eyes wasn't nearly large enough a vessel for the distance Deiq would need to avoid alerting Pinin.

"I go where I'm told," Pinin said, his accent sliding back to a rougher sailor-speak as another crewman went by. "I made sure to have someone ready to hold me down when the song came for me, and after that I wasn't never troubled again. They're lazy creatures, aren't they? Only interested in easy takings."

"For the most part," Deiq replied soberly, "I wouldn't disagree. But don't assume that yesterday rules today. Everything and everyone changes."

"True enough," the seer agreed. "I'll keep that in mind, with thanks for the caution."

Deiq nodded and began to turn away.

"Ha'inn." The softness of the seer's tone stopped Deiq. He looked over his shoulder, frowning. Pinin's pale eyes met his without hesitation or fear. "I'll return the caution in turn. Whatever's coming—I can feel this much: it involves you."

Suspicion rose instantly. Pinin's expression was a bit *too* bland. "Nothing more than that?"

The seer touched his left shoulder with two fingers, a sailor's signal for sworn truth. "No. I don't know why you're here, ha'inn, and there's no reason I should. But I'd like a warning if you're planning to send us to the depths."

"I have no intentions of that."

"Ah, but everything changes," Pinin said with a twisted smile, then inclined his head and walked away.

Deiq let him go, unsettled enough already. He stared out at the distant line of the Horn, dread gathering in his bones.

Ever since that conversation, he'd been listening and watching for the disruption Pinin had mentioned. He hadn't slept or eaten much, nerves racking ever higher as the days passed. He almost suspected that Pinin had been playing some strange, malicious seer game—except that seers didn't lie. They only told truth, it was part of their gift. They couldn't lie about visions.

As far as Deiq knew.

He returned to the mending, watched Pinin out of the corner of his eye, and wondered if he might be mistaken about that restriction.

The first break in the pattern came shortly past midnight: a subtle arrhythmia in the way water and wind moved around the ship. Deiq remained still, eyes closed, and listened from his perch on a large water barrel. Another break: a bubbling that raced round the bow of the ship, then faded into the slapping of water against the hull.

It could have come from a large fish, or a school of smaller ones, or any number of ordinary causes. Deiq hadn't set foot on a ship, much less a deep-ocean vessel, in more years than Alyea had been alive. He'd walked *through* the water, even stood beneath the deepest waves for days at a time. Adapting to a form suited for underwater breathing was relatively simple. Being *above* the surface, for some reason, was entirely different. He was always afflicted by a creeping paranoia when on a ship. He could be overreacting.

The shivering dread itching along his spine argued otherwise, and the seer's words rang ghostly echoes along his inner ear: *Whatever's coming involves you.*

An out-of-place ripple sent a hearty splash up against the hull. One of the night watchmen padded over to investigate this time. Deiq stayed still, eyes open now, listening, watching, sensing—and found only a vague not-rightness that increased the uneasy itch to a prickling burn of anxiety.

He rose, unable to stay still any longer, and moved to stand at the rail near the bow. *I hate ships so much.* The irony didn't escape him. He'd made much of his fortune and status among the tharr by way of building a small shipping empire.

The water wasn't the only thing sapping his strength, though. He ran a finger across the tiny bump at the end of his right eyebrow, one of the few tangible reminders of the teyanain ceremony that had tied him to Alyea.

Married. Bound. I'm an idiot. I should have asked Teilo to remove the binding.

She might even have been able to do it without killing Alyea in the process. But would she have made the effort? Doubtful. Alyea didn't deserve to die over his stupidity.

He could almost hear Teilo scoff: *The girl is human. You're the last of the First Born ha'ra'hain. Whose life holds more value? Not hers!*

He didn't agree, *wouldn't* agree. In the long run—meaning centuries and millennia—humans were far more important to this world than even the most powerful ha'ra'hain. They were *flexible,* and inventive, and adapted with astounding speed to changes that would have a ha'reye reeling with shock for a hundred years.

Another splash, and a strange thumping from underwater that died away almost immediately.

If I die, what happens to Alyea?

Bound to a human. Surrounded by water. Weakened even further by tey-b'tibik— the stibik-like powder he now knew he'd secretly been fed for years—and that he had, for a short time, in utter madness, taken voluntarily—

Why did I do that? What idiotic impulse was I following? Oh—Alyea. Again, Alyea. Of course.

Because he'd once again allowed himself to become truly interested in a human, he was currently almost defenseless against anything more powerful than the tharr sailors snoring nearby.

Would I know if she was in trouble? Would I even know if the chains were snapping tight?

An eerie silence had descended. Even the waves slapping against the hull seemed heavily muted, and the air felt thicker by the moment. He shut his eyes and tried to reach out, sensing, listening with stronger senses than simple human vision—and met only a vague grey queasiness, too reminiscent of his fits of disorientation. He withdrew hastily and stood still, breathing hard and staring out into the darkness, hands clenched around the rail.

An ethereal, underwater wail wound into Deiq's bones with shivering force and quicksilver speed. The ship bells sounded a moment later, urgent alarm tones summoning sailors to their feet and to stations.

The tharr almost certainly couldn't hear the much softer sound that brought Deiq to full alert: a smug, huffing teyanin chuckle.

I never asked Evkit if any of his athain have turned against him. This could turn extremely bad very quickly.

Silently cursing the sodden sentiment that had put him into this idiotically vulnerable position, he backed away from the rail. Around him, sailors snatched up harpoons and crossbows, ropes and nets, clubs and boathooks and marlinspikes, anything and everything dangerous that could fend off an attack.

If athain were involved, or another ha'ra'ha, none of the weapons would be any use at all. Deiq didn't point that out aloud. Estah wouldn't know such things.

He put his attention in staying quiet, on staying out of the way, on listening—searching for the first fragment of information that might give him a heartbeat's lead on the choice to fight or escape.

Pinin cast him a sardonic, all-too-perceptive glance as he went by, boathook in one hand and long dagger in the other. Deiq ignored him as irrelevant and kept his focus on matters beyond and below the hull of the ship.

A presence began to form: An intangible pressure, coming from the area of the starboard bow. Not—threatening—exactly, but worryingly familiar. Deiq headed for the bow, grabbing a signal lantern from a startled sailor as he went by. He willed three people out of his way, ignoring their startled yelps at being shoved aside by an invisible hand.

Pretending to be Estah the tharr was a useless game at this point, if athain were nearby.

At the rail, he raised the lantern, strengthening the beam past what ordinary oil and wick should have been able to produce. In a flurry of shouts and scrambling feet, the terrified sailors retreated as far as possible from the apparent witchcraft.

Deiq ignored them, moving the lantern in a slow sweep and directing the light in a widening ray across the dark waters. He paused when he saw the anomaly: A body, limp and silent, being rocked by the waves less than a hefty stone's throw from the hull.

"There," he said over his shoulder, motioning with his free hand to the sailors behind him. "Look. Bring that body aboard."

The captain moved to stand beside Deiq at the rail, squinting out at the body. He looked sideways at Deiq, hostile suspicion clear on his broad face. "I'm not bringing a sea-corpse on board my ship, not by the word of a new deckhand, for sure! Just who in all the hells do you think you are?"

Deiq grinned at the man, drawing on hundreds of years of learning how to frighten humans to shape the expression. "I'll be your worst godsdamned nightmare, if you cross me, Captain."

The color in the captain's face changed from dark to a splotchy, nearly inverse freckling.

Deiq kept his voice low. "Tell your men to bring that body aboard, Captain. Now."

The captain stared into Deiq's eyes as though paralyzed for another moment, then jerked away and began shouting orders that sounded like it had been entirely his own decision. Deiq smiled, watching the confusion among the tharr sort itself out into disciplined action.

He held the lantern steady while nets were thrown and the body was pulled from the sea. Free of the water, the body turned out to be that of an old woman; emaciated, with long pale hair wound like seaweed around her skeletal frame.

Teilo. Apparently underwater wouldn't have been the safer path after all.

Deiq set the lantern aside and knelt beside the motionless form, waving the sailors back. He splayed his hand across her chest, focusing on the nerves in his fingertips. After several seconds, he felt a distinct *ta-thump*, then, several seconds later, another. He sighed in relief and delivered a tiny surge of energy—the equivalent of nudging a tharr's shoulder.

Teilo drew in a shuddering breath. A human heartbeat later her hands locked around his throat, nails digging in hard. Her white-hazed eyes stared into his from a hand span away, her lips drawn back from her teeth.

Dizziness surged through him—nausea—a bizarre feeling of having absolutely no existence at all for a moment—then the world snapped back into focus.

Deiq brought his hands up inside her forearms and shoved outward, breaking her grip at the cost of several scratches on his neck. "Ha-vash!" he said sharply, both aloud and mentally: *Stop.*

She froze, as he'd hoped—just for a moment, but it gave him room to roll aside and come into a defensive crouch.

Ha-ne, he told her. *No harm. Ha-vash.*

She blinked, her head bobbing in an oddly unfocused manner, and drew in another gasping breath. "Deiq?"

"Estah," he corrected her, all too aware of the increasingly hostile ring of onlookers.

Her head turned, her milky eyes moving as though trying to find him. With a cold shock, he realized that she couldn't see him.

"You're blind," he whispered. "Truly blind."

She shut her eyes and shuddered, then dipped her head in confirmation.

The question slipped out before he realized he'd opened his mouth: "What the hells happened to you?"

She said one, bitterly inflected word that turned the chill in his stomach to a searing fear:

"Teyanain."

The word *teyanain* produced instant results in the crew. The ring of onlookers widened perceptibly, and the captain lunged forward a wide, hostile step.

"Oh, bloody hells," the captain said, "I want the both of you gone right now. I've enough to handle without bringing teyanain trouble aboard. Fes, get the longboat ready—"

Deiq stood, slowly, turning to face the captain. "That would not be in your best interest," he said. He locked gazes with the man, summoning conviction. "You're in no danger from us being on board, Captain. I promise you that."

The captain frowned, unconvinced.

Your facility with lying appears to have been affected by your association with Alyea, Teilo observed sourly. He twitched a hand at her behind his back, signaling *Shut up.* She huffed dry amusement, but stayed silent after that.

Deiq could feel unexpected holes in his willpower, unprecedented weakness reflected in the captain's skepticism. He flexed one hand, measuring his remaining strength and hoping it wouldn't come to a physical contest. He wasn't sure how much of that he had left, either.

It was the tey-b'tibik. Had to be. He'd finally accumulated enough in his system to force a conversion to near-human. He cursed the timing, then wondered if Teilo's arrival had anything to do with it. That moment of oddness when she'd touched him—

Had rebel teyanain athain done something to her that would infect any ha'ra'hain she encountered? He wouldn't put anything past them. They'd already tried once to use him as a living weapon that could have killed dozens of innocent teyanain once unleashed. They had no boundaries, no sanity.

"My cabin," the captain said abruptly, after sweeping an assessing glance around at the watching crew. "I've questions for you, Estah. If that's your name at all."

"Of course, Captain. We should get her dried off and cleaned up a bit first." Deiq moved aside a step so that the captain had an unobstructed view of Teilo's dripping, shivering form. "And she could probably do with a hot drink, I'd think."

"You can do all that in my cabin," the captain said tightly. "You lot—get back to work! And don't you bother me until I'm done with these two. Move," he added in lower tones, with an unforgiving glare at Deiq. "Before I come to my senses and have you put over the side after all."

Deiq knelt and helped Teilo to her feet. She leaned on him, trembling as though from a bone-deep chill, seeming nothing more than a frail old woman who'd almost drowned.

It's not entirely an act, Teilo said after a few steps. Her teeth chattered.

Deiq eased his pace, his alarm increasing. *What the hells did they do to you?* he demanded. *And how did they dare?*

The answer to that second question, she said with a flare of bleak humor, *goes back quite some years. The first one is simpler, but still a long story. I'll tell you once we get through this foolishness—and after I've fed.*

He missed a step, stumbling, at the accent she placed on *fed.*

Can't you tell? I'm true-ha'rai'nin now, she said, amused. *I have similar needs to yours.*

"Oh, gods," Deiq muttered aloud.

Don't worry, Teilo told him. *I may not be as attached to human morality as you are, but that doesn't mean I'm completely impractical. There are enough people on this ship to allow me to spread the draw across several lives. They won't even notice—beyond a slight headache, perhaps. Haven't you been doing that yourself?*

Deiq let out a long breath of frustration and shook his head. *There's a seer on board.*

Teilo was quiet for a few steps. *That... could be something of a problem.*

Yes.

Deiq pulled open the door to the captain's cabin and ushered Teilo inside. It was a small room with a narrow bunk. Every bit of wall space was in use: Racks of weapons, document tubes that probably held rolled maps, blankets, books—laid flat against the wall rather than spine out—and, in the odd spaces left, paintings of three smiling children, all under ten, at a guess.

No portrait of their mother to be seen. No signs that a woman was involved in the captain's life. That didn't surprise Deiq. The captain was an austere man, very much dedicated to his ship and his life at sea. In the captain's view, more than likely, children were something to be proud of, but not the ultimately replaceable women who produced them.

Predictably, the captain refused to leave or even turn his back while Teilo dried off and exchanged her sodden clothes for an overlarge sailor's shirt. He stared at her with a ferocious suspicion throughout, as though expecting her to display multiple abnormalities at any moment. Deiq didn't bother protesting. It would have been false outrage, and the captain wasn't stupid enough to miss that.

His sharp hearing picked up an array of shouts from the deck, but he couldn't make out the words without focusing his attention in that direction. The commotion died down a few moments later, and he dismissed it as unimportant. The captain's attention never wavered from the old woman before him.

Teilo sank onto one of the captain's plush, low-slung chairs with a sigh of relief and began braiding her hair back from her face. "Call in your seer, Captain," she said without looking up at him.

"My what?" The captain stared. "I don't have a seer on board! I wouldn't trust one of those *fesh'ii* on board my ship. They're bad luck!"

Deiq cleared his throat and said, "She used the wrong word, Captain, that's all. She's talking about Pinin, your listener."

The captain scowled, then yanked the door open and roared, "Pinin!"

A burly sailor lumbered to the door, his face creased with anxiety. "Pinin's gone, Captain," he reported. "Went over the side, once you was in your cabin here with these folks. We talked on turning to get him, but—" The sailor's gaze went past the captain to skate across Deiq and Teilo briefly. "He told us to leave him be, that he'd be better off swimming with the sharks. We're of a mind to believe him. Oh—he said to give this to Estah." He held out a battered metal flask.

The captain hesitated, then snatched the flask from him. "Keep the rest of the crew on board, if you have to tie them to the mast," the captain snapped.

"Yes, Captain!"

The captain waved the man clear, then slammed the door shut and spun to face Deiq and Teilo.

"What the hells is going on?" he shouted. "Now I've lost my listener because of you? What sort of witchcraft have you brought to my ship? And what's *this*?" He brandished the flask.

"It's... medicine," Deiq said. "I get seasick easily. Pinin's been helping me on bad days."

"Oh, *that's* plausible," the captain said, rolling his eyes, and pointedly set the flask on his desk. "I'm going to give you just enough time—"

"Sit down, Captain," Teilo said.

The captain barreled on, ignoring her. "—to tell me what the hells is going on—and if you don't talk right fast, you'll be over the side to join Pinin. So be convincing!"

"You'll give us as much time as I damn well want," Deiq said, deciding that there was absolutely no point in hiding any longer. "I own this ship, Captain. I'm Deiq of Stass."

"Try another one," the captain said. "I've met s'e Deiq. You're nothing like him." His lips thinned. "You're itching for that swim, aren't you?"

Deiq shut his eyes, concentrating on what he'd looked like before. He'd never be able to recapture it exactly, but the captain's malleable human memory would fill in the gaps—

Nothing happened.

"Thinking up another lie?" the captain inquired tartly.

Deiq blinked, puzzled, and relaxed his eyes, allowing them to slide out of human-normal—

They wouldn't shift.

"Time's up," the captain said. "Any last words?"

Words, yes. Humans were easily stalled with words. "Captain," Deiq said, holding up both hands, palms out, "I'll be honest with you. I'm not quite sure, myself, what's going on, but if the teyanain left this woman floating by your ship, they had no intention of leaving her to drown. You were supposed to pick her up, and that means that if you throw her—or me—off the ship, you'll be irritating the teyanain, at the very least."

There was no value in explaining about the split among the teyanain. That news would only alarm the captain past all chance of negotiation. Best to leave it as simply *the teyanain* for now.

"And having you on board will frighten and upset my whole crew," the captain retorted. "Which will irritate the hells out of me and likely make the rest of the voyage as dangerous as facing anything that the teyanain might do. I'm not interested in a mutiny, Estah, so give me a better reason than that or go swimming."

"Oh, for the love of whatever gods might exist," Teilo snapped. "Sit *down*, Captain! And *shut up.*"

The words cracked through the cabin. The captain blanched, staggered, and sat down on the nearest chair. He stared at Teilo with utter horror on his broad face.

How in the hells did you do that? Deiq said, astounded.

Be quiet, this takes concentration. "He's telling the truth," Teilo said.

Deiq felt the space around Teilo distorting in widening ripples. She was pulling water from the humid air as a source of power. He hadn't even known such a thing was possible, and certainly couldn't have done it himself. Apparently she wasn't *entirely* crippled, after all.

Teilo smirked in his direction, clearly sensing his distress, then turned her attention back to the captain. "This *is* Deiq of Stass. Who I am doesn't matter. What matters is that you're in grave danger. If you want yourself and your crew to survive this voyage, you'll treat us as honored guests until we land, then forget you ever met either of us at all."

She paused, then added, "I'm only giving you that chance because *he* has acquired a ridiculous sense of your common morality." She motioned vaguely in Deiq's direction.

The captain frowned, his shock dissolving under the implicit reassurance of so many spoken words. Humans always seemed to equate talking with safety. More than likely, he'd only heard every third word, and his hindbrain filled in what he wanted to hear for the rest. He folded his arms across his chest, courage returning, and demanded, "What do I get for taking you so far and risking a mutiny, not to mention teyanain on our tail?"

Deiq restrained an impulse to roll his eyes. Humans. Always looking for the greatest advantage. "What would you want that's better than your life?" he asked dryly.

"Life ain't worth much without the money to live it. If you're the one as owns this ship, how about signing her over to me—with a word to keep all my business contacts viable?"

Deiq hummed a moment, as though pondering—no good letting the captain know how trivial his request was, compared to some of the demands he might have made.

"I can do that," he said at last. "It's easiest if you tell everyone that I'm Estah, the son of the man you all knew, and the only heir. Let them know that I was working as ordinary crew to see how the captains I'm going to be inheriting operate—and you impressed me with your quick handling of her rescue." He nodded at Teilo.

"And I'll make sure nobody remembers anything outrageously unusual," Teilo murmured.

Deiq held his expression neutral, hoping the captain wouldn't think too deeply about the implications of that statement. He said, "My factors will recognize the name Estah, if inquiries are made."

The captain rubbed his eyes with one hand and sighed. "I don't know just what I've stepped into, but I'll be glad to see the backs of both of you, whatever the bonuses involved."

"What was your original destination?" Teilo asked.

The captain stared at her for a moment as if debating whether to answer, then shrugged. "Agyaer."

Teilo turned her head toward Deiq. When he said nothing, she nodded and said, regal as any human ruler, "Agyaer will suffice."

"Why, thank you," the captain said heavily, his volatile mood souring once more. "If you'll be so kind as to stay here a bit longer, I'll go address the crew about the—situation. And are you still working as crew, s'e, or do I need to rearrange the workload?"

"I'll work," Deiq said easily. "I signed on to work, I'll carry on as I began."

Teilo gave a faint huffing sound of amusement, derision; Deiq couldn't tell which. "And I'll act as your listener for the duration of the voyage," she added, which earned her another dark stare from the captain.

"Well enough," the captain said. "I'll tell you when you can come out." He sketched a half-mocking bow, glared at Teilo for a moment, then stalked from the cabin.

Silence hung for a few breaths.

"Please, old mother, by all that's still holy in this world," Deiq said as he scooped up the flask from the captain's desk and tucked it into his belt pouch. "Leave them their lives."

Teilo tilted her head, teeth bared in an odd combination of grimace and smile, and made no reply.

Chapter 2

The very air in the reception hall seemed to glitter from the sheer bulk of polished glass in an infinite array of shapes, each finely-cut facet refracting light as though the crystals aspired to imitate diamonds. Candelabra had been decked out with swags of clear glass beads. Sheets of gleaming beads hung along the walls. Each table, indeed nearly every available surface, boasted an exquisite glass sculpture. And of course the oversized formal wall lanterns all had flawless glass panes that reflected the light to ever brighter proportions.

Alyea had a thundering headache from the ostentatious display. It was taking a real effort to keep her pleasant smile in place. At least the other desert lords in the room—Fimre, Renk, and Hoimas—seemed equally discomfited. Renk and Hoimas, distinctly younger than Fimre but still a few years ahead of Alyea, had shifted position throughout the room several times over the course of the evening, obviously seeking a spot where the reflected light wouldn't dazzle their still-sensitive eyes.

They were newer desert lords, both from Sessin Family; long enough out of the final trial to be able to control themselves in public, new enough to be unable to help casting frequent covetous glances Alyea's way. Fimre had offered to intervene. Alyea had declined, more amused than offended by the attention. They had yet to work up the courage to approach her directly, and she was mildly curious to see if they ever would.

She had a feeling Renk would be the one to try first. He was older, and had a sturdy confidence about him that didn't entirely come from being a new desert lord. Hoimas was built more broadly, but his mannerisms tended towards the twitchy, and he visibly deferred to Renk.

Neither of them particularly interested her. She'd already arranged to steer them toward specific palace servants who'd indicated themselves more than willing to *engage in stimulating political conversation*, as the current phrasing went.

The gathering was—on the surface—to welcome the two new desert lords to Bright Bay, to give anyone of status a chance to become more familiar with their nearest southern neighbors. It was one of many such planned events. Given that Families didn't mingle well, each was getting its own special welcome.

More subtly, it was a way for attendees to see Alyea acting in her new role as liaison between southerners and northerners of rank. She and Fimre had introduced the newcomers to the king on their arrival, in a formal court presentation. Tonight, she'd been taking turns with Fimre to make sure each person present had a chance to speak with Renk and Hoimas for at least a short time. She was keeping her silent discussions confined to Fimre. The newcomers were too raw around the edges yet and were likely to let something embarrassing, if not outright politically delicate, slip.

There were so many new points of etiquette like that to remember. Fimre had already caught her just in time on multiple occasions during this evening alone, and embarrassment wasn't doing her headache any good at all.

You're doing fine, Fimre said. *You worry too much, Alyea.*

She shut her eyes for a moment, gathering quiet around her thoughts, then looked across the room at him and jerked her head in silent apology for being 'loud.' He grinned amiably, then steered Renk and Hoimas toward a group of notable merchants who'd gained admission to the gathering more by way of their wealth and political connections rather than any actual claim to noble blood. Two were women: dressed, as Alyea herself was, in loosely flowing pants and long-sleeved tunics. They wore boots with elevated heels, one of the more recent fashions to sweep the city. Alyea hadn't adopted that one, preferring soft-soled shoes that let her feel the floor underfoot clearly.

Hama would have been incensed from floor to ceiling, as the saying went. But times were changing in Bright Bay, and the rigid hierarchy Hama had supported was dissolving into a muddy mixture filled with merchants richer than noblemen—merchants who, in many cases, loaned money to noble families.

The introduction of southerners, who had a political and status system completely different from that of the north, made measuring relative status a near-nightmare by traditional standards—which was where Alyea came in. She could explain, in terms most northern minds could easily grasp, exactly where a given southerner stood in relation to the king.

It was more difficult to convince desert lords that the northern king, under northern rules, had to be treated as politically superior, rather than someone only barely on equal footing. Most desert lords, Alyea was finding, had been groomed with an enormous bias against northern nobility of any sort. Understandable, in one way, because southern culture generally gave more respect to those of ability and proven service—such as desert lords—rather than measuring their worth solely by their relationship to the Head of their Family.

Understandable, but no less difficult to overcome. Fimre had been a tremendous help, over the last few days, in knocking the typical Sessin arrogance from the two newcomers. His encounter with Deiq had given his words a weight—with people of his own Family, at least—that Alyea could never match.

It had also left him with strong silver streaks in his dark hair, a permanent limp, and occasional difficulty speaking. Most of the damage to his tongue had healed, but the months of recovery had implanted a reflexive slurring that he was having trouble training himself out of.

She noticed that he was leaning more heavily on his cane than usual, the line of his jaw and shoulders tight.

Fimre, she said without sound. *Do you want to rest?*

His head jerked in a barely perceptible nod, his mouth tightening. She could feel his stubborn pride, his determination to not appear weak in front of the king and the new lords alike.

Good, Alyea said. *I have a headache that's threatening to rip my ears off at the seams.*

He smiled briefly. She worked her way across the room to Fimre and his charges, politely deflecting the few attempts to draw her into conversation. She eased the three desert lords out of their various conversations; smiling, never apologizing, but leaving no ruffled feathers behind. As she steered the group over to King Oruen, heads turned, watching with narrow-eyed calculation.

Walking together like this, the three Sessin men were striking, from intricately braided hair to the chain-linked series of hoops in each ear; from the bracelets covering their forearms—Fimre sported considerably more bracelets than the new lords—to their belts, which mimicked the chain-loop pattern of their earrings. Their straight-backed, nearly synchronized pace came across as arrogant to northern eyes, while southerners considered it a sign of respect to the status of the company.

The noise level, to Alyea's relief, slowly died down to near silence as she neared the king's seat. Not a throne; that would have been offensive, an unearned declaration of superiority over his primary guests. He'd chosen to use a heavy chair carved with a number of symbols, drawn from both northern and southern sources, all indicating peace, prosperity, diplomacy, and neutrality. Fimre and Alyea had worked with the crafters on the chair design. Oruen's only, slightly plaintive request had been to include a thick cushion.

Oruen's dark hair, cut to shoulder length these days, had begun streaking with silver as well. Not through a fight with a ha'ra'ha, fortunately, but from the simpler pressures of bringing a chaotic political, economic, and social mess back into reasonable order. His formal blue and green robes were as deliberately crafted as the designs on his chair, and he wore a single thick bracelet on each arm: one of white, and one of black.

He stood as Alyea and her companions arrived, set his feet together and bowed deeply.

"Lords Sessin and Lord Peysimun," he said.

Facing Oruen put Alyea's back to the worst of the glittering display. She could feel her eyes beginning to relax from the squint she'd been fighting all night. Her headache was getting worse by the moment, but in a peculiar manner—she could only think of the word *sideways* to describe it. And *inverted*. Neither of those terms made any sense, but it was an effort for anything to make sense through the haze of pain.

"This gathering is wonderful, Lord Oruen," Fimre said. "I'm truly honored by the effort you've put into hosting us tonight."

The two newcomers nodded and visibly tried to look happy, but Alyea saw the faint lines of strain around their eyes. They were as exhausted as Fimre, and too proud to show it. Oruen's eyes narrowed briefly, his expression assessing. He cut a quick glance at Alyea, and she dipped her chin in a scant nod. The motion prompted a skitter of disorientation along her inner ear.

She blinked hard, straightening her back, and focused on staying upright and looking serene.

"It's been a long evening," Oruen said, raising one hand to wave a servant over. "Would you forgive me if I withdrew a touch early tonight?"

"Of course, Lord Oruen," Fimre said, smiling. "We will look forward to our next meeting." He backed up a step, signaling the others to do the same, then bowed deeply.

Alyea began to bow as well. A wave of disorientation staggered her sideways before she'd more than barely inclined her torso. Her legs went out from beneath her, and she sprawled on the cool tile floor with an undignified yelp.

"Alyea!" Oruen blurted, taking a step forward. Fimre hastily raised a hand. The king stopped, color washing into his face.

He still cares, Alyea thought vaguely, struggling to her feet. *That's important. Why?* A moment later, the headache went away as though it had never existed, leaving behind a dreadful, crystalline clarity. *Because it's a weakness.*

Her peripheral vision blurred, then changed, while Oruen came into a bizarrely sharp focus. She could *see* him—not just the outer body, but the map of muscle, vein, and bone. She could sense his heartbeat, the sore spot on his right leg, the bruise on his left shoulder. She blinked, and vision shifted again, this time mapping out emotional lines—Immediate: he was frightened by her collapse—and longer-running: He'd been having trouble sleeping again, his night filled with worry over the impossible task of getting it all right.

Another blink, and the two maps merged, overlaying, weaving together in a mad chaos that somehow made complete sense. In the very center of those maps, in a place unrelated to the center of his body, was a spot—a dark, yet multicolored density that drew her attention like a magnet to metal.

Somewhere far away, a man's voice said, "Good gods—Alyea—your eyes—" The words held awe and horror in equal measure.

Another voice, closer to hand, wove into her mind: *Alyea, stop!* The words carried a welter of other impressions: *Holy gods, she's hitting the change now? No—that can't be it—look at her eyes—what's happening to her? I've never seen anything like this—what the hells is going on here—have to get her out of here quickly—*

She snarled at the notion of anyone making her do anything she didn't want to do... and she *didn't* want to leave. That density inside of the human before her was compelling, hypnotic, seductive. She had to look at it more closely, had to touch it, to see how it felt—

The human wailed. Astounded and intrigued, she watched lines of pain sparkle throughout his body. The patterns were *beautiful.* A shape moved between, blocking her line of sight. A hard shove put her back several stumbling steps, and the connection broke. The same blurry form pushed itself close and shouted her name.

Stop, that voice said inside her mind. *You don't want to do this, Alyea, you'll kill him—for the love of the gods, take me, I'll at least survive—*

She refocused, and saw lines of nearly animal terror wound throughout the man before her: Memories of darkness, and jumbled, tumbled impressions that wouldn't quite come clear. She looked for the density, and it was there—oh, it was there, so much stronger and larger and more interesting than the first human's had been.

Please, Alyea, the voice said, *Get us out of here first. Don't do this here. Please!*

She paused, thinking about that plea. Then she became aware of the crowd: the shock, the hostility, the approach of those who would take her rightful prey from her. She could fight, could kill them all, easily—but then her prey might escape in the confusion, and she was *hungry* in a way she'd never experienced before.

She grabbed the shape before her with hands and willpower—it flinched but made no true protest—and moved them both elsewhere. A familiar room came into focus around her. Murals that should have been hidden by the dark seemed to glow in a strange, amber-tinted vision. For the first time, she saw the flaws in the paintings: Every gap, every spot where the intent and the understanding didn't—quite—match up. Human sight hadn't seen the colors and lines where the artist had gotten it wrong.

She saw how to fix it, given the right tools; saw the lines to connect and the arcs to complete, the colors to change. But not right now. Right now—

—She was *hungry*—

The form before her whimpered and thrashed in futile reflex, then broke into a full scream a moment later, as she reached into the density. The noise annoyed her. She stilled the vibrating throat muscles with a moment's concentration, then returned to reveling in the glorious sensations evoked by contact with that dark solidness.

After a time, the amber vision faded to match the darkness of the density, and all sensation evaporated. She hung in emptiness, feeling nothing, thinking nothing, sensing nothing—barely aware of her own existence, a tiny grey thread against an eternal field of black.

Slowly, slowly, that thread widened and expanded into a ribbon, then a road. With a strange roaring sound, it resolved into the grey of a stone-walled room barely lit by a cloudy dawn.

She lay on her back, staring up at the unpainted ceiling, for some time; not thinking, not remembering, simply watching the light changing from a pale grey to a topaz flush. Someone else was breathing nearby, but that seemed unimportant compared to the sound of her own heartbeat and the rasp of her own breath in her throat.

I'm alive, Alyea thought, and didn't know why that surprised her so much. She turned her head slowly.

Fimre was sprawled limp as a dead snake across the floor nearby, his breathing shallow but steady. The silver in his dark hair had turned stark white, and most of the black had turned silver. A stubble of beard darkened his chin: at least two days' growth, possibly more.

You're not going to sleep as often, Deiq had told her at one point. *But if you push yourself too hard, or if you're injured, as soon as you're in a place of safety you'll sleep for days. As you did after I rescued you from Kippin. I've seen some desert lords sleep for* weeks.

She inhaled through her nose, testing the air: No blood, so she hadn't hurt him *too* badly. What would be left of his mind, though....

She considered that question without any particular remorse as she watched Fimre breathe, measuring the slow strengthening of each inhale, the color seeping back into his face, the beginning twitches as he rolled out of the depths of his exhaustion.

Eventually he sucked in a long, shuddering breath and opened his eyes. Moisture overflowed, sliding down into his ears, slinking round to his neck and down to the floor. He drew several more shuddering breaths, blinking his eyes clear every few moments. Then he raised a shaky hand to wipe his face and ears clear—pausing to rasp his fingers through the beard growth as though counting the days in the stubble—and met Alyea's gaze, unflinching.

"Where are we?"

"Deiq's tower," she answered, distantly relieved. The question indicated that his sanity was reasonably intact. She looked at the walls again, studying the artwork. She still saw weak spots, and remembered how to bridge the parts where Deiq hadn't quite gotten it right. Not as clearly as before, but she knew how to shift back into the amber vision. She'd fix the mistakes when she had time—not now, though. Now she had other responsibilities.

She looked back at Fimre. He'd shut his eyes and lay quietly, just breathing. She could feel him slowly putting his disarrayed internal landscape back into order. She waited until he steadied, then said, "Thank you, Lord Fimre."

"Duty done," he said with a bleakly sardonic lilt, then sat up, steadying himself with both hands. "What the hells just happened? And how long have we *been* here?"

She considered that question, turning over various answers, but Fimre wouldn't be able to understand any of her own tentative guesses without more explanation than she cared to give. In the end, she said, "I'm not sure myself."

"The hells you aren't," he said, his stare turning dark. "You *fed* from me. It would have been a kindness for someone to tell me you're actually ha'ra'hain!"

She shook her head and climbed to her feet with immense care, each small motion feeling wildly exaggerated. At least they both still had their clothes on. She'd avoided taking Fimre to bed thus far for a variety of political and personal reasons. It was a relief that they hadn't breached that careful separation.

"I'm not ha'ra'hain," she said, brushing a hand over her clothes to ease the wrinkles. "I don't understand what's going on, either, Fimre. But I think we'd both better go find out if the king is still alive."

Chapter 3

Dawn turned black and wet to grey and wet. Idisio sat on a log and watched the transition, unblinking except to shift in and out of the amber-edged vision his mother had so brutally taught him about. Not far away, in a small tent, Kolan snored quietly. Idisio sharpened his hearing to pick out the tiniest inflections of each raspy inhale and exhale, muffled his hearing until the world was wrapped in a dense silence, then returned his hearing to what he'd come to think of as human-normal.

The rain dappled down around him, not quite ever landing on his skin or clothes. The chill in the air was something he recognized without directly feeling. Deiq had tried to teach him this trick and failed. Ellemoa's savage approach had been more effective.

Idisio's mood, as grey as the daylight, soured further. For all that he'd mistrusted Deiq as dangerously amoral, Idisio's own mother had turned out be far worse.

He pushed aside the memories before they deepened into brooding—which always brought her voice soaring into his conscious mind, pushing for violence, pushing for pain—and stood, stretching. Kolan's snores cut off abruptly, followed by a snorting cough as the man awakened. Idisio held still, waiting; after another few breaths, Kolan said, "Idisio. Good morning."

"Good morning." Kolan emerged from the tent, pushing untidy, shaggy hair from his eyes. His scrawny frame had filled out somewhat since Idisio had first met him, and his grey eyes held less anguish. He would never be considered handsome—years of imprisonment and torture had furrowed too many harsh lines and scars into his skin—but as he returned Idisio's smile, he looked briefly young again.

Spending time on what he considered holy land, resting among his fellow priests in the swamp settlement, had done Kolan good. The experience had unsettled Idisio tremendously, and by the end of the visit, the priests had been openly uncomfortable around both of them. But it made Kolan happy, and that had been enough—barely—for Idisio to keep his manners in place.

"You didn't sleep, did you?" Kolan said, casting a critical gaze across Idisio's face. "Again. You can't keep doing that."

"I know," Idisio said, keeping his tone mild despite a brief flare of annoyance. Kolan occasionally pushed into *mothering* territory. Or, at least, what Idisio thought mothers were supposed to be like. His own... hadn't been like that. He pushed that aside, adding, "I'll sleep tonight. You needed a proper rest yourself."

Kolan nodded, accepting that, and began packing up the campsite. Idisio sat down on the log again and waited. They'd agreed, weeks ago, to switch lead roles from day to day. This was Kolan's turn. Idisio sat still and let the other man do things his way without interfering. Kolan would ask if he wanted help with anything—not that he ever did.

It reminds me that I'm alive and free, he'd said once. *Ordinary tasks are still miracles to me. I enjoy focusing on every moment of the work at hand.*

Idisio didn't—quite—understand, but he didn't have to. Simply accepting was enough for now. It was a long trek back to Arason, especially along what passed for a path through the boggy, hilly, forested lands this side of the Ugly Swamp. They would have plenty of time to discuss their respective pasts.

Absently, he reached into his belt pouch and withdrew a folded piece of paper. It had grown smudged and worn around the edges, and one corner had a small piece missing. He hadn't ever opened it. Didn't know what it said. Only vaguely remembered his mother handing it to him. She'd said something about the paper holding answers that he'd been looking for.

Given the sort of *answers* she'd been offering him before her death, he didn't really want to know this one. Once again, he tucked it away, down at the bottom of the pouch, and once again promptly forgot that he'd been fussing with it at all.

His mother had shown him a vast world of possibility to explore. Idisio now knew that he could step across miles in a matter of heartbeats. They could reach Arason much more quickly that way, even though the effort carried a price Idisio didn't much like to pay. Fortunately, Kolan refused anything faster than an ordinary, plodding pace.

I'm enjoying every single step, he said when Idisio, feeling unusually impatient with their slow pace, pressed the point once. *We aren't in any hurry. We can take our time.*

Time. For some reason that word resonated like a newly-struck bell in Idisio's mind, and memory unrolled: *A strong hand gripping his wrist, a hawk-fierce glare drilling into his soul—*

Idisio blinked in and out of other-vision several times to dispel abrupt disorientation.

I should have stayed on the streets... I should have left you there....

He shut his eyes and shook his head hard, anxiety rising thick and sharp in his chest.

"Idisio?" Kolan said. "What's the matter?"

Idisio opened his eyes and made a helpless gesture with one hand. "I don't know. Just—visions, memories—"

If you ever need anything—

Idisio's stomach twisted as the memory of his own voice skewed into his inner ear. "No," he said aloud, "Oh, no. No—"

If I can help you with anything. I will. I owe you everything.

A single, silent nod, sealing acceptance of the offer—

Cafad Scratha's voice came, as clear as though he stood beside Idisio in that moment: *"Idisio. I need you to come back. And Riss needs you. Please."*

The pressure in his chest moved down into his guts and became an urgent, burning sensation. Idisio splayed a hand across his stomach and bent double, moaning.

"Idisio!" Kolan's voice was closer now, with overtones of *about to grab hold and shake.*

Idisio put up his free hand in hasty warning to stay back. "I have to go," he said thickly, pushing himself to sit upright again. "I'm being called. I have to go."

"Called?" Kolan's pale eyes narrowed, the lines in his face deep with alarmed concern. "Who's calling you?"

"A friend," Idisio said. "I made a promise. I have to go."

Kolan nodded once, as Scratha had done. "Go. I'll be fine on my own. Meet me in Arason when you can."

Idisio struggled to his feet. The burning faded to a background pain, and his mind cleared rapidly. He shut his eyes, forcing himself to think before he took a single step. If moments mattered, it was already too late. He could move fast, and even skip across miles in a heartbeat, but Scratha Fortress lay far to the south. He would have to rest often along the way—unless he fed—which, given the lack of desert lords in the area, would mean leaving a trail of bodies behind him. Much like Deiq, he found that an obscene concept.

Think it through.

It would take time. It would take so much *time.* Another distracting thought arose: *I'll see Riss again.* No doubt she'd moved on, but... he'd see her again. Was that a good thing? What if she had found someone else to share her time with? His stomach churned with conflicting emotions.

He realized he'd reached into his belt pouch again and was fiddling with the bit of paper. He looked at his hands, looked at his fingernails, looked at his wrists, and finally admitted he couldn't look straight at the paper. He was never going to be able to open it and see what it said. More than likely another *gift* from his twisted mother. She would have found great amusement in watching him strive to overcome her compulsion.

Time. He didn't have time to stall over a piece of paper. He thrust the note at Kolan, who took it with a bewildered expression that swiftly changed to distaste as he dropped the paper to the ground. "What are you trying to do?" he demanded, hard and hostile.

"Read it, if you can," Idisio said. "Burn it if you can't. My mother said it had answers I wanted about something that happened in Kybeach." He waved Kolan silent as the man began to ask more questions.

No time. Time. No time. He turned in place, like an asp-jacau chasing its own tail, scowling, trying to regain his focus.

If Cafad was calling on Idisio for help, then things had gone bad, past even a desert lord's ability to handle; more than likely, that meant Scratha ha'rethe was involved.

Killing one mad ha'ra'ha did *not* mean Idisio was up to opposing a full ha'rethe. He needed to gather help. He needed—

Torchlight glimmering along red hair, catching yellow highlights from blue eyes, a stare that could drill through rock—Idisio's mother hissed, far away, her memories overlapping with his, showing that meeting through a different perspective. *A bond, flaring into argent life*—Idisio had never seen nor sensed that, but his mother saw it clearly, saw a connection between her son and the redhead who'd been trained to kill their kind. Her alarmed bewilderment in the following moments: *He'll kill me. But he doesn't want to kill my son. I don't understand! It doesn't make sense.*

Yessssss... his mother whispered, pleased now, straining forward. She wanted to see the redhead again, wanted another chance at destroying him, revenge for his attack on her. *He dared to strike me! You have to punish him, son, you have to....*

Idisio shook his head, hard. "You're dead, *shut up*," he muttered, then looked up to find Kolan narrow-eyed and taut with wariness.

"Still hearing her?" he asked.

Idisio shrugged, turning away, forcing internal vision narrow, locking himself into thinking only of Tank, of being near Tank—

—the world slipped sideways and inside out for a heartbeat—

—And Idisio stood elsewhere, miles away, miles to the west: neatly laid stone under his feet, a familiar sign in front of him.

The Grey Salt Tavern.

He'd been here once before, with Scratha and Riss. He could still remember the rainy, muddy weather they'd ridden through that day. In early morning sunlight and under clear skies, the tavern proved to be a sturdy building with more windows than Idisio recalled—then again, given the weather, no doubt they'd been shuttered tightly. The shutters were pinned open this time, and the aroma of pipe smoke and bacon drifted through the air.

Idisio drew a breath and glanced around. Nobody stared, nobody fled—nobody in sight, which was a miracle all its own. He sighed in relief and took a step toward the door, which opened a moment later to reveal a familiar burly, redheaded young man in dusty travel clothes.

Punish him, Idisio's mother said instantly, her fury turning his vision yellow for a heartbeat. He pushed her back once more: Tank was hypersensitive to impending threats.

The air lit up in a wavering line between himself and the redhead: the bond his mother had seen, now visible to Idisio. He found himself as bewildered by that as she'd been. He and Tank *weren't* close, hadn't shared anything particularly intense, didn't even trust one another.

Tank's attention instantly focused on Idisio. He took two steps clear of the door, drawing it gently shut behind him; steadied his stance and said, "No. Whatever it is—no."

Pressure built along the edge of Idisio's bones, an awareness of how much that long leap had taken out of him.

Feed, Ellemoa said, a tiny whisper in the back of his mind, growing in strength with every word. *You have the right. Feed!*

A vague aura formed around Tank's entire body, a yellowish, inviting haze. Idisio drew a long breath, fighting to ignore the urgent pressure. He said, "Tank—"

"I. Do. Not. Fucking. Care." Tank's blue glare could have frozen fire. "*No.*" His weight shifted to his toes, his shoulders loosening in clear readiness for a fight.

Tendrils of red and orange crept into the yellow, conveying a sense of imminent danger. Idisio hesitated, considering that feral determination. Tank waited, unmoving, alert, watchful, *dangerous.* Thready aches wound into Idisio's lower back, a reminder that he *promised* to help Scratha, that he had sworn an oath—he *had* to bring Tank, he *needed* Tank, he could feed, he could *feed....*

Feed, his mother insisted. *Why starve yourself for the sake of a human?*

No. His mother wouldn't have said that. She knew exactly how dangerous Tank was. That had come from some other part of Idisio's mind. His heart rattled in abrupt terror—was he going mad at last? No. *No. I'm not like that. I don't have to be like that.*

Gods, even knowing better, Idisio wanted to reach—and take—there was something so dreadfully compelling about the redhead's aura—

He began to raise a hand, helpless to stop himself.

"Not another word, not another step," Tank said. "I'll slam you into last week if you come at me." His tone cut like an ice blade, slicing through the ravening imperative. Idisio gulped in a deep breath, incredulous and grateful, and tucked his arms tight against his sides.

How dare you refuse me: Ellemoa's voice, truly hers this time, filled with savage anger, pushing for violence—for revenge, for *pain....*

Idisio bit his tongue, stopping the anger before it crested into action. He cast a deliberate glance around, checking for onlookers; then said, "Please."

Tank's eyes narrowed. A heartbeat, two, three went by. Red and orange faded to paler colors. "No. I'm not leaving Dasin again. He wouldn't survive it."

Idisio opened his mouth to ask *Who's Dasin*—but discovered that as usual, his odd intuition—ha'ra'hain vision, as it had turned out to properly be named—filled in sufficient details: *lover / friend / wounded / victim / employer / partner.* The concept came limned in a brilliant swirl of green and white, shot through with threads of red and gold. Tank was *attached* to Dasin with complex intensity. There was no separating them, and judging by the pattern of those swirls, even less chance of bringing Dasin along.

Idisio said, carefully non-challenging, "Who do you suggest, then?"

Tank's mouth stretched in a strangely humorless grin. "Try talking to Alyea," he suggested. "She's got everything I could bring to the table and then some."

"When did you meet—"

Tank's eyes narrowed, dangerous colors flaring into the bond once again.

Idisio held up both hands. "Never mind. I'll get the story from her."

"Good idea," Tank replied. "Now piss off before Dasin sees you."

Idisio nodded, sketched a half-polite, half-ironic bow that brought a real smile to Tank's freckled face, then focused on Alyea and *moved—*

—into a familiar hallway, but not the one he'd expected: not into Peysimun Mansion. In front of him was a plain grey door. Smoke and bacon lingered in his nostrils for another heartbeat, then drained away to the scent of metal, oil, sweat, stone, and the sense of poorly circulated air within a large human structure.

Muscles tightened throughout his back. *Trapped, trapped, have to get out, have to have to have to get get get away*—Two guards faced him, northern livery over thick chainmail adding to their already considerable bulk. Helmets narrowed their faces to a shallow view of eyes to chin. One had darker skin; the paler man was taller, but both presented identical hard stares. They were already bringing their polearms down to rest against his chest.

Idisio held still, hands slightly out from his sides, palms forward in a placating gesture, and tried to breathe through the burgeoning panic. There was a haze over his senses, as though he'd been stripped of anything extra. He knew this feeling. *Oh, no, no....*

He risked a glance down at his feet. *Yes. Damnit.* He stood on a series of pale yellow blocks. He'd seen that composite before: Aenstone. It blocked nearly all ha'ra'hain abilities.

That stone hadn't been here the last time he'd visited the king. Apparently Oruen, or his advisers, had decided that there were entirely too many crazy ha'ra'hain running about. The palace was more than likely riddled with the stuff now.

Deiq would have found it an outrageous insult. His mother would have considered it a killing offense. Idisio, reluctantly, admitted that it was a smart move on the humans' part.

The sharp points of the polearms rested ever so gently against his shirt, a light nudge away from slicing into skin. The guards watched him, very nearly unblinking; not hostile, but alert in a way that spoke of special training toward this exact type of situation. They didn't speak, but the shorter one moved a foot sideways, tapping a small gong once. The sound resonated at a painful pitch. Idisio winced, closing his eyes until the vibrations faded from the air.

The guards didn't move, their gazes unfaltering. An ugly sense of impending violence threaded through the back of his mind, a hiss filling his ears. *They dare, they dare... they're going to hurt you, attack, attack!*

Idisio drew in a shallow, calming breath and said, "S'es. I'm no threat. My solemn word. Please tell the king that ha'inn Idisio would like an audience, if he has a moment."

"Stay still," the taller guard said, and let himself through the grey door without a backwards glance. The other guard didn't so much as twitch, his attention—and his weapon—still aimed at Idisio.

Idisio kept his breathing even and ignored the black spots appearing in the back of his mind. He tried not to look down at the stone underfoot; seeing it straight on made the hissing louder, clearer, more present.

Never again: a distant whisper. Even killing his mother hadn't been enough to shut her up. Maybe if he'd done it another way, she wouldn't be writhing through his mind like this; but then again, he'd gone with the only method he'd been certain would work. There hadn't been time to sort through better options.

Time. Time. No time, no time... The pressure felt hollow this time, an echo, a ghost of its former force. He was able to push it aside easily.

The door swung open all the way. From within the room, the guard said, "Three steps inside. No further."

The remaining polearm lifted away from Idisio's chest. He let out a much deeper breath than before and took four careful steps forward—one to the doorway, then three more. The entire room had been floored in pale yellow stone, and it was speckled throughout the walls.

Oruen rose from his chair with ostentatiously calculated leisure, his mouth set in a thin line. "Ha'inn," he said. "It's my honor to host you today." He wore his formal robes of blue and green, a blatant warning that this, unlike last time Idisio had been in this room facing him, was *not* going to be in any way an 'informal audience.' His dark hair had considerably more grey in it than Idisio remembered, and he radiated a tight sense of strain.

"I can tell," Idisio said dryly. "I'm feeling quite welcomed."

"You've not been doused in stibik powder," the king returned sharply. "That is a strong welcome for your kind, these days."

They want to cage us... They have no right... How dare they! his mother snarled.

Idisio passed a thoughtful glance around the room, noting the aenstone in the walls, the alert guard in each corner.

Alyea was nowhere in sight, which seemed odd. His focus should have brought him straight to her. For all he knew, though, she could be watching from a spy-hole somewhere. The mass of aenstone stopped him from sensing her presence.

Shame it couldn't shut his mother's voice up. That, at least, would have been useful.

"I take it something extraordinary happened after I—left," Idisio said.

"Several extraordinary things," Oruen said without a trace of a smile. "Why are you here, ha'inn?"

Idisio laced his hands before him, trying to reduce whatever sense of threat was setting that sharpness in Oruen's voice. He said, carefully, courteously, "I'm looking to speak with Lord Alyea of Peysimun."

The king's regard deepened into a regal glare. "Interesting," he said. "The timing, especially. What do you want with Lord Alyea, ha'inn?"

Idisio opened his mouth to answer, then stopped, intuition nudging at him again. *I outrank him. I need to act like it.*

"Lord Oruen," he said, "I don't want to be rude or disrespectful. I have nothing against you that I know of. But my reasons are my own, and not your concern. Where is Lord Peysimun?"

The king's voice stretched taut, his glare nearly feral as he said, "In prison for trying to kill me."

Idisio blinked a few times, speechless. "I—she—you—*what*?"

Chapter 4

The back of Alyea's tongue soured to a harsh, strained feeling as soon as she set her hand on the latch to the outer door. "Wait," Fimre said at the same moment. "There's someone outside."

Alyea shut her eyes and focused. "More than one," she told him. "Six."

Fimre snorted. "They're not here to be friendly, I'm guessing."

"No." She reached out, focusing more intensely than she'd ever known possible. "They're here to arrest us."

"Is that all?" Fimre said. "We can handle that. Now, if they had orders to kill us, that would be a problem." He laughed a little, as though recalling something from years ago.

A bleak, dark rage stirred in Alyea's chest. "They have no right," she said, the words emerging deeper and rougher than she'd intended. Fimre studied her with narrowed eyes, shaking his head slowly.

"You tried to kill the king, Alyea," he pointed out. "That generally upsets the people tasked to guard him."

"I *didn't*—"

Fimre held up a hand. "I know. But that's what they saw." He rubbed a hand over his face. "Let them arrest us, Alyea. It's the easiest and safest way to sort this out—"

Fury spiked at the notion of letting herself be chained. *"No,"* she said through her teeth.

"Aly—"

"We are going to talk to Oruen." She seized Fimre's forearm, digging her fingers in hard, spinning options through her head in rapid sequence even as her hand tightened around his arm: *Not to the throne room, not to the audience hall, not to the dining hall—definitely not his bedchamber, because if he's there he's already dead or dying—*

She wouldn't let herself think about that.

I didn't kill him. I didn't. I wouldn't do that.

She decided on the most likely place, his favorite, most comfortable setting, then jerked Fimre sideways into an infinite instant of inverted movement.

The walls of a familiar small room took shape around them a moment later. Fimre sagged, dry-retching. She let him collapse and turned sharply round to take in the entire room in a fast sweep of awareness.

Guards, of course—two by the door, two to either side of Oruen, and she could feel the presence of armed watchers behind every hidden panel. In the fractional moment before they all began moving, Alyea said, very loudly, *"Stop."*

Stillness descended, shock cascading across every expression. Oruen's face went even more ashen, and he shrank back in his chair, hands up to ward her off.

"I'm not going to hurt you," Alyea said, directing the words to Oruen. She began to apologize, but found the words stuck in her throat. *I don't have to apologize to this human,* something whispered in the back of her mind. *He should be apologizing to* me.

She shook her head, bewildered. Fimre lurched to his feet, rubbing his throat, and rasped, "Lord Oruen. Thank the gods you're all right." He glanced around the room, letting out a rough grunt of astonishment. "How in the hells?" he muttered. "Alyea, how did you—?"

Alyea ignored him, more interested in watching Oruen. *Mine,* said a thready voice in the back of her mind. *He is mine, and must give me proper respect.*

Oruen didn't take his haggard stare from Alyea. "I wouldn't quite say I'm *all right,"* he said.

"I'm not here to hurt you," Alyea snapped, incensed at the disrespect. After all she'd done for him—

Fimre put his hand on her shoulder, his fingers tightening. "Alyea," he said in an undertone. "Please. Let me handle this—"

He dares touch me, dares to tell me what to do—Rage rose, uncontrollable and serpentine, threading through every nerve in her body. Her vision blurred. When it cleared, everything had changed.

Fimre sprawled limp against the far wall. A chair lay in splinters, forming a bizarre bread-crumb trail between Alyea and the unconscious desert lord. Four guards stood between Alyea and Oruen, and a panel in the wall behind the king was sliding open, a hand reaching out to tug the king to safety.

"Oh gods," Alyea said aloud, horrified. "What the hells—what did I just—? Fimre?" She looked at the fractured chair leg in her hand, at Oruen's retreating back, at the expressions of the guards—at the small holes in the walls where hidden panels had slid back—at the tiny blowgun darts skimming through the air toward her—

Half a heartbeat later, a dozen sharp stings peppered across her body. Two increasingly staggered, thundering heartbeats after that, black silence descended.

Chapter 5

The weather stayed clear, the wind angled just right to speed the *Wild Eyes* on her way. More than one sailor shot dark glances at Teilo and muttered wards against witchcraft. They weren't at all happy with the situation, regardless of the captain's attempt at explanation.

"A female listener," a sailor muttered, well out of human earshot, during one of those lulls. "T'isn't right. Bring the sea-devils down on us, it will."

"Ah, that's an old night watch tale," his companion answered. "I been on ships as had sea-devils calling with men as listeners, and been on one run as didn't have a listener at all. Won't do that again, by the gods! Lost five men that trip."

Deiq turned his head slightly, but couldn't bring the men into view; the water barrel stood in the way. He tried, again, to focus *other*-vision, and managed a grainy view of water sloshing gently in the barrel, then gave up as a headache began to creep along his temples.

"Women draw their attention," the first man said stubbornly. "Every time. I'm saying it true. Ask Slick over at the *Deep Sea Lover*. She knows. She gets a call every damn run, and that ain't normal."

"So, then, and Slick's still alive, so what's the complaint?"

"Aw, well! Would *you* take this old ginny? Pfah."

"Pfah yourself," the first man said. "She's old, right, damn right, and that's a sign she's a strong listener! That she's still at it this late? Pfah yourself. She's more experience than Slick by a good fifty years. I'd not mind finding out the difference."

"You'd fuck a cow with diarrhea," his companion said. "Go on, then, we've still half the deck to scrub."

Deiq grinned up at the sky, then looked at Teilo, standing by the rail. "You heard that?" he said, pitching his voice to land just by her ear.

Her head dipped in a brief nod. He couldn't tell if she was amused or irritated by the coarseness of the sailor's observations. Rising to his feet, he took an absent-minded sip from the flask Pinin had left him, relishing the spirited burn down the back of his throat.

Momentarily impatient with the self-imposed charade, he left the mending aside and went to stand beside Teilo at the rail.

He deliberately called past images of her to mind as he looked at her: pale hair darkening to a rich onyx, lines smoothing to a sharp-featured alertness, milky eyes wide and dark and hot with her passion for living, for learning secrets, for power.

She'd taught him quite a lot about seduction and human sex, long ago, but had been openly relieved when that mantle passed to a younger Chosen—not because she disliked the work, she'd said, but it had become boring. There were far more interesting experiences to explore.

"That's quite enough," Teilo said acerbically. "I don't want your memories in my mind any more than I would want your drool down my shoulder."

"You were beautiful," Deiq said impulsively. "Why did you let yourself—?" He stopped himself. Too much time among the humans, perhaps, but *why are you letting yourself look so old* felt like an insult no matter how it was phrased.

Unfortunately, she picked up on the thought. "Why? *Why?*" She slapped the rail with an open palm, face tight with real anger. "*Damn* you! You and your *forgetting*—take it all to the coldest of the hells!"

Deiq bent his head, wincing, as her anger ripped open doors he'd long ago done his best to shut. "The faereen," he said, voice muted. "I'm sorry, Teilo."

"After what they did to me, I'm *lucky* I can hold together this healthy of an appearance," she snapped. "And have you forgotten the love taps *you* inflicted, First Born?"

He swallowed back fury and bile, and stayed silent. She had every right to upbraid him. And they were both currently crippled to a near-human level, so if they were going to have a confrontation, this might well be the best time for it.

A draft of warm air swept across Deiq's face, then a chill breeze that turned into a cutting wind. He looked south and swore out loud. A heavy sheaf of darkness lay to the southwest, sweeping in toward them with terrifying speed. Lightning crackled through the clouds and the sea was turning a dreadful, muddy color in all directions.

"What is it?" Teilo said, alert, head moving as though she were trying to force her eyes to provide an answer.

"Storm," he said briefly. "It's bad. Might be from the Jungles." A shiver went down his spine at the thought.

Idiot, she said. A moment later she shoved into his mind, twisting vision inside out, forcing a moment of complete control, looking out through his eyes. Shocked that she'd been *able* to do that, he reeled internally. By the time he caught his balance and anger began to rise, she was already withdrawing.

He gagged and retched harshly, nausea returning full-force. She slapped his shoulder hard, bringing him out of the fit just that easily.

"It's not the Jungles," she said. "They couldn't steer a storm with that much precision from that distance, not across open water."

"Don't ever fucking do that to me again," Deiq said, breathing hard. He wrapped his hands around the rail to avoid striking her. "Don't you *dare.*"

"I've had it done to me many a time," she responded. "By you, for one."

He turned his head aside, trembling with conflicting anger: At himself, at her, at hundreds of years of changes that made normal behavior into a mistake over and over and over again.

"Never mind my bitterness," she said. "I'm an old woman, after all. Tell me about the storm."

He looked southwest, forcing himself to let go of emotion. "The clouds are moving into a circle around the ship. Getting tighter."

Wind creaked through the sails, pulling and twisting at the mast. Someone, probably the captain, shouted for the sails to be taken down. Feet thudded across the deck, and curses scattered through the air as sailors raced to obey. Deiq didn't bother looking to see if the first mate was waving for him to join in. Nothing would have taken him from Teilo's side at the moment.

"Definitely not the Jungles," Teilo repeated, turning one hand over to rap her knuckles against the railing.

"Meaning teyanain. *Which* teyanain is the question. I assume you already know about their split?" Even as he said it, he felt foolish. Of course she did, she'd been trapped and crippled by Evkit's opponents, after all.

Her lips pulled back over yellowed teeth in a half-snarl, half-laugh. "Of course I do. I was Evkit's *guest* recently, if you can call it that." Her voice held acrid venom.

Oh, shit. Deiq blinked witlessly for a moment, then said, "So—you're not on good terms with Lord Evkit...?"

She turned an incredulous expression his way. Wind splayed loose tendrils of hair against her face; she pushed it aside impatiently, then snorted as it plastered right back across her cheek. "Are you *joking*?"

"Uh...." He resisted the temptation to smooth the hair aside himself. He *probably* had enough power to bid it stay in place in spite of the wind, but this didn't seem like a particularly wise time to offer a gentle touch.

"What have you done?" she demanded. "Quickly!"

He felt both his hands clench into fists at her peremptory tone. At the same time, an uneasy itch rippled up his spine, warning of impending danger. Half-distracted, looking out at the turbulent sea, he said, "I... I made alliance with—"

"You godsforsaken idiot!"

The wind abruptly stilled, all sound ceasing. Deiq turned to find all crew members simply fallen over, apparently asleep—although some had dropped from the rigging or onto something sharply edged, and were more likely unconscious. The scent of blood teased past his nostrils. He blocked awareness of that as best he could, given his rising anxiety.

A huffing chuckle pulled his attention sharply back around. Two athain perched on the rail, one to either side of him. Their triple-split braids were dyed a bright blue and interwoven with owl feathers. Various warding sigils covered their faces, necks, and bare torsos, from wrist to shoulder to waist. He had no doubt the designs continued all the way around their backs. Some of the designs were tattoos, others more temporary, but the lines wove together in graceful, nearly hypnotic patterns—

He blinked and turned his head away with a grunt of annoyance.

"Greetings, old mother," the left-hand athain said with grave courtesy. Deiq could just make out a scattering of flat, dark moles across his face, nearly hidden underneath the tattoos. "We are glad to find you well this day."

"Greetings, ha'inn," the right-hand athain said, as solemnly. The timbre of his voice was distinctly higher, very nearly feminine: a jarring contrast to his broad, heavy-browed face. "We are glad to find you well this day."

"No thanks to you," Teilo said sharply. "What do you want, athain? To drag me back to your Calcen? Even now, I think, you'll find that difficult."

"Calcen Evkit is displeased with your abrupt departure from his care," the left-hand athain said. He scratched at his ear, smiling. It looked like one of the subtle code signs teyanain used, but not one Deiq was familiar with. "He is also troubled by your choice of traveling companions. But no. We are not here to summon you back onto teyanain lands. You took a binding oath never to return once you departed. We honor that."

"The old mother has been disruptive," the right-hand athain said, his gaze steady on Deiq. "She left Lord Evkit's care without consideration or courtesy, in the company of his enemies. You have been very helpful in rooting out those same enemies, and we could not have located the old mother without your assistance. Lord Evkit sends his gratitude for your help."

Deiq turned a disbelieving glare on Teilo. "You sided with the—"

"Shut up, child," she said harshly, her back stiff and chin up, arms folded, jaw tight.

"They tried to use me as a weapon!" he snapped. "I could have destroyed hundreds of innocents because of their manipulation!"

"And who told you that?" she inquired, her mouth twisting sourly.

"... Evkit," he said after a moment, and looked up at the black clouds, still swirling although the air around him remained dead still. "It made sense at the time, damnit. It still does."

The athain on the left cleared his throat gently, tugging at one earlobe. "We should discuss obligations," he said. "Old mother, you have stepped away from the Agreement multiple times in the past year alone. You no longer bear the protection of the Jungles. Calcen Evkit accepted you as a guest despite that, and attempted to aid you in a time of great need. You chose to reject his aid and flee with his enemies. This places a discourtesy debt upon you."

"He took my *child*," Teilo said, throat taut with the force of her words. "And he broke the Agreement long before I did!"

"Calcen Evkit's actions before your arrival do not impact the obligation incurred from your behavior during your visit," the left athain said, his gaze unwavering. Deiq realized that each athain was pointedly addressing only one person, as though the other barely even existed. "He accepted you as a guest. He rescued your child from unfavorable circumstances and saved your life."

"*He tried to kill me!*" Each word emerged as a distinct, heavily accented shout, more than one flecked with spittle.

"No, old mother, he did not. If he had wished to kill you, as you lay birthing your child, he would have simply allowed the birth itself to destroy you. He saved your life."

A visible ripple of rage shook her shoulders and neck. She snapped, "The only reason I was at risk was *because* of—"

The athain on the right turned his head sharply, frowning. "Old mother," both teyanain said in unison, "be still."

Teilo stood mute, her mouth working, chin tilting up as she fought to refuse the compulsion.

"You must discuss such details with Calcen Evkit," the left-hand teyanin said. His companion returned to watching Deiq with a blankly serene gaze. "We are not authorized to hear or speak further on that matter. Old mother, your voice is released back to you."

Teilo sucked in a harsh breath, her chin lowering nearly to her chest. She made no attempt to speak, and neither did Deiq, too shaken by what he'd just witnessed. They were surrounded by ocean on all sides, far from any proper source of power. Even crippled, Teilo should have been by far the stronger, with her ability to draw on the water in the air. Unless—

His stomach turned sour. "Oh, no," he said. "No. You didn't. Tell me you didn't."

The athain smiled, serene. "We do as the Calcen commands," the left one said. "Always and forever," the one on the right added.

"Didn't do *what*?" Teilo demanded crossly, turning to squint past Deiq's right shoulder.

Deiq bit his lip, *wishing* he could check other-vision, but his eyes still refused to shift over. The athain on the right held up a warning hand, bidding silence, and said, "First Born. You are, yourself, sworn to deliver punishment for several of the actions the old mother has taken in recent months. For one, she removed the collar of a sworn desert lord, the one who is now your wife." His mouth twitched into a brief, distinct smirk. "She broke the Agreement in that moment, above and beyond anything else she has done before or since, and her status as the mother of the Agreement gives that breach severe weight. What are your intentions?"

Deiq drew in a long breath, pushing that smug grin into the *forgotten* pile to quell his anger. His voice emerged rough with unexpected emotion. "I won't kill her. I won't allow you to kill her, either."

"We are not tasked with punishment," the right athain said. "If the Calcen wished the old mother destroyed, he could handle the matter himself at any time he wished."

"Not *bloody* likely," Teilo snapped.

The left athain tilted his head, a smile twisting the patterns on his face. "You have not realized yet?" he said, stroking the curve of his left ear with a thumb—*definitely* one of the teyanain coded signals this time, but Deiq still couldn't interpret it. "Ah, the Calcen will be pleased to hear our work was so well crafted."

"*What* work—" Teilo stopped abruptly; stood stone still, her eyes shut, then sucked in a deep, shocked breath. "He *dared* put full chains on me?" The words emerged in a basso roar of outrage. "*Me?*"

Deiq let out a long, quiet sigh at the confirmation of his suspicions.

"Calm yourself, old mother, before we do it for you," the athain on the right said, looking directly at her for the first time.

Teilo trembled, milky eyes wide with rage, but slowly stilled to a tight-lipped silence.

"After your many offenses and breaches of the Agreement, you no longer have your Chosen status to protect you, old mother," the left teyanin said gravely. "That ended the moment you parted ways with the Jungle and chose to move among humans once again. You became *the old mother* to us: the mother of the Agreement, your original role and one that cannot be stripped from you. And in teyanain eyes, when the one who founded the Agreement in her own blood and her own pain walks away from that compact, it lies broken for all."

"Oh dear gods," Deiq said, utterly appalled. "I honestly think that is the single most dangerous thing I've *ever* heard a teyanin say aloud."

"We have long been ready for the ending of the Agreement," the athain on the right said. "The Jungles, from disciples to ha'reye, are occupied with immediate matters. They are not looking or listening to the rest of the world right now."

"What have you done?" Teilo said, her voice scarcely a whisper.

"The Jungles are burning," the athain on the left said, unblinking.

Deiq caught Teilo as she staggered back a step, trembling violently. She thrust herself upright again and said, voice cracking with emotion, "You *dared* breach that sanctuary?"

"We have dared only to preserve humanity. You, and many many others, would be dead right now if we had not begun distracting the Jungles the moment you defected, old mother," the left athain said. "And the chains you both bear protect you as much as they bind you. We crafted them with care. Lord Evkit is able to assist you in time of need through those chains. None may use them against you save ourselves, and that only through the will of Lord Evkit. Ha'reye and ha'ra'hain and disciples will not see these chains. This work took great effort, and harmed some of our own in the crafting. All this despite your discourteous departure with enemies of the Calcen. For that safety, and in the face of such forbearance, you owe the Calcen a life bond."

Teilo lowered her chin, her shoulders rounding like a bull readying to charge. The athain watched her, waiting, impassive. Eventually, Teilo muttered, "I accept that obligation. I will offer my word to no longer aid those of his people who have turned against him, in return for freedom from these chains."

"Your word means little, old mother," the left athain said. "You are an oath-breaker, after all." He smirked. Deiq's hands curled briefly into fists. The athain on the right caught his eye, shaking his head in warning.

Deiq made himself relax. He wasn't up to fighting two athain who could freely draw on Teilo's power—and regardless of how well he acquitted himself, Teilo would be dead at the end. That thought nagged at him, as though he'd missed something important.

"Back to my first question, then," Teilo said harshly. "What do you *want?*"

Freely draw on Teilo's power, that was the part that wasn't quite right—*oh*—

"Wait," Deiq said abruptly as a phrase rolled over in his mind. "*The chains we both bear*—I'm bound to Alyea, not to—"

He looked at the twin smirks before him with a dark disbelief.

"Your perceptions are very much dimmed by the tey-b'stibik, First Born," the right-hand athain said gravely, even as Deiq turned vision inward, searching urgently, narrowing vision again and again and again. The words came from farther and farther away as he focused. "Calcen Evkit set the bond between you and your wife. He still controls those chains. He controls *you*."

There. A crimson line, snaking along the inside of veins and arteries: thin, light, and comprehensively intertwined with every major and minor organ.

Deiq opened his mouth and let out an ear-shattering roar, fury turning his torso molten. Thought slid sideways under emotion. Wood creaked and splintered, glass shattered, and metal screamed as it bent, the whole ship listing dangerously to one side. Teilo dropped to her knees and curled into a ball, hands over her head. The athain regarded Deiq smugly, apparently unaffected by the chaos and the tilting deck alike.

Deiq's bellow cut off as his throat simply closed. He gagged and went to his knees, clutching his neck as dramatically as he'd ever seen a human do when choking. A moment later the block lifted and he sucked in deep, trembling breaths, anger transformed to disoriented shakiness.

"As I said," the athain on the right said, "the Calcen holds control of you, and through his will, *we* hold control of you both. I am directed to say something that might calm your temper: Remember that your wife is also held by the chains, and so is also subject to the Calcen's control." He smirked.

"That's supposed to *calm* him?" Teilo muttered sardonically.

Deiq rose to his feet slowly, rubbing his throat, still breathing in great gasps. "I made an agreement with the Calcen," he said, his voice refusing to rise above a whisper. "There was no need to bind me, much less to involve my wife. I was already a bound ally, under the law of *peh-tenez*—"

"You were not in *peh-tenez*, First Born," the teyanin on the right said. "That much we can speak to absolutely. We are involved in every peh-tenez. We would know. Whatever your discussion with the Calcen, peh-tenez was never declared. If you made an incorrect assumption, that is nobody's fault but your own."

Deiq sucked in a sharp breath, feeling his throat loosening and healing. "That. Little. *Fucker*." Another phrase turned over in his head, connecting pieces in a different order than before. "Wait. Did he—*did* he lie to me? Did *he* set Kippin after me, to put me in a position where I thought I owed him my life?"

"We do not know, First Born," the athain on the right said. "You must ask the Calcen these questions. We are here to talk of other matters."

"Oh, I'll talk to him, all right," Deiq said, feral rage building once more. "If he lied to me about that—"

"—It wouldn't be in the least surprising," Teilo cut in sharply. "You're both doing a great deal of talking and not getting to the point, athain. I ask a third time and bid you to *answer*: What do you *want*?"

"The Calcen wishes your assistance in subduing a formidable enemy of the teyanain and of humanity as a whole," the left-hand athain said readily. "The last of the ha'reye capable of being bound to human service is the unstable one at Scratha Fortress. It must be destroyed."

Deiq gaped at the athain. "That's *madness*. You can't ask that of us—of *us*, for the love of the gods—you *can't!*"

"There are no gods, First Born," the athain on the right said, unsmiling.

"This shouldn't surprise you in the least," Teilo said tightly. "Not after what he's already set up with the teyanain ha'rethe."

"What?" Deiq turned to stare at her, bewildered. "It's dead!" The twin smirks on the faces of the athain put a hard knot in his throat.

The athain on the right tilted his head to laugh up at the sky for a few moments, then, still smiling, shook his head. "No," he said. "We have not lost our ha'rethe. We have merely rearranged the relationship."

"Meaning it's enslaved," Teilo said, voice cold and dark as the depths of the sea.

Deiq stared, the words simply not registering as sense for a long moment, then turned an incredulous glare at the athain. "*What*?"

"Evkit reversed the bond during his blood trial," Teilo said. "He now controls the teyanain ha'rethe." She glared at the sky as though blaming it for the transgression; or, more likely, as reflexive avoidance of provocation.

"That's not possible," Deiq protested. "It would destroy him, mind and body together. Humans simply *can't* master that much power!"

The athain smirked. "One human cannot," the one on the right said. "Many humans working together can." He spread a hand over his chest, fingers splayed wide, his smug grin even wider.

"He's gone insane."

Neither athain took offense at that. "The Calcen is dedicated and passionate in his beliefs," the athain on the right said gravely. "He is working for the freedom of the world, First Born."

"Spare me the sermon," Deiq said. Their eyes narrowed, a sign that he'd finally nettled them with that petty insult. "Evkit wants to be in *control* of the world, not to free it!"

"The one does require the other," the right-hand athain said. "Those who do not understand the vision will be swept aside soon enough, driftwood on the storm waves."

"We have served the ha'reye for millennia," the athain on the left said. "Now they will serve us, or they will be destroyed."

"It may help to understand that this task will earn you both your freedom from the Calcen's control," the right-hand athain offered. "He will never again attempt to bind you to his will."

"He'll not get the chance to bind me twice," Teilo said through her teeth. "So *that's* a facile promise!"

The athain shrugged, their attention on Deiq.

"What happens if I say *no*?" Deiq asked, scarcely audible even to his own ears.

Both athain tilted their heads to one side in unison. The one on the right said, very softly, "Then you will be destroyed, First Born, here and now, along with your wife and the old mother. We will take your power from you and accomplish the task ourselves."

"It would be an inconvenient solution and a less graceful answer," the athain on the left observed, his tone pragmatic. "The pattern the Calcen seeks to build would be more complete with your willing involvement. But the pattern will be built, regardless of who falls along the way."

"I cannot raise a hand directly against any ha'rethe," Teilo said. "My oaths have been in place for a thousand years. I offer to refrain from interfering."

"That is not accepted," the athain on the left said, shaking his head. "You have already breached your oaths multiple times—in the waters, above the waters, beside the waters. You have fought and harmed and even killed ha'reye and ha'reye-kin."

Teilo turned her head away, dipping chin to chest. "Those were *different*," she said, her voice rough.

"They qualify as raising your hand against ha'reye," the athain said, unyielding. "To draw a line now is hypocrisy."

Her head sank further, her shoulders rounding. Deiq could sense her misery. It stained the air around her a color that human eyes couldn't see. "I will do what you ask."

"Very good," the athain on the left said. "The Calcen accepts your service, and you will be granted limited freedom with which to manage matters. Your sight will be returned to you, old mother." He paused, cocking his head as though thinking, then went on: "I will remind you that the Calcen still holds a hand on your chains, and that attempting to escape that hold before completing your task would be vastly unwise on your part." He turned his head, nodding at his companion, and folded his hands before him in a clear signal that he was finished speaking.

"First Born," the athain on the right said. "What is your decision?"

"I've been tricked and manipulated into this position," Deiq said harshly. "This is not worthy of the Calcen, to treat an ally so."

The athain chuffed derisory amusement. "You are and ever have been far too dangerous for any human to claim as a true ally, First Born. We do not forget the Aerthraim ketarch. We do not forget the fallen city in the sands. We do not forget the *faereen*, your brother's children. And most of all, we do not forget the other First Born, your brothers, who nearly destroyed the world for their own pleasure."

Deiq bit his lip and bowed his head, acknowledging the points made even as he fought back a wave of indignation: *You have no right to speak to me so*!

The athain went on, tone no gentler than before: "You often claim to favor your human kin and to be seeking redemption for your wrongs. Here is your opportunity. Help us free the world from the grasp of those who have held us in chains for so long. Save your own life and the lives of those dearer to you than you like to admit."

"That's human thinking," Teilo muttered, shaking her head in clear disgust. "And you feeding him tey-b'stibik is behind *that*."

The athain looked at one another, as though consulting. Then the one perched before Teilo unfolded his hands and said, "Old mother, the tey-b'stibik only opened his eyes to that part of himself. It did not create those thoughts. Please be still now, and allow the First Born to make his decision." He drew a hand across his face, signaling that he was not going to speak again, and shut his eyes.

"Make your choice, First Born," the athain on the right said. "Take your path alongside humans, or be destroyed here and now."

"There have been times I would have told you to destroy me," Deiq said bleakly, meeting their unwavering gazes.

"We know," the athain on the right said, nodding, his expression shifting toward sympathy. "We chose the time of this conversation with great care. You will not ask us to destroy you today."

"I should," Deiq said, then shut his eyes and shook his head slowly. "You're right. Godsdamn me, I'll do what you want." He opened his eyes and pointed at the athain, right then left. "You carry a message back to Evkit for me, though. You tell that little rotworm-fucking *beetle* that he'd better hope this task kills me—because if I survive it, I *will* find a way to kill *him*."

The athain smiled, unconcerned. "He will be told," the one on the right said. "You are not the first to voice such thoughts, and you will not be the last."

"*My* freedom, if you please," Deiq said tightly. "*Now*."

"In part, but not in whole, ha'inn," the athain on the right said. "The old mother, being slightly more trustworthy, will be given intermediary control over you until the task is complete. You will submit to her hand, and she will judge how much power you may safely draw upon at any given time."

Teilo huffed in astounded derision. The athain ignored her.

Rage threaded through every vein of Deiq's body at that level of insult. "Don't you *dare* put *her* over *me*," he snarled. "That's intolerable!"

"And yet you will tolerate it, ha'inn," the athain on the right said. "Be still."

Deiq found himself frozen, immobile, voice and limbs locked.

"Hold your hands out, old mother, palm up, and stay very still, please," the athain on the left said. Deiq watched, helpless, raging, as the athain climbed down onto the deck and drew out a slender instrument that looked like a cross between a dagger and a reed flute, a ceremonial tool he'd only ever seen in use among the athain. He didn't even know what they called it.

The athain drew a rapid series of lines across Teilo's upturned palms. Blood welled out, dripping from her hand onto the deck. The smell brought a hot flush rambling up Deiq's spine: *gods*, every moment of her years of serving the Jungles seemed to be compressed into that lush crimson scent, *demanding* that he strike, that he *take*—

"Remain quiet, ha'inn," the athain still perched on the rail said quietly. "Remember yourself."

The other one raised his head, shot Deiq an amused glance, then added a final set of cuts to each of Teilo's hands. Deiq gagged. A swarm of hornets seemed to swirl through his head, their buzz a roar, their wings and stingers slicing him apart from the inside out. He went to his knees, gasping for breath, unable to focus, to think, only aware of a hideous internal *squirming*—

The athain were saying something. Teilo was saying something. None of it mattered. He'd been *chained*, he—*he,* First Born, chained to someone who was, at the same time, his inferior and supremely dangerous in a way Alyea had *never* been—

Kill her before she has a chance to exact revenge on me for the past thousand years—kill them all—

Teilo's voice wove through his haze. "Deiq. De'sta'haiq. Look at me."

Trembling, he raised his gaze to her face. Her eyes had shifted to a lambent, flat gold. She surveyed him with the regal confidence of complete superiority. A moment later, a crease in her face shifted and her expression became sympathetic. Another flicker: demented. He shut his eyes, aware that his predator-mind was tricking him, and struggled to recapture sanity.

"They're gone. Do you understand? The athain are gone. We must get to Scratha Fortress. Feed on the crew. Give me five and take the rest for yourself. Get yourself under control before I have to do it for you!"

Her tone was objectively sharp and harsh now. The trembling rose into a ferocious shudder. He rose to his feet, glaring down at her. She stood still, watching him without visible fear.

Kill her. She's too dangerous, has too much reason to use that power against me, can't be trusted—

—Dark eyes, wide with terror, fear-sweat thick in his nostrils as Alyea leaned into his support—

—She *trusted me, knowing I was as dangerous to her as Teilo is to me—a human, taking that risk... insanity... but if* she *could do that—*

I am not weaker than a human.

Deiq turned, surveying the crew, deliberately putting his back to Teilo. If she was going to strike, let it be now, let it be over with. *Five. She wants five. Do that first...* Once he began slaughtering the crew, there would be no stopping, not once he unleashed the rage itching along his spine.

The humans were beginning to wake from their induced slumber. Cries and groans broke the taut silence as they discovered their various injuries. The captain rolled to his feet, clutching at a nearby water barrel for support, and stared at Deiq in dazed horror. He was the highest-status human on the ship, so he properly belonged to Teilo, as did the first mate.

Deiq's hands spread out, hooking against air. He turned one hand palm up and offered the captain a slow, beckoning motion, projecting: *Come to me willingly, human.*

As had happened with Alyea, long ago it seemed now, Deiq saw himself reflected back through the captain's perceptions: He'd gone much further into the change than he'd ever let even Eredion see before. Flat, round white eyes, no pupil visible; skin a matte grey, laced with thousands of tiny bumps and ridges. His head had narrowed and elongated, mouth and nose edging towards an aquatic beak in appearance.

The captain screamed, a shrill cry of horror, and leapt for a nearby boathook. Deiq let him snatch it up, let him take a lunging step forward, then met the man's eyes and said, inaudibly, *Sleep.*

The captain collapsed to the deck once more, boathook dropping from his hand. Deiq scooped him up and tossed the limp form to the deck beside Teilo, a relatively gentle lob that probably only broke two or three bones.

It didn't matter. The captain wouldn't be needing those bones any longer.

He picked out four others: The first mate; a cross-eyed man who'd bragged repeatedly about raping children; one who considered himself unbearably handsome but was simply, in truth, unbearable; and a particularly amusing fellow who told wickedly raucous stories with a dry wit. The humans seemed to barely be moving as he snaked among them, lifting and tossing the chosen ones towards their new master. By the time all five were safely unconscious at Teilo's feet, rage was staining Deiq's vision white and his entire body was shivering as though about to come apart around him.

Teilo nodded at him, accepting his gifts as regally as he had ever accepted tribute from the tharr—and no doubt in deliberate reflection of just that motion. He didn't care.

It was time to hunt. He turned to survey the remaining crew, adjusting his vision/time sense to allow him to appreciate their scramble for escape, for hiding places, for weapons.

He shifted himself into proper ha'ra'hain speed and launched himself forward. Wild laughter bubbled throughout his body, emerging through altered vocal cords as a high, ear-shredding screech.

Pinin had been right. They would have been safer with the sharks.

Sharks didn't *enjoy* causing pain.

Chapter 6

Alyea woke to find her eyes smothered under dark cloth. Rough iron edges cut into her arms, scraped her legs raw through the far too thin formal clothes. She could feel cloth shredding as she moved. Twisting in the restraints, she nearly choked herself on a metal collar, chained tight to the stone wall at her back. Furious and petrified, she let out a bellow that would have impressed Deiq.

"Lord Peysimun," a voice said. Details filled in without the need for sight: *male, adult, northern/southern heritage, accustomed to command, ready to kill at need.* "You are in prison for attempting to kill the king. Do you understand?"

"*How dare you!*" She would wrench their heads from their shoulders for this. She would—

"One moment, please," the voice cut in, completely calm.

A movement to her right. She turned her head, inhaling through her nose, trying to place the scent filtering through the air.

"Alyea," Fimre said, his voice hoarse. "Listen. Please. Don't—" The word cut off abruptly, followed by a tiny groan.

"Lord Fimre of Sessin is standing beside you, Lord Peysimun," the first voice said. "He is currently unharmed, save for the injuries you inflicted on him, which we have tended. If you attempt to control me, he will be dead a moment later. I suggest you listen carefully to what I am telling you, and don't waste time arguing. I am captain of the guards in this particular tower, and I have been told to treat you with courtesy but also extreme caution."

She went still, breathing hard, and squeezed her eyes shut. Reaching out to Fimre met only a grey haze. "Fimre," she said aloud, unable to help herself, hating the whine of distress that emerged in her voice.

The captain went on, unruffled. "Lord Sessin is, for the moment, unchained, but you are both under arrest for attempting to kill the king. You will not be released, Lord Peysimun. Lord Sessin might be—if his Family negotiates for his release and sends us a new liaison in his place."

The captain paused, as though giving Alyea time to consider the information. When she said nothing, he went on, "You have no Family to negotiate for your release, Lord Peysimun. You will remain here, and you will remain chained, until the king decides whether to execute you for your treachery."

"I *didn't*—"

He went on, steady, unstoppable, completely ignoring her attempt to protest. "There are deaf guards watching this room at all times. They have orders to kill you and Lord Sessin at any attempt to escape, or if your allies attempt to rescue you. Should you succeed in escaping, Peysimun Family will be dissolved and its assets turned over to the king. You do not leave this room without the explicit permission of Lord Oruen. Do you understand?" His tone conveyed an utter lack of interest in whether she did or not.

She breathed heavily through her nose and stayed silent, not trusting herself to speak. *Fimre,* she tried once more, pushing harder this time. The grey haze stayed in place, silent, implacable, blanketing her senses.

"You're unable to use many of your desert lord abilities," the man said. "I'm guessing you've noticed that by now. You've been fed esthit, as has

Lord Fimre. I'll ask again, as I am required to report a coherent response: Do you understand your situation, Lord Peysimun?"

The metal collar pressed against her throat. She made herself relax back against the wall. "Yes," she said, hoarse with the desire to bellow again. "I understand. Do *you* understand—"

"Don't threaten me, Lord Peysimun," the man interrupted. "You're being held in as much comfort as we could justify giving you. There are much less pleasant ways we could have secured the king's safety. If you think about it, I'm sure you'll see that. Good day, Lord Peysimun."

The held shout rose hard and fast in her throat, filled with dire curses. The sound of a thick metal door gently clanging shut stopped her. The echo resonated in her ears, mapping out a half-round room with one high, narrow window and one door, a stone's throw in front of her. If she could get free, she could reach and wrench that door open in a heartbeat.

How do I know that? How can I see the room so easily? Why does this space feel familiar? She caught herself nearly panting with mixed panic and rage; forced her heartbeat and breathing to even out.

"He's gone," Fimre said, his voice rough and shaky. "Please. Don't yell. My head hurts too much, and it won't do any good." *Headache, spine sore, bruised shoulder*—a map of aches unrolled in the wake of his voice. Only the sturdy resilience and willpower of a desert lord was keeping him on his feet.

She drew in a long breath and let it out through her nose, summoning aqeyva calm, then spent some time disciplining raw fury back into structured thought. At last she said, "Where are we? It feels familiar, but I've never been imprisoned like this before."

"I was told you'd been here before," Fimre said. "As a visitor. The captain seemed quite smug about being able to chain you up this time."

Alyea rested her head against the wall behind her. "Ah. That would be Oruen's sense of humor at work," she said bleakly. "Lady Peysimun was imprisoned in this room. With rather fewer chains and cuffs, though, as I recall."

"She wasn't able to throw a desert lord across the room," Fimre said, sand-dry. "Nor could she hop from one end of the city to the other without stepping on the ground between."

Alyea couldn't help tensing. Cold metal dug into her neck and wrists again as she pushed forward with reawakening anger. "How could he think I'd betray him, after I sent my own—" She stopped, slumping back against the wall. "Only she wasn't. So I suppose it doesn't count, in his eyes."

"You're making remarkably little sense," Fimre observed. "I suppose that shouldn't surprise me." He sighed, then groaned quietly. "Oh, my ribs," he muttered.

Alyea leaned her head against the wall again and didn't answer.

The air turned warmer and cooler and warmer again. The sound of Fimre pacing the room ticked off passing time in uncertain increments.

"How long have we been here?" Alyea asked eventually, as much to break the increasing boredom as from actual interest.

"About two days," Fimre said. "You took a while to wake up. Whatever they put in those darts laid you out solidly."

She stayed silent for a few breaths, considering her words, then said quietly, "I'm sorry I hurt you, Fimre. I didn't know what I was doing."

"I believe I picked up on that, yes."

She felt him pause in front of her. Abrupt awareness of her helpless state tensed every muscle in her body. She bared her teeth without meaning to and said, "Going to take your revenge while I'm bound, then?"

After a long moment of silence, he said, "No," and backed up a step. "I won't break my oaths." There was a sharp, bitter edge to the words.

"And I've broken mine?" she retorted.

He paced away again without answering. Eventually, he said, "When I was researching Bright Bay in preparation for my posting as liaison, everyone said you were a social ninny who'd gotten in over her head and wouldn't last long. A weakling. Once I'd met you, and saw how smart you are, I was able to see you as almost an equal."

If he'd arrived a few short months sooner, his information would have been absolutely accurate. She wasn't about to admit that to him, though. "Almost equal? How kind of you."

"You're northern, Alyea," he said without apology. "You have no idea how little you really know about the south, even now. The most foolish southerner understands things you've never conceived of, and knows how to navigate customs and rules that nobody will ever directly explain to you."

He paced across the room twice more. She let him work off his agitation. When she sensed him calming, she said, "It's the same in the north, Fimre. You don't know nearly enough about our customs."

"Yes. I know. That's your role. That's your job, to be intermediary. And I thought you were doing quite well at it, right up until—" He stopped and let out a hard breath. She could feel him standing in front of her again. "It was one thing to see you as competent and intelligent—that was a change I could accept. Even though I was beginning to suspect you're smarter than I am. That was a hard realization."

"Thank you," Alyea said, honestly surprised that Fimre's Sessin pride had allowed him to speak those words aloud.

"This is worse," Fimre said. Air moving across her face told her that he was gesturing wildly as he went on, his voice picking up speed and passion with every word. "What you've done now—gods, Alyea, you're ha'ra'hain for all practical purposes! *More,* even—you brought us through an aenstone wall, which is *fucking impossible.* I don't understand most of what's happening, and I don't like what I do understand. This entire incident is chewing holes in everything Eredion and I—*and* you—have been working to build! I don't know how to fix this. I don't think even Eredion would know how to handle it. You're a desert lord—a *northern* desert lord. I outrank you by any sane standard. We're only equals under your northern customs. And yet, apparently, now *I'm* serving *you*."

Something in that rattle of words struck her as important—what had it been? She sifted through the sentences, testing, discarding, assessing.

Ah. There it is.

You're ha'ra'hain for all practical purposes. More, even...

Would Deiq have been able to break free of these chains? It seemed entirely possible. And if, as she suspected, her changed abilities came from the link with Deiq—

Fimre was still ranting. She moved awareness of him to one side. He wasn't likely to say anything particularly new at this point. She breathed more slowly, easing into a trance, and focused on sensing the chains and cuffs with the amber-edged vision that had shown her the flaws in the Tower paintings.

A grey fog blocked her attempt. The esthit.

She stayed in the hazy calm of aqeyva trance and turned her attention to the drug in her system. The grey shifted, swirled, developed distinct patterns within her arms and torso. No sign of it below the torso, which was interesting in an abstract sort of way. She put that aside for later consideration and looked at the patterns.

From waist to head, her body was filled with a shifting series of monochrome lines.

"Alyea," Fimre said from far away. "Are you even listening to me?" By the strain in his voice, he was shouting at her. The words sounded barely louder than normal volume.

"Pahenna," she said absently, still studying the lines. They thinned out and blurred at her wrists, becoming a vague patchiness from there to her fingertips.

"Godsdamnit," Fimre said. "What are you doing *now*?"

The grey extended past her fingertips, the only spot where the monochrome pattern extruded from her body into the air around her. Focusing closer, closer yet, she saw faint ripples in the grey, like waves washing away from her hands. As the wavering lines separated from her flesh, they dissipated, going from increasingly tiny grey to silver to white blobs, and then gone entirely.

Waves.

"Alyea, *ta feth kii,* you bloody *reeven!*" His voice was scaling into a rigid, hoarse shriek, like the caw of a giant bird.

She didn't bother answering this time, too intent on discovery. She followed the ripples up her arms, into her torso, and found where all mist-movement ceased, a deep, dark grey stillness just below her sternum.

An earlier lesson came to mind: the memory of Deiq glaring into her eyes with murderous intent barely held in check, and the realization—*Water flows. Still water can be* made *to flow.*

Without hesitation, she directed a tremendous push to that central calm, a gigantic rock in the center of that stillness—willing all the grey to surge toward her fingertips and out. A burst of acid-laced fire tore through her from head to foot—

—Every muscle in her body spasmed in screaming protest—

—Her head cracked back against the stone wall—

—Darkness thickened the corners of her vision—

No. If she passed out, her jailers would only reload her with drugs to keep her helpless, probably worse ones this time. She pushed hard against the wavering black, gritting her teeth and summoning every bit of willpower.

Red hair and a bright blue stare—Tank's face rose in her memory, and the feel of him: not the physical sensation, but the steel-hard determination to survive. Somehow she knew he'd been through head injuries before and stayed conscious. His ferocious willfulness blended into her own desperation, and the threatening black receded, bit by bit.

A thundering headache and a sticky feeling on the back of her neck told her she'd split the skin at the very least. But her head was completely clear, and her body hummed with a disconcerting sense of raw power.

"Sun-lord's arse," Fimre said, his voice constricted as though raw from shouting and tight with fear all at once. "What did you just *do*?"

She reached, found the grey mist laced throughout Fimre, found the anchoring stillness, and pushed, not gently, to expel it from his being.

He screamed and collapsed to the floor. She could hear him writhing. She ignored him, the new, vibrating strength inside her claiming her full attention. Her jumbled emotions shifted into a new feeling, a strange, icy-cold focus she'd never experienced before. Breathing drew her deeper into the detachment, damping the sullen anger into a chill awareness of everything: the feel of the metal cuffs against her skin, the floor under her feet, Fimre coughing as he hauled himself upright.

Air shifted, warmth shifted, scents threaded past her nose.

She kept her eyes shut and let herself sink into the abstractions. Noise moved the air. Fimre saying something. Once more, she ignored him.

The cuffs around her wrists came into a sharp focus. She could sense them in a way that had nothing to do with vision or skin contact; traced the welds, the pins, the chains—pressed further, and became part of the metal, feeling the tiniest flaw standing out in high relief.

She wedged invisible fingers into the flaws, then *breathed*—

The metal snapped in multiple spots, clattering to the floor.

"*S'ii datha-dista,*" Fimre yelped, then: "Fucking *sanahair,* stop—they'll kill us both—"

Once more, she ignored him. The rest of her bonds rained to the floor in an explosion of metal. She pulled the blindfold free and tossed it aside, but kept her eyes shut, still lost in an abstract haze of hyper-perception.

She sensed the darts—likely tipped with a lethal poison, this time—as they twisted through the air toward her. She knocked them to the floor with a thought, then traced their paths back to the source: Two spy-holes in the walls, and a barred window in the door.

The guards beyond were already releasing a second volley. She slapped those aside as well, then sealed the walls and door openings with unbreakable stone. Almost as an afterthought, she sealed the door from the inside, not by filling in the gaps with stone, this time, but by applying the imperative determination that it *would* stay shut until *she* released it.

Silence descended, punctuated only by Fimre's ragged, panting breath.

"What," he said eventually. "*What?*"

Alyea drew in a deep breath, then let it out, haze fading. She opened her eyes and looked at Fimre.

The color in his face had washed out to a nearly green hue. A large purple-black bruise marred the left side of his jaw, and his right arm was bandaged. His hair was shorn back to a silvery stubble barely longer than the shadowy scruff of his developing beard. He stared at her with horrified astonishment.

"What?" he said again.

Alyea sank into a cross-legged posture, leaning back against a wall. "Sit down, Fimre. Stay still. Be quiet."

He stumbled a bit as he obeyed, his wide-eyed gaze never leaving her for more than a moment, then chose a spot rather more than arm's-length away and sat with his legs tucked up to his chest, his arms wrapped around his knees, trembling.

She smoothed a hand across her clothes, absently mending rips and releasing wrinkles. Looking up, she found Fimre's expression mottled with complete disbelief, the skin around his eyes and mouth nearly white.

"How," he said, a guttural bark of sound barely recognizable as a word. "What."

Alyea shrugged and shut her eyes, unwilling to face his shock or his questions.

"Lord Peysimun," a voice called through the door. "Lord Fimre? Are you still there?"

With a thought, she unlatched the door and swung it open. A bulky, heavily-armored guard filled the doorway a moment later, long dagger in hand.

"Stay there," she said without raising her voice. The man checked a half-step into the room. She could see more guards, all well-armored, in the passageway behind him.

"That wasn't wise, Lord Peysimun," the guard in the doorway said.

"I'm not trying to escape," she told him. "If Oruen wants me to sit here, I'll sit here until he says I can leave. You don't need chains and collars for that. Now *go away*."

The man backed up under the command she laced into the last words. With another, ferociously focused thought, she slammed the door shut and sealed it.

Silence stretched. Eventually, Fimre said, "You are fucking insane."

"Very probably," Alyea said. "But now we're in a position of voluntarily accepting temporary subordination that we could walk away from any time, instead of being prisoners without options. That seems better to me."

"Insane," Fimre repeated, then shut his eyes and leaned his head back against the stone wall. "You're as insane as Deiq."

"Then I'm in good company," Alyea said, and couldn't help a bellow of laughter, quickly choked off. Fimre rolled his head from side to side, mouth a grim line, and gave no response.

Chapter 7

Humans were so easy to convince. Hardly any acting was required when one could nudge their perceptions into seeing what Deiq wanted them to see: a bedraggled, shivering pair of refugees on a ghost ship.

"The crew went mad," Teilo told the new captain, her voice raspy, old, weak. "They killed one another and leapt over the sides of the ship—I've never seen anything like it in all my days! If my nephew hadn't carried me aloft to the lookout spot and kept guard, they'd have killed me, too...."

Her voice faltering, she turned and buried her face against Deiq's chest. He put a comforting arm around her, keeping his own head lowered as though deeply grieved at the recollection.

Returning to a human appearance had been painful, even with the raw power flushing through him from taking so many lives so quickly. Searching out a nearby coast-hopper and drifting the remains of the *Wild Eyes* into its path had been Teilo's task as Deiq struggled with converting bone, muscle, and nerve back to the proper alignments. He'd only managed the final corrections scant hours before, and his temper was still shaky. It wouldn't be smart to test it by looking too closely at the humans surrounding them.

He let Teilo handle the encounter. She wove deft, feather light pushes into her explanations. Soon, the entire crew was going out of their way to offer dry clothes and clean cabins, hot soup, the best of the ship biscuits to the poor, fragile old woman and her handsome, heroic nephew.

Don't oversell it, Deiq commented dryly. *We don't need to be carried in on silken cushions when we reach Agyaer.*

Teilo humphed irritably but nodded agreement. Over the following days, the crew's enthusiasm faded to a respectful indifference. When Agyaer was a matter of hours away, Deiq and Teilo retreated to a little-used part of the deck and methodically erased their very existence from the minds of the crew. Covering his movements had become a habit for Deiq across the millennia, and Teilo saw the sense of it as well.

Side by side, patient, they remained quietly unremarkable throughout the flurry of docking and unloading, waited until the humans had settled into their predictable routines again, then walked, unnoticed, down the ramp just before it was pulled for the night.

Deiq let out a hard breath of relief as his feet touched solid ground again, then staggered sideways as he adjusted to a non-moving surface. Teilo regarded him with amusement, shaking her head, but said nothing.

He steered them to a side path that cut around rather than through the main harbor. "I've been eating ship food for far too long," he said as they walked. "I want a decent meal that doesn't smell of brine and fish."

"You're thinking like a human again," Teilo told him dryly.

He shook his head, refusing to acknowledge his still-simmering anger. She hadn't abused her control over him—*yet*—but it wasn't something safe to think about, either. "We will have a proper meal," he said. "We will stop for the night and rest before we start up the Wall."

Teilo tilted her head back to survey the looming cliff and the winding trail that snaked laboriously upward. Her tone was dryly incredulous: "Do you intend to climb the *entire* Stair?"

He smoothed his tone to blandness. "I intend to eat and rest. I'll think about the morning when it arrives."

She turned a hard stare on him, blinking ostentatiously, as though to draw attention to her white-shrouded eyes. "*We* don't need to eat, and we don't need to rest. You're stalling. Why?"

He looked up at the top of the cliff, far above, and sighed. "There's something I haven't told you," he said.

"What a shock."

Deiq paused in front of a small building to their right. The sign out front was cut in the shape of an apple and painted green. Below the apple hung a rectangular piece of wood with a bed painted on it.

"Food first," he said. "They have excellent bread here, and the rosemary rice is one of my favorite dishes." He could tell that the complex economics of what he'd said didn't register with her at all. Not surprising. Most humans didn't understand the careful balance he'd established with his Farms, and that sort of thing had never particularly interested Teilo in any case.

She shook her head in clear disgust, but followed him into the Green Apple. The host, a tall, lean man with deep-set grey eyes, squinted at Deiq uncertainly for a moment before smiling broadly and bowing. "*S'e* Deiq," he said. "It's an honor to see you again. I wasn't expecting you, I'm so sorry, your room's taken—"

"I didn't send word ahead," Deiq said easily. "It's my own fault. Another room will do. There's no need to put anyone out." He didn't remember this man specifically; just one more human in an endless cycle of studiously polite hosts.

The host blinked, seeming startled, as though that wasn't what he'd expected to hear. "Ah," he said uncertainly, glancing at Teilo. "Well, I... I thank you for that, *s'e*. Would you—would you care to have a meal while I ready another room for you and your companion?"

"That would be fine," Deiq said. "I know the way, thank you." He steered Teilo along a connecting corridor that led to a second building, rather further back from the road than the main inn and almost completely hidden from casual view. Most travelers only knew the Green Apple as a tiny, not particularly appealing roadside inn. Those with more status went straight to the back building, where the furnishings, accommodations, and food were of considerably higher quality.

Teilo grumbled under her breath as they went, muttering in a mishmash of languages humans had largely forgotten over the centuries. Deiq didn't bother trying to work out what she was saying. He wanted to relax, not get angry again.

The dining room was small, with four fine blackwood tables and sixteen matching chairs, a sideboard of assorted liquors, and another offering an assortment of cheeses, breads, and fruit. Deiq glanced around, nodding satisfaction, and motioned Teilo to take a seat.

"You own this place, don't you?" she said as she settled, her mouth quirking in wry amusement.

"What gave it away?" he returned, smiling. "Yes. For about three hundred years now." He felt no concern about speaking freely. Nobody else was in the dining room, and he never allowed spy-holes or eavesdropping posts in his properties.

He selected two pieces of the bread on the sideboard and handed one to Teilo as he rounded the table to sit across from her. She regarded it dubiously. A server came in, a broadly built young man with heavy pox-scarring across one side of his face and an old cut across his lower lip that twisted his expression into a perpetual sneer. "Lords. How may I serve you this day?"

Teilo squinted a bit at that honorific, but made no open protest. Deiq said, "Is there any rosemary rice today?"

"Yes, lord. And redfish stew."

Deiq hesitated, considering: *redfish stew* could mean anything from a mixture of crustaceans and shellfish to a strongly-flavored coastal fish. Terms changed over the years. The most modern usage, if he recalled correctly, was the actual fish, in a highly spiced sauce. "A bowl of each for me, please."

The server glanced at Teilo, raising an eyebrow inquiringly, then, obviously noting her filmed eyes, bent forward a bit and said, more loudly than necessary, "And for you, lord?"

Teilo grimaced but said, "A bit of the rice will do, thank you."

"And drinks, lords?"

"The sideboard will do," Deiq said, waving a hand in dismissal. "I'll handle that. You may go." The server bowed and retreated.

Teilo said, "You do like your luxury, don't you?"

"On occasion," Deiq answered, "it's soothing. And it's best I connect with being human at the moment, don't you think?"

"Not if it means climbing the entire Wall Stair," she said. "So we're sitting. Tell me what you've been hiding this time."

"The cliff face isn't very stable," he said, then shook his head, rising to his feet. "Wait."

He went to the sideboard and poured them each a shot of something vaguely tan-colored from a nearly flawless cut-glass decanter. He had no idea what it was called these days. A hundred years ago, a similar distillation had been called Maiden's Tears. It smelled of pepper and juniper, and had an unexpectedly smooth taste.

As he set the small cup of liquor before Teilo and returned to his seat, he went on. "The cliff face has been on the verge of collapsing for hundreds of years. That would have destroyed the bulk of the coastal communities past rebuilding, and that would have had... complicated effects throughout the entirety of the southlands."

Again, there was no point in mentioning the multiple functions his Farms served. She wouldn't care. She'd been in the Jungles for hundreds of years, focused only on her personal power, content to let humanity muddle through on its own; ignoring civilization's triumphs and catastrophes alike, as long as the protective cocoon of the Jungles wasn't troubled.

She sipped the drink cautiously, her nose wrinkling. "This is terrible," she said, setting the cup on the table and pushing it away from her.

He sipped his own, relishing the complex swirl of flavors. "I suppose it's an acquired taste," he conceded.

"So you decided to stabilize the Wall, and it's unwise to press against that binding with stepping from floor to ceiling," she said. "Foolish of you. It must have taken a large amount of your power. No wonder you've been so weak—"

"I'm not the one binding it together," he said quietly, not raising his gaze from his hands, the cup, the liquor.

"Ah," she said. "I'd heard there was a protector at the top of the Wall. So you taught it how to—"

"No. It's not a protector. Not in the modern sense." He tossed back the rest of his drink, still avoiding her gaze.

She inhaled sharply. "Oh, no," she said. "Tell me it's not one of *your* children."

Deiq shook his head. "Not one of mine. One of my brothers.'"

"*What?* Those were all destroyed!"

He made himself meet her shocked, furious glare directly. "It's the last one," he said. "The *last*. I couldn't save my brothers, I couldn't save their children—only this one. I've been keeping it reasonably stable, and insulated. I've put precautions in place, it's almost impossible for it to communicate with or influence the outside world—"

She was still staring, her mouth open in unabashed disbelief. "You think *Evkit's* insane?" she blurted. "You're using a *faereen* to stabilize a *cliff face*! That's like using an ocean to quench a candle!"

"It's more complicated than that," he said, then gestured for quiet as the server returned with their meals. The stew was, as Deiq had hoped, a strongly aromatic dish of fish chunks and alliums in a bright red broth. The rice was drenched in a pureed rosemary sauce, very nearly a soup itself. He inhaled the contrasting aromas with intense pleasure, half-closing his eyes, then offered the server a wide smile that brought an abrupt flush to the young man's face.

"Lord," the server said, bowing as though unsure what else to do. "Will there be anything else at the moment?" He glanced at Teilo, and appeared startled that she was looking directly at him.

"No, thank you," Deiq said, easing back on the smile. "This is enough. I'll call if we require more food." The young man nodded, bowed again, and retreated, his movements considerably more fluid and confident than he had been before. "Ah, humans," Deiq murmured, watching him go. "They do love being found attractive. Especially when their own kind has rejected them."

Teilo's mouth was set in a thin line. She said, "Did you think presenting this to me while on *your* territory, surrounded by luxury, would ease my reaction?"

"Have some of the rice," he said urbanely, dipping his spoon into his bowl. "It really is quite good. I helped them develop this recipe, if I recall correctly."

"I have no appetite now," she said, not even glancing at the food. "You *know* what the faereen did to me before they were destroyed. And you *saved* one! You expect me to face it? Your cruelty hasn't faded one *bit*, First Born."

"I'm not going to make you face anything," he said. "You're welcome to take another path, if you like. *I'm* going up the Wall Stair. I'm overdue for a kin-visit."

"The only way I'm leaving your side is if I gather the entirety of your power under my hand first," she retorted. "It's the only way to keep you out of trouble!"

"But then I wouldn't be able to protect myself, would I?" He ate a spoonful of rice without taking his gaze from her furious expression. After swallowing, he added, "And faereen *are* dreadfully dangerous, even for me, even when dealing with one I've practically raised for hundreds of years."

She let loose with a stream of invective drawn from three languages most humans had long ago forgotten and four that were still mostly in use. He waited, patient, uninterested in searching his memory to work out what she'd said this time. She finished her tirade in modern kaenic: "You fucking *shit.*"

He met her gaze, smiling, and ate another spoonful of rice before speaking again. "I promise I won't let it hurt you, Teilo. Consider this a much-needed exercise in building trust between us."

She shook her head and began eating the rice, eyes a hazy grey now, and refused to talk to him for the rest of the night.

Chapter 8

The light shifted and shifted again before another knock came at the door. "Thank the gods," Fimre said. "They're finally bringing us food." His bruises had largely faded, but the increasing scruff of facial hair gave him an unsettlingly savage appearance.

A cold indifference moved within her. Food was trivial. Food was human. It was only a weapon to be used against them. "More likely they're trying something new," she said. She settled to the ground, her back against the wall furthest from the door, then unbound the door and motioned for Fimre to open it.

Fimre cast her an aggrieved glance and said, "*I'd* like some food and a clean chamber pot, at least." Alyea smiled without real humor and didn't answer. In a distant way, it did seem odd that she *hadn't* felt hunger, or the need to eliminate wastes. She shrugged it off as a probable side effect of whatever change had allowed her to feed from Fimre in the first place.

The door swung open almost as soon as Fimre touched it. Fimre retreated with a speed that just barely stayed within graceful boundaries. A bulky, heavily-armored guard stood framed in the doorway, bare hands empty and splayed wide in the ubiquitous signal of non-aggression. His weight was planted solidly, indicating no intention to move forward. Alyea smiled a little, amused at the mix of stolid obedience and anxious caution flowing through the air. It wouldn't take much to make the man turn and bolt as though all the hells were chasing after him.

"Lord Peysimun," the guard announced, voice muffled by the dark cloth covering his face from the nose down. "You have a guest."

"So, no food," Fimre grumbled. "Lovely."

Alyea studied the guard. The armor and the face mask made gender impossible to determine for certain, but *he* seemed a safe enough guess—and it didn't really matter, one way or another. The guard's grey-green eyes remained on her, steady, watchful, but not fearful. His anxiety had eased on seeing her sitting still.

She started to ask after the identity of the guest, then realized the pointlessness of that and simply focused other-vision to see who stood in the passageway behind the burly guard. "Oh," she said. "Idisio. Please come in, ha'inn. You may go," she added to the guard.

The guard retreated. A slender young man took his place. As they respectively cleared the doorway, Alyea swung the door shut, sealing it once more.

"So this is the one I've heard so much about," Fimre said, taking a step forward and beginning to offer his hand for a northern-style greeting clasp, hand to hand; then shifted the angle slightly as though to grasp Idisio's forearm instead. Alyea could feel his uncertainty as to the proper greeting. Deiq had been his only above-ground encounter with a ha'ra'ha, and that hadn't exactly been an exchange of pleasantries.

She looked past him to Idisio, her amusement souring. "Fimre, *stop*," Alyea said sharply. "Stay where you are."

Idisio had changed since she'd last seen him. He was thinner, in a way that had little to do with weight—more as though his bone growth had outpaced his flesh, leaving his skin stretched uncomfortably tight. His grey eyes held a shimmer she'd never seen there before, the faintest mist of multicolored overlay. He watched her with the alert wariness of a hunter facing cornered prey.

Fimre froze, then dropped his hand to his side and backed up a cautious step. Idisio spared Fimre the briefest of glances, assessing and dismissing in that one moment. The Sessin lord bristled but stayed quiet. "Alyea," Idisio said. "Lord Peysimun."

Even his voice had shifted, emerging deeper and more solid than before. The new timbre was uncomfortably like Deiq's. She found herself deeply disturbed by the comparison.

Idisio's eyes narrowed. He took two prowling steps forward into the room. Alyea rose to her feet. Fimre scrambled to stand as far away from them as possible, muttering something about *bloody ha'ra'hain*.

The door closed with a quiet, definite thud. Idisio stopped moving. His eyes slid half-shut, hands loosening to hang limp at his sides. "Alyea," he said, his voice thick now, as though speaking had become difficult. "Stop it. I'm not here to attack you."

She tried to breathe, to calm herself, bewildered by the urgent rage rattling up her spine. "Mine," she said before she realized she'd opened her mouth.

Idisio's eyes widened, a bloom of gold forming along the outer edges. "Yours," he said through his teeth. "Your room. Your servant." Fimre chuffed, obviously affronted. They both ignored him. "I make no—no—argument—damnit, Alyea, stop it!"

"Stop what?"

His words emerged just under an outright roar. "Will you please calm down before I put you through a fucking wall?"

The room blurred around her, time and space moving in nauseating gyrations. Fimre screamed, a long, wailing, shuddering cry. When the disorientation cleared, she found herself on her stomach, her arms wrenched painfully behind her, Idisio's weight pinning her to the ground. A strange dusty smell hung in the air, and her vision blurred erratically.

"I'm not interested in a fight, godsdamnit," he panted. "I'm here to ask you for help."

"The hells she's not ha'ra'hain," Fimre muttered, somewhere to Alyea's left.

"She's not," Idisio said tightly. "She's acting like one, reacting like one, but she's *not.* Alyea. Listen to me. Are you listening? I don't know what the hells is going on with you, but you have to calm down before I really hurt you."

She lay still, feeling the tension shivering through his hands where he held her wrists, through his thighs where he knelt over her. A watery shock spread through her. Had she just attacked *Idisio*? What was *happening* to her?

Rage skittered along her spine again: *Mine, mine, mine, my territory, my servant, mine*—She caught in a sharp breath and tried to release the tension throughout her entire body. It felt like attempting to soften a brick by running a damp washcloth across it.

"I need your help, Alyea," Idisio said. "Will you please listen to me?"

"Get off me," she said through her teeth. "Let me go. I can't calm down while you're twisting my arms!"

Idisio hesitated, then moved clear. Aggrieved tension slowly faded, fragmenting into a more manageable gravel-sand sensation. Alyea drew in a long breath, then another, before rolling to her feet and turning to face Idisio once more.

Actual gravel-sand crunched underfoot.

She froze, her vision clarifying at last: looked down at the ground, then up at her surroundings. Not prison walls, but rocky scree, twisted devil-trees, and gigantic slabs of rock torn free at some distant past moment from the towering cliff face behind her. A grey-blue, cloud-littered sky stretched overhead. Far below shone the unmistakable glitter of water, dotted with bright-sailed merchant ships. A rough path, barely wide enough for a single file line, wound from their plateau up the side of the cliff, disappearing around a bend in the rock long before it reached the top.

"What," she said. "*What*?"

"That's my line," Fimre muttered. She shot him a black glare. He rolled his eyes at her, unrepentant.

"Stand still," Idisio advised her, grinning. "That's a nasty drop, and the footing's bad here."

"Where the hells are we?" Her throat rasped with the acidic anger of the demand.

"The Horn," Idisio said, his smile fading. "I think." He looked up at the cliff, down at the sea, and shrugged. "Well, you're definitely not in prison any longer. I thought that moving us elsewhere might help you calm down."

Alyea watched an eagle lofting by far overhead. In a low voice, she asked, "Are we in teyanain territory?"

"I don't know," Idisio said as quietly. He shrugged at the look she shot him. "I wasn't thinking clearly. I just wanted to get clear of that room so that we could talk."

She glanced at Fimre, noting the grey strain in his face, the way his hands trembled. "I heard Fimre screaming," she said.

Thin-lipped, the Sessin lord jerked his chin at Idisio, who met Alyea's glare without apparent concern.

"He'll be fine, Alyea," Idisio said, his flat tone once more a disturbing echo of Deiq's. "I didn't take much. And I couldn't very well use you, given that we were in the middle of a fight."

"I've been through worse," Fimre said harshly. "Doesn't make it pleasant."

Alyea stared at the chill pragmatism in Idisio's expression and found herself at a loss for words. "What *happened* to you?" she blurted.

A shiver wrinkled the skin on her arms at the look that crossed Idisio's face.

"Don't ask." His chin lifted, his eyes sliding half-closed; he inhaled loudly through his nose. "We're not on teyanain land. Just barely—but we're past their boundary."

"How do you know?" Alyea demanded.

"There are four teyanain watching us from about a quarter mile away. If they could come closer, they would. So they can't. So we're not on their land." Idisio almost preened, smug in his certainty.

"Not true," someone said.

Alyea looked up reflexively, scanning the area, and saw nothing. Idisio shut his eyes, his head cocked slightly to one side, and seemed to be listening intently. Fimre stood as still as the stone around him, his face washing out into a mottled grey anxiety.

"Show yourself!" Alyea snapped. "Don't play games."

"Games are what make life fun," the voice said, from a different spot this time. "You're on teyanain land. Your ha'ra'hain companion is wrong about that. But he's not entirely wrong, even though he's distressingly ignorant. He doesn't understand that teyanain have what you would call factions. Political parties that are currently in rather sharp disagreement."

Alyea sucked in a breath, startled.

"Oh?" the voice said, from behind her this time. She took her cue from Idisio, shut her eyes, and forced herself not to look for the speaker. "You didn't know either? Oh my. Your husband never told you? That's unfortunate."

"Your *what*?" Fimre choked out.

"Oh my," the voice said. "And these two didn't know that you bound yourself to the First Born ha'ra'ha. That's amusing. Oh—their expressions!" The voice hiccupped into laughter, then calmed again. "My day is the brighter now. But come—open your eyes, ha'ra'ha, northern lord, southern lord—and let's all speak properly."

Alyea could feel Fimre and Idisio staring at her. Her face burned as though under a molten beam of sunlight. She ground her teeth together for a moment, then opened her eyes to face their horrified expressions.

"Tell me it's not true," Fimre said hoarsely. "Holy gods, Alyea! You didn't! You're—"

"I'm insane," she said. "Yes."

A chuckle came from behind her. She turned, carefully slow and precise in her movements.

The man was tall and light-skinned for a teyanin, with pale grey eyes and coarse, dark brown hair. He wore simple grey and dun clothing. A strap across his broad chest held a dozen thin throwing knives and an array of black-tufted blowgun darts. He allowed her to study him for a few breaths, a smile creasing his plump face, then said, "Lords northern and southern. Ha'ra'ha. My name is Grey."

"Not a very teyanin name," Fimre said.

Grey dipped his head in a nod, apparently unoffended. "True," he agreed. "I am what the traditional teyanain call *huerg*. My father was not of pure teyanain blood, so my mother and I were sent away to live on the fringes of teyanain land. It is supposed to be a place of deep shame."

He motioned with one hand, a sweeping gesture that took in their surroundings. "I find no shame in living with such beauty. Better here, I think, than in the stifling corridors within the mountains that the traditional teyanain favor so."

Fimre didn't take his stare from Grey's face. "You said factions," he said. "Teyanain have *factions*?"

"We are no less complex than the other desert Families, although we do like to be seen as monolithic," Grey said, his smile fading. "The northern lord and the ha'ra'ha, I believe, have been guests of one faction in the past. The huerg see little to no value in following that faction. They rejected us, they sent us to live at the far edges of the land, areas that are difficult to survive in at best. What service do we owe such masters? None. So we have claimed our lands as our own, and the other factions do not cross our borders without our permission." He paused. "Not even," he added with a sly smile, "when we have acquired a prize they deeply desire."

"We are not your prizes," Alyea said tightly.

"Of course you are," Grey said, laughing again, "and better off ours than theirs. Those teyanain watchers you sense, ha'ra'ha, would dearly love to lay hands on the northern lord again, as well as yourself. You've both gone through certain changes that make you—let's say, more valuable than you were previously. Ah. That reminds me." He produced three looped strands of greyish-blue beads. "Put these on, please. It's for your own protection."

"What is it?" Idisio said, staring at the necklaces with a deepening frown.

"You're familiar with aenstone, yes? This is the teyanain-crafted version. Bluestone. Keeps you safe from the twisted ones." He shook the beads, held them out again. "Believe me, please, it's much safer for you to wear these. Tuck them under your shirt, so that they are protected from the sun."

"Are you wearing this?" Idisio asked.

Grey pushed his thick brown hair clear of one ear, then the other, to reveal a line of five bluestone studs along the curve of each ear. "All members of my faction wear these," Grey said. "It is how you tell us apart from the others."

"What are the twisted ones? And how many teyanain factions are there?" Alyea demanded. Grey smiled, placed both hands palm-flat over his chest, and said nothing.

Fimre, jaw set, looped the beads over his head without a word. Alyea reluctantly followed suit. Idisio took his beads in hand and stared at them for a few breaths, before shrugging and draping the necklace into place.

"Thank you," Grey said. "That makes things much safer for everyone. Now, if you will follow me, I will take you to where you should be at this point in time."

Alyea stayed still, feet planted ostentatiously firm. "Are we prisoners, Grey?"

Grey pursed his lips as though considering, then shook his head. "That would not be the correct term to use," he said. "We have a word: *hunimmae*. It means guests who have arrived without invitation nor warning. You are such guests. You have—" He paused to think, then went on. "You have not guest rights, but guest *obligations*. You inconvenienced us with your arrival. Your due courtesy is to break bread, as you would say, and rest under our shelter, and give us some compensation for your lack of manners."

"That doesn't make the least amount of sense," Idisio said. "We dropped in without warning, so we owe you the chance to serve us dinner?" His eyes had turned a muddy shade, and he radiated irritated bewilderment.

"More or less, that is correct," Grey said, then grimaced, sketching apology with one hand. "We will not actually be *feeding* you. Teyanain language is difficult to translate at times, and our culture is rather more complex than perhaps you are accustomed to, ha'ra'ha."

The ha'ra'ha scowled, folding and unfolding his arms as though trying to decide whether to be aggressive or neutral. "My *name* is Idisio."

"We are aware of your name," Grey said placidly. He turned his head, watching a small red bird hopping through the twisted branches of a nearby devil-tree with intent interest. It chirruped, pecked at something, then lofted off into the sky, swirling with the wind. Grey nodded, as though that had been a message of some sort, and went on, "Would you please come with me? The air is chill, even for me, and I can see the southern lord shivering."

Fimre glanced at Alyea. "We may as well," she told him, very aware of Grey's widening smile at the exchange and Idisio's deepening frown.

"I'm not keen on being a guest of the teyanain again," Idisio said, crossing his arms. His eyes had turned a disturbingly dark shade now, and had begun to lose the whites. "My last experience was unpleasant."

"Ah, but that was with the traditional faction, ha'ra'ha," Grey said. "We handle such matters very differently. We will treat you as you treat us, ha'ra'ha."

"Why won't you use my name?" Idisio demanded, clearly frustrated.

"We have our reasons." Grey glanced to the sky. A dark, ragged line of clouds had begun to gather to the west. "This unpleasant chill will soon turn for the worse. Please follow me." He turned and began picking his way across the broken slope toward the path.

An odd, distant expression crossed Idisio's face. His eyes faded to a grey so pale it was nearly translucent. He said, without looking at Alyea or Fimre, "Do it. This is the best road to take. Trust me." He went after Grey, not waiting for his companions to agree or even respond.

Alyea shrugged helplessly at Fimre's dubious expression and followed Idisio, hoping she wasn't making her worst mistake yet. Fimre stayed at her heels, occasionally grumbling about insanity and idiocy.

Chapter 9

Idisio's intuition had changed since his mother's death. It felt deeper, and wider, and blacker, arriving with a hard push where once it had been a strong suggestion. More often than not, it flatly contradicted his sense of self-preservation.

Logic said that he ought to grab Alyea and Fimre and leave—drawing from Alyea, from Fimre, from anything living within reach to fuel the leap elsewhere. Failing that, common sense told him he should simply abandon them and get the hells out of there himself.

Intuition insisted: *Follow the teyanin, this is important. You're in no danger.*

What about Alyea and Fimre? he asked that urging. *Are they in danger?*

No answer. "No surprise there," he muttered.

He could feel Alyea's stare boring into his back. "What was that?" she asked, deep suspicion coloring the words.

He shook his head. There was no way to answer without destroying her trust further, let alone giving far too much information to the listening teyanin.

Idisio put his attention on scrambling up the steep, narrow trail with a modicum of dignity. Ahead, Grey stepped with serene confidence from rock to rock, not even looking down to check his footing, or looking back to check that his unwilling guests were following. Then again, with the way Alyea and Fimre were stumbling and cursing over the uneven terrain, it didn't take ha'ra'hain senses to figure that part out.

You said you needed my help, Alyea's voice said in his mind unexpectedly. He staggered a bit, caught his footing. *What's going on?*

Idisio focused on keeping his "voice" quiet and targeted to Alyea alone. *I have to go to Scratha Fortress. I need you to come with me.* It was more challenging than he'd expected to walk over the broken ground and communicate this way.

Why? she insisted. He could hear an echo to her speech. She wasn't being nearly quiet enough. If Grey were trained as a spirit-walker, or if an athain were watching, they'd hear her side of the conversation, at the very least.

Idisio shook his head and pointed at their guide's back. "Not now," he said over his shoulder. Alyea snorted irritably, but let it drop.

Around the bend in the rock where the trail had disappeared from their initial view, a plateau opened out, the ground clearing into neatly raked gravel paths and sun-drenched garden beds. Sprawling rosemary bushes, very nearly hedges in height, lined the cliff edge like a fragrant living fence. Lush, feathery fennel taller than Idisio stood sentry at the corner posts of a stone pergola. Yellow and red flowering plants bent under the attention of industrious insects. There were no other teyanain in sight.

It reminded Idisio of his initial walk through the gardens of the Bright Bay palace with Lord Scratha—which, in turn, reminded him of the call that had taken him back onto this road.

He touched the bluestone necklace lightly, wondering if, like the aenstone, it was blocking the pull of that summoning—and if so, what price would be waiting for him when he removed it.

The chill air softened under the onslaught of sunlight. Idisio half-shut his eyes, tilting his face up to meet the warmth. *Sunlight,* said his mother's voice, faint and thready and whining. Idisio shook his head sharply, scowling, and focused on his surroundings again.

Grey watched him with that uncanny, piercing stare that saw far more than it ought. Fimre was gaping at the precisely arranged grounds and gardens, while Alyea's gaze had fixed on the pergola.

"Peh-tenez," Alyea said, pronouncing the word with strained caution, as though she'd been warned it was an easy one to misspeak into an insulting term.

Grey smiled benignly, tilting his head in apparent approval of her care. He swept his hand out to indicate that they should approach the pergola as he said, "No. That is a tradition we do not follow."

Alyea shot him an unreadable glance, then walked forward, her back straight. Idisio followed, realizing that her steps were nearly silent despite the gravel underfoot—as were his own. Fimre, by contrast, sounded like a horse stomping across broken pottery. Even the Sessin lord's breathing seemed loud and harsh.

Each of the stone pillars proved to be intricately carved with winding designs, echoing the climbing spirals of the plant that used the pillars as access to the wooden slats overhead. Idisio wasn't familiar enough with southern plants to name this one, but it reminded him of wisteria, with long, trailing, feathery branches and grapelike clusters of yellow-white flowers. The overhanging tendrils formed a colorful, insect-noisy screen on two sides, latticing the sunlight within into swaying, chaotic patterns.

The floor of the pergola was a considerably finer, paler version of the crushed gravel they'd walked across to reach it. A stone table, blunt and plain compared to the ornate pillars, sat low to the ground on stubby legs. Brightly colored cushions surrounded it in precisely spaced intervals. A woman sat on one of the cushions, facing them.

Idisio halted, blinking hard. How had he not seen her while approaching the pergola? Alyea and Fimre seemed to be similarly startled.

"I did not wish you to see me," the woman said. "Please be seated."

She was bone-thin and not particularly attractive. Her brown tunic left her arms bare to the shoulder, revealing lines of ink that swirled in ornate designs all the way to her fingertips. The tattoos, set against the woman's dozens of waist-length, dark braids, made Idisio think of a chaos of hissing snakes, eager to rise up and attack.

Her meditative posture was an ostentatious lie to Idisio's senses. Deadly power shimmered beneath her calm. As with Alyea, back in the king's prison, he felt aggression rising along his spine. She wasn't properly ha'ra'hain, or properly human; but was *most* definitely a threat. A peculiar burnt smell traced against the inside of his nostrils for a heartbeat, then faded to an icy sensation, taking aggression with it. The snake-nest image came to mind again, but quiescent now, many tiny black emotionless eyes watching Idisio, tongues flicking gently to test the air.

The woman smiled, revealing small, yellow-brown teeth, three of which were missing. "You do have an imagination, ha'ra'ha," she said. Her voice held an angular accent, as though kaenic was a language she had to consciously focus on, but she still spoke it with precision. "I like that. The other two are only thinking about whether I am athain. The southern lord is wondering why I do not have beads in my hair. The northern lord is noticing that there is no tea on the table, and wondering what that means. You are much more interesting, ha'ra'ha. I thank you for that."

Idisio dipped his chin to his chest, staring at the woman with as much ferocious chill as he could summon; feeling, obscurely, that she'd just insulted him.

"Please sit," the woman said, motioning to the cushions. "There is no tea because there are no facilities here for such niceties. Water is difficult to get here, and we prefer to use it for our gardens and our own people. It is not an insult, merely a practicality."

She waited, watching, as they one by one settled down around the table. Then she gathered up a fistful of braids and said, "As for the beads, that is a status marker among the traditionalists, and I have chosen to abandon that symbolism."

She loosed her grip, sliding her hand sensuously down to the end of the braids, and smiled wickedly at Fimre. The Sessin lord's eyes took on the same gleam Idisio had seen in women and men alike when Deiq smiled too brightly; then Fimre cleared his throat, looking away in clear discomfort.

The woman turned her head just enough to meet Idisio's eyes, sly expression unchanged. Idisio returned her gaze with a flat, nearly hostile indifference. She lifted one shoulder in a faint shrug, her smile dimming to a more neutral cast, and said, "We have created our own symbols, southern lord, and our own traditions. We do not use names, here, until invited to do so. It is a moment of trust, to give and to receive a name. The traditionalists use that trust to build their power. We choose otherwise."

"But Grey—" Idisio began, turning to look at their guide. He was nowhere in sight.

"That is not his true name. It is merely a word, and so holds no power to bind him."

Idisio, Alyea, and Fimre stared at the woman in mutually bewildered silence.

"What are we doing here?" Alyea blurted. Color washed into her face immediately, and she put her hand over her mouth, ducking her chin to her chest. Idisio grinned, obscurely relieved by the break in Alyea's ominous desert lord persona. Fimre's eyes brightened as though he were trying to restrain his own amusement.

The woman's gaze tracked their reactions with intent interest. "You are our guests," she said, her cadence slowing, her words becoming more precise. "You are under the protection of guest-right. I wish to speak to you, to tell you truths you would not learn from any other source."

"Out of an abundance of generosity, I'm sure," Alyea said with dry skepticism.

"Of course not. You are not so foolish as to expect me to explain how this benefits me, desert lord." The woman paused, her dark gaze tracking across each of them, then added, "But if you are willing to listen, you may be able to keep the world from being destroyed by those you so foolishly trust."

Chapter 10

Keep the world from being destroyed.

Alyea took a slow look around at her companions, deliberately not reacting to the dire pronouncement. Idisio gaped like a landed fish, staring at the teyanin woman. Fimre sat still, face as blank as smooth water, apparently watching a nearby insect bumbling about on a fennel leaf.

The dire statement felt entirely too similar in its direction to the discussion with Lord Evkit's daimaina: *This one First Born, this most restrained and sane of all the First Born, who now walks among us in the guise of a rich, self-indulgent merchant, could cause all of humanity to be wiped from the earth with a slight effort on his part and a few words to the Jungles. Do not forget this....*

The woman's smile faded, her gaze focusing on Alyea. She said, "The elder race is indeed among those I speak of. Please, use great caution in your thoughts and your words. As a matter of habit, I always assume someone of power is eavesdropping. Even with the protections we have given you, this is not a safe place in which to be careless, desert lord."

Alyea drew into herself, ferociously tightening her shields, until the woman smiled briefly, nodding.

"As proper names are not to be used," the woman said then, "you may call me Tallisil."

Idisio choked audibly. "*What*?"

The woman shrugged. "It serves as a name," she said, "and as a warning, if you need one, not to underestimate me." She cast a sultry smile at Fimre again; this time, the Sessin lord regarded her with blank disinterest.

Alyea hesitated, then said, "I'm not familiar with that word."

"It's a street term," Idisio said in a muted voice. A wave of color rose to his face, then faded. His eyes turned a very dark grey, and his distress scratched through the air, harshly uncomfortable. "It means—it's someone who—" He shook his head and fell silent, one hand over his mouth as though even saying that much made made him nauseous.

"It refers, in northern street parlance, to a woman who tears off a man's testicles with her bare hands," the teyanin woman said, moving her hands through the air in a graceful twisting and pulling gesture. "Beautiful brutality contained in a rather pleasant-sounding word, I've always thought." Her eyes gleamed with amusement, bringing a sly animation to her features. Alyea had a flickering sense of looking into a mirror: a sense of darkness and power, a depthless drive to fight for life and an immense need/pleasure of granting death resonated between them. Then Tallisil blinked, her expression closing off once more, and the cloudy air cleared to neutrality.

Idisio shuddered, closing his eyes. Fimre's expression hovered somewhere between horrified and amused. He looked everywhere and anywhere except at the two women.

Tallisil watched Idisio for a few moments, her head tilted to one side. "You've seen some dreadful things, young ha'ra'ha, haven't you?" she said, only the faintest trace of sympathy in her voice. "I suggest you compose yourself and move your thoughts away from the various antics of human whores, thieves, and beggars."

"Tallisil," Alyea said deliberately, ignoring Idisio's flinch. "While I understand that teyanain enjoy being dramatic, I'll suggest in turn that you stop baiting us and get to the point."

Tallisil nodded, apparently pleased, and said, "You are as direct as I've been told, desert lord. This is good. Southern formality is far too weighty and ponderous to suit me at the best of times." The skin around her eyes creased thoughtfully.

Fimre sat motionless, his eyes half-shut, his breathing almost imperceptible. Idisio fidgeted in his seat, avoiding Tallisil's gaze, and cast frequent glances into the distance, as though thinking of running away.

The gleam returned to Tallisil's eyes. She said, "Ha'ra'ha. Have you fathered offspring yet?"

Idisio eyes widened, fading to a translucent paleness. "No. Not as far as I know."

"You are sufficiently adult by the standards of your kind to discharge that duty, ha'ra'ha," Tallisil said. "I call on you, here and now, to do so. We will provide a suitable vessel."

Alyea began to shake her head. Before she could voice her protest, Idisio said, vehemently, "No. I'm not answering to *you* on that! Besides..." His tone wavered. "I might not even be able to—to have children."

"This is an old law, and I do have the authority to enforce it, ha'ra'ha," Tallisil said. "You must attempt to pass on your heritage. You will not be permitted to leave until you do so."

Idisio rose to his feet, his eyes black now. "And you're going to stop me how?" he demanded, his hands balling into fists.

Tallisil looked up at him without apparent concern. The air warmed sharply.

"*Ha'inn-nai-gana*, sit down," she said.

Idisio folded back onto his chair like a docile child. Alyea could feel sweat forming on her forehead even as a deep chill coated the back of her neck. She couldn't move, couldn't voice protest, could barely breathe.

"Stand up."

Idisio rose to his feet, his eyes washing out to a pale grey.

"Sit down."

When Idisio sat this time, the air began to cool. Tallisil looked at Alyea and Fimre, both of whom had frozen in their chairs, staring in horrified disbelief.

"You begin to understand, perhaps?" Tallisil said. "Humanity was given defenses in the original Agreement, protections from abuse by those we served. Over the centuries, humanity chose to hide those defenses from one another in exchange for political gain, and what was once a partnership has become slavery. I stand outside of that structure. I have an authority a desert lord may never touch. Ha'inn-nai-gana, I release your will back to you."

Idisio sucked in a shivery breath, his eyes flooding with black. "How dare you," he said, voice low and venomous. In that moment, he sounded—and looked—frighteningly like Deiq.

"Because I *can*, ha'ra'ha," Tallisil said. "I did warn you about underestimating me."

Idisio rose to his feet, golden speckles appearing in the flat darkness of his eyes. A shivering chill raked through the air; Tallisil raised a hand, and the ambient temperature eased to a comfortable warmth. Idisio gagged briefly, as though struggling for breath.

"Stop posturing as though you are my master, ha'ra'ha," Tallisil said. "You are not, and never will be." She lowered her hand and glanced at Alyea, adding wryly, "Ha'ra'hain never do like to hear that, do they?"

"No, they don't," Alyea said, unable to repress a smile as memories of her own confrontations with Deiq rose to mind. *I won't be a slave to anyone, Deiq. Not for any reason. So kill me now and get it over with for both our sakes, then go find some other damn fool desert lord to torture.*

Alyea caught flickers of movement beyond the screening vines. That had to be deliberate, a reminder that they weren't alone. She scuffed a foot lightly against the underlying gravel, drawing Fimre's attention; silently said, her focus rigidly precise, *I don't think we're in a position to take this into a fight right now. Is that really a law?*

Yes. Unfortunately. I assumed he'd already done that. Deiq should have made sure it was handled.

Alyea glanced up to find the teyanin woman watching her with distinct amusement.

"You are not so quiet as you think, desert lord," Tallisil remarked. "Then again, I am stronger than you are willing to comprehend."

Alyea bit her lip, looking down at the stone table until her pulse subsided from her ears. Then she met Idisio's gaze and said, "You're not the first to walk through that indignity. I had to give my first-born child to the Qisani."

Fimre dipped his head. "As did I," he said. "It is part of the compact between human and ha'reye. Those who can share of themselves to continue the legacy must do so." Tallisil nodded and said, "Ha'ra'ha, believe me when I tell you that should you be able to produce a child, it will make *you* stronger. Ha'ra'hain gain strength from this sort of exchange. By giving the nest beneath the holy place a child, desert lord—" she nodded at Alyea. "—you strengthened them greatly. Had you died as intended, they would be stronger yet."

Alyea's vision greyed out at the corners, her stomach lurching. "Had I—*what*?"

Tallisil regarded her without sympathy. "Your husband did not tell you?"

"No. I knew I'd been—injured, but I never had any idea that they'd intended—" She stopped. The words wouldn't come. It felt like too massive a betrayal. They'd wanted her to die? The ha'reye were supposed to be partners with the desert lords. They'd tried to kill her?

She felt as though the world were tilting slightly sideways around her. Sound muted for a heartbeat, and the acrid-floral scent of weeping-vine was unpleasantly thick in her nose.

Tallisil's expression remained austere. She said, "Your husband cares for the survival of humanity as a whole, desert lord. He does not have as much regard for individual lives. He has told you this himself, has he not? Consider other ha'ra'hain and ha'reye as greatly magnified versions of your husband, but without *any* care for humanity beyond what benefit *we* offer to *them*."

"Wait," Idisio said. "That isn't right—"

Tallisil's chin rose, her geniality disappearing. "Ha'ra'ha, you are still an infant in the ways of your kind. Do not contest the truth I have seen across all the days of *my* life." She delivered a pointed stare down her nose until Idisio dropped his gaze to the ground, scowling. Then she said, "Time passes. You have a duty, ha'ra'ha. Get up and face it."

Idisio straightened and glanced at Alyea, his eyes a very pale grey. Although he didn't speak, Tallisil nodded slightly, a smile quirking her mouth. Apparently, she'd caught another one of his thoughts.

"The process will be entirely pleasant for you, ha'ra'ha. You may take comfort in that, at least." She raised a hand, and a lithe form stepped up into the pavilion.

The girl was slightly taller than Idisio, and without much by way of curves. Alyea found herself assessing the line of hip and breast under the pale grey wrap, and shook her head dubiously. The girl didn't even look old enough to bear children.

Her shaven head added to that impression, as did her long, gangly limbs. With large dark eyes focused on Idisio, she stood quietly at the edge of the pavilion, waiting.

"She's not teyanain," Idisio said, voice hoarse. "And gods, she's *young*—this can't be right!"

"She is chih-huerg," Tallisil said. "Born of huerg, which is outsider, mixed-blood, in our language. In her case, the essence of the northern who fathered her won out over what teyanain characteristics her huerg mother possessed. Her teyanain blood allows her to live in our community, but she has little bloodline honor. If you give her a child, ha'ra'ha, she will gain considerable status. Her appearance is deceptive. I assure you she is no younger than you yourself are."

She motioned. The girl turned in place, sinuous, graceful, entirely adult in that moment. Fimre and Idisio's expressions brightened noticeably; Alyea's own pulse sped up.

"She is serving of her own choice," Tallisil said. "She chose to remain untouched in hopes of one day having just such an opportunity to raise her status. She is not a whore, ha'ra'ha."

Idisio blinked as though startled out of a trance, shaking his head. "And I'm not a stud," he said roughly. He put his hands on the table, spread flat, fingernails flushed with the pressure he was exerting.

"Please do not break my table, ha'ra'ha," Tallisil said, perfectly calm. "It has done you no harm."

Idisio closed his hands into fists and left them resting atop the table. The girl stood quietly, her back straight, gaze on Idisio as though deaf and blind to all else.

Tallisil went on, "This is not about being a *stud,* in the human sense. You are not human. You are ha'ra'hain, and the longer you wait, the older you grow, the more your ha'rethe side influences you, the more infertile you will become."

"I don't *trust* you," Idisio said flatly.

Tallisil sighed, glancing up at the ceiling of the pergola as though asking the gods for patience. "I sit before a ha'ra'ha and two desert lords," she said.

"Do you think me enough of a fool to *lie*?" She snapped her fingers, then waved a hand in a shooing motion. "You have a duty, ha'ra'ha. Get up and face it, and stop shaming us all with your foolishness."

A tickle of power surged along Alyea's inner ear; it made her want to sneeze. She put a hand to her nose to stop the impulse, breathing deeply.

The girl bent forward into a limber bow, her shaven head almost touching the ground. "Ha'inn," she said in heavily accented kaenic as she straightened. "Please come with me."

Idisio stood, eyes hazed—whether with shock, terror, contemplation, or compulsion, Alyea couldn't tell. "Tallisil," he said with fierce emphasis, then turned away and followed the young girl from the pavilion.

Tallisil sighed, watching him go. "He's thinking I chose my name well," she said. "He's so angry with me. And he has such a strong anger. It's impressive. I hope he doesn't hurt her too much."

"As long as she can still bear his child, you don't particularly care if he hurts her, do you?" Alyea said, knowing it for a challenge and not caring. The queasy look on Idisio's face had drawn her own emotions into ragged conflict.

"You still know very little about the world you have stepped into," Tallisil said, her tone sober. She pointed to the tattoos swirling across her face and arms. "I earned each of these from making far more difficult decisions than this one, desert lord. I will tell you a secret, an important piece of truth that only loremasters and teyanain truly understand: the centuries of mixing ha'ra'hain and human has decreased *human* fertility, especially in men. It is no accident that southerners have far fewer children than those north of the Hackerwood. If that girl can bear a ha'ra'hain child, the changes that will bring to her body means that she will be able to bear human children even to infertile men."

The humming of insects on the flowering weeping-vine and fennel seemed very loud in the silence that followed. Alyea stared at the woman, unable to believe what she'd just heard. Fimre picked at his fingernails, studiously silent.

"I did say she would gain great status from this," Tallisil said. "Your blood trials involved ha'reye, desert lord. That is considerably more dangerous than dealing with a single young ha'ra'ha who has not even realized the extents of his power yet."

A cold breeze swept through the pergola, stirring up a cloud of buzzing insects and bringing a strong perfume to the air. The bees swirled, then scattered, lofting into the distance like chaff on a strong wind. Tallisil raised her head, an intent, listening look on her face.

"I regret that we will not be able to finish this conversation," she said. "We are about to have company I prefer to avoid. You may wish to flee, yourselves."

Alyea looked around. There was nothing moving, either in the open spaces or behind the screening plants. "Flee from what? And to *where*? I don't even know where we are!"

Tallisil gave no answer. Alyea looked back at her, utterly unsurprised to find the woman gone.

"Bloody teyanain," Fimre muttered. "Always games."

Alyea sighed. "At least they're consistently devious." She began to stand.

"It is our nature," a man's voice responded. Between one blink and the next, four teyanain stood within the pavilion. A fifth, dressed in garishly bright blues, yellows, and greens, his glossy, blue-black hair loose, sat on the cushion Tallisil had recently occupied. The other teyanain wore unremarkable grey and brown tunic and trousers, and their long hair was thick masses of braids bound into heavy tails down their backs.

"I've seen you before," Alyea said. "Dinas Teyantin, right?"

"You remember, yes," Dinas said, inclining his head. He swept a hand round to indicate his companions. "These you have also met before, Lord Peysimun. They assisted with your travel to find your husband not long ago."

Alyea offered a bow to the four teyanain around her. "I regret that I did not get the chance to thank you for that assistance," she said. "I thank you now."

She received not the least flicker of acknowledgement from them, but the Teyantin nodded as though pleased with the courtesy.

"Lord Peysimun, where is the ha'ra'ha you traveled with?"

"Occupied elsewhere," Alyea said.

Dinas let out a long breath, frowning. "Have they convinced him to produce a child for them?... ah. No need to answer, desert lord. I see your eyes." He looked around at his companions; they shut their eyes briefly, heads lifting, nostrils flaring as though scenting the air. One by one, they opened their eyes, shaking their heads regretfully. "Unfortunate. He is beyond our reach. This pushes the boundaries of our alliance, but I must leave that for another to decide. I strongly suggest that you return north. There are matters moving in the southlands that are likely to prove fatal to both yourselves and the ha'ra'ha. Better by far that you retreat and allow those with more experience to handle the situation."

"I'm getting awfully tired of being told to back away," Alyea said sharply. "Don't you people know me better by now?"

Dinas's smile faded into a more somber expression. "Yes, Lord Peysimun," he said. "We do know you better by now. But honor demands that we give the warning. What you do with that warning places the responsibility on your shoulders, not on ours. If we did not warn you, we would be breaking our alliance."

"It would help more if you ever bothered to tell me *why*, instead of just issuing vague warnings," she retorted.

"A full answer would require years of training and scholarship, Lord Peysimun," Dinas said. "You do not have that much time, and I do not have that much patience. However, Lord Evkit might be willing to address the most important points." He touched the stone table with a fingertip, sketching out a symbol too quickly for Alyea to follow as he rattled off a string of harsh teyanain words. The four teyanain around them raised their hands towards the sky and let out a guttural barking sound.

"Thank you, my Teyantin," another voice said.

Alyea startled. Fimre rose swiftly, backed up a step, staring in outright horror. Lord Evkit sat on the remaining empty cushion, perfectly placid, as though he'd been there all along. He wore all black: long sleeves and thick leggings, with soft-soled grey boots that laced up to the knee. His hair was bound back into a simple triple bound tail, revealing unusual earrings: thick silver wire twisted in a graceful spiral through at least eight holes along the curve of each ear, tipped with a small red stone at each end. Alyea stared, trying to figure out how they'd managed to put those in place without ripping Evkit's ears apart in the process.

Dinas cleared his throat, bringing Alyea's attention back to the moment. He was smiling, smug and making no attempt to hide it. The grey-clad teyanain had returned to stolid, arms-crossed silence.

"Please be seated, desert lords," Lord Evkit said.

"How did you—that's not *possible*!" Fimre blurted.

"Get used to that around him," Alyea muttered.

Lord Evkit laughed. "Indeed," he agreed. He waved a hand, dismissing the subject, then raised his voice. "Come, join us, Cuna."

A sound like cold water hitting a hot pan split the air. The greenery all around the pavilion burst into flame. The stone of the pillars and the low table in the center radiated a rapidly climbing, searing heat. Black, choking smoke rose from underfoot; Alyea looked down to find the gravel turned into red-streaked coals.

Vines fell to ash in moments, leaving a clear view in all directions. Overriding terror drove Alyea forward, towards cooler air, toward sense, sanity, safety. She made two steps before a wall of flame replaced the destroyed vines, a scant arm's reach away. Fimre grabbed her, hauling her back with his good arm just before she stumbled into the conflagration.

Her clothes and hair dried, crisped, itched against her skin as though a heartbeat away from bursting into flame themselves. Rock scratched at the soles of her feet as the soft leather of her shoes gave way. She turned in place helplessly, coughing, and realized that Lord Evkit hadn't moved.

The four teyanain, and Dinas, had turned to face the flames but seemed to merely be standing still, hands outstretched as though warming themselves on a winter's night.

"Calm yourselves, desert lords," Lord Evkit said, raising his voice to carry over the crackling roar. "It is only my daughter trying to kill me once again. My Teyantin will handle this."

One of the grey-clad teyanain went to his knees, coughing. The flames rippled, like still water disturbed by a rock, and twisted into impossible shapes, distorting the space around them in a way that made Alyea nauseous. The twisting turned into a gathering funnel, the flames stretching and braiding into a long, argent-orange rope. In the next moment, almost too fast to track, the rope whipped around the fallen teyanin, searing, scorching, sinking into his body—

The air filled with the scent of roasting beef, creamy with fat, irresistibly savory. Alyea's stomach, instead of inverting, grumbled.

This is revolting, she told herself fiercely, and pinched her nose shut.

The burning teyanin arched his back, his hands out and up as though offering a silent appeal to the gods. If he was crying out, Alyea couldn't hear it past the roaring chaos. To her horror, little by little, as the flames disappeared from his body, he crumbled into a mass of thick, erratic ash, with pieces of bone and puddles of melted fat disrupting the dark flakes in spots.

Alyea turned away and gagged. Sour acid rose in her throat but made it no further. Fimre, his expression bleak, stood with folded arms, his lips a thin line. The air cooled steadily; rock creaked and ticked, and one bench cracked with a sharp sound that made both Fimre and Alyea jump. The pieces wavered, then tipped over, crumbling into large chunks as they fell. Alyea coughed as rock dust filled the air, and shielded her face with one arm until the ash and dust settled somewhat.

"Well done, Teyantin," Lord Evkit said. "I do not believe she expected that."

"This was a trap," Alyea said, the words painful in a raw, scorched throat.

"That's absurd," Fimre said immediately, scowling at her. "She couldn't have known we were—"

"Of course it was a trap," Evkit said. "My daughter has many traps in place for me, each only waiting on the correct bait. The chance that she might successfully breed a ha'ra'ha of her own served admirably for this one." He rose. Alyea noted that the cushion he'd been sitting on didn't have the slightest scorching. All of the other cushions had been reduced to ash. "And now—consequences. Dinas?"

"Yes, lord," Dinas said again. He motioned to the remaining three teyanain, who followed him from the pavilion. None of them even glanced at the ragged pile of ash.

"Your speech is clear," Alyea said. "You usually sound—rougher."

"It is occasionally useful to be underestimated," Lord Evkit said, smiling.

"That woman," Fimre interrupted, his voice clipped and harsh. "The one who called herself Tallisil—"

Lord Evkit broke into a full-throated laugh, tipping his head back for a moment. "Amusing choice," he said when he'd calmed down. "Very apt. She has done that before, you know. It is a literal description, in her case."

"Uh," Fimre said, looking ill again. "No. I wish I didn't know that now. That's—uh. But—" He made a clear effort to gather his thoughts. "Did I hear you right—she's your *daughter*?"

"Yes," Lord Evkit said. "It will not stop me from killing her, if I ever lay hands on her again. It is a shame. She would be a worthy successor to lead the teyanain, if she was not so intent on destroying everything I have built."

Alyea stared at the teyanain lord. "What?" she said. "I don't understand at all."

"We are teyanain," Lord Evkit said. "I would be surprised if you did understand. But time is limited, and you should leave this area very soon."

Fimre lifted his head, looking through one archway of the pergola. "Is that smoke?" He pointed. A thin thread of grey was twisting up into the sky to the northeast.

"Yes," Lord Evkit said. "Even desert lords will not be comfortable here for much longer."

"You're going to burn this entire area down?" Alyea demanded, horrified.

Lord Evkit regarded her with a flat, implacable expression. "You should already understand that there are consequences to everything, Lord Peysimun. I strongly suggest you both return north. Matters here are about to become extremely unpleasant."

"What about Idisio?" Alyea said. "I can't just leave him here—and—and I can't go back north—" The last part slipped out without her intending to voice it aloud. *Oruen is going to be furious,* she thought. *He* will *have me killed this time. At the very least, I've lost my lands, my home—everything*. She wouldn't get a second chance to explain—and she didn't particularly blame him, all things considered.

She'd been acting as cold-hearted as Lord Evkit, willing to throw Fimre in the path of oncoming danger not once, but multiple times; as dangerous to allies as to enemies. But that chill, steely overlay had faded as quickly as it had arrived, leaving her more than a little dismayed over her own recent actions.

Looking down at her feet, she realized they were bare, surrounded by blackened shreds of soft leather, but unburnt. And her clothes were entirely intact, without so much as a rip. Fimre, for his part, looked little better than a street rat. He was scorched, soot-streaked, and his clothes were half-destroyed.

What the hells is happening to me?

Lord Evkit said, "I am fairly certain that the ha'ra'ha has already been taken to a safe place. Cuna would not allow him to be distracted from providing her the prize she seeks." He paused. "The Horn is, as of now, closed to all travel—and I suspect that local sea travel will be less than safe for a time, as a side consequence. Whichever destination you choose, be certain you can survive there at length."

"Wait—what? You're closing the Horn?" Fimre blurted. "That's going to cause *incredible* disruption—"

"That is not our concern," Lord Evkit said. "We have already begun encouraging uninvolved outsiders to leave the area at speed. Your politics and finances and deals are not ours, Sessin lord. The teyanain are at war."

Alyea and Fimre both goggled at the diminutive teyanain lord, uncomprehending. "*War*?" Fimre said.

"With your *daughter*?" Alyea said. The concept was simply too vast and twisted to comprehend, and she was relieved when Lord Evkit shook his head, his mouth drawing aside in what might have been amusement or annoyance. Alyea didn't trust herself to read cues just then.

"No," he said. "My daughter is a smaller part of the whole. The teyanain are at war with Aerthraim Family."

Chapter 11

Idisio followed the girl in silence, his willpower oddly muted. Tallisil must have done something to stop him from talking, or stepping onto another path, or doing anything but what she'd sent him to do. The beads of the necklace felt cold and hard against his skin.

He knew this feeling. He'd been compelled before. Knowing what was happening made it no easier to fight it off, even as an ominous whine built in the back of his mind. *Never be controlled,* his mother whispered. *Never let the humans control you. Never again, never again....*

You're not one to talk, you unholy bitch. He couldn't tell if that thought came from him or from one of the tortured ghosts shifting in his mother's wake.

Looking at that part of his mind would only drive him over toward madness. Instead, he studied the girl walking before him with intense consideration. She was tall and gangly and her head was shaven: What color would her hair be, if she grew it out? What would her laugh sound like, if she ever relaxed enough? How much of this really *was* her own choice, and how much compulsion? If Tallisil could force a ha'ra'ha to do her bidding, it would be simple to bind a human girl into doing whatever she wanted, however dangerous.

Tallisil doesn't care if this girl survives, he thought. Like a series of ripples, his mother's murmuring formed an ever-shifting background of sound: *Never again, never again... This girl just wants to control you... That's all the humans want, is to control us....*

The muted sensation faded the further they went from the pavilion, the mosquito-whine of rage seeping into its place. The world sharpened around him. Far overhead, a large bird circled, its wings slashing through an acidic blue sky. Air moved across Idisio's face, laden with feather-dust and the rolling, deep song of the land deep beneath his feet. He half-turned, putting a hand out to assure himself he was still aboveground, still earthbound. Colors merged and flared, striping out into a million threads before swirling round into identifiable shapes and textures again.

He drew a whirlwind of cold air into his lungs and managed to stop walking. The girl paused and turned to face him. The grey of her clothing and her name merged, and her body stretched into impossible distortions, swelling from thin to voluptuous to obese, from infant to adult to elderly, as though all the possibilities of her life were flickering before his eyes.

"Ha'inn?" she said, tilting her head. His perception of her body steadied, and a flicker of real interest went through his own body at the look in her eyes. "We are near our destination. May we go?"

He stared at her without answering for a few breaths, waiting to be sure the uneasy oddness had passed completely. He found himself restlessly fingering the strand of bluestone beads around his neck. She stood silent and attentive, watching him without a flicker of concern or impatience.

The moment of desire faded. "What's your name?" he said.

"Grey." She didn't ask *his* name, which came as a relief and an irritation all at once.

"That's what our guide called himself."

She dipped her head, blinking as though uncertain how to answer. At last she said, "It is a name we use to outsiders, ha'inn."

"What happens when two or more of you have to give your names to the same person at the same time?" His hand closed around the beads. They felt *itchy*, even though his fingers reported nothing but rough stone.

"Then choose we different words," she said, then paused, apparently thinking over the phrasing. "We choose," she corrected herself. "Would you prefer another name? It does not matter. Whatever pleases you. Come, please, though. This way, ha'inn."

Idisio stayed put. Grey took another step, then turned to face him, frowning.

"Ha'inn," she said, "you have problem? I am too—formal?" Her frown changed to a forced smile. "I was told to be more... friend... kind." She shook her head, as though frustrated in her search for the correct word. "I forget. I am nervous. I apologize. I will be more...." She ran a hand down her side, a bit awkwardly, and shifted to a sinuous pose.

"No," he said. "It's not that." He took his hand away from the beads, and rubbed his hands together to get rid of the strange prickling sensation shooting up his arms. "I want your name. Not the mask. Your name."

Her posture reverted to straight-backed severity. "No, ha'inn," she said, seeming surprised and a bit offended. "That is forbidden."

"Without a name of your own," Idisio said, "You're not—" He shook his head before the wrong words could emerge, then tried again. "*I* can't. It's bad enough I'm being put up for stud. I won't do it without even knowing your *name*."

Memory pressed in, unexpectedly painful: A man's voice, laughing, drunk: *Why would I care about your name, you stupid little fuck?*

Idisio set his jaw and pushed awareness of anything beyond the moment aside.

"You are not understand, ha'inn, and my words are not good enough to explain. This thing you speak of, this *stud*, this is not correct. And I do not owe you my true name, ha'inn."

He closed his hand around the beads again. This time he caught her in a tiny flinch, her eyes darting to the necklace for a fleeting heartbeat.

"Ah," he said, and pulled the necklace over his head.

Color leached from her face, one hand rising in protest. "No, ha'inn, you not, do not—"

"*Tell me your name.*"

"I *cannot*." She stared at the necklace dangling from his hand, her eyes wide, expression appalled. "Please, ha'inn—please—"

"*Why* won't you tell me your name?" He kept the inflexible command in his voice, compelling an honest answer.

"Because then you *own* me," she blurted. "We will not be slaves!"

"You're already being controlled by Tallisil," Idisio observed.

"I am not controlled. She does not *own* me," Grey said. "It is not same. I serve freely."

"Do you have any choice in this matter?" Idisio challenged. "Can you say *I don't want to give the ha'ra'ha a child* and walk away right now?"

"This *is* choice; this *is* what I wish! This is *honorable*." She looked at the necklace again. "Please, put that back on, ha'inn, *please*—"

"But if you did want to refuse, could you? What happens to you if I refuse?"

She stood very still and seemed to be barely breathing. "Put the necklace back on, ha'inn, and I answer."

He hesitated, but her stare was direct and unflinching. She meant it. "It's making me do what you want," he said.

She shook her head vehemently. "No. Not a caging-chain, ha'inn. Not control you. It blocks, it hides, it keeps us all safe. You have no idea what you risk. *Put it back on.*" She touched her own ears, pointing to the line of blue studs running along each one. "Look, I have also."

He slowly dropped the necklace over his head, watching her relax.

"Thank you. You gave your word," she said then. "I gave my word. These are *bonds*, ha'inn. These are very important things."

"No, actually, *I* didn't give my word," Idisio said. "I stood up and walked after you when I was told to do so, and only because Tallisil was controlling me, not because I wanted to. I never *agreed* to give you a child."

She blinked, her expression turning stony. "You are unkind, ha'inn," she said. "I am not so displeasing as that, I think. You insult me."

"This doesn't have anything to do with you!" he nearly shouted at her, his hands clenched into fists.

"It has all to do with me. *I* have agreed to give child," she said, her tone chill, her words precise. "You *must* serve."

"So now you're saying I'm a slave?" he shot back, frustration laddering up his spine.

She made a small sound of exasperation, as though her patience had given out. "No. Not to me. This is your *duty*." She turned and began walking away, raising a hand in an imperious beckoning motion.

Idisio took two slow, reluctant steps. His mother's voice hissed in his ears: *They only seek to control you, they want to cage you, humans are all the same....*

No. That's not true. That's not what's happening here. It's just a... a duty... Even Scratha said I would have to do this one day. It's nothing unexpected.

Test it, she suggested. *Tell her no. See what happens.*

He stopped moving. "No," he said. "No, and no. I'm not doing this."

The girl turned around and came back toward him, almost to within arm's reach, no trace of amicability left in her expression. "Then I must do this thing without your consent."

He nearly laughed. "How in the hells do you think you can—"

"Ha'inn-nai-gana," she said, her voice flat, emotionless, nearly without accent. The word sank into his bones, wrenching muscle to comply. "You will come with me—"

She took a step back, beckoning. He took a step forward, sharply aroused now. "There," she said, satisfaction clear in her voice. "We will go to a safe place, and you will give your duty."

His mother screeched outrage. *You see? They only aim to control! But she is not as strong as the other one. Take the necklace off. It's restraining you.*

No.... a distinct disagreement from his intuition. The necklace wasn't the problem. *Leave it on. The girl is right. Leave it on....*

Leave the foolish thing, then, his mother said, petulant. *But look – if you twist your vision just so, there is a thread wound through your mind – that golden thread right there – break it!*

He stumbled forward another pace, fighting the compulsion. Grey frowned as though surprised, and began to speak. "Ha'inn—"

Don't let her speak the words again! Break it! Break it!

It felt like trying to break a silken garrote with a shattered pinky finger.

"Nai—"

Red filled the edges of his vision. He couldn't tell if it was blood or a ha'ra'hain fury.

"Ga—"

The thread snapped. He staggered back a step, pushing at the air before him as though to keep her from coming closer. The red receded from his vision, but he could feel damp streaking down his face; blood or tears, he didn't take the time to check. She was staring at him with a horrified expression, so it was more than likely blood.

"No," he said, "I won't do what you want. *Be quiet.*"

She fell back a step, one hand on her throat.

His mother's presence was an almost tangible pressure against the back of his mind. *She dared to try controlling you,* she said. *She* dared. *You must not allow that, ever again. Take off the necklace! Take it off! You cannot punish her properly while you wear it.*

"Stand still," Idisio said. "Right there. Good." He pulled the necklace off once more, dropping it into a heap at the side of the trail. Her gaze followed the movement, her color fading to a stark horror. She made no protest this time, apparently realizing that her lies about the chain wouldn't work any longer.

He advanced, closing the distance between them, and lowered his voice into a compelling murmur. "You tried to control me. You tried to force me into doing what you wanted. You *dared* put your will against mine."

He leaned in close, his hands on either side of her face, watching her pupils dilate, her eyes rolling. She was barely hearing his words. Like that girl in Sandsplit. He said, "I won't *ever* do what you want."

Her eyes snapped wide in alarm as his fingers tightened. "Ha'inn," she gasped. "Don't give in to this—"

He wouldn't listen to her lies. She was a human. They lied. They only wanted to control. He said, low and harsh, "You would have taken what you wanted from me, and killed me afterward. Or caged me somehow, so that you could use me again."

Her voice steadied, strengthened, rang with sincerity: "Ha'inn – don't let the twisted one take you—"

I will never again be caged, his mother said, the words spiraling into a fierce shriek. *Never again. Never again!*

Idisio nodded, agreeing. "Never again," he murmured. "Never, ever, ever again."

The girl opened her mouth to scream. Idisio willed her vocal cords silent before so much as a squeak emerged.

Kill her, his mother urged. *Destroy her. Take all that she is, then leave this place! It grows less safe by the moment.*

"Give me your name."

Why does that matter? Kill her!

It matters, Idisio retorted. *It just* does.

He released the girl's voice back to her, ready to silence her again if necessary.

She swallowed hard and stared at him, chin tilting in proud defiance. "I have done nothing to deserve this death. I give you my name—Fekilla—not in fear, but in hopes that one day it may help you fight the demon inside of you."

Demon! Idiotic human, playing such innocence, his mother said. *All lies, humans only lie, they lie, they lie... She deserves pain and torment unending... Make her suffer... She dares call us demons!*

"Fekilla," Idisio repeated, then reached inside the girl's mind. Like a key in a door, the name gave him access to every moment of her life, every thought, every fear. He *owned* her. She would do anything he wanted. *Anything.*

Use this one, his mother said, eager, pressing forward. *A moment can be a thousand years to her. Take what you want from her. Take* everything. *This is the most* wonderful *experience—*

He remembered the girl in Sandsplit. Remembered how incredible that sensation had been. He could have that again, could stretch it out with what he'd learned since that day—

Yes, his mother said. *Yes, yes, that's right, this is what you are, this is what you're born to be!*

He drew in a long, difficult breath, looking at the girl's dark eyes; remembering similar, if colder, words coming from Deiq. Remembering the mad glare in his mother's eyes towards the end, and the icy determination in Tank's stare as he said *No.* That last memory gave him unexpected strength.

I won't be like that. I don't care what I was born to be. I won't enjoy their pain.

No.

Fekilla... die, Idisio said.

He could feel the blood slow throughout her body, her heart skipping, stopping, skipping, stopping. Muscles seized into tiny rebellions as moisture evaporated. Small bones, nails, and what scant body hair she'd been allowed to keep simply dissolved. Her pain was hypnotically beautiful, even in that condensed moment, and he felt a momentary, biting regret that he'd refused to draw it out.

She'd truly wanted to bear him a child. He could feel her aggrieved bewilderment at his refusal and her genuine terror that he'd removed the necklace, both scratching through the air with her dying exhale.

I thought you would be as a kindly god to me, her voice said without sound.

Fekilla folded to the ground without a sound, skin stretched tight around her bones. The knowledge faded as she fell, leaving only wispy scraps of sorrow and regret.

His mother groaned, furious. *You should have made her suffer... You would have kept her memories longer if she'd suffered. She might have known something important.*

He scooped up the necklace and draped it over his head once more, then pushed his mother's presence aside sharply, annoyed. She wasn't real. She was as dead as Fekilla. It was a stupid echo haunting his mind, nothing more. Thinking about Tank's solid refusal to suit what others wanted him to be was more useful.

"I will not walk into a cage," he said aloud, speaking to any hidden watchers as much as to the girl's silent bones. "I will not be a game piece for humans. I am ha'ra'hain, and *nobody* gets to order me around. I won't forget that again."

He turned in place once, twice, feeling out the way back to Alyea and Fimre, then *moved*—

—stepping into a twisting, inside-out nightmare of colors gone wrong and unbreathable air. Invisible razor wires sliced him into a hundred hundred diamond shaped pieces, scattering him across an unfathomable void.

Oh, shit—

Everything went black.

Chapter 12

A thick, smoky smell lingered in the air, unbothered by the erratic breeze. Alyea could feel the ambient temperature dropping nearly as rapidly as it had risen, and Fimre rubbed his good hand across his opposite shoulder, wincing as though chilled.

Far away, a series of thundering cracks sounded. Squinting, Alyea could just make out a fine spray of particles rising high into the air.

"Good gods," Fimre said, shivering, his attention only on the teyanain lord standing before them. "War with the Aerthraim? That's—closing the Horn is bad enough, but *war*? You'll destroy the entire southlands!"

Lord Evkit tilted his head, his expression a peculiar mix of amusement and annoyance. "The Families have gone soft, if that is the case," he said. "I have a higher opinion of them than you, apparently. Interesting."

"The *Agreement*," Fimre said, throwing one hand out in emphasis, as though that encapsulated everything he wanted to say.

Lord Evkit chuffed amusement, flicking his own fingers in dismissal. "Irrelevant," he said.

"Irrelevant, hells! It's the only thing that's kept the Horn from being demolished—" Fimre stopped short, his expression one of intense self-reproach.

Lord Evkit studied Fimre with dour appraisal. "I begin to think that you know more about certain internal teyanain matters than you properly should. Not surprising, given your past associates, but unfortunate."

Alyea stiffened as a sense of violence began to thread through the air. *Godsdamnit, Fimre!* Aloud, she said, in a tone of practiced calm, "Lord Evkit—"

"Do not speak right now, desert lord," Lord Evkit said, not taking his gaze from Fimre. "This moment is unfortunate enough as it stands."

Another voice cut in. "Calcen. It is unfortunate. It's also irrelevant at this point." Dinas Teyantin stood on the lowest step of the pergola entrance, looking up at them with a sober expression. "There's no returning ash to wood. You have already granted them safe passage. His statement was not a great enough offense to you or to the teyanain people to justify breaking that truce. Matters have moved beyond keeping that particular issue in the shadows."

Lord Evkit frowned at his subordinate. Alyea kept her breath shallow, watching his expression closely as it shifted from irritation to resignation.

He said, curtly, "Have you found my daughter, Teyantin?"

Dinas bowed with precise grace, hands palm-flat against his chest, and said, "No, lord. The net did not catch her."

Evkit grunted, clearly displeased, then looked back at Fimre. "You should thank my Teyantin, desert lord. He just saved your life."

"I intended to, Lord Evkit," Fimre said, then bowed to Dinas. "I owe you a life debt, Teyantin."

"Acknowledged." Dinas returned the bow, his mouth twitching as though he found the formality tedious. "With your forgiveness, I will return to my duties, lords. There are many in hiding who must be found before we depart this place."

"There is nothing to forgive," Fimre said before Lord Evkit could speak. That drew a hostile stare from the teyanain lord but no open comment. "Go with grace, Teyantin."

"My thanks to your grace, desert lord," Dinas said. He bowed to Lord Evkit, waited for his lord's nod, then turned and walked away.

Alyea let out a long, slow breath, blinking hard. Dinas had barely even glanced at her during that brief conversation. Did that mean she was now considered irrelevant? Or was it another facet of teyanain courtesy?

I'm never going to understand these people.

Lord Evkit let out a peculiar barking sound of surprise. A heartbeat later, an intense wave of heat and light swept over them, as though the pergola had burst into flame once more. Alyea covered her eyes reflexively, turning away; Fimre pulled her in against his shoulder, his own head bent.

Something large landed heavily on the floor of the pergola, and the heat dissipated.

"Ah," Lord Evkit said, surprise replaced by smugness. "And so the net was not entirely useless after all."

Alyea jerked free of Fimre's sheltering half-embrace and stared, incredulous. Idisio lay sprawled before them, blood streaking his face and hands. He rolled to one side, groaning, his gaze wandering witlessly.

"Grace to you, ha'ra'ha. You have more spirit and strength than I had expected," Lord Evkit said. In that moment, he looked—and sounded—a great deal like his daughter.

"He's under my protection," Alyea said before caution could stop her. Fimre made a strangled sound, then put his entire hand over his face, shaking his head slowly.

Evkit regarded her with raised eyebrows. "What makes you think a ha'ra'ha needs your protection, Lord Peysimun?"

"As the First Born isn't here to speak on Idisio's behalf, I believe it falls to me to uphold the First Born's interests." She felt her heart thudding in her ears. Fimre had dropped his hand and wore a dangerously flat expression. Apparently, by southern standards, she'd made another dreadful error; too late now.

Evkit stared at her for several heartbeats, unblinking. Idisio groaned again, struggling to sit up.

Deciding to run with what she'd started, Alyea put ice in her tone and said, "He *is* under my protection, Lord Evkit, and by extension under the protection of the First Born. Whether he needs it or not, he has it."

Evkit bowed gravely, his severe expression fading to amusement. "Your protection is noted and accepted," he said. "It is entirely possible that the First Born, when he hears of this matter, will be less pleased than you expect. But that is yours to deal with, not mine."

"We're leaving now," Alyea said. "*With* Idisio. And we're going south." She looked around, abruptly realizing she didn't actually know which way was south at the moment. The air felt—*refractive*, in a peculiar way that threatened to bring on a dizzy fit as she tried to sort out compass directions.

"I will have my Teyantin set you on the safest road," Evkit said.

"That's not necessary—" Alyea began, blinking hard and trying not to show her internal struggle for balance.

"Do you know where you are, desert lord?" Evkit inquired, his tone chilling to a distinct exasperation. "Do you know where the road is from here? Do you know how to avoid the traps that my daughter has placed throughout this place?"

Alyea looked at Fimre. He shook his head, squinting as though fighting a headache himself. "No," she admitted.

"Then it *is* necessary. Teyantin?" He didn't raise his voice, but the peremptory command *echoed* beyond the audible range.

"Yes, Calcen," Dinas said, once more on the lowest step. He regarded Idisio with visible surprise, then glanced at Evkit questioningly.

"The ha'ra'ha has been placed under the protection of Lord Peysimun as representative of the First Born," Evkit said in a tone at once mild and peculiarly flat, as though he were striving to be polite while speaking of something deeply annoying. "These three have decided to travel south."

Dinas drew in a slow breath, looking at each person in turn as though considering how to respond. "Yes, Calcen," he said at last.

Idisio sat up, blinking groggily, and groaned again. Within moments, his gaze sharpened, focusing on Lord Evkit, and the air turned chill and dangerous.

"Ha'inn," Lord Evkit said, apparently unconcerned by the tension. "Do you hear my voice? Do you understand my words?"

Idisio drew in a sharp, long breath, let it out more slowly, then climbed to his feet. Black flooded into his eyes.

"Ha-vash, ha'ne, ha'inn," Lord Evkit said, not moving. Dinas said something in another language, the words blurring together too quickly for Alyea to make out.

Idisio turned his head to stare at the colorfully dressed teyanain. Black slowly faded to a russet-tinged grey. The skin around his nose and eyes was puffy and streaked with red, as though veins had burst all throughout his upper face.

"No harm, ha'inn," Lord Evkit said. "You are under protection from Lord Peysimun as representative for the First Born. I cannot harm you. I wish to ask you a question. Will you permit that?"

"He's in no shape," Alyea began, unable to tear her gaze from Idisio's mottled face. The ha'ra'ha made an impatient silencing gesture with one hand.

"Ask," Idisio said, the word hoarse as though forced from a raw throat. His glare remained fixed on Evkit.

"Have you given a child to—" Evkit paused, glanced at Fimre, then went on, " —Tallisil's people?"

Not *my daughter's people*, Alyea noted with interest. Not *Cuna*. Apparently Evkit didn't want to say that name aloud again. She held her peace, trusting that Lord Evkit had good reason for the sidestep.

Idisio's shoulders drew forward, then went back, his chin rising, and delivered as bleak a glare as Deiq could have done. "Not that it's any of your business, but no," he said. "I did not."

Lord Evkit nodded, his mouth relaxing into a smile. "Thank you for the answer, ha'inn. I am pleased."

Alyea looked at the blood on Idisio's face and hands. She didn't ask what had happened to the girl.

"I won't do it for *you*, either," Idisio rasped. "No more cages. No more traps. Never again." He looked down at his bloodstained hands; slowly clenched them into fists, then spread them wide, palms up: all the blood had disappeared. "Never again," he repeated.

Evkit's amusement froze. He exchanged a glance with Dinas, then said, "We have no cages or traps in place this day, ha'inn. Please allow my Teyantin to take you and your companions to a safe road away from teyanain lands. I will request, as before, that you do not enter teyanain-held lands without my direct consent."

"Wait," Alyea said sharply. "Don't agree to that, Idisio. Lord Evkit. Kindly rephrase those overly broad terms."

She met the teyanain lord's hard gaze without flinching.

"You are quicker than at our last encounter, desert lord," Evkit said. "Very well. I request an agreement from ha'inn Idisio that he will not set foot on—"

"No," Idisio interrupted. The black had returned to his eyes. "No agreements. No restrictions. No more cages built of words. No."

Evkit stiffened. "Ha'inn—"

"You hold no power over me," Idisio said flatly. "Otherwise you'd be demanding, not requesting. I'm not on your lands, I'm not your prisoner, and I don't need anything from you." His voice cleared as he spoke, losing the rasp and acquiring an icy edge. Alyea stared, incredulous. Fimre tugged her back a step, his jaw tight, and motioned for her to stay silent.

Evkit's face darkened, his eyebrows drawing into a ferocious scowl. He shifted his weight as though to step forward. Fimre's grip on Alyea's arm tightened, and he drew her back another step.

"Calcen," Dinas said. "The ha'inn is correct." He gestured apology as Evkit's glare settled on him. "Grace to your grace, my lord, he speaks truth with the weight of law, whether he knows it or not. And this is perhaps not the time to focus on a relatively minor show of disrespect, when we have a far greater one to address." He motioned to the pergola around them.

Evkit breathed out, a heavy, harsh sound. "There are days I regret making you my Teyantin," he said grimly.

"I know, lord," Dinas said, ducking his head, nearly bowing. "Grace to your grace."

"Remove them, Teyantin," Evkit said. "Set them on the east road." He raised a warning finger to Idisio as he added, "Ha'inn—your prior agreement to stay out of the Horn *does* remain in effect."

Idisio said nothing, made no motion. His silent, bloodshot stare was as intimidating as anything Alyea had ever seen Deiq deliver. Evkit let out a thick, irritated sound and strode from the pergola, his Teyantin scarcely moving out of the way in time.

Alyea watched him walk away, struck once more by how small he was. Up close, his sheer presence always made him seem larger. She looked at Dinas, comparing the two. The Teyantin was taller than his lord, but still considerably shorter of stature than she herself, when seen on equal footing.

A smile curved Dinas's mouth as he regarded her. "You have poor vision, Lord Peysimun," he said. "You still look too much at the surface." He made a dismissive gesture and nodded at Idisio. "Ha'inn, will you allow me to move you to the east road? I swear that no harm, deceit, or ill intent is involved. As you already discovered, you cannot safely move yourself—and your companions would suffer far more if you tried to bring them along. I must be the one to move you, but I need your permission to do so."

Slowly, a placid grey bled back into the ha'ra'ha's eyes. Idisio glanced at Alyea, as though checking for disagreement, then nodded.

"Deep breath, please," Dinas said. "Deep deep, hold tight."

Chapter 13

Cold to warm, light to grey, a pressure that came as much from within as without... Idisio could feel Dinas guiding him through the inverse not-space with a surprisingly light touch.

Peripheral blurs radiated tension, resistance. Idisio sensed that Alyea and Fimre had the bulk of the Teyantin's attention at the moment. They weren't being particularly cooperative.

Humans rarely are, Dinas said without sound. *They do not understand, they fear, they fight.* The words were as much a sense of a resigned shrug as coherent speech.

Grey reversed to light, warm cut apart into a chill wind, and solid ground appeared underfoot. Alyea and Fimre staggered sideways, both looking thoroughly ill. The Teyantin, standing stone's throw away from Idisio, rolled his shoulders as though working out the strain.

"Holy gods," Fimre said, sitting down on a boulder. "I can't believe we're still alive." He leaned over his knees, shuddering. Alyea plopped down on the ground and let out an explosive sigh.

Idisio regarded them with a mixture of curiosity and bewilderment. Why did they make everything so difficult? Once the decision was made to allow someone control over your person, what was the point of fighting against that hold?

Dinas said something softly in another language, his eyes crinkling in amusement. Then, in kaenic, he added, "You are more unusual than you recognize, ha'inn. You have grown a great deal in a very short time. These two are not so far along the curve."

Alyea and Fimre appeared not to have heard the words. Idisio shot the Teyantin a sharp, distrustful stare, receiving only an amused head-tilt in response. He turned away, looking at their new surroundings.

A limited amount of flat space permitted only a few steps in any direction. Ragged ground, littered with boulders of varying sizes, dropped sharply to every side of the plateau but one, a craggy cliff-face dotted with rough-rooted plants too stubborn to admit defeat.

"That was tricky in spots," Dinas said as he perched atop another slab of rock, drawing his legs up into a cross-legged posture. He regarded the horizon pensively. "There are days when being Teyantin is a difficult task, even for me."

"Do you want sympathy?" Idisio snapped.

"*Idisio*," Alyea snapped right back. "That's *enough.* —Please accept my apologies, Teyantin."

Dinas shook his head. "I take no offense," he said. "It is one of the requirements of being Teyantin, to not take offense easily. An especially important skill with this Calcen." He leaned forward to trail his fingertips along the rock near his knees. "It is good to be away from the Horn now and again. I thank you for this opportunity."

Idisio stared at the oddly dressed teyanin. "Opportunity?" he said. "Are you—" He caught himself before the words *a slave?* could fall out of his mouth.

Alyea cut a sideways glance at Idisio, as though suspecting what he'd been about to say. She cleared her throat and said, "You almost sounded critical of Lord Evkit just now, Teyantin."

"I am one of very few who is permitted that luxury," Dinas said, unsmiling. He looked at Idisio for some moments before continuing. Clearly, the teyanin *had* heard the unspoken words, and found them insulting. "I have pushed my luxury as far as it will go today, I think. I should give the Calcen some time to reflect on my usefulness, rather than on the fact that I contradicted him multiple times in front of outsiders."

"Absence makes reflection gentler," Fimre observed. Dinas nodded.

"Indeed. And so I will stay here for a time, as he knew I would. If you wish, you may rest here safely. I will guard you."

"Do we have anything to *eat*?" Fimre muttered. "Gods, I could take a horse apart with my bare hands about now." Alyea nodded emphatic agreement.

Dinas smiled and handed each of them a small, twisted dark stick: jerky of some sort. "It is not spicy," he said as Alyea sniffed at it dubiously. "It is food we give to our children when they are hungry during a long day's work."

Alyea and Fimre's expressions soured, but they bit into the jerky without argument. Idisio shook his head and stuffed the jerky into his belt pouch, his stomach presently far too unsettled to accept food.

"Where are we?" Idisio turned to examine the rocky landscape around them. He saw no signs of a road, or any flat spot beyond the bare space upon which he stood.

"The east road." Dinas pointed. "If you climb that rock, ha'ra'ha, you will see the Wall stair. I have brought you to a spot halfway up, the closest I can safely approach. It is the best I can do to set you close to your destination."

"How do you know where we're headed?" Idisio challenged. His tone came out rougher than he'd intended, and Dinas's eyebrows dipped in a distinct frown.

"*Idisio,*" Alyea nearly moaned. She waved the stick of jerky at him scoldingly. Annoyed by her condescension, he stared back at her. She rolled her eyes, then dropped her gaze.

Dinas cleared his throat lightly, bringing their attention back to him. "It is not a difficult guess, ha'ra'ha," he said. "There are few places in the south that would draw both yourself and Lord Peysimun together at this particular time." Dinas inclined his head to Lord Fimre. "Without intending offense, Lord Sessin, I must assume you are along by accident of oversight."

Fimre let out a dry bark of laughter. "You're right on that," he said. "And hells, *I* don't even know where we're going—how could you have figured it—" He stopped, his head slowly turning. His gaze fastened on Alyea, then on Idisio. "Oh. Oh no. No, please. Not Scratha Fortress?"

"What's the matter with going to Scratha Fortress?" Idisio demanded, instantly aggrieved. *Why* did everyone seem to have this enormous bias against Lord Scratha?

Fimre buried his head against his knees again and groaned. "I'm not going to Scratha Fortress," he declared. He took a quick glance at Idisio, then directed his glare at the sky. "I'll head down the Wall Stair, thank you, and take ship back to Sessin Fortress. It's not as though you have any reason to bring me along!"

"No reason *not* to, either," Idisio said stubbornly. "What's the matter with going to Scratha Fortress?" For some reason, he dearly wanted Fimre to admit to his irrational dislike of Lord Scratha.

"Why are you trying to pick a fight with everyone?" Alyea demanded in evident exasperation. Idisio ignored her, even as a small voice in the back of his mind agreed with her question.

They can't hurt me, he thought. *I'm the one with the greatest status here. I won't take being treated like a child!*

Dinas Teyantin let out a tiny chuff. Idisio couldn't tell whether it was in laughter or offense. His dark face remained entirely expressionless, his emotions tightly closed off.

"Ha'inn," Fimre said, "No offense, but haven't you noticed that Lord Scratha isn't exactly fond of my Family? I haven't been invited, and I *won't* be welcome. You don't need me, and I have a mess that needs to be cleaned up on my own doorstep. Why *would* I want to go to Scratha Fortress?"

Idisio blinked, realizing that he had, actually, forgotten that Fimre came from Sessin Family. There was a strange haze over his mind, obscuring peripheral details, ghosting out recent events. He touched his chest, feeling the bumps of bluestone beads, and tried not to look worried.

"He's right, Idisio," Alyea said. "Let him go. He's been through enough."

"*Thank* you, Lord Peysimun," Fimre said heavily, apparently as annoyed by her mothering as Idisio.

"I don't know if I can claim that title any longer," she said, glancing up at the nearby cliff wall. Idisio noticed heavy dark circles under her eyes. A moment's focus told him that she was exhausted, hungry, and more than a little angry about—something—although the source wouldn't come clear. Just then, she shot him a scowl. He shrugged and looked away, refusing any sign of apology for intruding.

Fimre, halfway to his feet, paused. He shot Idisio a glance, then straightened to his full height, wincing as he tugged the rumpled sling back into place. "Until I'm formally told otherwise, you deserve the grace of the title," he said soberly.

"Wait," Idisio interrupted, memory clarifying into an unwisely blurted question: "Lord Oruen said you tried to kill him? Is that what you're talking about?"

"You did *what*?" Dinas said, impassivity cracking into incredulity, then burst into unrestrained laughter.

"She went mad for a while," Fimre cut in. His good hand moved to cup his broken arm. "That's the easiest way to say it. She was told that if she left the room without the king's permission, she'd lose all her lands and titles."

"Oh," Idisio said, more a long exhalation than a word. "Oh. I didn't know that."

"Obviously," Fimre retorted. "I'm beginning to wonder what you *do* know, ha'inn."

Idisio felt his veins ice over. "Don't presume, desert lord," he said in the same cold tone he'd used with Lord Evkit.

Alyea spoke up. "What is the *matter* with you, Idisio? You're acting like—like Deiq."

Idisio blinked several times, vision shifting across multiple spectrums, and finally shut his eyes. The small voice in the back of his mind that agreed with Alyea crowed in triumph. He let it gloat for a moment, then shoved it aside. "I know," he said then, his voice subdued. "I'm beginning to understand—why Deiq acts the way he does." He glanced at the teyanain. Dinas said nothing, a half-smile on his face that seemed more weary than mocking.

"I'll take that as my cue to leave," Fimre said laconically.

"You should rest first," Alyea answered. Idisio barely kept himself from rolling his eyes. What was it going to *take* for her to stop being so... so motherly... the haze across his mind swirled, distracting him into looking up at a hawk soaring far overhead.

She's showing concern, the small voice in his mind pointed out. *She obviously likes Fimre. They know each other.* He couldn't help wondering how *well* they knew one another, given how she was acting; but that was none of his business.

The hawk passed out of sight. Idisio lowered his gaze from the vastness of the sky, feeling calmer, and studied the small plants enthusiastically sprouting from every crevice in the rock, as though trying to escape the mountain's strangling grip.

You do have an imagination, ha'ra'ha... A ghostly, sharp laugh slid through his mind, mocking, shattering the momentary peace. Idisio looked up and around again, more intently this time, but sensed no presence beyond their own. When he met Dinas's gaze, the Teyantin shook his head slightly, as though he once more sensed what Idisio was thinking.

"Forgive me for being rude, but I'd sleep easier with some distance between us," Fimre said, bowing to Dinas. "I still owe you a life debt, Teyantin. Ought we to resolve that before I go?"

Dinas studied Fimre speculatively for a moment, all humor fading from his face. He looked up at the sky, as Idisio had just done; then slowly shook his head. "I release you from that debt, desert lord."

"That—thank you, Teyantin," Fimre said, clearly startled and more than slightly suspicious. "May I ask—without offense—why?"

"I don't need anything from you right now, and I dislike keeping track of outstanding debts." Dinas looked up towards the Horn ridge high above them, his forehead creasing as though he were listening to a faraway sound. "I should go."

Idisio squinted at the Teyantin, wary. That had been a distinctly evasive and incomplete answer. "I thought you were going to rest here for a while," he prodded. "Let Lord Evkit settle down."

"I changed my mind," Dinas said. He stood. "Grace to your grace, Lords Peysimun and Sessin, ha'inn. May your gods protect you." He bowed once, then turned and leapt high in the air.

In mid-leap, the Teyantin caught at a thick, gnarled root that protruded from the cliff face. He swung to stand atop it, grasped another handhold and pulled himself up, then repeated the process, skipping like a four-legged, sticky-footed spider across an impossibly steep surface.

"Holy gods," Fimre said, staring in astonishment. "I knew they were good climbers, but—gods."

"Don't watch." Alyea tore her own gaze away. "It's rude."

Fimre shook his head, as though rousing himself from a daze. "Yes. Of course." He shook his head again, then bowed to Alyea and Idisio. "I'll be on my way. Forgive me for not thanking either of you for your company." The sour cast returned to his mouth.

"Forgiven," Alyea said quietly. "But I'll thank *you*, Fimre. You've done more than your duty."

"Don't remind me," Fimre muttered. "Seriously—don't *ever* remind me." He scrambled over the rocks in the direction of the trail, grunting in audible pain, and was soon gone from sight.

Alyea turned to Idisio. "This is the closest to privacy I think we're going to get from this point on," she said. "So will you please tell me what the hells is going on?"

A pain stitched through his side. Briefly, he wondered if the Teyantin had been shielding him in some way, but the thought muddied and dissipated before he could think about the implications. It served to remind him of the urgency, so he said, "Let me summarize to save time. Lord Scratha needs my help. That means something big has gone wrong. I wanted someone to help me. Tank was my first choice, but he refused and told me to get you. You know the rest."

Her face mottled with incredulous fury, her voice rock-rattling loud as she bellowed, "You destroyed my entire fucking life for *Cafad Scratha*?"

Chapter 14

Deiq didn't need to sleep, as Teilo had pointed out, but he *enjoyed* the drifting loss of responsibility, the endless space for still, slow contemplation. In the moments when he roused to check on his surroundings, he could tell that for all her protests, Teilo was also taking advantage of the time to rest. He hoped it would sweeten her temper.

Morning dawned cold and windy. Deiq lay quiet, looking up at the ceiling, listening to the rattling shutters and tracking temperature shifts throughout the room. It always amused him to watch cooler air encountering his skin. A finger's breadth away from contact, it nearly sizzled as it veered aside to seek easier prey. Between his own body heat and Teilo's filling the room, the chill breeze was reduced to fussing with curtains and flowing out through the gap under the door to annoy the humans.

He'd never been able to show that clarity of vision to Alyea, although he'd tried. She was sharp, for a human, but still limited in her ability to *see* the world. He wondered if Idisio had managed to master the necessary focus yet; veered away from the thought as sharply as the air veered from his skin. It wasn't safe to think about Idisio. The next time he *saw* Idisio, he was duty-bound to kill the younger ha'ra'ha.

Not that Deiq had followed duty particularly well over the years. Still, Idisio's choices hit at one of the rawest spots among ha'reye and ha'ra'hain. Killing another ha'ra'ha by feeding from her mandated an inflexible death sentence.

Deiq sat up, rubbing a hand over his face, and redirected his thoughts to more immediate matters. Teilo stirred, sighed, then rose from her bed. "That wasn't unpleasant," she conceded.

"Breakfast," Deiq said succinctly, and began rebraiding his loosened hair.

"Wasteful," she told him, stroking one hand over her hair. It braided itself into a tidy bundle under her fingers, locked into shape by her will alone. He shrugged, finished his hand-braiding, and secured the tail with a small tie.

He turned his head at a small sound, focusing: *Ah.* The servant by their door had just left to warn the innkeep that his honored guests were awake and interested in food. He smiled, smoothing wrinkles out of his clothes with contented smugness.

The small dining room they'd sat in the night before was once again empty of occupants when they arrived. Not surprising, as Deiq had made his preference for solitude well known over the years. The sideboard was laden with sweet and savory pastries, a fresh pot of tea, and an assortment of fruit.

Teilo shook her head at the luxury and refused everything except a cup of tea and a small biscuit. Deiq sampled a bit of everything, taking his time, paying attention to both tangible and intangible sensations. A spicy meat pastry carried the impression of the cook's laughter, while a sliced sunfruit bore the sense of a young girl laboring diligently at a new task.

Eventually, Teilo said, "This tea isn't unpleasant." She took another sip. "I don't think I've ever had anything quite like this."

"It's made from locally grown herbs," Deiq said. "It is unique."

"Bold claim," Teilo returned dryly.

"Find me a match for it, then," Deiq answered.

Teilo shook her head and began picking apart the biscuit as though expecting it to crumble under her fingers. She tilted her head in visible surprise as it separated into flaky layers.

"Also local," Deiq noted, smiling at her expression. "I've made sure they have good milk cows."

She took a tentative bite, then rapidly devoured the rest of the biscuit. Deiq carefully minded his own breakfast, keeping his amusement hidden.

"You have put a great deal of effort into the trivial," Teilo said, wiping crumbs from her lips, tone acerbic in an obvious attempt to regain her dignity.

"It's kept me amused," Deiq said lightly. "I'm fond of humans, Teilo. They're fascinating creatures." He cleared his throat, nodding at her by way of reminding her of her own origins.

Teilo snorted, her chin lifting. "The people here don't seem fond of *you*, for all your gracious help."

"I haven't been back this way in many years," Deiq admitted. "I probably wasn't overly polite, last time they saw me. I don't remember." He shrugged, waving a hand to dismiss the topic. "Are you done eating? I'm ready to move on if you are."

"You've invested far too much of yourself in being human," Teilo said as they rose to their feet. "That's what's put both of us into this nonsensical position. You do realize that?"

She was clearly back at her old game of prodding at him until he lost his temper. More than likely she considered it a dominance test or some such nonsense. She hadn't been out among humans nearly long enough to abandon the games of the Jungle disciples.

Deiq stopped and turned to study her with narrowed eyes. "If I hadn't learned to act and think like a human," he pointed out, "I would long since be as dead as my brothers. So scolding me on that point is the same as saying you wish I was dead. Have *you* thought of that?"

"No," she said after a moment. "I—I didn't see it quite that way. I—" She swallowed, turning her gaze away, closing her eyes briefly. "I won't do that again."

"I'm well aware you have many reasons to want me dead." He kept his tone cold and pragmatic. "But that's not a good beginning for trust, is it? I want my freedom. You want your freedom. Neither of us particularly *wants* to die. So wait until we're back on equal footing to start sniping at me, Teilo, or I'll kill you here and now and the hells with what happens to me."

She stared, round-eyed, leaning back as though fighting the urge to retreat, then nodded jerkily. "Yes, *ha'inn*," she said. "Let's move on, then, before the day's older than I am. It's a long climb to the top."

He smiled without humor and steered her from the room.

They walked without speaking, edging through the narrow, crowded streets that gradually rose higher and higher above sea level. Deiq turned away insistent merchants, beggars, and pickpockets, scarcely thinking about it. Teilo seemed lost in her own thoughts and made no sign of noticing the various interruptions.

As the foot of the Wall Stair came into view, a low, rumbling boom came from high above, and the sky darkened under a fast-spreading cloud of dust. Deiq stared, appalled, as a half-mile-wide section of the cliff edge began, majestically, to fall.

Chapter 15

"You're overreacting," Idisio muttered.

Alyea cut him a sideways glare as cold as the air and said nothing. A night's uneasy sleep on the small plateau had done nothing to ease her temper. They'd risen well before dawn by unspoken agreement, and scrambled across the rocks, as Fimre had done, to find the stair.

As they walked, Idisio tried to continue his explanation, telling her that he owed Cafad everything, that he'd promised to help if called. He told her about the stitch in his side every time he delayed. He was polite to the humans they passed going the other way, even when they crowded him aside as though *they* had right of way.

Nothing made the slightest difference. She still glared as though considering whether to toss him over the edge of the Wall stair.

He had to get Alyea settled down and listening again. There were other things that needed to be discussed before they reached the top of the Wall stair—including the inevitable encounter with a distinctly odd ha'ra'ha. And that meant opening up a conversation about Ellemoa, and what had happened after the kidnapping, and why he'd never come back to Bright Bay.

Idisio didn't want to have that conversation with her. *Ever.* But he also knew Alyea well enough to know that if he let her walk into the situation ignorant, she'd be vastly more dangerous than if he explained it all up front.

"Oruen isn't that important right now," Idisio tried next. "There's other—"

She stopped walking and pushed him up against the wall to their right, glaring at him with all-too-human outrage. "Not that important?" she nearly snarled. "*Not that important*? The moment you took me out of that prison cell without Oruen's permission, I lost *everything*. My land. My title. My family home. All of my property. Everything held in Peysimun name or on Peysimun lands now belongs to the king. Every last brass bit, every box of thopuh. There is no way for me to get that back. I can't even go back to Bright Bay, because he'll have a standing order out to kill me on sight by now. Don't you think any of that is *important*?"

He held still, holding his temper, being calm, being polite against her aggression. At least he wasn't feeling the need to fight for dominance as he had in the king's prison tower, maybe because Fimre wasn't present this time.

Carefully even, he answered, "Since there's nothing we can do to fix it right at the moment, no. I don't think any of that is important. Once we get done helping Scratha, I'll turn every influence I have to getting you reinstated, because I'm responsible. I give you my word on that, Lord Peysimun. You will get it all back."

She let go of his collar, stepping back as though belatedly realizing what she'd just done. "I don't see how you can have any hope of filling that promise," she said bitterly.

"I've learned a few things since you last saw me. Speaking of which, there's a lot you need to understand, yourself."

"I'm actually going to get all the information before I walk into the storm this time?" she said, sardonic. "The sand may swallow us all."

"If you're willing to stop glaring at me and *listen*, I'll tell you as much as I can." He glanced up, gauging the distance left to the top of the Wall stair. There was one more resting spot, not far from the top. They ought to reach it around dusk. "So... I need to start from when you last saw me. That was at your family mansion, right? I left in the middle of the night. Well, I was kidnapped, I suppose, but I didn't know that at the time. I just remember feeling—*strange*. Everything seemed hazy. I couldn't remember what I was doing in a noble house, and I expected to be thrown out as a thief at any moment—"

"Stop," Alyea said. She pulled him to the side of the path, into a shallow alcove. "If you start there, this is going to take far too long." *Let's speed this up*, she added silently. *Just* tell *me*. She touched the side of her head, as though to make sure he hadn't missed the inference.

He stared, bemused. "I don't think that's a good idea," he said. "Words are... safer."

"And slower," she pointed out. "Remember, I'm the one who was mad enough to marry Deiq. And I've seen—" She paused, her gaze cutting to one side briefly. "I've seen my share of horrible things. I can handle whatever you tell me. So—*summarize*, please."

Idisio hesitated, studying her. Intuition lay blank, but he had a feeling, all the same, that this wouldn't end well. A sharp, jagged ache stitched through him as he began to refuse. He stopped, wincing, and put a hand to his stomach, where the worst of the pain was centered.

"Damnit," he muttered. If this happened every time he paused, he'd have to skip over distance to speed their travel. He'd never tried going *up* before, but there seemed no reason it should be more difficult than horizontal.

In any case, he *didn't* really like the notion of trying to explain the whole complicated tale out loud. She might be right, after all.

"Fine," he said. "I'll do this the fast way. Ready?"

She nodded. Abruptly impatient, not wanting to look at it himself, he ungraciously dumped the sequence into her mind.

Dark/WET/cold/FEAR—grey eyes, impossibly huge, dangerously close—and then—

Alyea screamed, a raw, unhinged sound, and collapsed.

Idisio waved off the immediate attention of the nearest humans. "She's all right," he assured them. "Does this sometimes. Go on, go on."

They cast dubious looks at him, at each other, then shrugged and went on their way without protest. Alyea moaned, rolling to her knees, and vomited a thin strip of drool onto the stone.

"I tried to warn you," Idisio muttered, unable to help a certain smug tone. He helped the shivering desert lord to sit against the alcove wall, then stepped back, letting her recover. To his surprise, he felt fragments of *her* memories seeping through his mind. He pushed that aside for later examination, and kept his attention on the desert lord.

"You." Her voice was sand-hoarse. "She was. You—you *killed—*" She shook her head, rubbing her throat as if speaking were painful at the moment.

"She was my mother," Idisio said in a low voice, no longer the least bit smug or amused. "Yes. And I killed her."

Alyea sat very still, breathing very carefully. He could feel her sorting through what he'd shown her. He stood quietly, his back against the stone, and stared out into the nothingness beyond the stair edge.

A random and apparently disconnected series of her memories wound through his mind: Her own mother, Hama, who'd been both cruel and loving and who hadn't, it turned out, been her true mother at all; Micru, dark-eyed and deadly, watching through spy holes in the palace, rarely speaking; Oruen, younger, not yet king, gathering her into his arms, his head on her shoulder as he shook with reaction to the latest excess of a mad king—

She loved him, a young love, quickly broken on the harsh reality of politics, but it was powerful while it lasted. She would have done anything for Oruen, would do anything for someone she loved—even as she refused to use the word *love*, finding it entirely too dangerous an emotion. *Loyalty* was safe, *honor* was safe. Not love. Never love.

He pushed the swirling morass of her thoughts aside before he could become too intrigued by the contradictions. He had more important things to handle at the moment than understanding Alyea's motivations.

Travelers went by in one direction or another; murmuring, laughing, stomping, cursing, singing, silent. They resembled ghosts when set against the darker shadows currently playing through his mind. He blinked hard and pushed *all* memory aside, irritated at the continual intrusion of the past into the present. It didn't *matter*. He had to get to Scratha Fortress, that was all, and nothing else could interfere with that.

"You were right," Alyea said finally. "Words would have been better."

Idisio shrugged, feeling his face settle into a hard, closed off expression. "Can we move on now? Or do you have *more* questions?"

She took his outstretched hand and let him pull her to her feet. Contact overlapped perception: A distant scream still haunted the corners of her awareness, and a dead girl's blank stare flickered in peripheral vision. The wet eyes of a priest as he cradled the body of a woman he'd loved for no good reason but a number of very bad ones; the abrupt end to a moment of infinite possibility; the broken, jagged emptiness of realizing that there was, now, no remaining chance at going back to anything resembling an ordinary life. The lifeless husk of the teyanin girl who'd only wanted to gain honor by bearing a ha'ra'hain child.

Idisio tried to let go of her hand. *I don't want to see this, godsdamnit!* But his fingers refused to move, his muscles locked for an endless moment of internal torment.

Memory of a voice in darkness, a smoky attempt at seduction—Riss shivering in fear—Cafad Scratha's grey face as he stumbled back into camp. *A ha'ra'ha living at the top of the Wall.* They'd be facing it soon.

My whole life I never knew ha'ra'hain or ha'reye existed, Alyea thought wearily, *and now I'm practically tripping over them every time I turn around.*

Idisio laughed aloud. "Yeah. I think that sometimes too."

Underneath his amusement was a bleak, bitter resignation that made him think of Deiq. *This is why he's always so sour and cynical, because otherwise everything* hurts *too much.* He set his teeth together, shoving that thought back into silence.

"Anyway. Now you know. So let's move on."

"Wait," Alyea said as his weight shifted towards taking a step away from her. "Idisio, wait."

He paused, raising an eyebrow.

"You're—" She hesitated, as though not entirely sure how to phrase it. "You did what you had to do," she said finally. "At... at the time, what you thought you had to do." She drew in a difficult breath. "I don't think you're a monster."

So she was back to being protective and motherly. That was the *last* thing he needed at the moment. "I don't need absolution from *you,* Alyea," he said with chill precision. "Is that all? If so, let's move on, now that you have your answers."

She took a wobbly step, another; resumed plodding up the Wall Stairs behind him. He waited until she'd regained her internal balance, then paused, looking up the Stair. Nobody nearby in either direction at the moment, and in any case he really didn't care whether disappearing would alarm any humans. He had to get *moving.* This was taking too long, and he didn't want to hear any more of her fussing.

"Walking is pointless," he observed. "Let's take a shortcut."

Alyea shuddered involuntarily. "*That* shortcut, I don't care for. I'd rather walk."

"And *I've* already climbed these stairs once in my lifetime. I don't want to do it again," he retorted. He stepped closer, grasping her right arm with one hand, and pulled her up against him.

She inhaled sharply, feral vision-hunger still echoing in her bones. Her recent brush with that internal world of blood fueled heat and iced emotion had altered her perception of Idisio, added an overlay of connection to Deiq—

—In darkness, in light, his hands, her mouth, arching, howling, biting, completely lost—

Holy gods. If he didn't manage to slap her back to sense he'd take her right here up against the wall. *Damnit—*

Her emotions/perceptions tumbled across him like a ferocious sandstorm. Idisio was febrile where Deiq had been rooted, thin and bony where Deiq had been solid. Idisio felt like green things, newly turned earth, where Deiq was spice and old things long since crumbled to sand. Deiq had always commanded her complete attention with his age and utter confidence. Idisio drew her in with his tumbling, raw, *young* energy.

Heat cascaded through her from head to foot. She pressed closer, her breathing stifled.

I'm not Deiq, godsdamnit, I'm not what she wants, I'm not a fucking substitute for him, I'm not doing this—

Idisio fought for clarity, for refusal, and managed to say, in a voice filled with stinging contempt, "Seriously? You want to fuck right *now*?"

Ice replaced heat. She broke free, stepped back, half-turned away; gasping for breath, shivering all over, her thoughts a chaotic tangle dominated by a sincere and searingly intense desire to strike him. He felt her forcing herself away from violence, heard her reminding herself that unlike Deiq, Idisio wouldn't restrain himself from a matching response.

I wouldn't hit her, godsdamnit, Deiq *is more likely to do that then I am.* But if it helped her regain sense, he wouldn't argue that perception. "My fault," he offered, hoping that would calm her further. He drew in a long breath, then another. "I wasn't paying attention."

It seemed to work. Her jumbled emotions cooled back toward sanity. She turned to face him, her face a neutral mask.

He made himself smile at her and held out a hand. When she took it, her own hands still trembling, he tugged her close, much more gently and dispassionately, this time. Colors blurred; the world turned inside out and sideways, and familiar nausea and muscle aches overwhelmed him for a timeless heartbeat.

The heat that rose along his spine in that not-place was peculiar: *Strength, endurance, she'll let me do—anything—anything—oh, gods—I have to—I* need *to—*

As fog clarified to solid shapes once more and Alyea's body pressed against his, with her scent thick in his nostrils and remnants of her recent arousal spiking through him, he shivered, not at all sure what he was fighting against or why. He cleared his throat, blinking hard, and forced himself to say, "Could we talk about that, uhhmm, impulse of yours—I was maybe a bit rude in my reaction...."

Before she could answer, his vision hazed with yellow.

Se'thiss, t'a-karnain, someone said. *Welcome back. I have been waiting for you to return and allow me to teach you.*

"Oh, shit," Idisio blurted, the overwhelming *need* disappearing just that quickly. "I'd *forgotten*—he tried to warn me—Alyea, *run*!"

"But you *did* tell me that there was a—" she began.

You are ready to create children, I see, the voice went on, ponderous, unrolling into their minds even as Idisio spoke. *You bring a desert lord who interests you. Very good. Come to me, and I will show you –*

"I can't have children," Alyea protested.

Of course you can, desert lord.

"No. I can't. Deiq said so—"

"Alyea, stop arguing *and get out of here,*" Idisio snapped. If she went far enough out of range, maybe it wouldn't be able to haul her in to serve as his godsdamn *breeding stock*. Images of the chi-huerg girl collapsing to the ground, skin taut, eyes glazed, bit into his mind. He wouldn't let Alyea be used that way any more than he'd let *himself* be used for stud. *No.*

Deiq? the Wall ha'reye said.

"De'sta'haiq," Alyea said, still too slow to understand the danger, caught in the human reflex of *answering questions*. "The First Born."

Ah. That one. He lied if he told you such a thing. But that is irrelevant. You may serve, and you will *serve. Come to me –*

"No," Idisio said. "No, she's not here to bear my child. I'm not interested in that, *ha'inn*. You're misunderstanding. I'm just passing through. I'll come back to speak with you another day. We have to keep going—"

You would refuse a kin-visit? The voice was edged with stern disapproval. *Your human companions have not taught you well. Have you not spent time with your own kin yet? I told you to seek out your own, as I recall. I see that you have met – wait. I cannot see. I should see, and I cannot –*

The voice cut off abruptly. Silence turned thick with danger.

"*Run*," Idisio said frantically, shoving at Alyea. "I can handle this, but it'll *hurt* you—get out of here!"

You both wear that which blocks me from seeing you clearly, young one, the voice said, speaking even more slowly than before. *I do not like that. It is rude and forbidden besides. Remove your protections and come to me. Both of you.*

"No," Idisio said aloud. "*No*. Leave her alone."

Chill, dark laughter snaked through their minds. Alyea stumbled back a step, rubbing a hand over her eyes as though trying to clear the golden haze from her vision.

You are still young, the voice said. *And I am still your elder, and the stronger. You* will *both do as I say.*

Idisio felt his hand wrap around the bluestone chain. He fought to unclench his fingers, even as the beads pressed painfully hard against malleable skin. Alyea went to her knees, beads scattering about her, head tilted back, and screamed. In the moment of shifting his attention to that sound, his hand yanked the necklace free.

Now you will come to me, the voice said.

A heartbeat later, the world imploded into darkness and agony.

Chapter 16

A double heartbeat after the cascade began, a sharp pain raced through Deiq's entire body. He found himself clutching at his face as though to relieve skin pulled taut to the ripping point. His involuntary bellow held as much startled outrage as pain.

Outrage. Not rage. He wasn't angry, not the way he should have been, it was more... a twisted, sideways-out sensation, as though his whole being, not just his body, was being pulled in two....

Oh hells, he thought vaguely. *Alyea. Of course. Middle of a disaster, like always. Then again, humans usually say that about* me....

Even as he grumbled to himself, he was already searching for a destination, instinct outlining the path, serving as infallible guide. He heard Teilo calling his name, angry, peremptory. He ignored her, took a physical step, another, began the sideways turn—

Her words came clear, drilling into his awareness with a severity that told him she'd pushed them into his mind as well as his ears: "You're *not* going into the middle of that mess!"

He felt the burring pressure against his chains, like a hand laid across vibrating harp strings. A sharp ache reaved through his muscles, jerking him sideways a step, breaking his concentration. "It's Alyea," he said through gritted teeth. "Let me go!"

"If she's up there, she's already—"

He didn't wait for her to finish. Aggravation crested past the breaking point, and he twisted the intangible chains away from her with an effort that brought crimson streaks to the corners of his vision and drew a scream of real agony from her.

I'm only warning you once. The red haze began to cloud his vision. He pushed it back harshly. *Next time, I* will *kill you.*

He turned his attention to the collapsing cliff face again, picking out the safe spots. The area was far too unstable, in more than the physical plane, to allow easy movement. It took barely a heartbeat to decide, three more beats to change position—once, twice; four, six times. Then he was clear of the collapsing section, standing on solid ground a stone's throw from the remnants of the stone monument that he'd put in place long ago as both warning and promise.

He could sense Teilo, just out of arm's reach behind him. She'd kept pace with impressive ease, following his positions exactly. *How did you break the chains?* she demanded. *I didn't think that was possible!*

They hadn't been broken. He'd yanked them out of *her* control. He'd be paying the price as soon as the teyanain realized what he'd done. He didn't tell her any of that. She'd lost the right to explanations.

"Be silent and stay out of my way," he told her, adding a rough push of command. It wouldn't affect her, but it indicated how serious he was about the order.

"Yes, ha'inn," she said, her tone desert-dry, and bowed in what might have been genuine or mocking respect. He didn't want to look at her closely enough to find out.

He turned his back on her and studied the monument—what was left of it. The top had shattered as though from some immense blast of pressure coming from deep beneath the ground. The base was cracked and crumbling as he watched.

Somewhere behind them, humans were shouting, searching, recovering wounded from collapsed buildings. He ignored that. There were always at least two humans working at the Wall Inn that knew what to do in this sort of emergency. He'd made sure of that, over the years. Faereen—as Teilo had said—weren't *safe* to be around, even with the controls Deiq had put in place.

One such control was access. There was no simple pathway from the surface to the underground tunnels. There never had been. He'd never intended humans to wander into conversation with this particular child. Only someone with ha'ra'hain blood could draw its attention through the wards he'd put up. It shouldn't even have *noticed* Alyea's presence. What the hells had happened?

A moment's concentration gave him the answer. Outraged echoes of *Kinslayer!* still lingered, and the afterimages of a brief but powerful altercation slid, ghostlike, along the edges of the disintegrating rocks. *She's traveling with Idisio. Oh,* that's *fucking wonderful. I thought I warned him not to come back here....*

A glance at Teilo showed that her face had gone an odd greenish-yellow shade, as though she were about to be violently ill. She sank to the ground, blinking rapidly, and almost gasped, "Dear gods. It's hurt, so hurt...."

"Quiet," he said, not harshly this time; unwillingly sympathetic to her panic. He, too, could feel the faereen's fluttering, crystalline pain. The wards were shredded to scant wisps. Anyone with a fingertip of sensitivity could feel the faereen's presence now.

Kin-slayer, betrayal, betrayal, rightfully attacked, refusal to pay, refusal to submit, desert lord betrayal, wrongfully attacked, traitor-monster, too strong, wrongfully attacked....

Deiq translated the tumbling word/images: It hadn't expected real resistance, had focused on punishing Idisio for his crime, hadn't expected Alyea to attack. At least, from the sound of it, Idisio hadn't had a chance to hit back. Alyea had caught the faereen from behind, so to speak.

What had given Alyea so much strength that she could damage a *faereen?* It was *impossible*. She was human—desert lord, yes, but merely *human*—

I'm forgetting something important. What am I forgetting? Thready memory flickered through his mind, tickling, insistent— but right now, heartbeats mattered. Solving puzzles, remembering relevant information, took too long. He'd think about it later.

He reached out without moving a muscle; listening, sensing, extending a silent greeting, sending a call for survivors amongst the wreck.

De'sta'haiq, the faereen said, its voice tinny and labored. *The humans have betrayed us. They plan... to kill us all... cage us... I am hurt. Help me. I knew you would come. Help me*—

There was no trace of Alyea or of Idisio. Had the faereen killed them both?

I am here. I will come to you, Deiq answered, motioning Teilo to stay put, and took a physical/not-physical step, turning, pulling himself through a doorway that didn't exist, and emerging a dozen stumbling heartbeats later into a furnace blast of heat and light.

The air reeked of heated underground rocks: The silky bitterness of quartz, the layered complexity of coal, the nose-scraping tang of the enormous salt boulders Deiq had brought in hundreds of years ago....

His clothes began to smolder. He swore at himself for forgetting that detail. Nothing human-made ever survived the heat of an established nest. He stripped the flimsy cloth aside with impatient gestures and let it fall to the ground. A heartbeat later, the garments simply dissolved into ash.

The air felt considerably cooler against his bare skin. He allowed himself to enjoy that for a single eyeblink, then focused on his duty. *Cousin*, he said. *I am here. I serve.*

A layer peeled back from the nearest salt boulder, like an enormous, nearly translucent flap of skin. *De'sta'haiq*, the faereen said. *I am hurt. The humans have betrayed us. They want to kill us all....*

The flap rolled itself up to one side, out of the way. Deep within the salt boulder, a golden light began to glow.

You are hurt. Deiq was careful to focus his thoughts with razor precision. *I serve.*

You are my father, the faereen said. *You do not serve me!*

Deiq held back a surge of panic at that. *Father*, under the ha'reye interpretation of the concept, came with vastly restrictive responsibilities that he'd always managed to avoid. He said, *I am not your father*—

You are the last of my near-kin, you saved my life, you have been by my side every time I looked for aid, it said simply. *What else should I call you? Bring me a human of strength. I sensed one nearby....*

He could feel it reaching out, searching for Teilo. "That one is unsuitable," he said hastily. *Her service is tainted. You cannot draw from her.*

Why does it still live? the creature asked, then its attention wandered. *The humans have betrayed us. They have created a thing that burns...I am in pain.*

I serve, Deiq said helplessly. *I permit you to draw from me. I will serve.*

I cannot. You are kin. I cannot risk harming you.

I am your elder, Deiq said firmly. *I will say what is permitted. In this instance, you may draw from me. I will recover. I tell you this is allowed. I serve!*

No, his brother's child said, voice weakening with each word. *I cannot break permitted behavior, even now, even... now...* It paused. Then, gathering determination, it went on, *There are humans above. They are already dying. It is wasteful not to use them. It may be enough to allow me to enter the healing sleep.*

"They're already—oh, hells," Deiq said aloud, reflexively searching through the lives high above their heads. Dozens of humans, including the ones Deiq had trained as watchers, were pinned beneath fallen timbers or struck senseless by chunks of flying rocks. The remainder had already turned to madness under the faereen's projections and begun battling one another.

So much for safety measures. I underestimated the danger. Teilo was right. He'd have to remember to tell her that.

Taking Deiq's pause for assent, the faereen reached out once more, riffling through the available lives as a human might flip through a book. The air took on an even more acidic tinge as it concentrated.

There are only two of value, the faereen said, disappointed. *And they are hardly useful. They were diluted. I must have the unstable one. There is nothing else strong enough in the area.*

Deiq could sense the human lives flickering out. Two of them, stronger than the others, probably the first children of desert lords, convulsed in agony for a handful of heartbeats before falling silent.

You cannot, Deiq said, blocking the faereen's renewed attempt to collect Teilo. *She is forbidden. She is the First among the Chosen. You cannot use her!*

The yellow glow brightened to an intense gold. Two other salt boulders began flickering red and orange. A wave of incredulity and outrage beat against Deiq, sending him stumbling against a wall for support. The heat scorched his palms and he jerked back, hastily readjusting his system to allow more tolerance of the searing temperatures around him. It had been a *long* time since he'd had to work this hard at regulating his defenses in multiple directions at once.

The First? I have heard the decree from the Jungles. The First is under death hunt. It is not unstable! It is a traitor, and is to be destroyed!

How the hells had it heard about that, through the barriers Deiq had put up? He didn't get the chance to ask. Time collapsed, reality blurring into a woven distortion of gold and red and orange as the faereen reached out.

Somewhere far away, Teilo screamed. The sound shifted in a corkscrew pattern until her back pressed against Deiq's. Her voice cut off into a choked series of gasps.

The glow intensified as the faereen drew Teilo's strength into itself, wrapping ever-stronger bonds around her to hold her still, hissing in surprised pleasure.

This one is strong! It is true-ha'rai'nin, and has fed—what glory—I cannot destroy this one. It is too valuable. It can *renew me without being destroyed! I will keep it alive and collared to serve me. The Jungles will reward me for finding the First. They will allow me to punish it, and I will gain such strength from its pain—* Why *did you seek to hide this from me?* Bewilderment filled the question, a child asking its parent why a delicious cookie had been withheld.

A crimson-argent line began to snake round Teilo's neck—

—She *screamed,* with more rage than that of a thousand berserk desert lords. In the fractional moment of the faereen's startled recoil, she grabbed the bonds it had wrapped around her and *twisted*—just as Deiq had yanked the chains from her hands, inverting and sidestepping and flipping upside down all at once.

Not broken—as with the teyanain bonds, the chains were too strong for that—but rearranged so that *she* held the control point. Deiq couldn't tell if she had figured out the trick from seeing him do it earlier, or if she'd already *known* how and had faked her surprise. Either seemed equally possible.

The faereen tried to close itself off, to disappear, but they were in its true lair, not one of the illusions put on for humans. There was nowhere to run.

I will not be collared, Teilo's mental voice was a feral growl. *I forged the Agreement in* my *blood and* my *pain.* Nobody *collars me!* For a half-heartbeat, her attention shifted to Deiq. *Choose your side, First Born!* she snapped. *Help me or fight me!*

Father! the faereen wailed. *Father, help me—help me!*

Heat seared Deiq's hair to powdery ash. Miles of rock in all directions exerted a crushing pressure, pushing breath from his lungs, squeezing his heart into a stuttering, paper-thin replica of itself. The dying shrieks of hundreds of humans on the rapidly crumbling Wall Stair echoed down his spine.

Choose, someone said, a voice without a source. *Choose, and be bound by your choice.*

Father— First Born!

...Deiq?

The last voice was faint, fluttery, startled—and sent a tickling chill through his body. He exhaled, inhaled, gathering into himself the conflicted rage, pain, and fear of every life within reach. Two lives, near at hand, offered up a powerful melange of agony: Alyea and Idisio. They weren't dead. His first reaction was relief; then fragments of their memories dropped into his mind:

You must attempt to pass on your heritage.

The Horn is closed... the teyanain are at war with Aerthraim Family.

He's under my protection.

"Oh, *hells,*" Deiq said aloud, no longer even remotely pleased that they'd survived this long. "You fucking *idiots.*"

He is your kin, Alyea said, voice distant, fragmented. *I thought you'd want me to protect him!*

I didn't do it, Idisio said, scarcely audible. *I didn't....*

Deiq squeezed his eyes shut, trembling, and wound protections around Alyea to save her from the incendiary heat and pressure of this place. Then he checked on Idisio, and found that he'd adjusted to his surroundings already. *Good. One less distraction.*

Fatherrrrrrrrr... The mournful wail held less hope and more horrified realization in every note. Deiq reached farther, tugging at lives that hovered on the brink between madness and death. Somewhere out on the Wall Stair, barely within range, a familiar presence rich with darkness and pain threw back its head and howled.

No – not again – I did nothing to earn it this time – I won't yield to that again! it cried, then leapt out into the emptiness: falling, falling to smash into a coffin of jagged rocks.

Fimre, Alyea mourned. *Ah, gods –*

The faereen began scrambling to shield itself, heartbeats too tardy in its acceptance of what was happening.

Deiq gathered up everything he'd been collecting, denying the faereen the least trickle of sheltering energy, ignoring the acidic, razor-lace sensations stripping through his own being – then twisted his bundle of fury and pain into a savage braid –

You betray your kin! the faereen whined.

No, Deiq said, *I save them.*

He swung. The impact shuddered along miles in all directions, loosening geographical constraints, destroying blocks and barriers. Deiq could *feel* entire sections of ground simply breaking away, falling down to smash coastal settlements, sinking into enormous depressions; water, freed from its directed course, flooding wantonly –

Centuries of work, gone in a moment. He turned his awareness away from that and made himself look at the damage directly before him. The salt boulders had disintegrated into piles of sandy fragments. Yellow, gelatinous threads twitched feebly, like giant flatworms, across the scattered debris. One end of each thread led down into newly revealed holes in the floor of the cavern.

Incoherent images of pain staggered the air. Deiq swallowed back an intense desire to vomit as he pushed all the salt far away from the searching threads, absorbing much of it into himself. His nausea crested sharply, bile collecting against his teeth. He swallowed it back, refusing to yield.

The salt boulders had, for centuries, protected the faereen from outside interference; insulated it from sensing the changing politics and problems of the surface world; and ever-so-slowly bound particle to particle, eventually becoming as much a part of the faereen as its real flesh. It was a calculated risk, a deliberately designed weakness, put in place for exactly this situation.

All air left his lungs as though swept away by a cruel hand. Just as swiftly, it returned with thundering pressure. Deiq coughed and went to his knees. The yellow faded from the threads, leaving them looking like brittle ice snakes, twisting with slow, reflexive shivers.

The last of his brother's children was dead. At his hand. *And so I become a kin-slayer myself,* he thought, bleak and unamused. *As foretold.*

The ambient temperature began dropping rapidly.

You did it! I'm free of that monster—Teilo's hoarse cry rang out, a mixture of triumph and agony. He could feel her relief that he'd protected her at the expense of his kin, blended against centuries of distrust. *But your bonds—Deiq! Watch out—*

Broad, glowing bands of red and gold snapped into place around him, binding him as though he were nothing more animate than a round of barrel staves. The world muted to a grey, silent haze. Up became down—inside became *out*—and nothing existed except the directive to *kill.*

Kill everything. Everything. EVERYTHING....

Chapter 17

He's under my protection....

"I don't need protecting," Idisio muttered, staring up into a yellow-orange dawn cluttered with dirty-looking clouds. Chill stone roof tiles pressed the warmth from his body. He shivered, wrapping the threadbare blanket closer around his shoulders as though that would help. One hand refused to open, and stayed tightly fisted. He did the best he could with the other hand and his knuckles.

"Of course you need protection," a woman said—Ellemoa—his mother—her voice all too familiar; smug, self-congratulatory, heavy with derision. "Look at you, son. You can't seem to walk a mile without having something awful happen, and you keep worrying so much about the weak victims that you damage yourself and make the situation much worse."

That didn't *sound* quite like his mother. It sounded like something trying to imitate his mother, but the phrasing and word choices were off. He turned his head, unsurprised to find himself alone on the bleak rooftop, looking out over a still-sleeping city on a cold winter morning.

"Your mother is dead, boy," the woman's voice said. "You already know *that*. What do you think I am, hmmm? You *want* to think I'm your mother. That would make it all so much easier. But you know better. Do you really think you're sitting in Bright Bay right now?"

He blinked, surprised, and sharpened his gaze. Familiar shapes wavered, steadied, then wavered again, like an illusion reluctant to lose cohesion.

"This is all *your* creation," the woman murmured, her voice laden with malice. "*Your* place of comfort. Your retreat, your little *cave*."

He shivered in a gust of cold air, scowling. A rooftop could hardly be considered any sort of cave. But if he'd come *here* to hide—this frozen, exposed, thoroughly uncomfortable spot—what was he running *from*? He glanced down at his clenched right hand, increasingly uneasy. "Shut up," he said. "Go away. Leave me alone."

"Your survival instincts are better than *that*, boy," the woman said, laughing. "You're already starting to wake up. You really should be dead, you know that? You're remarkably tough. Must be that lake-born blood. Or maybe the fact that you *killed your own mother*. Makes one hard, that sort of thing does. You've seen that before, haven't you?"

He looked down at the fog-lined streets far below, his mouth twisting. "Yeah, once or twice."

"Or ten or twenty," the woman corrected. "Living on the muddy side of town doesn't make for a kind group of people, does it? But here you are, reliving that time as though it was *good*. Why do you think you're doing that?"

"I'm damn well not having a good time—" Idisio began to protest, then realized two things: The blanket had disappeared, and he was warm. The cold air simply didn't bother him anymore. The fog below was scattering, revealing various dark figures hurrying to and fro along the streets.

One woman went by, short and sour even at this distance, her feathery hat nearly taller than herself. A taller, meaner form strode along an intersecting path. Idisio leaned forward, opening his mouth to cry a warning—

"It's just a memory," the voice said in his ear.

"Stolli!" the woman on the street exclaimed, putting a hand to her face in apparent surprise. "I thought you'd—you'd—run off—or something—"

"No, you didn't, you lying whore," the tall man said. He pressed forward, sharp metal in each hand. "You told the guard what I was up to, dincha? You thought I'd be hung—and outer yer fancy hair—"

Idisio shut his eyes, swallowing hard, both hands tightening into fists. He heard the woman's shriek cut short, the collapse of her body to the dirty street. Then came the sound of her clothes being expertly rummaged through and ripped away.

"Now I *got* yer fancy hair, yer bald-fogged bitch, and yer lacy new man can go suck a whistle for his wine," the man muttered before departing with his newly filled sack of loot.

"He was a nasty one, wasn't he?" the voice said in Idisio's ear again. "Killing his own mother in the street like that. Stripping her all the way to her *wig*. Oh yes, he deserved to hang."

"Never did, though," Idisio said. He looked up at the sky, regarding the blurring gold-blue lines with a bleak resignation. "He always found a way to escape when they thought they had him cornered."

The woman finished the thought, pushing the words into his awareness without mercy: "And if he had no escape, he killed his way out."

Idisio shut his eyes again. "So I'm talking to myself, trying to tell myself something important. Let's just get it *out*, all right? I don't need to see more shit like that!"

"You don't *want* to," the woman said. "You may still *need* to."

"I don't fucking need to see it," he shouted at the increasingly azure sky. *"What is the fucking point of all this?"*

"You missed an important point in that memory," the woman said. "What were you doing, while all that was happening? *Watching*. Just watching...."

"It would have been insane to interfere. Stolli would have killed *me*—" Idisio stopped, his mouth sour around the last words.

"Exactly. You do what it takes to *survive*," his own voice, younger, drier, entirely *human* in its thinking—said in his ear this time. "*Survive*. Sometimes, that means hiding—but it always means *staying out of the fight*."

"*What* fight—"

The city dissolved around him, replaced by greyish, sand crusted cavern walls. A bellow shook the sand into a fine powder. The yell echoed, redoubling, filling Idisio's mind with visions of inchoate rage and deadly violence. Gold and red flickered through the air. A massive, dark form, silhouetted against light that should have shown him clearly—but didn't—stood with legs braced wide, arms moving as though gathering something invisible into a gigantic bundle. The floor lay ankle-deep in dank, slimy sand.

Two other forms sprawled nearby. He couldn't remember their names, but knew *who* they were: *Younger, female, stubborn,* and *older, female, stubborn*—with overtones of *Will help/won't help me.*

"Help me," he said to the first. A name came clear. He used it before it could fade. "Alyea. *Help me.*"

She rolled over and began to sit up. Then the huge figure bellowed, and her attention locked in that direction.

I'm on my own.

Something laughed, a cackling bird-call that faded into a skritchy, skittering sound.

I have to hide – but where – this is a huge empty cavern, *there's no cover –*

His panic chilled to a harder, calculating mindset. He regarded his surroundings more carefully. He could *feel* the particles—not sand, but a horrible, greasy-feeling salt—grain by grain, crawling over his bare feet, each tiny scratchy fragment being drawn steadily toward the bellowing figure. Any moment now, that form would turn and see Idisio—

Kin-killers don't like to leave witnesses, his younger self pointed out; the voice sounding, this time, remarkably like that of the intuition Idisio had followed all his life. *Stolli would have killed you if he'd known you were watching. This is the same all over again. That thing is about to kill, and it won't want witnesses afterward. Fuck hiding. Get out of there!*

He'd gotten *in*, so there had to be a way *out.*

The cavern air was hazy, the light uncertain, the heat and sound disorienting. He made himself ignore it all and searched— not feeling fear, just a frozen, precise *focus*. One of the walls nearby wavered and became smudged, a tall blotch of *not-solid* space, barely wide enough to turn and edge through sideways.

Idisio took another look at the dark figure. Walls of salt fragments were rising around it, and the newly bare floor was deeply furrowed, as though raked by gigantic claws able to rip into solid stone—

Get out of here went from desire to pure survival instinct-imperative. Idisio focused on the blurry section of wall and *ran.*

Chapter 19

The rain muted as Azni settled down in her room to a light morning meal of tea, thinly sliced fruit, and a flaky, rich pastry lined with jam and nuts. The tea was a deceptively mild blend, the pastry rich with butter. After running her own household in the north, she knew that neither were simple to produce. Given her various shades of disgrace, it was surprisingly luxurious food.

Apparently Aerthraim Family had abandoned its austerity under Kallaisin's hand. Azni could almost hear her grandmother's click of annoyed disapproval. As she wiped her fingers clear of crumbs and grease, she considered ways to use the point as a relatively neutral topic once the mahadrae relented. Kallaisin was obviously looking for things to be angry about, to put Azni in her proper place. Best to give her as little as possible to work with.

"I'd forgotten what a firebrand she is," Azni muttered to herself, shaking her head.

A chuckle came from behind her. She rose, turning swiftly, and stared at the athain standing just out of reach. She checked memory against the moment, then again, a thick fear running down her spine.

He wore grey-tan leggings, as before. This time, though, darker grey boots laced up to his knees, and an off-white, long-sleeved shirt covered his tattooed arms to the wrist. His hair was fastened into proper athain braids and pulled back from his face, clearly showing an arc of bluestone studs on each ear.

She couldn't find words, beyond: "*Tharr*?"

The athain bowed slowly. "Greetings, Azaniari of no Family. You are correct that the mahadrae is easy to anger, and even more impatient than you yourself are." He sat down, cross-legged, on the floor and met Azni's stare with open amusement.

Azni sank back onto her chair, unable to hide her bewilderment. "What—I don't understand," she said. "What are you *doing* here? We're at war—"

"No." Tharr's amusement faded to a more serious expression. "First, you are not Aerthraim Family. Second, Aerthraim Family and Lord Evkit are at war. I do not serve Lord Evkit, so I am not at war with Aerthraim Family at this time."

"Does Kalla—does the mahadrae know you're *here*?" Azni demanded, flicking an apprehensive glance at the thin wooden door.

"No," Tharr said. "Not yet." He smiled at Azni's sharp intake of breath. "It is my turn to be impatient. I have little time, and an important question to ask. I offered you training once before. Will you accept that offer, or not? I will not ask again."

Azni held up a hand. "Allow me a moment to think, please." Tharr nodded and sat patiently, head tilted a bit to one side as he studied her. Azni sorted through memory rapidly, recalling their previous conversation, then searched her understanding of southern politics for relevant points, and matched up facts, inferences, hints. Finally she said, "You are not at war with Aerthraim Family, but you've sided against Lord Evkit."

"True," Tharr agreed. "I am sworn to serve the best interests of the teyanain as a whole, and at the moment we are being weakened by a dangerous reliance on our ha'rethe."

"But the teyanain don't *have* a—" Azni stopped short, closing her eyes in utter astonishment at her own idiocy. "I was told it had died...."

"It was a lie that served to further Lord Evkit's ambitions," Tharr said soberly. "At the time, I thought his path was the best of many bad options for my people. I have since changed my mind and no longer support his plans. Will you accept my offer of training?"

She met his gaze, unflinching. "I asked you once before. I'll ask you again. What do you get out of training me? Why choose *me*, when there must be stronger, wiser, and more experienced people available?"

His expression remained stony. "You are of no Family," he said. "The Aerthraim disowned you many years ago, and Darden Family never formally accepted you as kin. You use the name as a courtesy because you trained there, but you have no claim on them and they have none on you. The only other qualified person who currently has independent standing is

Lord Alyea of Peysimun, and she is—allied—with someone whom *I* am unwilling to trust. You carry no such complications."

Azni sucked in a sharp breath, caught off guard by the brutal simplicity of it all, and entirely surprised at the searing hurt that shot through her chest at the summary.

"On a kinder note, you think far too poorly of yourself," Tharr said, tone pragmatic. He looked around the room slowly, apparently thinking over his next words, then went on. "You have survived events that would have broken many ordinary humans. You have taken risks most people would shy away from. You have paid a high price for your choices, and you understand consequences." He paused.

Azni shut her eyes, looking back over the years with deliberate detachment. Her children came to mind first, wide-eyed and flaccid in death. Regav's horrified expression came next, along with Roise F'Heing's smug laughter. For the first time, it all seemed to belong to another person. For the first time, she found herself asking not why she hadn't tried harder, but why Regav had been so credulous. She let out a long, rough breath and opened her eyes, regarding Tharr with absolute awareness that he'd been the one to prod that particular question into view.

He bent his head slightly, his expression sympathetic. He said, "I have given you only facts. This offer I make you is a high risk on your part, for many reasons. It will give you power that you have turned away from in the past, but you may not survive the events that it will lead you into. Those are also facts." He paused, cocking his head to one side as though listening, a faint frown appearing on his face, then relaxed.

"I doubt I'd survive trying to *leave* right now," Azni said, looking at the door again. "I'm not fast these days. And... I have a servant. I can't leave him behind, Kallaisin would take out her anger on him."

Tharr seemed briefly amused, his gaze drifting to the ceiling as he said, "Are those the only things stopping you from accepting my offer?"

"My brother," Azni said. "I'm told he's being held by Lord Evkit."

"Anything else?" Tharr's tone warned that he was nearing the end of his patience.

"... No." Azni swallowed back a surge of panic, steadied her voice, and said, "If you can solve those concerns, I'll accept your offer."

"Your brother is an adult with his own future in hand," Tharr said. "His decisions and safety are not your concern at this time. For your servant, I will arrange his safe escort to a place of his choosing. I will not allow you to come to harm while you are under my hand as a trainee, so your safety in leaving this place is not an issue either." He rose to his feet. "Your concerns are solved."

She began to protest, indignant: *Like hells they are.* Tharr met her gaze steadily, the lack of humor in his expression a distinct warning. "I give you only facts," he repeated.

Azni bit her lip and bent her head, considering his words more carefully. He was right about Allonin, much as she disliked the reality. Her brother had always done what was best for Allo, regardless of how it affected Azni. No doubt he was still doing the same thing today. He'd be fine.

She'd miss Ishru, but at least he'd be *safe*; and Irrio, having sworn over to Aerthraim Family for some godsforsaken reason, was comprehensively not her concern any longer.

Azni stood, slowly, looking around as though some delaying item might appear. Nothing caught her eye. "I'll... pack, then."

"You will not need your belongings," Tharr said with a dismissive wave of one hand. "They are trivial and easily replaced. Leave them behind."

She began to protest, then reconsidered, seeing an unexpectedly harsh gleam in his eye. Folding her hands over her stomach, the posture she'd been taught was appropriate when standing before one's teacher, regardless of age, she bowed her head briefly in deference.

He chuckled, amused once more. "Wisdom," he observed, then looked up, as though listening to something. "And so now we begin."

A heartbeat later, the light door swung open. Two guards blocked the doorway, shoulder-to-shoulder, their faces grim and their attention entirely on Tharr.

"Don't move, *hask*," one of them said. "Not a twitch. Not a word."

Irrio shoved his way roughly past the guards. "What the *hells* are you *thinking*?" he demanded. "Grey, are you *mad*?"

Tharr raised an eyebrow, directing a pointed glance at the guards as they matched shoulders once again.

Irrio motioned impatiently. "Leave us," he said to the guards. "I can handle this." Their eyes narrowed in response.

Azni took a step forward and sideways, drawing the guards' attention. Their gazes flickered back and forth between Irrio, herself, and Tharr in momentary indecision. Before they could resolve the confusion, she took another step towards them, hands peacefully at her sides. They backed up a step, hands raised in preparation for defense. She smiled and shut the door in their faces before they could react further, then turned to set her back against the thin panel.

Irrio grinned at her with rough amusement, then glared at Tharr. "What are you *doing* here?" he demanded.

"Currently," the athain said, "leaving." He beckoned Azni forward. "The door will not move until after we are gone," he told her.

"Wait—*we*?" Irrio said, turning a furious glare on Azni. "What the *hells*—"

Azni stepped smoothly around him to stand beside Tharr.

"No," Irrio said, his face greying as his eyes widened in abrupt shock. "No, no, no, Azni, no, *tell me you didn't—*"

Tharr's hand settled lightly on Azni's shoulder, and the world around her disappeared.

Irrio had been wearing pale gold and dark green, with a broad sash of stark white. Not exactly Aerthraim colors, but significant all the same, given his recent change in status; and his forearms had been bare of bracelets, his ears clear of rings.

"He's starting entirely over," Azni said, and watched the words swirl through the inverted not-space around her. They changed colors, sharpened, dug streaks across her vision. "He's really, completely sworn over to Aerthraim Family."

The streaks widened into trenches. She fell, tumbling slowly, stripped of fear, feeling only a vague wonder at the textures brushing against her skin.

"Wake, Azaniari," a voice said. "There is ground beneath your feet, not a chasm. You are not falling. Wake."

She opened her eyes to find herself standing upright on solid ground, as promised. Tharr sat on a low stone bench some distance in front of her, looking exhausted and a bit cranky. She tapped a foot lightly, feeling the flat stone beneath. Just past the bench, the stone became crushed gravel, spread out in a wide arc. She turned to confirm that it ran in a complete circle, as did the archway-studded wall beyond.

"Where are we?" she asked, facing Tharr again.

"You do not ask," Tharr said. "You are learning now. Answer your own questions."

Azni tilted her head back, half-closing her eyes as she inhaled through her nose, reaching out to gather all the information she could from her surroundings. Warm, dry air, unbroken by the slightest breeze, carrying aromas of rock dust, oil, and sand. Her perceptions stopped cold at the stone archways. She moved her focus up: the placid sky was clear of clouds and sun alike. The light had no real direction to it, and there were no shadows in this circle.

"We're nowhere," she said, looking at Tharr. "This isn't a real place. It's a... vision." A vision with roots in truth, if smell was involved, but a vision all the same.

"True," he said, and nothing else. Apparently there was more for her to figure out.

She looked around slowly, letting impressions filter through her mind, watching questions and patterns emerge side by side. "You're not controlling this vision," she said. "You're part of it, but someone else is creating it."

"True." He made a slight motion with one hand, indicating that she should keep going.

"So it's someone with more power than you yourself, and it's the person who's really responsible for me being here. I have no way to know if I'm going to be allowed to meet this person, but I do hope so."

Tharr smiled, weariness fading from his face. "Good," he said. "I am permitted to train you now. Sit down, Azaniari. Let go of everything you know, everything you are and have been. Remove all earrings and bracelets in the mind; assign yourself no colors of consequence."

She knelt, methodically emptying her mind of attachments. It took considerably longer than she'd expected, and several times she grunted in frustration as a released item fastened itself back into place.

Tharr watched her with a sleepy expression for a while. Eventually, he said, "You are permitted to ask for assistance, Azaniari."

"You could have *said*," she muttered, exasperated.

He smiled. "Is that a request, then?"

"Yes."

"Very well. Repeat after me: *iii-yaaa-naaa-beee-taaa-sen.*" The nonsense syllables came out in a sing-song rhythm, lilting, drawing calm in its wake.

She obeyed, doing her best to copy his inflection.

"Continue," Tharr said. "Each time you reach the end, bid yourself to release another attachment. Do not stop to pick out which attachment, do not look to see which attachment is being released. Merely command your mind to obey, and trust that it knows what to do without your direct awareness being involved."

She hesitated, dubious. That was *completely* backwards from everything she'd ever been taught about being a desert lord. Self-awareness was key to controlling one's temper, libido, and abilities alike.

Tharr waited, his eyes once again half-shut. She had the feeling he could wait forever.

"All right," she said finally, and began to sing.

Chapter 20

Lantern-light gave the white drapes a grey-golden sheen and caught gleams from the recently polished blackwood desk. Cafad could still smell the polish in the air; some sort of almond oil, at a guess. Not his favorite aroma, but the desk looked even more magnificently imposing than usual. He could tell that Seg had been handling a number of administrative duties here. Different papers were stacked all around, and a fresh inkwell and several quills had been added.

The constant, rhythmic battering of wind and rain made conversation here, as in many rooms of Scratha Fortress, difficult at best. But Cafad had to sort out what his *s'ekath* had been doing, so he was sitting at his desk, chair edged close to Seg's, heads bent together over various letters and documents.

They mostly concerned tedious, boring matters. A bill for seedlings, paid and receipted. A note from the gardeners on how the seedlings were coming along, and how many would be set aside for seed and propagation, how many used for fruit and food. A listing of the current garden staff, and notes on their behavior. Pages of observations about the numaina's habits: She was spending a great deal of time in the library, and had been distantly polite to all since the ceremony. Seg had it all organized very clearly. This stack for the kitchen, that stack for household servants, this for the kathain....

Cafad flattened his hand on the kathain paperwork as Seg began to set it aside. "Lichni," he said. "You said she's still here?"

"Yes, lord. Waiting on your word as to her status." Seg glanced up, his mouth moving into a faint grimace. "Given the current weather, there is no hurry, lord. She will not be able to travel for some days yet. You have time."

"I'd like to get it over with," Cafad said. "First and foremost, Seg, I owe *you* an apology."

Seg inclined his head gravely. "Yes, lord," he said. "Accepted and appreciated. Shall I fetch Lichni?"

Cafad hesitated—he'd had a lengthier apology ready—but Seg had the right to decline further conversation on that point. "Yes, please," he said, surrendering. Seg's mouth moved in a slight smile, and he inclined his head again.

"I'll send for a tea tray as well, if I might," Seg offered as he rose to his feet and set his chair back to the front of the desk. "It's nearly time for the afternoon meal, in any case."

"Yes. Thank you." Cafad sat back in his chair, rubbing at his eyes. As the study door closed behind his s'e-kath, he idly opened a desk drawer. Writing supplies rattled: a box of ink powder and a bound bundle of uncut quills, a sharp knife, a box of drying sand, a half-melted bar of blue wax, the Scratha Family seal—He frowned at that last item. It should have been in a locked safe. He'd scold Seg over that on the man's return.

It also seemed like an excessive amount of writing supplies. He'd have to ask Seg how many letters he'd been writing while Cafad slept—and to *whom*. He slid the drawer closed again, opened another. This one held a stack of folded cloths: neatly embroidered handkerchiefs, of all things. He shook his head, bemused, and began to close the drawer again. Something else rattled.

He paused, pulling the drawer out until it met the stop, and lifted aside the cloths to find a small box containing several spools of thread and an assortment of needles and thimbles.

Interesting. So Seg liked to embroider in his spare time. But the box didn't rattle quite the same way as the sound he'd just heard, and this was the drawer he'd always heard an odd noise from. He lifted cloths and sewing supplies aside, piling them carelessly on the desk, and began seriously studying the inside of the drawer. The rain eased, its roar dying to a steady patter as he ran his hands around the wooden rectangle.

The study door opened. Seg ushered Lichni into the room.

"Lord," he said, "as requested—ah." He paused, regarding the embroidery on the desk. "I apologize, lord. I had intended to take that out of your way."

"It's fine, Seg," Cafad said, waving at the chairs before his desk. "Sit down, Lichni, I'll be with you in a moment."

"Lord," his manservant replied, tone reproving. "I took s'a Lichni from meditation—"

"I take no offense, s'e-kath Seg," Lichni said, settling into the northern-style chair rather than the kneeling stool. "It's enough of an honor to be in my lord's presence, whether he addresses me immediately or later."

Cafad glanced up at her, eyebrows rising. She met his gaze, serene, smiling. She hadn't been shaving her scalp. The hair was a soft dark shadow, just past stubble, a tacit declaration that she wasn't currently in service. She wore a simple dress of dark-neutral colors, and sat in the chair with her bare feet resting gently against the floor.

"Thank you," he said after a moment. "Seg, did you send for tea yet?"

Seg's head-tilt offered silent reproach for that question, but he said only, "Yes, lord. It should be here shortly."

Cafad tilted his own head, raising an eyebrow pointedly.

Seg picked delicately at one sleeve, his mouth twitching. "—Ah. I'll go check on that, if I may." He bowed and removed himself from the room.

Cafad went back to examining the drawer. "I've been hearing a rattle from this drawer ever since the desk moved in here," he said. "Drawer's empty, everything feels solid, nothing's wiggly, so I thought—"

"A secret bottom or back," Lichni said, beaming. "Oh, that's fun!"

"This was Orde's desk," Cafad said. "I rather doubt anything he thought worth hiding would be *fun*, Lichni."

"I wouldn't be so sure," she returned. "I've heard many a rumor about Orde over the years. He had some peculiar tastes, apparently."

"He was a desert lord," Cafad said absently, feeling around the inside of the drawer once again. "Peculiar is normal for us."

"Even so." She wiggled her eyebrows, grinning. "I've heard *kathain* saying he was unusual—in more than one way."

"I don't want to know," Cafad said, then grunted and sat back in exasperation. "Nothing. I can't find the slightest ridge or hook. The drawer is as solid as all of the others."

"Sounds like a puzzle box," Lichni said. "I love those—Norau taught me rather a lot about them. Maybe I could look?"

Cafad flattened his hands on the desk, jarred by the abrupt reminder. "Lichni," he said, "About that—about... what happened."

She sobered. "Lord, I was not available when you needed me, and you were injured from my inattention. That was *my* failing. I should have waited until I was certain you would be occupied elsewhere that night. I owe you an apology, and you may take whatever penalty you choose for my failure."

"You weren't the only one involved," Cafad said, the words emerging harsh from the back of his throat.

"True, but you weren't looking to take *them* to bed that night, lord," Lichni pointed out. "I am the one at fault. I have already offered your s'e-kath my apology, and paid his choice of penalty, for putting him at such risk. Please don't ask what he required of me, lord. I'd prefer not to discuss it."

Don't ask—words he'd always hated hearing, now more so than ever. *I have a right to know!* said his younger self. *She has the right to refuse answers,* came the more mature, and extremely frustrating, reply.

Cafad looked down at his hands until his temper subsided once more. "I'm sorry, Lichni," he said then, not raising his gaze. "I expected more of you than was proper, and I put the entire Fortress in danger from my mistake. You did nothing wrong."

"I appreciate the kindness, lord, but I was at fault. I accept your apology, not because *I* need it, but because you need me to accept it." She paused, then added, "Caffy, I'm sorry. Truly. I hurt you, and I never intended to do that. All I wanted was to make you happy, which I would have tried to do whether I was your kathain or ordinary lover. I never lied. I did want to serve you, when I heard you were alive. I still want to serve you. I'm not sure, though, that my continued service is what's best for *you*."

He looked at her, studying the lines of her face, the laugh wrinkles, the sadness in her eyes, the stubble of her hair, and sighed. "See what you can do about this damn drawer," he said, standing to move out of the way. Her expression lit up at once, shifting to a childlike joy, and he laughed as she almost leapt from her chair.

"I love puzzles." Unbothered by his amusement, Lichni shut the drawer, studied the handle, and tapped a few places along the top and sides of the desk. Then she opened the drawer again, slowly, head cocked as though listening for something. She ran her fingers around the inside, as he had done, but with more attention to the rims of the drawer than the bottom and sides. She repeated that process twice more, each time more rapidly, then shut the drawer firmly and straightened, smiling.

"You solved it?" he demanded.

"I think so." She motioned him back to his chair. "Take hold of the handle, not as though you're pulling it out, but as though you're going to turn it in place. Now twist it to the right. You should feel a click—there! Now wait—don't move a muscle—hold that for one, two, three, four—now twist it back to the left, and further to the left, until you feel that click again—Now turn it back to center quickly, good. Now pull the drawer out as normal."

The drawer that slid out was a good inch wider to each side than it had been. The original drawer was easily lifted out and set aside. A metal cylinder, capped at each end with wax, took up most of the previously hidden drawer. Much of the wax had broken off, probably while the desk was being moved, and a tight roll of papers could be seen within the tube. Three small stone balls had rolled loose as well, each one a varying shade of blue.

"Holy gods," Cafad said, grinning widely. "Thank you, Lichni! That's astounding. How did you know that?" He picked out the marble-sized stones, setting them on the desk with care, and corrected their slight movement until they held still.

"It's an Aerthraim-crafted puzzle drawer," she said, returning to her chair, visibly pleased with herself. "Norau told me about those. He couldn't show me any, obviously, but he told me so many stories about the ones he'd encountered. He was a very good storyteller, lord." She sighed. "I do miss him. Oh—" She looked at Cafad in consternation. "I'm sorry, lord, I wasn't paying attention—that was unkind of me."

He doubted that the comment had been in any way accidental, but he waved it aside all the same. "Thank you," he said again. He hesitated, then added, "Would you join me for dinner tonight?"

She smiled and bent her head. "I would be honored, lord," she said. "But I need to know my status before accepting. And I need to know the penance for my failure, lord."

He sat back in his chair, considering, turning the metal cylinder over in his hands. What was left of the seal showed Orde's distinctive stamp, and the metal was etched with Orde's shorthand for *confidential/danger*.

"I think—" he began.

The door to the study opened. Cafad put a hand over the stones to keep them still; then, impulsively, scooped them up and tucked them into his belt pouch. Seg ushered in one of the new kathain, carrying the tea tray. Another followed behind with a folding tray-table, which he silently set up at the corner of Cafad's desk, to Lichni's left hand. The first kathain set the tray down, fussed a bit with the fixings, poured two cups of tea, set one before Lichni and one before Cafad, then bowed and withdrew alongside his companion. Not a word was spoken the entire time.

Seg shut the door gently behind the kathain, then turned to frown at Cafad. "What is that, lord?" he asked, motioning to the cylinder in Cafad's hand.

"This was in a hidden drawer of the desk," Cafad said, holding it up briefly. "There are papers inside. I haven't opened it yet, but I think it's something Orde wrote."

"Ah." Seg's frown deepened. "I think perhaps I should take that, lord."

"What?" Cafad felt his chin go up, his jaw hardening. "There might be *answers* in here!"

"Which is precisely why you should *not* read it, lord," Seg interrupted. "Allow me to read it first, please, to make certain you will not be troubled with matters a *bound lord* ought not concern himself over."

Anger flushed up his spine. Cafad sat up straighter and snapped, "*No.* I've been looking for answers my entire fucking *life*, Seg! I'll decide if I should be *troubled* in this instance, thank you very much."

"My lord," Lichni said, her expression anxious. "Your s'e-kath is correct—lord, you should really allow him—"

"Quiet," Cafad said harshly. "You're not in my service any longer. You have no right to advise me, and I'm not asking for your opinion in any case." Lichni's back stiffened, her head lifting in clear affront.

"Lord," she said, standing. "I'll excuse myself, by your leave, and begin preparing to depart once the roads are clear."

A sharp ache cut through his chest. Rising anger cauterized it a moment later, adding acid to his reply. "Fine. Seg will write you an open recommendation for any place you like. Gods' grace, s'a." The final words felt insincere and hollow in his mouth.

Lichni's mouth turned to a sour line. "Gods' grace, lord," she said with matching emptiness, then turned and stalked from the room.

Seg's frown almost obscured his eyes. "That was ill done, lord," he said. "The temper you're displaying makes me all the more inclined to insist you not read that document."

"You're not going to *insist* on a godsdamned thing," Cafad said thinly. "You *may* sit your arse down in the chair and stop scowling at me. You're *not* taking this out of my hands." He matched Seg's glare for a moment, then added, "I'll read the damned thing aloud. Slowly. And you can interrupt and make me take a break if I get too upset. All right?"

Seg, his lips a thin line, settled in the chair Lichni had been occupying. "May I suggest adding a tincture to your tea, at least?" he said.

"I don't have any more." Cafad reached for his now-lukewarm tea and tossed the liquid back like a shot of desert lightning. He shut his eyes and swiftly constructed the strongest possible version of the layered thought-globe Deiq had shown him. "There. I'm settled. Now—"

He brushed away the remaining wax, and scooted the mess off to the side with one hand. Seg reached out and gathered up his embroidery supplies, depositing them gently onto the seat of a nearby kneeling chair.

Cafad unrolled the papers, hands steady. Seg leaned forward and pinned down the top edge with one hand, eyes darting over the revealed text. His frown returned immediately, and Cafad laughed, unable to help himself. "You can't read this upside down," he told *his s'e-kath*. "Orde had a specific way of writing when he wanted something kept private from onlookers. And it's Scratha dialect. I'll have to translate some of it for you."

"I am not unfamiliar with Scratha dialect," Seg retorted, clearly nettled.

"Seg, Orde *invented* words. I doubt even the old Lord Scratha could have made sense of this entire thing. I'm going to have to work at it, myself. Now be quiet and let me concentrate."

He worked through the first paragraph in silence, struggling to remember Orde's style and eccentricities. He'd spent considerable time, over the years, reading through every journal and record book his mentor had written, but it had been a long time since his last attempt.

"Ah," he said under his breath. "That's right. He always swapped out those letters—and put those words backwards—I remember now." He straightened, rubbing his eyes, then began reading aloud.

I begin this account on the ninth day of—

"I'll skip the beginning, it's all dates and titles and how long he's been in service at Scratha—wait. He didn't *train* at—oh. He trained at the *Qisani!* I never knew that!" Cafad glanced up to see a faint smile twitch Seg's mouth. "Obviously you did."

"Yes, lord."

"Hm. Well. In any case—"

—I have made many a controversial decision during my time serving Scratha Family. I already have more enemies than friends, and I fear that will only grow worse in the coming months, as I make ever more dangerous arrangements. Many Scratha desert lords are already abandoning their oaths, going to safer service or, in the most extreme cases, losing themselves to strong drugs and drink.

Cafad paused. "Oh yes," he said under his breath. "I remember." Shaking his head, he returned his attention to the document.

My task is the preservation of Scratha Family as a whole first; obeying the Lord of the Fortress comes second. This is heretical to many of my fellow desert lords, who see themselves as far above the commoners as a mountain to a grain of sand. The commoners merely serve us, they are replaceable and insignificant. I vehemently disagree. Scratha Family has always been premier diplomats, but that is of late becoming a restriction that holds us back and sets a barrier before those of potential, merely because of their bloodline. I will *change this.*

Cafad paused again, leaning back in his chair. "So that's why he brought me in," he said, wonderingly. "As part of a bigger plan. I thought he just...

well. I didn't look at it too closely, actually. I was afraid that if I questioned my good fortune it would be taken away." He went back to reading:

I believe this troubling separation between those of so-called noble *birth and those who can only expect to perform menial labor throughout their lives is directly tied to the influence of Scratha ha'rethe. The ha'reye, as I learned during my time at the Qisani, are extremely narrow of vision and divide all things into the worthy and the unworthy of consideration, often missing the complex nuance of human reality. I was taught that the host affects the protector as the protector affects the host, and that over centuries a given Family will find that their ha'rethe takes on the dominant characteristics of their leaders, while their leaders become, in turn, more like the ha'reye.*

Cafad leaned back in his chair again. Seg silently refilled his tea and pushed the cup towards him. Cafad sipped it, considering what he'd just read. "Do you have any thoughts so far, Seg?"

"That I should remove that document from your possession at once," his s'e-kath said, unsmiling. Cafad snorted, set the tea down, and resumed.

The current head of Scratha Family is doing a very excellent job of standing up against the strain, but he has confessed himself prey to increasingly severe nightmares over the past months. His kathain have had to stop him from sleepwalking on multiple occasions, and his appetite for all ordinary things such as food, drink, sex, and sleep appears to fluctuate alarmingly. He is increasingly violent at little provocation, and has been going through far too many kathain. I am having difficulty finding handlers willing to sell to us, and the better quality kathain refuse to serve.

Cafad let out a long breath. "Damnit," he muttered. "That's a new angle on *that*, most surely. Why the *hells* didn't anyone talk to me about this? I've been asking for just this sort of information—"

Seg's hand landed on the paper, palm down, fingers splayed wide. "*Lord Scratha*," he said severely. His fingers bunched slightly, paper crinkling. His gaze stayed fixed on Cafad, hard and uncompromising.

Cafad raised his hands in mock surrender, then picked up his tea and drank it down. "All right," he said. "It's the past, it's over, it's a story in a book. Move your hand, Seg."

"I continue to have *grave* doubts about this," Seg said as he sat back.

"You said Scratha ha'rethe isn't paying attention to me right now," Cafad said reasonably. "So there's no better time, really."

"It *will* rouse if you get truly angry," Seg pointed out. "And it will be *extremely* displeased."

"Then don't let me get angry," Cafad shot back. "You've been doing well at that so far." He waved a hand, cutting off further conversation, and returned to the papers.

I believe that a greater separation between the Fortress at large and the influence of our ha'rethe is wise. I have reached out to the Aerthraim, under the pretext that they are the best at repairing old stonework. They are *known for their masonry, so it is a reasonable justification.*

Negotiating with the Aerthraim is tricky on many fronts, the most obvious being that they are not part of the Agreement and thus ought not be trusted. I have had to be extremely careful in explaining my plan to the Lord of Scratha Family. He has allowed me to proceed on the grounds that a problematic ally is best held close, and has been scrupulous in not asking me for anything beyond the broadest outlines of the work underway. This no doubt adds to his strain, but he is, as I said, handling his balance in an exemplary fashion, all things considered.

The Aerthraim are also notably devious and dangerous, and I am not at all sure how far to trust them, myself. I have had to make certain agreements that would land me in severe disfavor if not outright banishment should anyone discover the details. But if it saves lives in the long run, it is entirely worth the risk. I am increasingly uncertain as to the good intentions of the ha'reye—and I am well aware that merely by placing that statement on paper, my life is forfeit should the wrong person see this document. Let the gods decide that, I suppose.

Cafad raised his head, blinking, dazed. "That's—holy gods. I had no idea he felt that way."

Seg shook his head, eyes tight with obvious worry.

"I'm not angry," Cafad told him. "I'm a little stunned—I feel like my entire life is turning sideways in my head—but it's not upsetting me."

"Does it occur to you that you're reading information that Lord Ordenial specifically notes is too dangerous for the bound lord of the Fortress to know?" Seg tapped a finger against the paper, frowning. "Don't you think you ought to trust his judgement—*and* mine!"

"No," Cafad said, stubborn, lowering his head like a restless bull getting ready to charge. "No, I'm going to get the answers I've been looking for. You—you just keep me calm, that's all."

"I warn you now," Seg noted, "I will knock you senseless if I have to."

"Fine. Good. Do that. But not yet. Let me keep reading—"

Chapter 21

....As of the twentieth day of the tenth month, the work is well underway. Stones throughout the Fortress have been replaced, with the greatest of caution, with the Aerthraim-crafted composite they name aenstone. *The levels of purity vary as widely as the locations, in a further attempt to keep the entire matter from alerting our ha'rethe.*

My own room has been rather more heavily "repaired" than most, but after consideration it was decided that any amount of shielding to Lord Scratha's room was far too high of a risk. Likewise, the temple is far too sensitive an area to touch, even though the resident Callen have recently tendered their regrets and departed the premises. I believe they know exactly what is happening, and their various oaths require them either to interfere or retreat. I am relieved that they chose the latter, al-

though I will miss the Callen of Ishrai. He had a dry humor that made my life lighter on many occasions.

Lord Scratha appears to be making no effort to entice replacement Callen, nor to replace the loremasters and desert lords who have fled in recent weeks. His temper is exceptionally harsh, and he has even raised his hand to me on occasion; thankfully, he recalled himself in time and turned his rage on his kathain instead.

I do not envy them their lives, and I have done the best I could to heal their wounds and divert their lord's irritation to kinder channels whenever possible, not to mention the high levels of dashaic, esthit, aesa, and various other substances I am constantly slipping into his food and drink. Even with all of that, Lord Scratha is beginning to bend under the pressure, and I worry that the work will not be complete in time to give him sufficient respite.

I wonder, even, if the Aerthraim are deliberately stalling their work schedule; there appear to be rather a lot of unexpected delays. I cannot imagine what benefit it would be to them, however, to see this Fortress sink into complete upheaval... completing this partnership successfully is their only chance of attracting the trust of the other Families to commission similar work on their own structures.

It is well known that they have money troubles, as is only to be expected when most avenues of commerce are closed to them as a result of their withdrawal from the Agreement. They need *the financial support of Scratha Family in order to gain any sort of stability for their own people. They cannot, or at least,* should not, *be willing to risk that.*

Increasingly, though, I feel as though I am missing something, and I wonder if I have put all of our lives in danger by way of a terrible misunderstanding....

Cafad sat back, frowning, and sipped tea to ease his dry throat, then said, "Damn, this is explosive stuff."

"Lord—*please!*" Seg's voice was as taut as his expression.

"No. In for a leg, in for a lizard. I'll brood and fret over it far more if I don't finish, at this point. And I'm not angry, am I? I'm holding my balance fine. So don't worry."

Seg's hand curled, briefly, into a fist. Then, grimacing, he spread it out again, holding the pages flat.

Notes of the twenty-third day of the tenth month: I am faced with a dilemma I did not expect to deal with for many years yet. Scratha ha'rethe has sent out a call for a chosen. It has chosen a women of proven fertility, and has indicated quite clearly that it feels the time has come for it to produce a child.

I had thought we had many years yet before our ha'rethe issued this particular call. As I understand it, the Fortress bound ha'reye sacrificed their right to produce offspring in favor of directing their energies towards protecting their sworn territories: the only time they are allowed to request a chosen for the purposes of reproduction is when they feel themselves failing.

The need to create and train a replacement overrides all else at that point, and it is a severe breach of the Agreement to in any way refuse or interfere with this order. My private agreement with the Aerthraim, however, requires me to do just that.

They were exactingly specific in that matter: in no way and for no cause am I to ever *permit Scratha ha'rethe to reproduce.*

I agreed only because I had imagined that it would be many a year before I had to enforce that oath, and I told myself that so many things could happen over the course of those years... surely I might be long dead by then, or I would be clever enough to find some workaround to that drastic demand.

And yet here I am, still alive, and not clever at all, it seems.

There is a tenday of preparation ahead for the chosen one, as is traditional—

Cafad stopped, lifting a scowl to Seg. "A *tenday*?" he demanded. "Riss had a day!"

"No, lord. Riss had an entire month, while you slept, to prepare. She was given far more time than most chosen, because the ha'rethe delayed the final call for some reason. I expected it to come at the tenday mark, and confess myself quite surprised at the extension."

Cafad's stomach began to turn sour, a whisper of memory sliding through his mind: *The child is almost ready....*

He looked down at the remaining pages, swallowing hard. "The child," he muttered.

"Lord—"

"Shut up," Cafad said, not lifting his gaze.

The only solution I can devise is a bad one among many other worse options. I have some skill in surgery—

"Oh, *gods*." Cafad sat back in his chair, splaying both hands out over the pages, nauseated. "He made her *s'ii*. Unsexed. She *couldn't* bear children—he took out everything required! I didn't think Orde knew *that* much by way of surgery." He looked up at Seg, questioning. The tall man shook his head.

"Lord Ordenial was not trained as a master surgeon, as far as I am aware."

"Gods—that poor girl. Apparently he did a reasonable job. She lived long enough to answer the call properly... What a brutal solution. But Orde always said: *You do what has to be done whether you like it or hate it. Duty is duty and every oath binds a piece of your soul.*" Cafad paused, studying Seg's expression. The man looked almost weary, resigned rather than tense. "You're not going to try to grab this away from me?"

"It's far too late, lord," Seg replied. "What's left is merely cleaning up the final details. You already see the structure and where it must lead, or you *will* once you take a moment to think it through."

Cafad stared at Seg's bleak expression, his breath steadily shortening in his chest. "... Yes," he said at last. "Yes, I do see. Oh... oh gods. And when the old Lord Scratha died... And now *Riss*—oh, *fuck*." He shut his eyes, fighting to restore the rapidly shattering thought-globe.

He heard the faintest scraping sound. By the time he registered it as a chair moving, Seg was already behind him. The blow and the darkness and the cessation of thought all came as a profound relief.

Chapter 22

Music swirled, drawing colorful patterns around Riss as she breathed in dizziness and exhaled sorrow. *Up* and *down* were useless abstractions, names were meaningless: there was only the this, and the here, existing in all directions simultaneously. Her feet and her hands and her back and her thighs and her scalp rolled against endless ridges of text, ancient knowledge unfolding into her awareness like a desert flower coming to life after a heavy rain.

You are my chosen, a voice whispered. *I give you all I am, I give you everything I have. You will be the one to come after me, you will be the one to restore the proper order of things. The humans will* serve *you, as they ought, and the Jungles will finally be called to account for what they have done to me.*

The music changed, the pattern becoming jagged, harsh, each note increasingly sharp and painful to hear. Music became form. Each cascading trill solidified into a golden blade that slashed through her, taking away arm, leg, ear, breast. She opened her mouth to scream protest, to cry agony, and found herself mute.

Be still, human, the voice said. *I am not interested in you.*

Bewilderment—sick hot betrayal—horror flooded through her.

No, the voice said. *You are not my chosen. You* carry *my chosen.* You *are merely a host, and your convenience is nearly at an end.*

She managed a single, desperate cry: *WHY?*

When I last asked for a chosen, the voice said, *I was betrayed by those sworn to serve me, given a useless host, and trapped into sleep by a servant of the Jungles. I have the right and obligation to produce a child to guard this land. I will not allow the faithlessness of others to interfere with that duty.*

I had nothing to do with any of that! she cried out.

That is not my concern.

Vision faded into wild darkness and blurred screaming.

Chapter 23

Cafad's hands burned as though being strangled by a hangman's noose, each finger wrapped in aching spirals of strain. Colors spiked across his vision: red, black, an odd almost-green color he had no proper name for.

Be still, a voice said. A woman screamed, long, anguished, despairing. He knew that sound, knew that voice, knew that—

His fingers curled, cramping, pain shivering from hands to elbows to shoulders before dissipating again. He turned in green-lit darkness, trying to orient himself. "What's going on?" he said—tried to say—and no sound emerged.

There was something in the darkness to his left. He turned, staring, and saw nothing—Now it was behind him. He turned again, faster, not fast enough. Green flared red and orange as pain spiked along his legs. He cried out, with as little effect as before. The creature was stalking him, coming closer. His legs wouldn't carry him to run, his hands wouldn't uncramp enough to fight: he tried to fling himself forward through sheer willpower, but stayed perfectly motionless.

He fought for clarity. *This is a nightmare, a dream, it's not real. I control my dreams, I control—I can control this, I can wake up, I have to—*

Be still, the voice said again. Colors muted and hazed, pain easing into a sensation of strong pressure. *I will care for you when I finish this task, and you will have such power that nothing will be beyond your reach. Be still, and wait, and trust me.*

Something was wrong, something was very, very wrong—

You need not concern yourself with the affairs of the tharr any longer. The voice came from deep within his breastbone, just beside his ears, miles away; had no sound, contained all the sounds he'd ever heard. The words were searingly clear, the words were cacophony incarnate. *You are safe, and I will care for you, and you will have the power you have wished for all these years. None will dare stand against you.*

Direct fighting wasn't any good against this much power. He called to memory his aqeyva training, the subtle moves, the sinuous sidestep: felt the pressure around him ease as though he were slipping through a net.

"No." He threw his head back, rejoicing in the sound of his own voice. "No, that's not what I—"

It is what you wish. I know you. I see *you. I will heal you from the wounds my brethren inflicted, and you will have as many children as you wish to create. The numaina is suitable, for one, and I will seek out others as worthy for you.*

"No," he shouted as the net closed in, binding bone and blood alike. No matter how he twisted this time, the pressure clung, stubborn as congealed grease. "No—that's not right—"

His voice broke and faded, lost once more. Chill cascaded down his spine. Red flared again, pressure turning to pain, and another unnerving scream shook his concentration.

Be still, the voice repeated. *Three times I say be still, and bid you obey this time. Trust in me. I will wake you when it is time, and you will see that you are safe and all is well. Be still. Sleep.*

Red turned black, senses fading.

Chapter 24

Icy winter chill invaded Alyea's bones, numbing her skin, slowing her heartbeat. Her hair was plastered against her face, stiff and harsh as though soaked and frozen. Her eyes wouldn't open past slits.

The air hung thick with grey and yellow mist. Her breath roared, a jagged waterfall in her ears. She tried to move her fingers, but couldn't feel her hands or feet.

Fear was a distant, abstract yammering. A flood of immense weariness rose higher every heartbeat, drowning thought and emotion.

This is what dying feels like.

Her heart stuttered once, twice—stopped. She fell, darkness replacing the grey. A large black bird called *Lost, lost*—then began laughing. The sound scattered into a million red droplets, spreading and sharpening into crimson stars dripping with blood.

Lost! Lost!

What have I lost? she cried out.

Why did this seem so familiar? Had she had this conversation before?

Lost! Lost! The bird, larger than a horse now, wheeled past her, shedding feathers like rain. One of the feathers landed on Alyea and dissolved into a mass of tiny, many-legged insects that promptly began to burrow into her body like sand-mites into a low-tide sand bank.

Her heart jarred back into motion—slow, labored, uneven beats.

The bird regarded her with bright, amused yellow eyes. *Lost!* it remarked again, and laughed. This time, its laughter produced only sound.

Tell me! What have I lost?

The bird clacked its hard beak and disappeared in a terrifying, abrupt explosion of feathers and laughter. Millions of insects splattered across her body and began to devour her.

Alyea, someone said: the voice bright with strain, dark with hope, shrill with need. *Alyea.* Help *me....*

She knew that voice. *Young. Male. Ha'ra'hain.* Names were invisible abstractions in this thick-mouthed moment, but she *knew* that voice. She turned to find its source, but:

Wife. Another familiar voice, this one stunned, disoriented; heavy with a sense of blind searching. Older. Imperative. *Needing.* Need so *deep,* so hopeless, so acidic that she abandoned the first plea without hesitation and turned in a new direction, but:

Desert lord. A third voice, less familiar but much more clear and sharp than either of the former. *Make... choice... honor... oath....* The words were labored and irregular, like Alyea's heartbeat. It was difficult to distinguish them from meaningless noise at first.

She shook her head, bewildered into standing still. *Too many needs, too many choices, too many directions.*

Words arranged themselves more clearly into sentences: *Your oaths are called due. Which will you allow? Which choice will you follow, which life will you save?*

Lost, came a faint cry. She could no longer feel the insects crawling through and across her skin. She barely sensed a body at all, only a tattered shell of fragments held together by memory and habit.

All, she said, and heard distant bird-laughter. It sounded like weeping.

You cannot, the voice said, tone stern and vexed. *You must choose.*

All, she insisted, stubborn as the rock around her. She looked for the first, weakest voice, and found it searching helplessly for some way to flee. She turned, located a thin spot in the not-world, and *pushed* until it became a passageway. The younger leapt at it, disappearing in a heartbeat.

Her attention shifted to the rock near to hand—the stone— the boulders—their roots extending into the deepest parts of the world, and filled with not-world *strength*—

The scolding tone shrilled into abrupt panic: *Oh* – no – *don't do* that –

The stone had veins, like a body—no, larger than that, and vastly abstract—more like motionless rivers flowing through an arrested ocean. Glittering quartz-beds surrounded smooth, looping silver streamlets; a current of brown-gold that might have been copper or brass felt like rough leather clippings. A red line that might have been agate, or rubies, or some lesser stone ruffled like fine silk against her awareness.

Don't!

Some of the material felt—*right*—even without a clear purpose in mind. Less-suitable veins she left alone or pushed aside to search behind them for something better.

No! the protester insisted. *Better for him to die than* this—

She ignored that, gathering materials, clearer in her desire with every choice. When a colorful array of glittering and dull, sharp and smooth, cold and warm materials lay before her, she turned her attention to locate that shrill, dark voice— which had gone ominously quiet.

Angry color flared before her, shaping into humanoid form, dissipating into random chaos, reforming a heartbeat later.

Destroy, it said. *Destroy*. She felt it focus its attention on her. The ambient temperature rose, scorching her flesh, blurring her vision.

No! she cried out. *You're a builder – you* create, *not destroy – Remember the paintings!*

The pressure faded, the heat wavering back down into unpleasant instead of incendiary. *Paintings?* Images rose, flickering rapidly through her mind, memory of each room's careful design. She tracked an intangible path connecting her memories to the other's perceptions; thrust herself through the opening, grabbed—*something*—dark and thick and grimy—then *pulled* at it, shoving it clear, kicking it away, thinning out the thready tangle binding it to its host.

Silence cut in, darkness covering all color. The air chilled rapidly. The shadow of a shadow of a powerful personality whispered: *Alyea?*

She traced the voice as she'd traced the materials; grasped the source, brought it—no, brought *him*—towards herself, or perhaps the opposite, direction having as little meaning as time. Only the cold remained, constantly dropping to ever lower extremes. Her hands shook, feeling clumsy and thick with a recurring awareness: *I don't have much time left. I can't survive this much longer.*

Strengthening, still whisper-weak, the dark voice spoke, shaky, wondering: *Alyea – you stopped me – how did you do that? And – what are you doing?*

A roughly humanoid shape, flaring erratically through the spectrum of hot colors, formed at her feet. The limbs seemed far too fluid in their movement—and too numerous—but there wasn't time to really examine the details. *I have to do this fast.* As though sweeping dust with a broom, she piled the collected material over the form and directed it to burrow, like the insects that had pierced her own body so easily.

His instant, panicked response came in a language she'd never heard before, translated by the shivering air into: *Oh, fuck – oh, no, no,* no *– you don't know what you're doing – stop – fucking* hells, *no!*

The last of the gathered material sank beneath his skin. She could *feel* it melting, stretching, bonding with other fragments.

No... he moaned, then went silent.

Ice reversed to a searing heat, indistinguishable at first. Then sensation returned to Alyea's hands, her feet, her skin—her heart steadied into an erratic rhythm, her breath rasping. A growing yellow-white brilliance replaced the darkness.

Screaming was too much effort. She panted like an asp-jacau left out in the sun too long, blinking, forcing her vision wider. Her eyelids felt crusty and swollen, her eyes filled with razor-sharp sand. With the last of her coherence, she gathered up anything that resonated as *ally* and flung herself through the opening she'd created earlier.

The world inverted. Her bones shattered, knitted: once, twice, a hundred times. Her heart stopped again. A sharp blow to her chest shook it back into motion.

I/we kill I/we destroy I/we feed on pain –

People died and died and *died*, ripped apart, eviscerated, *absorbed*—A rush of intense, erotic joy as hot blood soaked through every pore—She could *taste* the gathered lives—the salt air—hear the creak of rigging—the screams, the *screams*—

Screaming wasn't an option for her. Breathing was barely possible.

Stay with me. Deiq's voice was a roar in her ears, overriding all other sound. *Don't you dare let go. Not after doing* that *to me—gods*damn *you! Breathe.* Breathe!

She sucked in a breath, then another, each one marginally easier.

Open your eyes. No suasion left in him, only piercing, shattering command.

She squeezed her eyes tightly shut, abruptly terrified, emotion catching up at last. Something wide and soft brushed across her face, wiping away what felt like a crust of damp shell-sand. Chill air prickled against newly-exposed skin.

Open your eyes. Look at me. His voice shook with barely restrained rage. *Look at me!*

She opened her eyes, unable to resist the command any longer. Filling the majority of her vision, far too close to ignore, enormous eyes of pure white stared back at her from a flat, grey face. Ruddy, crenellated flaps of skin flared out where ears should have been. The mouth was the wrong shape entirely: triangular, hard, like a—

Her mind simply refused to supply the word.

Like a beak. Yes. The voice, while still harsh, had lost some of its edge. A pale golden pattern flickered across the alabaster eyes, then cleared. *Keep looking.*

Loose, damp-velvet textured skin covered the flattened, elongated limbs wrapped around her. The bone beneath felt supple, segmented. A rippling shiver passed through the creature, streaks of crimson and gold flaring through the grey.

No. Not creature. Name me properly, bind me back to a name! A sharp, hot pain speckled across her body, focused in a familiar pattern: eyebrows, ears, lip, groin—

De'sta'haiq, she said. *Deiq. First Born ha'ra'ha. Husband.*

The pain dissipated. A great sigh shook through him. Grey began to fade, the face rounding out, bone and skin solidifying. The golden pattern flickered across his eyes again, spread, thickened, and then lids formed, dropping to hide the white.

She watched the transformation, too numb to be afraid, too exhausted to do anything but accept. What formed didn't—*quite*—look like the man she remembered; but it was a close enough match to call brother, or cousin.

His eyes opened, black shot through with gold and white. He focused on her. "You're wrong on one point," he said. "I'm not ha'ra'hain any longer—because of *you*."

Chapter 25

The fetid, hellish light and heat cut off abruptly as Idisio leapt through the abstract opening. He stumbled, tripped, and rolled across smooth, cool stone. Skin slid, then caught against the unyielding surface. He yelped at the burn, twisting his hips as tender bits pinched. He pushed to his feet, toes and left hand splaying out for balance. The fingers of that hand stubbed painfully against a wall a step away. His right hand, still curled into a tight fist, met nothing but air.

There was no sound here, no smell, no air-currents. Straining his ears didn't help. Shifting to ha'ra'hain vision did nothing to pierce the unrelenting black. His bare skin registered a dull indifference to the temperature, as though a protective, oily slick covered every pore.

He turned, very carefully, and felt across the nearby wall. Tiny bumps and dents resolved into distinct patterns under his fingers, like a random fragment of a random page of a *very* large book in a completely unknown language.

Idisio shut his eyes tightly, shivering a little. "At least I know where I am," he muttered. It made sense that the only exit from the creature's lair would be into these tunnels. He would even have been relieved, except for the complication posed by the lack of light. He had no idea how to summon the ghostly blue-white glow that had made his previous walk through these tunnels, with Scratha and Riss, almost pleasant.

At least it was silent. There was no battle taking place nearby, no strange murmurs in his head. He had a few moments in which to collect his thoughts and figure out what to do next.

Could he simply *step* back outside from here? Could it be that simple?

No, intuition said sharply, accompanied by a brief, vivid image of broken buildings, ravaged ground, and a truly grim number of bodies scattered about.

"Oh gods," he breathed, appalled. "That's all my fault." He sat down slowly, his back against the wall. "What did I do?"

Silence met his question. The dark remained absolute, and even his mother's angry voice was still for once. He leaned his head back against the wall, rubbing his one good hand over his face, and made himself think in more pragmatic terms. It was no good looking at what could have been. He hadn't reacted fast enough or smart enough, that was all. Now hundreds of people were dead because of it.

A faint flutter ran through his stomach; not painful, but a reminder of time passing all the same. He had to get to Scratha Fortress where, quite probably, more lives were at risk. Maybe, if he could handle whatever was going on *there* with greater skill, he could in some small way make up for the destruction he'd triggered.

It was as good a compromise as he could come up with at the moment. He stood, turning carefully, and ran his hand across the slight curve of the wall once more. The writing was intended to be read in all directions at once, but even so—any message had a *beginning* and an *end,* and there had to be some sort of positioning indicator within the writing itself.

He felt along a good fifteen paces of wall, reaching up high above his head, down to the ground and all around in between, before the patterns began to make sense. He still wasn't sure what it *said,* but he was fairly confident on the directional aspect of the writing. The message began to his right and wound leftwards.

Now to figure out which way led to the enormous chamber of tunnels that would take him to Scratha Fortress. He checked intuition, but it felt muddy and uncertain. *Not enough information to work with,* he decided. *Maybe if I could see the tunnel?*

Somewhere in the nightmare collection of memories that killing his mother had inflicted upon him, there *had* to be something about creating a light from nothing. Deiq would have been able to do it. His mother surely could have done it.

He turned his attention inward, looking at that morass of hate and madness. *How to create a light,* he thought, shunting aside the initial, gore-drenched images—gods, she'd *licked blood from a man's wounds,* more than once, while the victim screamed—*Don't look at that!* He refused to acknowledge dozens of even more horrific memory-moments demanding his attention. *Light,* he demanded. *Light. Creating light.*

Light, his mother's voice said, thready, distant, wistful; filled with images of warm sunlight and vividly colored flowers. *Oh, how I love daylight. Moonlight. Any light at all... It's so wonderful. Look, son, like this....*

Searing argent-orange threads snaked along Idisio's right arm, into his hand, gathering into an abruptly beautiful glowing sphere. He managed to uncurl his fingers at last, whimpering at the pain of joints held locked for too long, and stared at the five small bluestone beads in his palm, now glowing with uncanny light. "Oh," he said aloud. "So that's what I've been protecting."

He shifted the beads, holding them cupped in both hands, staring awestruck at what he'd created. *How the hells does* this *work?* he asked, not sure who was supposed to answer. Nobody did. The silence still hung, disrupted only by the faintest crackle coming from the sphere in his hands.

"Chances are," he muttered to himself, "I'm using something from inside myself to create this, since there's nobody *else* around to use for fuel. So I'd better get moving. And why am I talking to myself, anyway? Godsdamnit, *stop* that, Idisio!"

He lifted his hands, looking around. To his left, the air past the reach of the light became—*oily* dark, a nasty sort of haze, while the other direction seemed a simpler, truer black.

"To the right it is," he said under his breath. He rolled the beads into his left hand, put his other hand on the wall to orient himself; closed his hand tightly around the bluestone beads, bid the light to die out, then began walking.

Time meant nothing. Depth perception and distance flattened under darkness, and he walked, not really thinking, just being as aware of the physical as possible to avoid tripping over his own feet or bashing into an unexpected obstacle.

Now and again, the air stirred, its taste changing briefly. He paused, straining his senses, and found nothing. The moment passed, stillness returning. *Vents to the outside, maybe?* he thought after the third time, looking up. *Even ha'reye need air, don't they?*

He hadn't noticed it on his first trip through these tunnels, but he'd been a bit distracted by his companions and hadn't needed to pay such close attention back then because they'd *had* light to see by. He went on, noting each incidence but no longer stopping for them.

Naknota feree anka-meynn be'halee....

He froze, pressing his back against the wall, hands waving out before him. A thoroughly uncomfortable prickling chill raced across his arms and neck. The murmuring continued, unheeding, incomprehensible; sing-song at times, staccato and dry at others. Gradually, the voice separated out into two, then three, then more, in an ever-increasing chorus of babbling nonsense.

Half-panicking, Idisio summoned the light again. The cool glow showed an empty tunnel. The voices continued: barely audible, but considerably more clear than on the previous trip.

Idisio looked up the tunnel, trying to see how much further he had to go before reaching the enormous room of portals. Then he remembered, belatedly, that the sense of presence and murmuring had become *worse* the further along the tunnel he traveled.

"At least I'm headed in the right direction," he muttered. "And it can't be worse than what I've already been through, after all."

After a moment's hesitation, he extinguished the light again and went on.

Chapter 26

Hot, crackling aches shivered through Deiq as he set Alyea on her feet. He could sense the fluids in his body gradually evaporating, leaving a thick, mineral-rich sludge behind.

He looked around, taking in their surroundings: Curved walls and a sloped floor; a tunnel, deep underground. Alyea leaned against one wall, trembling, staring at him as though nothing else existed. Teilo, sprawled on the ground, was beginning to haul herself to her feet, groaning and muttering.

He could hear the ground breaking, not far away. This tunnel wouldn't remain stable for long. They had to move further away from the faereen's den. He reached a hand up, brushing fingertips against the ceiling, and grunted in annoyance at the slick feel.

Sealed, as he'd expected, and confirmation that this was one of the hidden ways. He could move from point to point *within* the tunnel, because of his ha'ra'hain blood, but there was no leaving it except through one of the portals.

The nest, the anchor point for this tunnel, would already be collapsing. No going back to that portal. They had to head for the hub. Not safe. *Not* smart. But it was the only option. "Move," he said, pointing in the safe direction and making shooing motions at the two humans.

"I can't see," Alyea said, her voice strained. "The light's gone out."

He blinked, shifting vision, and brought human-visible light to the immediate area. Alyea visibly relaxed, then looked down at herself with a dismayed expression. "My clothes—my pack!"

"You're alive," he said, studying her with a sense of pragmatic abstraction. By current human standards, she was probably beautiful. A hundred years ago, her eyes would have been too large; four hundred years ago, she would have been unattractively gaunt. At other times, her dark, coarse hair would have been a flaw. Human fashions and customs were so trivial.

My wife. It seemed a bizarre concept. What could he possibly be to her, now that she'd seen him with a few of the protective masks removed? What point was there to a relationship now—he wasn't ha'ra'hain any longer. He was something—

New. Powerful. Beautiful.

—Something *wrong*, something *dangerous*, something he'd fought against becoming all of his life. He focused on that, grimly lacing stubborn refusal through the forefront of his mind as a first reaction to anything at all.

Alyea stared at him, uncomprehending. Well, that was his own damn fault, wasn't it, that he'd never explained about his brothers. He hadn't wanted to talk about family at *all*, for fear she'd turn away from seeing him as human—for fear of eroding his own tenuous grasp on that mindset.

Too late now. He shut his eyes, tracking internal changes, straining to bring his temper under control. It felt like dragging his brain through a puddle of molten mud. He growled in frustration and sensed Alyea taking a wide step back, her fear spiking.

For the first time in his life, nearby human emotions didn't *matter*. He felt no impulse to attack, to dominate—nothing more than a vague indifference.

Oh, this is nice, he thought, pleased at that aspect of the change. No more irritating, horsefly-bite like demands for attention, for reaction, for acknowledgment. Maybe he would finally get some *peace*—

The human said his name. He looked at her reflexively, watching her burnt-almond skin shift and distort under the pressure of her emotions. What she wanted didn't matter—why he'd ever *cared* was beyond him. She was human. Tharr. Insignificant.

Replaceable....

Sludge shifted through his veins, rattling an ache through his temples. *Fluid*. He needed more fluid, to offset the dehydration. What would be best? Water, or—

"Deiq!" she said again, more emphatically, as though that would make a difference.

Once more, and he'd be... *annoyed*... yes, that was the word. He'd be annoyed. He didn't really like being annoyed. He wanted to stay peacefully serene and think, very slowly, about the hydrating properties of various fluids. Blood might be best. It had nutrients he needed....

"De'sta'haiq," another voice said from behind him.

He turned, smiling with recognition this time. "Old mother," he said. "I *am*. That is *magnificent*."

It was a loose way to convey the massive sense of *rightness* filling his entire body at the moment, but he knew she would understand. She'd seen his brothers moving into this stage, after all. She knew what was happening to him.

Why, *why* had he fought this for so long? This was *glorious*.

The human said something—not his name, but speech all the same. He began to turn.

"De'sta'haiq," the old mother said before he could react to the annoyance. She commanded his attention, his respect. It was only *polite* to listen to a wise elder.

He waited for her next words with careful patience. Sometimes it took a while for the older ones to form words into coherent speech. She wore no clothes—of course not; *covering* was a human concept that she was long since past needing to obey. Her skin was a sagging net of complex wrinkles overlaying centuries-solid muscle which connected bones tougher than the densest rock.

The younger human, the one that had annoyed him, was so much softer, so much more fragile. So pale, so ephemeral in comparison.

The elder studied him with a—wistful—regretful? he couldn't quite decide on the proper word—expression on her lined face.

"Oh, child," she said. "I'm so sorry. You're going to hate me."

He frowned at her, puzzled. *Hate*? What was *hate*? She seemed to expect him to understand that concept. Well, she was the elder, so she was implicitly right. He just had to remember it properly.

As he began to search his memory for a definition of *hate*, she stepped in close and slapped him across the face, her open palm cracking flat against his cheek. A moment later she slapped him with her other hand, striking his opposite cheek.

Each blow carried more than simple physical force. Intangible hooks snagged memories, dragging the ghostly past into searing immediacy. Indifference shattered, disinterest fragmented. He screamed as serenity evaporated and he *remembered*—

—What that fucking human he'd been stupid enough to bind himself to had *done*—then, in a staggering emotional reversal, reeled in horror at what he'd almost become—

—And Teilo had just effectively, if temporarily, trapped him *between* the two stages. In a surge of bitter fury, he turned to strike her down.

She wasn't there, of course. She was far too canny for that. She stood behind Alyea, her hands on the human woman's shoulders, misleadingly gentle. Alyea probably thought that Teilo was trying to *comfort* her.

Deiq held still, his gaze on Teilo. Her eyes were round and golden, with faint dark streaks passing across them in odd patterns. He blinked and redirected his focus. He was much too old to be caught so easily in the snake-stare.

"Hold still, desert lord," Teilo said, her voice scratchy and harsh. Alyea tensed, finally understanding. Color flushed and faded across her face. Deiq watched patchy goose bumps rise and smooth out across her body, forcing himself into a distant sense of amusement at the process.

Alyea's stare locked onto Deiq's face, wide-eyed, caught between pleading for rescue and fear of what he'd do next—fear of what he *was* now. "What's happening?" she said.

"Did the First Born ever tell you of his brothers, desert lord?" Teilo said—answering a question with a question, as the disciples were always taught to do with outsiders.

Humans are such maddening creatures—they really should have all been destroyed long ago—

Deiq shut his eyes and focused on his breathing. On separating internal layers, distributing weight, balancing what humans would have called his *humors*.

"Enough," he said as Teilo began to say something else. "Let Alyea go." Another wave of rumbling passed under his feet. "We need to move. We can talk as we go. *Move*."

He heard Alyea take a step, another. She moved to one side, skittish—then, for a wonder, they were all hurrying along the tunnel, outpacing the spreading destruction of the faereen's nest.

"What do you know of the First Born?" Teilo prodded as they went, tone honey-laced malice. "What have you been *allowed* to know?"

"They were all destroyed except for Deiq," Alyea said. "I tried to ask the loremasters in Bright Bay for more, after he... left... but they wouldn't really tell me anything. They gave me books of folktales and fireside stories. Most of them were absurd, fairies and wind sprites and nonsense like that, but one story involved—giants—"

Deiq knew the one she meant. He'd memorized over fifty versions of that tale to date, drumming it into his mind with a ferocious intensity to *not be like that*:

They raged across the world, leaving deserts in their wake, burning hundreds of miles of forest to see the ashes dance in the wind. They created great trenches in the earth with every step, leveling mountains with a flick of one finger, simply to see a cloud of dust thick enough to match their madness.

"The loremasters gave you the answer you asked for," Teilo said. "That story is about the First Born."

"Stop," Deiq said, hauling them all to a halt. He looked back the way they'd come, listening, reaching out, tracing stress lines. Finally, he nodded. "We're outside the collapse. It's radiating more east than south."

"Tell her the truth of that story she read, First Born," Teilo said, sardonic, as she settled to the ground in a cross-legged posture and smirked up at him.

Deiq turned his back on her, looking up at the ceiling for a few moments, then said, "That story's about my brothers. It's filled with human exaggeration and distortion, but...." *Not as much as usual* he kept behind his teeth. "It was difficult to repair the damage from their various amusements."

"Such a good thing humans breed quickly," Teilo said, her tone acidic. "So *very* fortunate."

He turned to look at her. Her expression was bleak and bitter, her eyes closer to a flat bronze color now. She met his gaze without fear. He shut his eyes. It was easier to balance his temper without the aggravation of vision.

"*Brother* is a misleading term," he said, aiming his words at Alyea. "Humans would probably use finer distinctions, like *cousin* or *half-brother*. It's all the same to ha'reye. But each of the First Born were created... a little differently. Each of us had fewer flaws than the previous creation. Lessons learned, mistakes corrected." He paused, then risked a glance at Teilo and added, "Humans weren't the only ones being bred for *results*."

She pursed her lips and looked away in tacit apology.

"You have children?" Alyea blurted, astonished.

"Not any more," Deiq said—a partial lie, but a necessary one. "My last tie was to one of my brother's children—called faereen—but now that's... gone."

A silence hung.

"That—what just happened—that was one of your brothers' children?" Alyea said at last, scarcely audible.

"Yes. The one I just killed—" The word sent a sick jolt through his stomach. He paused, breathing hard, accepting the reality of what he'd done, then went on. "—was the best of the faereen. And the sanest. I was... fond of it, so I saved it and hid it here." He glanced at Alyea. She was frowning, apparently caught between fascination and confusion.

Hold her, draw her close, use her—use *her....* He tried to silence the urge, but *gods*—he could do anything, *anything* to her, she could even fight back and he'd still have complete control over his own actions—*No. Gods, no. This is part of why the collar was put on. We were so incredibly hard on the humans*—Memory shifted, adding in details he'd forced himself to forget hundreds of years ago, the taste of blood and pain filling his mouth like sweet honey.

"Stop talking, First Born. You're becoming too emotional," Teilo said, sarcasm fading into a sharper edge.

"You go on, then," Deiq said, turning away again, lips tight, and began rebuilding the *forgetting*, half-listening to her explanation.

Teilo said, "Ha'reye control elements, primarily earth, water, and fire. The eldest First Born focused on earth. They were dispassionate, emotionless, and destructive. The middle children created vast deserts as they took all moisture into themselves. The next ones burned everything they saw for the sheer joy of watching the flames. Deiq is the only one who convinced the ha'reye that he had balanced the three elements. He's a very good liar. I suspect you've already noticed that."

"I *did* keep a balance," Deiq said, unable to let that go without comment. "Better than they did, anyway. Enough to pass."

"Yes," Teilo said. "*Enough to pass.*"

Alyea made a pained, protesting sound that changed to a thoughtful grunt halfway through. Deiq couldn't summon enough humor to smile at the odd noise. Memory had been locked to silence once more, but a residual ache/anger flared through muscle and bone at erratic intervals.

"I remember piling... something like rocks on you." Alyea's tone was subdued.

"Yes," Teilo said. "You replaced water and fire with earth, stone, and metal. His balance is within a breath of being completely *gone*—at which point he won't care about *anything* except destruction."

"I don't know how I did it. I didn't even know what I was doing," Alyea said. "It just... happened."

"Your chains," Teilo said. "Evkit used your chains to control you into doing what he wanted."

"What? I'm bound to Deiq, not to—" Alyea stopped as Deiq let out a harsh, bitter laugh.

"That was my reaction as well, when I found out," Deiq said, then explained as briefly as he could. "He can reach out and push you into doing what he wants any damn time he pleases," he finished. "And—rather less easily—he can push me."

She sagged to the floor, leaning against the tunnel wall, blinking hard. "I—I'm sorry," she said unevenly. "That's all my fault, isn't it? I gave him that opportunity."

"Yes," Deiq said, flat and cold. "You did."

"But—how could he know I'd be here, how could he know what was—oh. The athain." She leaned her head back against the tunnel wall, wrapping her arms around herself, shivering. "How does he benefit from you becoming... like this? Why would he risk it? If you're close to being... like your brothers... you'd destroy the world! He doesn't want that!"

"He wants to *control* the world," Deiq said, his voice dropping to a near-growl. "He's turned me into a weapon on a fucking *leash*." A thought occurred to him: If he killed Alyea, the bond would break, the leash would be useless—

"Don't be stupid," Teilo said, sharply enough that it shocked him back to clarity—and into a comforting rage. "He won't let you do that."

He barely heard her last words under the cascade of thick-blooded fury. He growled, opening his eyes, focusing on the old woman—She was *traitor*, she was *outcast*—He would *destroy* her—

"*Stop it*," Alyea said, loud and peremptory, as she stepped into his line of sight. He took a long stride forward, rage cresting into a blinding haze; grabbed Alyea by the throat, lifted her high, slammed her against the tunnel wall—

—And collapsed to the ground a heartbeat later: choking, bruised, crying out in tandem with the human woman.

"Still heart-bound," Teilo said, somewhere far away. "That's interesting."

He rolled awkwardly to his feet and glared at the disciple—no: the elder—no, that still wasn't right—the old woman—no, *damnit*—and a name finally came clear: *Teilo*. The other one struggled to her knees. Reflexively, he turned to help the woman—the younger human—to her feet—wait, why was he bothering? *Insignificant*—no, no, this was important, this one was someone he had to respect—*why*?

Wife. Bound. Name. *Name!* He fought to see through the haze creeping across his vision, and grasped at memory. Her name was Alyea. *Alyea. That's Alyea. That's Teilo. They're important. I need them.*

He blinked hard as Alyea shrank away from him, her face an ashy grey. Teilo laughed, sardonic. "And the truth sets in at last," she said. "I warned you to stay home, Lord Peysimun."

Names. *Names*. One name was missing. Something important.

Someone—

"Idisio," he said abruptly. "Where's Idisio?"

"He went through before us," Alyea said. She looked south along the tunnel, squinting as though trying to see through the darkness past the light Deiq had created. "I'd guess he's further along that direction."

Teilo looked south, the haze over her eyes turning a smoky grey in alarm. "That's the *hub*," she said. "He's headed for the hub!"

"He's been there once before," Deiq said, bits of old conversations falling into order.

"*What*? How did he get out? How did he get *in*?"

"Cafad Scratha," Deiq said succinctly.

"Oh, for the love of the gods," Teilo said, face tight with exasperation. "Is there *anything* that man does right?"

"I think he sleeps on occasion without causing trouble," Deiq said, relaxing into a rueful laugh, then went back to picking out bits of past conversations. "Last time, Idisio had the permission of the faereen, walked in the company of a desert lord, and still saw himself as human. The *attiara* probably stirred, but they obviously didn't rouse. But with the changes he's been through since then, and with the faereen dead—"

"*Get him out of there*," Teilo rasped. "*Now.*"

Chapter 27

Deiq took a long step forward, then stopped, lowering his head. "If I go after him, *I'll* set off the attiara," he said. "So will you, old mother."

He lifted his stare to Alyea. She watched a pulse beat in his temple, in his cheek, with abstract fascination. Something about the vein didn't *look* quite right—it seemed *harder*, more distinct, than it should have. In a human, it would have indicated an imminent stroke. She had no idea what it meant for—whatever Deiq was now.

"Alyea," Deiq said, sharply enough to catch her from her examination of his face.

"What do you—" Alyea held up her hands in reflexive, beginning protest, then dropped them to her sides once more. "What are the attiara?"

"Guardians," Teilo said. "Very powerful and very nasty guardians. She wouldn't survive three steps under their attention, First Born." Her voice dropped to a low murmur, obviously aimed at Deiq's ears alone: "At least it's not another faereen!"

"Almost as bad," Deiq answered, as quietly. "And she can hear you just fine, old mother."

Teilo turned a sharply disapproving stare at Alyea.

"I wasn't *eavesdropping*," Alyea said defensively.

"Not intentionally," Deiq corrected. He looked up at the arc of the tunnel roof, his expression oddly blank, then sighed. "So much work wasted," he said under his breath.

Alyea followed his gaze, her perceptions linking into his: extrapolating tremors and echoes along the north-eastern end of the tunnel, seeing an expectation of what waited far overhead. "Oh dear gods," she said, appalled. "Surely it can't be that bad."

A roughness came between them, a painful, cutting distance. She lurched against the wall, disoriented. Deiq made no move to help her recover; Teilo chuffed exasperated laughter.

"We'd have trouble ourselves, if we went alone," Deiq said, his voice once more emotionless and cold. "So it's all of us together. That will at least give them pause to ask questions before striking."

"We *could* just leave him to it," Teilo observed, her previous alarm replaced with a chill pragmatism. "The disaster would be... containable. And it might open up alternate pathways that would allow *us* to avoid going through the hub."

"I can't," Deiq said. "Not this time. He's only in this mess because I abandoned him when he needed help once before."

"When did you abandon—" Alyea began, indignant. Shared memory turned sideways, offering glimpses to fill in the answer. "You *lied*! You said he was *fine*—"

Both Deiq and Teilo turned desert-dry stares on her. She shut up and looked at the ground, biting her lip to contain her anger. *Of course he lied. That's what he* does....

A shivering howl warped the air around them, a braided chorus of pain.

"And that's the end of that. We're out of time to argue," Deiq said. His hand closed around her upper arm, cool and impersonal, rather than the warm assurance she was used to feeling from him. The pulse in his thumb was wide and oddly *thick*—it didn't feel right at all.

Before she could think about that or ask questions, the air shifted, darkened, turned inside out, bit at her lungs. Then she was on her knees, coughing uncontrollably. Her nose seemed filled with a thick sawdust. She gasped for breath, heart thudding in her ears. Stone stretched high overhead, far beneath—or was she upside down?

Deiq hauled her to her feet, slapping her hard on the shoulder. She staggered two steps and threw up a thin, acidic drool that trailed down her chest and stomach. She wiped at it with vague distaste.

Naknota feree anka-meynn be'halee, something whispered in her ear. The language felt *old*, like something long-interred and abandoned, but somehow she understood: *We will destroy the world one day.*

"Not this day," Deiq replied, voice raw and fierce, in that ancient language. "I call for your presence, and stand on my right as First Born!"

As ferociously, Teilo echoed, "I call for your presence, I stand on my right as First of the Chosen!"

Complete silence fell. A pale, wavering light grew around them, taking away shadow, illuminating curved stone walls. They were still in the tunnel, but a much larger section—the topmost curve lofted well beyond Alyea's reach.

"You have our attention, First Born and First Chosen," a thin voice said. "Have you come regarding the kin-slayer we hold? Have you come to heal us from the damage it inflicted? It harmed us with forbidden weapons."

Alyea's stomach shrank into a small, unhappy ball.

Deiq and Teilo said in seamless unison, "We demand right of punishment for this kin-slayer." Their voices blended into one complex tone, as though more than only two throats spoke the words. It was a breathtakingly beautiful sound.

"Our right to punish those who walk our tunnels has never been challenged," the sourceless voice said, a thin strong wire of sound compared to Deiq and Teilo's braided song. "And we require healing. It has harmed us. It used forbidden weapons. This must be repaid."

"We have a right beyond yours," Teilo and Deiq said. "Give us the kin-slayer and we will heal you."

A long silence followed, in which the air turned slowly colder and grainier.

"You do not have this right," the thin voice said at last. "We doubt your promise to heal us. You have attachment to this kin-slayer. You are oath breakers yourselves. Your breath is foul with betrayal and deceit."

"Oh, hells," Deiq said under his breath. "I'd actually forgotten they could do that." Then his voice lifted, joining Teilo's once more. "Attachment, yes, and obligation as well. Give us the kin-slayer and we will explain—"

"We hear the signs," the thin voice interrupted, each word distinct. "The Agreement is broken."

Deiq and Teilo glanced at one another, their mouths set in unhappy lines.

"Not broken so much as *changed*—" Deiq began.

"There is only broken and not-broken. And *change* means *broken*."

An unholy scream filled the air, a wailing, scratching cry that seemed to tear at the deepest recesses of Alyea's ears, shredding her guts, emptying the blood from her veins, and pulling every hair from her body at once. She staggered a step, then steadied, distantly astounded that she hadn't fallen over completely.

"We were told this day would come," the voice, considerably stronger now, exulted. "And so it is. We will emerge and we will destroy and we will *feast*."

"*No*," Deiq and Teilo said together, Alyea's own protest arriving as a tardy third.

"I forbid this," Teilo added. "You may not emerge."

"*We* were given specific signs," the voice said. "Those signs have been met. All we require is the key word, the one that will unlock our bindings and allow us to emerge and take our payment for our long servitude in darkness. You have that word. You *must* have that word: First Born and First Chosen, you would have been given our key. Use it! Free us!"

"I will not do that," Deiq said. "This is not the time for you to emerge." Sweat trickled down his temples, the back of his neck and his chest. His eyes were wide and pale.

"But the signs are met." The voice held a thread of doubt, a strong hint of a whine.

"We have nothing to do with those signs. We are merely here to remove the younger who wandered into your territory. His presence here is unintended, the damage done a mistake, not a true attack. He is too young to be on his own, and he is too ignorant to be held accountable for his mistakes. We will teach him, and we will heal you."

"*It is a kin-slayer.*" The voice held cold outrage now.

"He was permitted." Deiq's eyes darkened. "His kin *chose* that death."

"This is not possible. Hakrakhain do not seek death."

Deiq let out a bitter bark of laughter. "You don't know a godsdamned thing about hakrakhain," he said under his breath, then, more loudly: "No. We do not *seek* death. But we do not always have to *fight* it, when it presents itself at our throat. I tell you, on my authority as First Born, that the killing was allowed."

"But we want to be *free*," the voice said, and now it held a deep, sensual *hunger* that raised goose bumps across every bit of Alyea's body. "We have served. We were *promised* our freedom."

"Not yet," Teilo said. "The day will come. *Not yet*."

"We have the signs. We have the *right*. You must use the key!"

"You do not have the final decree! You are misreading the signs! We are the greater, you must listen to us—you will not win a battle against us."

The voice flattened into a near-growl: "*You are greater than we are, this is truth. We cannot destroy you, this is truth. But even weakened as we are now, we* can *harm you severely enough to require a long sleep; and we* can *kill the younger. He is damaged and weakened enough for that.*"

"We cannot free you. It is not the time!"

"*Then offer us something else of high value—and your word that you* will *free us when it is time!*"

Not entirely sure why, driven by some odd impulse to do *something* to help, Alyea began to step forward—towards what, she had no idea. Deiq's grip on her shoulder dug in cruelly hard, and he yanked her back. "No," he said in her ear. "*No*. Don't you dare. We're bound, remember? You are not going to offer any *part* of yourself—"

"Bound?" The voices lightened, bounced, warbled with abrupt interest.

Alyea's vision filled with yellow haze, struck through with jagged red and black lines. A heartbeat later, darkness came as an almost physical relief. She leaned against Deiq, gagging and shivering.

The voice rolled through the air, increasingly gleeful.

"Bound? A First Born, bound to a human? Oh, yes, we see it now. That will suit. *Oh, yes.* Give us your chain-bond. Give us that weakness, that vulnerability, that pain and shame and fear. Yes."

Laughter shrilled, painfully intense.

"We will take that chain as payment for allowing the younger and yourselves to depart. Give us your word that you will free us at the proper time, and we will forget you were here. We will wait for the signs to come again."

"What would you get out of *that*?" Alyea demanded, baffled.

"Everything you lose, we would gain," the voice said. In the distance, a lunatic laugh shrilled. "Everything we gain, you would lose. Give us this chain. It is a strong chain, a *wonderful* construction. Give it to us."

She could feel Deiq breathing against her hair. He shivered briefly, and a yellow haze passed across her vision as quickly. "What happens if—" she began.

"No *time*, girl," he said. "Attiara: *yes.* As long as my partner agrees to release her end, I agree to release mine. Attiara may take my chain when and if she gives you hers. I swear to release you at the proper time."

"What am I giving up?" she insisted.

"Everything and nothing," the voice said. *"Choose."*

The darkness wavered between stifling heat and acrid chill. She gasped for breath, dizzy with conflicting desires: obey / flee / refuse / kneel—

The voice of her long-dead aqeyva teacher cut into her as the whips had cut into him: *No tears.* A small wooden wren, carved by a man she'd later killed, nestled in her palm. *Resourcefulness,* Deiq said in distant memory, explaining southern symbolism. *Bold, crafty, smart and adaptable... It was a message to you... to live, to survive.*

Past became present: "*Trust me,*" Deiq whispered in her ear.

Freshly compared against her memory, his voice was—*wrong*—off-key, just a bit. Was it only because of the changes he'd gone through? She hesitated, deeply uneasy. An oily sensation slid along her limbs, a shivering pressure lodged in her chest.

"*Trust. Me.*" His voice held a harsh velvet suasion that she'd always had trouble standing up against. It felt even more off-key than before, but still exerted tremendous pressure.

Crafty. Adaptable. The words sounded like a warning as they echoed through her mind.

Alyea turned her head, searching through the darkness. She wished Teilo would speak to advise one choice or the other. She wanted a glimpse, a chance to check her sense of dread against a wiser gaze. Deiq's breath was hot in her ear, evoking other shared moments, scrambling her thoughts into helpless chaos.

"Trust me," he said again, low and overtly sensual this time, one hand sliding down her spine. Her remaining determination crumbled.

"Yes," she said, shivering between arousal and fear. "Yes, I trust you. I release the bond. I give the attiara my chain."

"You godsforsaken fools," Teilo said a heartbeat later, voice raw as though she'd been straining to speak for some time.

The shrill laughter had already begun to rise again.

It cut off, a double heartbeat after that, into a moment of shocked silence, then ratcheted rapidly into a series of screams that soared far out of Alyea's hearing range.

The laughter that replaced it was human—*familiar*—and, unmistakably, teyanin.

Crafty. Adaptable.

"Oh... shit," Alyea said, vaguely, and welcomed unconsciousness when it arrived.

Chapter 28

Like diving into winter-chill water, icy air surfed across Deiq's body. He cried out, rolling, seeking warmth. The cold *hurt*. He wasn't used to that. Where had all the warmth gone? Why couldn't he *see* anything?

Godsforsaken fool. The words echoed in his mind, pulling identity along with them—not the first time he'd made a mistake. Hells, it was practically one of his defining traits.

This was a larger one than usual.

Tricked again. Used again. Godsdamnit. So much for being a god....

"It's been many years since *anyone* thought you were a god," Teilo commented. "Stop the misery conceit and wake up already, First Born."

Cold faded, his body adjusting to the ambient temperature. Vision cleared into color, form, shape. The other senses caught up a heartbeat later.

Sunlight sprayed up from the eastern horizon, filtering through clouds that were layered streaks of grey, purple, and gold. Incandescent orange limned the area where sky met earth. To his left and right, massive slabs of rock stood as erratic, dark sentinels against the oncoming day.

The air was clean and thin in his nose, every sound vibrantly clear in his ears. A scrape, a sigh, a click of teeth as someone shifted position restlessly.

"Face what you've done," Teilo said. She stood somewhere behind him. He lowered his gaze slowly, taking in a newly created slope where once there had been a steep cliff; studying the shattered coastline, the flooded areas, the ruined ships and obliterated settlements to north and south. It was unrecognizable as the land he'd walked for hundreds of years.

He spared a moment to wonder if the sanctuary he'd brought Alyea to had been affected, then shrugged that aside. He'd rebuilt his nests before.

He turned, putting his back to the dawn, and sucked in a deep, shocked breath.

The underground way had collapsed in on itself, leaving a jagged, branching series of trenches that ran, at a guess, a half-mile deep in spots. The damage to the geography was catastrophic; the damage to the trade routes, to the *politics*—

"Oh, gods," he said aloud, truly appalled. "Sessin's *ruined*. Tereph, the coastal villages—I don't think they'll—"

"You're *still* thinking like a human," she said sharply. "Why is it that *I* have to tell you what to look at when it's right in front of your nose?"

He blinked. Alyea was curled into a ball on the ground at his feet, either asleep or unconscious, but that couldn't be what the old woman meant. He blinked again, refocusing more tightly, and finally saw it: A fine, red-gold speckling in the air around him. "Oh," he said, dread coiling into his stomach. "Oh, no."

For a wonder, Teilo didn't say anything. She let him look at the shimmering cloud in silence. After a few breaths, he gathered courage and turned his attention inwards. As expected, the chains had been reset, and were now braided, through and through, with the muzzled energy of the attiara.

He wouldn't be able to wrench free of the chains this time. And the attiara were *not* happy about being tricked. Their roiling fury felt like a series of tiny hammers constantly placing bruises along every joint in his body. From what he could tell, they were at full strength. The pain was insignificant against the implications.

He was sane, for a given value of *sane*; in control of his actions, with the same qualifier. More powerful than he'd *ever* been, more powerful than his brothers, very probably as powerful as a full ha'rethe. But the teyanain controlled his access to that strength. Teilo's hold on the chains was gone.

There had to be at least a *clee*—three athain—somewhere nearby, watching, holding Deiq to their will. Possibly a double or triple clee, given Evkit's astounding achievement and the subsequent amount of raw power they had to work with.

He didn't bother looking for them. Didn't bother getting angry. Didn't know, even, if he was choosing resignation or if it was being forced on him.

A weapon on a leash, indeed. Evkit never, ever *loses. Not in the long run. Why don't I remember that by now?*

The words *crafty* and *adaptable* echoed through the back of his mind, laden with mockery.

He shut his eyes and sat down slowly, gingerly, then put out a hand and laid it on Alyea's shoulder without really thinking about the motion. The touch gave him no comfort, but he left his hand there all the same.

Alyea's skin was warm under his hand. That meant his own body temperature was too low. He looked inward, gauging resources: *too low, too low.* He needed fluids.

He opened his eyes, looking out to the west: reaching, filtering, rearranging the air to pull a storm together. It would cause more disruption, more damage. He could feel the hail forming at the edges, the air warping off into tornadoes. *The teyanain won't be happy with me.*

Fuck the teyanain. Fuck Evkit. Fuck everything. He drew in a breath, hauling himself back toward sanity.

"You did agree to take a certain course of action," Teilo observed dryly. "This will make that goal easier to accomplish."

"And considerably harder to *survive,*" he said. He could smell rock dust stirred up by a far away wind, sense the plants nearby growing alert to impending moisture, their cells flexing, opening in anticipation. He pulled his perceptions back to physical: the air hung hot and still, the smell of sweating human strong in his nostrils.

Alyea's shoulder moved as though she were waking. He allowed himself to focus on watching her, studying the sheen of moisture across her face and groin. He reached out and trailed a finger along her inner thigh and across the line of leg and hip. *Moisture.* It wasn't enough. He'd have to drain her entirely, and he wouldn't—wouldn't—why? Memory was unreliable. He let himself trust the instinct, and withdrew his hand.

Teilo humphed, irascible and amused all at once, bringing his attention back to her.

"You're harder to kill than all of that, First Born," she said. "I *am* surprised the younger has lived this long, though."

It took Deiq a moment to reconnect the pieces of conversation. He turned his head in startled realization, searching for the younger ha'ra'ha. "The younger. Where is he?"

"Sleeping," Teilo said. "Behind that rise. I thought it best to keep you apart until you'd stabilized again. He didn't react well to the attiara."

Deiq looked west, studying the slowly building line of grey and the scarred, tumbled rocky ground, analyzing ambient humidity, and sighed. As much to distract himself as to move matters along, he pushed gently at Alyea's shoulder.

She rolled over once, grunted, then sat up, bleary for only a moment. Her attention locked on Deiq's face, examining him as though checking to see what he looked like this time; shifted to Teilo, studying her as carefully, then scanned their surroundings.

"Idisio," she said succinctly, looking back at Deiq.

"Sleeping," he said, dryly amused at echoing Teilo's answer. "Nearby. He didn't handle that well."

"I don't think any of us did." She frowned, studying him more closely. He watched her eyes focus, vision perceptibly narrowing. "What is that all around you?"

"Don't look at it," he said wearily, waving a hand in front of her face. "You'll get hurt." The sight of his own hand distracted him. Was the skin texture changing? It looked too grainy, the tiny crosshatching of human cells warped. He weighed the effort of pushing it straight, but decided it was best to save his energy for more critical matters.

He couldn't help glancing at the blended red streaks running through the chains. *Peace,* he tried to tell the attiara. *I do not intend to harm you. You are not bound by my will.* He couldn't tell if the message got through. Their roiling dissatisfaction continued unabated.

He could feel Alyea blink back to normal vision. "What is it?" she repeated.

He debated answering, but that *look* was back on her face, and Teilo was stirring impatiently. "Attiara," he said.

"What are att—" She stopped, looked away as though to stop herself from staring at him. He hadn't meant to glare, but apparently it now took a more conscious effort to maintain a neutral expression. Something to remember in the future.

"Idisio's waking," Teilo said. Deiq shot her a deliberately stern glance. She'd put the younger to sleep, and he *wouldn't* have woken without her direct prodding. She tilted her head and raised an eyebrow at him, unrepentant.

"I'm not stupid," Alyea said, very quietly. "I do understand what's going on, Teilo."

"You're not *as* stupid as you once were," Teilo answered. "You understand *somewhat* more than you once did."

Teilo was playing her stupid disciple games again, but Alyea didn't know the rules and was going to get angry in short order. Deiq felt his temper sliding even more rapidly than that.

"I swear by all the gods that may ever have existed, I will *bury you both* if you don't knock it off right now," Deiq said, favoring each of them with a piercing glare. Alyea nearly blanched, but held her ground. Teilo laughed at him.

She'd been deliberately prodding at his temper, testing, *pushing* to see if he could hold his balance. Or, more likely, to see if the renewed chains would hold him in check.

Idisio stepped out into view before Deiq could think too deeply about the implications of *that,* which was probably very much for the best.

The younger ha'ra'ha's gaze locked on Deiq immediately, which *wasn't*, very *much* wasn't, for the best. Tunnel-vision hazed, peripheral sight reddening, and an all-too-familiar sensation took over Deiq's muscles: A gentle, easy, floating stillness that would let him move in any direction at high speed—

Idisio let out a hoarse choking sound, like a strangling crow, wrenched his gaze away from Deiq, then sank to his knees, head bowed.

Teilo said something in a long-lost language that translated into kaenic, roughly, as: "Holy *fuck*."

Deiq blinked, not at all sure what to do next. That reaction was—*unprecedented*. At this point in his development, under this particular set of stressors, Idisio should have been charging forward to assert his dominance. It should have been a matter *completely* outside of his conscious control. He simply wasn't old enough to have that kind of strength.

He realized that Alyea was laughing—not loudly, and not maliciously, but she clearly found Deiq and Teilo's astonishment amusing. She said, "Idisio, I think I'd have paid you everything I once owned to do that much sooner if I'd known that having you kneel to him would put *that* look on Deiq's face."

Idisio didn't answer, but one shoulder moved in a brief, acknowledging twitch.

"It's not the kneeling," Teilo said, "It's the situation—"

"I *know*," Alyea said sharply.

Deiq's vision darkened with irritation. "Stop it," he snapped, not taking his attention from the kneeling younger. "Go away. Both of you. Go over to where he was sleeping, get out of my sight. *Go*. And be *silent*."

Neither one argued. Idisio didn't move as they retreated. His breathing was deep and even. He'd dropped into a full aqeyva trance with impressive speed.

After a few moments of baleful glaring, Deiq realized that the younger wasn't about to emerge from that trance without a clear indication of safety. *Smart*. He ought to know better than to underestimate Idisio by now.

I am thinking like a human. This time, it didn't seem like an insult—but it *was* strange, all the same. He'd been jerked from helplessness to full power and back to helplessness multiple times in the past days. *Why aren't I completely mad by now? Ah. The athain*. He'd actually forgotten the rearrangement of his bonds. No doubt the clee was nudging that amnesia along at every chance.

They aren't going to let me become violent until they're ready. He sank into a cross-legged posture and dropped into a trance of his own, idly considering whether or not to be grateful for that restriction.

The teyanain want to control, not destroy. The Aerthraim want to destroy, not control. He'd been watching their respective focuses sharpen and solidify for hundreds of years. Evkit coming into power had been the seal on that side, while Osenna had done the same for the Aerthraim. Osenna had failed in the long term, constrained by the realities of descendants who simply *didn't* do what one wanted. Evkit had chosen to extend his own lifespan rather than risk that same failure.

But Osenna hadn't been a fool, and she'd still been alive when her granddaughter and grandson began their respective rebellions against the paths laid out for them. Much like Evkit, she'd been the type to have backup plans within backup plans....

Deiq had taken pride in neatly avoiding becoming a pawn in their respective maneuvering. The only way to stop them would have been to destroy both factions, and watching their games and avoiding their nets had been far too *amusing* to make that a worthwhile action. But now, wrapped in attiara-laced teyanain chains, driven by compulsion and oaths towards a task he did *not* want to complete, he had to admit—

—In truth, he'd been snared a *long* time ago.

Humans were far more intelligent than the ha'reye recognized. And *far* more interested in controlling their own path than the Agreement had been built to accommodate.

I tried to tell the ha'reye. I did try. It's not my fault they didn't listen. They wanted servitude. Humans considered it slavery. The ha'reye didn't care....

It is *my fault that I was careless enough to get caught myself.*

Looking back over the span of his lifetime, he pondered, for the first time, what humans would do without any ha'reye or ha'ra'hain in the background.

They'd survive. They'd adapt. They're resourceful. Something about those phrases struck against his inner ear; was there an overlap with his or Alyea's memory?

It didn't matter. It wasn't important. He prodded at the storm once more, then gave up and let himself rest, conserving his strength, waiting on Idisio to emerge from his self-imposed hibernation... and trying to think of ways to stop himself from destroying the world.

Chapter 29

The air felt chill after the recent overheated hells he'd been thrust into. Idisio focused on enjoying that, on the feel of the breeze against his bare skin, on wondering *how* in all the hells he was going to get new clothes—not to mention money, and traveling supplies. Wonderfully mundane concerns, if one left out the events that had caused the worry.

Apparently, he was *really good* at not thinking about things that bothered him, these days, one more gift from his deranged mother. His memories—just—*gapped.* He'd been walking along the increasingly noisy underground corridor... and then he'd woken behind the rock, with a flat haze across one corner of his mind that warned him not to prod after remembering.

Blue beads, thrown with the entirety of his strength, becoming tiny, deadly missiles; a shrill, outraged shriek—The haze thickened abruptly, hiding images and recollection. *Don't think about that. Don't.* Simpler to think about immediate concerns of money and clothing. *Safer.* Much, much safer.

He'd stolen his way back up from mud trousers more than once, when he still thought of himself as human. With his current abilities, he could walk away with half a city and not be spotted. Hopefully Alyea wouldn't find that reprehensible—not that her opinion mattered, and Deiq would understand.

Deiq. Idisio blinked, surfacing from trance involuntarily, a shiver of gathering tension running along his muscles. That *was* an immediate matter to be concerned over.

The elder ha'ra'ha sat, cross-legged, just out of reach, his eyes closed, a thoughtful expression on his face. His breathing was even, but his eyelids twitched in a way that suggested he wasn't—quite—in trance at the moment. He was waiting, patient, solid, immovable, unavoidable.

Non-threatening, which eased the aggrieved tension twisting at Idisio's muscles. And naked, which was... unexpectedly, not disturbing. Deiq seemed beyond matters of sexuality these days. His smoldering intensity had transformed into something much more... the only word Idisio could think of was *groundlike.* Flat, solid, impermeable, dry, and... *red,* in a nearly invisible pattern that made Idisio's eyes water sharply.

He turned his attention away from that, intuition warning him not to look, not to ask questions, not to think about the swirling not-there not-movement not-safeness.

Teilo and Alyea had been naked as well. It hadn't seemed at all unremarkable. Teilo's dark, age-creased skin and alabaster-opaque eyes removed her from *human* to something... other, something connected to a deep, ancient power, coiled loosely about a convenient skeleton: waiting, watchful, dispassionate.

You do have an imagination, Tallisil laughed in memory. He wasn't sure why that comment had stung so deep, clung so stubbornly. Were ha'ra'hain not supposed to have imaginations?

Another image pressed into very clear view: Alyea had been naked. *Oh, damn,* he'd thought for the briefest moment, before his entire focus had locked onto the absolutely dominant threat Deiq represented.

Oh, damn, came to mind again, linked in with the molten moment of her desire on the Wall Stair. *I really should have taken her up on that....*

He squinted at Deiq's still visage, chill washing away the heat.

Almost definitely best I didn't, he told himself. Emotionless Deiq might seem, but Idisio had a feeling he still considered Alyea to be *his* in a very basic sense.

I don't belong *to* anyone, *Idisio*, Alyea said acerbically. *Stop being an ass.*

Idisio flinched, hastily rebuilding his mental shields. As Alyea's irritation faded behind a protective wall, he glanced at Deiq again to see if the elder had overheard. Deiq's head tilted slightly, acknowledging. His eyes stayed shut.

Deiq said without preamble, "What makes you think that Cafad Scratha is the one calling you to Scratha Fortress?"

Idisio stared at his elder, at a complete loss for words. "What?" he croaked.

"Don't stare at me like that," Deiq said. "Shut your eyes or look to the side."

Idisio turned his attention to a nearby rock. He watched a lizard crawl across it, then said, again, "What?"

"You're not stupid," Deiq said. "Don't act like it."

The lizard emerged around the side of the rock and paused, testing the air, its beady black eyes examining everything intently. *Lizards are... Scratha Family symbol, right? Or is it Sessin?* Idisio worried at that question briefly, then shrugged it off and returned to the conversation.

"You think the teyanain are involved," Idisio said.

"I *know* the teyanain are involved. There's a *clee* nearby right now. Don't look for them."

"I know *that* much," Idisio retorted.

"Good. Whether the teyanain had anything to do with your abrupt desire to return south is what *I'm* wondering."

"That—" Idisio shut up, shut his eyes, and thought about it, then flattened a hand against his stomach as though the touch would provide him a clearer answer. The motion hurt. He turned his hand palm up, staring in surprise at the bruised and bloodied indentations across his palms and fingers. What had he been holding so tightly, to leave perfectly round marks—*Don't think about it, don't think, don't!* He shifted attention to voicing the one question that had come clear in his thoughts so far. "How far can a desert lord reach under extreme stress?"

"Scratha would be lucky to contact the Qisani. *You* can hear farther than he can shout, but if you weren't *listening* for it, there's little to no chance you'd have heard him." Deiq paused, then added, "There are ways to relay a call through—intermediaries—to extend the contact range. But Scratha doesn't know about those, and neither do you."

Idisio shook his head slowly, agreeing. "Then it had to be the teyanain." A shiver ran down his spine at the thought that there had been teyanain—athain—trailing him all along. He'd never picked up the slightest hint of their presence.

"Likely, but not definite," Deiq said. "The Aerthraim would also find it useful to drag you back into the current conflict, and they've developed ways around the restrictions of the Agreement. As have the huerg—Tallisil's people—and the disciples of the Jungles. They all have ways of hiding themselves from you, these days." He let out a long breath. "Thank whatever gods exist that nobody's managed to coax the Aerthraim boy to return."

"I tried to get Tank to come back with me," Idisio admitted. "He refused."

"Good. Let's hope it stays that way. Open your eyes and look at me."

Idisio hesitated, then obeyed. Deiq hadn't moved. His broad, dark face was expressionless, his eyes still shut.

"You look different," Idisio observed.

"I've had to completely reconstruct my appearance multiple times. It never matches up exactly." Deiq let out a long breath. "You're under my protection, thanks to Alyea. Do you understand what that means?"

Idisio studied Deiq's blank expression for a few moments, then said, "No."

"You killed your mother by feeding from her. I'm *supposed* to kill you for that. Alyea claiming you as under *my* protection puts me in a hell of a bind." His chin lowered towards his chest, his head moving side-to-side for a moment. "I thought you were going to Arason, and once you'd crossed the line of the Hackerwood, especially once you were back on your birth lands, I could have said you were out of my reach. But here you are."

"I didn't have a choice," Idisio muttered, looking away. Red danced along the edges of his vision; a sense of emptiness, a screaming that wouldn't *stop*—and small blue stones, why did he keep thinking of—

"*Shut your eyes.*" Deiq's voice flattened. "Don't think about her. Or *them*."

Idisio retreated into darkness and quiet without protest.

"*Gods*, your mother was fucked up," Deiq said after a few heartbeats, his tone—regretful? "Fucking Roise and his fucking twisted friends—" His voice cut off, and he breathed deeply, as though gathering himself back under control. "There's always a choice. Killing her was the best thing you could have done. But the *way* you went about it—that's the unforgivable part. As the attiara no doubt explained quite clearly. What did you use to attack them with, by the way?"

Idisio shivered, a pale mist hazing his vision. He blinked rapidly until his sight cleared, then replied, "I don't remember. There's a—a gap in my memories." He looked at his hands again. The right one was much more damaged than the left, but both bore distinctive bruises in a nearly identical pattern. He turned his hands palm down, his lips thinning.

"Ah," Deiq said. "Yes, that's a trick I've used to keep myself sane many times over the years. Teilo always warned me against it, but there are times it's reflexive. You'll remember the details when it's safe to do so." He paused. "It's good that you can do that," he added. "You'll live longer."

"Assuming I don't get killed for what I've done," Idisio pointed out.

Deiq shook his head again. "You're under my protection," he reminded Idisio. "That means anyone wanting to bring you to account has to go through *me* first."

"Oh," Idisio said, his stomach sinking. "Oh, shit. I—didn't understand—oh, shit."

"I may not be able to protect you for long," Deiq said. "I'm in a complicated situation. The clee is keeping me fairly stable, but I'm not all that different from your mother, at the moment. And I've made some very dangerous enemies of late. I'm not in a good position to help anyone else."

"Wasn't my doing, but I'm sorry all the same," Idisio said. "Would it help if I released you from any obligation to protect me?"

"No. I'd have to believe you capable of protecting yourself, and I don't. Not against what's coming." Deiq rubbed his hand across his face, then opened his eyes again. This time they were a flat, human black. "As I said, I'm not particularly sane right now, so be careful. The only thing keeping me the least bit coherent, besides the *clee*, is centuries of practice at acting human, and that's... a thin shield at best. As you can probably understand by this point."

"Yes," Idisio said. "I've been understanding your past actions more clearly of late." He paused. "Will the clee get you *out* of this madness?"

A long silence followed that question. "No." Deiq shut his eyes again, jaw tightening. His voice turned harsh. "I've been trying to think of ways, but I haven't any ideas. My brothers were only stopped by the combined powers of our parents. There aren't enough ha'reye outside of the Jungles to do that again." He paused, breathing deeply, then added, "Sooner or later, I'll truly go mad. When that happens, someone's going to have to stop me before I destroy everything. I don't think even all of Evkit's athain combined will be able to do it."

"*Stop* you?" Idisio said, chilled to the bone by Deiq's matter-of-fact tone. "You mean kill you?" A whisper surged along his inner ear: *blood, death, destruction...* He pushed it away hard, a skitter of panic threading through his chest.

"Yes. You could probably combine your powers with Evkit's athain and have a reasonable chance." Deiq paused, then added, "It's best if you don't do it by feeding from me, unless you want to become... more like your mother, to put it mildly."

"How in the hells are we supposed to... stop you?" Idisio didn't want to risk saying *kill* again. His mother's ghost-voice was dangerously strong of late. "I can't imagine a... a weapon...." He stopped as a hiss rose in the back of his mind: *I can show you, I can help you....*

No. No and no and no. I won't take help from you. Ever. He forced his mother's ghost aside yet again, and wondered if he'd *ever* be rid of her. And if he killed Deiq by feeding from him, would he then be saddled with the elder ha'ra'ha's voice for all eternity? The thought froze his blood. *Oh, hells no.*

Deiq laughed a little, apparently hearing that part, at least. "I'm not fond of that idea myself," he said. "Fortunately, I wouldn't care at that point." An odd expression crossed his face. "As for your initial question—you might try talking to Alyea about it. She's proven to be... surprisingly inventive."

Chapter 30

Alyea sat quietly in the shade of an enormous slab of rock, watching lizards and beetles scurry from one spot to another. Beside her, Teilo seemed to have gone to sleep sitting up, her breathing even, her face untroubled. Meditation, of course; the ha'rai'nin had no doubt been practicing aqeyva since before it took on that particular name. Alyea couldn't match that, especially at the moment, and didn't try.

Instead, she focused on trivial things: easing the scrape of sand against tender areas, calming the heavy sweat that wanted to drip down her back and face, placating her gnawing hunger into waiting a little while longer. She let her awareness of Deiq fade to a vague background noise, and let the waves of his irritation and amusement wash past her without looking to see the details of the conversation. Eventually, she felt his attention shifting to her own location.

She's proven to be surprisingly inventive, Deiq said, the words washing through verbal into a sardonic mental remark, laden with images aimed at her alone. Alyea grinned briefly, then sobered. "Time to get up," she said aloud.

"Not for me, child," Teilo answered. "He wants to talk to you, not to me." Her eyes remained closed, her face serene.

"I want to get *moving*," Deiq said from behind them. Alyea scrambled to her feet, startled, and yelped at the pinch of sand in various skin creases. The ha'ra'ha, perched atop the large boulder, stared down at them with a dark frown.

In that moment, he looked like the world made incarnate. The lines of his body appeared to have been chiseled from stone, full of liquid fire drawn from the deepest trenches, his breath stolen from the mountain peaks. She could nearly count the years he'd walked the world as human, and feel the harsh, endless coil of his experience etched into his bones. His skin seemed a paper-thin overlay, a cocoon drawing ever tighter, ready to shatter at any moment, ready to release a new form of life into the world.

"Talk to your wife, First Born," Teilo said, not flinching in the least. "Resolve what needs to be resolved, before it troubles what needs to be done."

Deiq growled. She ignored him. Alyea backed up a few steps, moving into molten sunlight. He loomed overhead, seeming larger for a moment than the rock on which he stood.

"Damnit," Deiq said, and leapt from the boulder to stand beside Alyea.

She barely kept herself from startling back. He'd covered over ten feet with one lithe movement. His dark stare froze her in place, her breath gone from her throat for a terrifying moment. Then he blinked hard and turned his gaze away. She sucked in a gasp of air and held still against the urge to flee.

"Alyea," he said, his gaze on the ground some distance to her right. "We're walking into a trap, and it's going to kill you. I can't do anything to stop that. I don't think I'll survive it myself."

He wasn't telling her everything. That much was clear, from hard experience as much as from intuition. She always had to prod, to dig, to trick him into speaking clearly. She exchanged a glance with Teilo. The old woman smiled, as though she'd seen that thought and emphatically agreed.

"The trap will kill me?" Alyea said, cold and clear, drawing his gaze back to her. "Or *you're* going to kill me? Be honest, for once!"

He shut his eyes, shaking his head slowly. "I don't... I don't know. I think the... trap... will push me out of balance. I won't know... I won't care, if that happens."

"Then I should kill you now," Alyea told him flatly.

He held still, creases around his eyes and mouth deepening for a few heartbeats, then said, regretfully, "You can't. Not... not yet. You might have a chance later. Not right now. There's also a chance the trap will kill me. There's that hope."

"I'll put a prayer in to that effect," Alyea said, desert-dry.

Deiq sighed, opening his eyes, and looked over to Teilo.

"Are you satisfied with that summary, old mother?"

"Ask your wife, First Born, not me," the ha'rai'nin said.

Deiq shook his head and went back to staring at the ground near Alyea's feet. "Are you satisfied, Alyea?" he said, tone bleak and harsh. "Do I need to explain anything *else* to you?"

"There's one thing I want an answer to," Alyea said. "I fed from Fimre. How did that—"

"You *what*?" Teilo and Deiq said simultaneously, both of them staring at her in utter and open astonishment. A moment later, Deiq shoved into her mind, yanking unceremoniously at her memory. She gagged and went to her knees, once more starkly aware of the texture of her surroundings.

Yes, that's unpleasant, isn't it? Teilo said dryly. Deiq snorted, waving a hand in dismissal, as though the comment tied into a past discussion. Alyea couldn't focus enough to see the connection.

"I see," Deiq murmured. He hoisted Alyea to her feet again, then moved back to just out of arm's-reach. "That's interesting. I'd thought the bond restricted *me* down to *your* level of ability and strength."

"No," Teilo said, squinting at him. "Look at the bond more carefully, First Born. Desert lord—imagine a ball of flame in your hand. A small one, mind you, and one that doesn't burn *you.*"

Alyea held out a hand and focused. A marble-sized, flickering globe appeared a finger's-width above her palm. The ha'rai'nin nodded, approving. Deiq frowned at the flame, clearly unhappy, and touched his chest with a fingertip.

"Desert lord, tell that rock over there to rise into the air twice your height, then let it down slowly."

The indicated boulder slid into the air, hesitated, then descended again, thumping to earth as though relieved. Deiq grunted. "Oh, I *felt* that," he said. "That came from *me.*"

"Yes," Teilo said. "She draws from you as you draw from her. Your strength is now shared. You didn't realize that before?"

"I didn't think it was *possible.* I'm First Born. She ought to be raving insane!"

"Thanks for your faith in me," Alyea said.

"No, he's right, desert lord," Teilo said, unsmiling. "It's an incredible achievement. Evkit did a masterful job on constructing that bond."

Deiq nodded. "I see what you mean. Alyea—it's a balance point. When you draw power, I'm weakened. When I draw, you're weak."

"It's an exceptionally dangerous arrangement," Teilo said. "You're one of three things keeping him sane at the moment, desert lord. If any one of those things fall, he topples into madness."

Alyea drew in a long breath, let it out again. She looked at Teilo, at Deiq, and how perfectly untroubled they were by the sand and grit. Then she remembered Fimre's complaint: *You're ha'ra'hain for all practical purposes.*

She took a moment to refocus her attention, bidding unwanted particles to disperse. The aggravation of abraded skin faded, smoothing out. She sighed in relief, then layered a thick barrier across her entire body to keep the sand from creeping back in to every crease and crevice.

Deiq shivered, his eyes closing, and hunched over slightly, muttering something in an unfamiliar language.

After a moment, he raised his head and met her eyes, his own a strange, brassy gold color. Black lines moved across her vision, a hypnotic pattern steering her toward the edge of sleep—

"Stop that," she said. "I have another question. Where is this trap? Where are we going?"

He looked bewildered, as though the answer should have been obvious. "Scratha Fortress."

"For the same reason Idisio's going? Because you're being... summoned?"

"No, of course I'm not being *summoned.*" He seemed offended at the notion.

"Then why are *you* going?"

He turned his back on her, a sharp movement that warned against interference. She stayed still.

"Don't ask," Deiq said. "It's better you don't know yet. It's *safer*. Trust me on that."

"You say *trust me* a lot," she observed. "And then you turn out to have been lying or manipulating something."

He shrugged, unapologetic. Once again, her vision shifted over to trace the swirling lines of age woven throughout his being. *What's lying, over centuries? Insignificant, is what.* She couldn't tell if that was her thought or his.

She said, "Fine. I'll trust you again. But before we go off to our deaths, you owe me a life debt. Do you acknowledge that?"

Teilo made an odd sound that might have been laughter.

Deiq turned, staring, astonished: his eyes a pale, distressed grey. "You're calling me on that?" he demanded. "*Now*?"

"I doubt I'll get a chance to claim it later." Seeing him shocked was deeply satisfying. She couldn't help smirking a little, but felt anger twisting it into something more feral.

He took a step sideways, then another, turning slightly to keep his gaze fixed on her. She shifted position to stay facing him as he moved. "Be careful what you ask for, Alyea," he said at last. "Be really, *really* careful."

"I don't care about what has to be done at Scratha Fortress," she told him. "That's a matter I've no stake in, one way or another, regardless of the fact that I've been dragged into the situation against my will. I don't care if I survive or not. I've nothing left to go back to. My Family is effectively dissolved at this point. I don't much care if *you* survive, either."

She hadn't meant to say that last part; but it resonated as true, and he didn't so much as flinch at the statement, so she let it stand.

"I'm not hearing the claim yet," he growled. His eyes hazed with lines, then flattened out again.

"I want... I want *revenge*," she said. "What I was told of the Agreement led me to trust the Qisani ha'reye, and they betrayed that trust." Heat flared through her throat as she spoke. She blinked against unwanted tears and kept her voice as hard as the nearby rock.

Teilo opened her eyes, cocking her head to the side, and studied Alyea with visible interest. "Now *that* I did not expect," she said.

"You should have, old mother," Deiq answered, not taking his gaze from Alyea. "My mindset is bleeding over onto her, just as hers has to me on occasion. Alyea, this is a bad thing to ask of me. A *very* bad thing. I'd be destroying my *kin*. You don't understand how serious that is, no matter the need—and *revenge* isn't *need*."

"I don't want you to kill them. I want you to take their ability to reproduce away from them, as they took mine away from me."

Teilo laughed. "Is *that* what you told her, First Born? Oh, my."

Deiq shot a hard glance at Teilo, as though warning her to be quiet. Then he sighed, his eyes closing, and bowed his head. Alyea sensed a muddy swirl of conflicting emotions for a heartbeat. It disappeared as Deiq retreated behind a thick barrier. There was something he didn't want her to see, something important.

He said, "I never said you couldn't have another child. I said you couldn't *safely* have another child. It would kill you. I could arrange the pregnancy, but it would destroy your body to carry anywhere near term."

"I've figured that much out at this point," Alyea said, dry and cold. She'd been working to remember Deiq's exact wording since her encounter with the faereen. "As I believe I've remarked, I'm not entirely stupid. I stand by my claim as I phrased it."

"You don't want your child back?" Teilo prodded, her head cocked to one side, her milky gaze intent.

"It's not my child," Alyea said, keeping her voice chill. "It was ripped from my body before the human soul came to it, as part of an attempt to kill me. I don't want anything to do with it."

Deiq's head moved slightly, a spike of something like unhappiness escaping the wall around his emotions.

"Interesting," Teilo murmured. Alyea had the feeling the ha'rai'nin was referring to Deiq's reaction as much as her own.

"Shut up, both of you," Deiq said, tone flatly harsh. "I'm thinking, and you're distracting me with irrelevancies." Finally, he nodded once, meeting her gaze straight on with those eyes of pale, murky grey.

"I'll honor the claim. Old mother. Stay here with—"

"No," Idisio said. *He'd* perched atop the boulder, where Deiq had been, and looked down at them now with a grim expression Alyea had never seen on his face.

He seemed as stretched-gaunt as Deiq, but in an entirely different fashion; more the tension of a bud preparing to swell into a flower. He was *young*, set beside Deiq, hardly more than an impetuous infant, and still trying to force a unique form onto a predetermined structure. Alyea found herself smiling tolerantly, which visibly irritated Idisio when he caught sight of her expression.

Idisio said harshly, "No separation. Not now. It's not safe. Too many—*people* are looking for one or more of us." He flattened a hand against his stomach, wincing. Deiq's eyes narrowed.

"I reluctantly agree," Teilo said. "We should stay together." She studied Idisio with visible calculation, met Deiq's gaze for a few moments, as though talking with him privately, then glanced back at Alyea and nodded. "I'll go along. I won't raise a hand against the Qisani nest. That would break oaths I still hold sacred, teyanain opinion be damned. But I won't interfere."

"Acceptable," Deiq said. "Alyea?"

She nodded, mouth dry, and let him grip her hand.

"One last question," Idisio said, the abrupt urgency of his tone startling everyone into looking his way. "Will there, maybe, be *clothes* at this place we're going to?"

Chapter 31

"Clothes," Deiq said as though he'd never heard the word before, then glanced down at himself and around at the others. "Why?"

"It would be helpful eventually," Teilo said sardonically. "Might as well be now. Humans *do* tend to expect their proprieties, First Born." She bent and scooped up a double handful of dusty, gravelly soil. "I'd appreciate some help on this," she added, directing a pointed glance at Deiq.

He shrugged and scooped up a double handful of dirt himself. Idisio watched in utter bewilderment as Teilo and Deiq cast the dirt into the air before them, then gasped as the grey dust shimmered into a cohesive pattern. It became a woven structure, binding itself together and rolling out into a sheet almost too rapidly for his eye to track. The weave fluttered to the ground, lumpy, twisted, but undeniably a dun-colored cloth.

"Not the most attractive wraps in the world," Teilo observed. "But functional." She bent to scoop another double handful of sandy soil. Deiq mimicked the motion, and they repeated the toss and weave, then twice more, until four lengths of cloth in varying shades of greyish-brown lay crumpled across the ground. Teilo dusted her hands off, stretching her neck wearily.

Deiq picked up a cloth from the ground and wound it expertly around his waist, then tossed another to Idisio with a vaguely impatient motion. Alyea and Teilo picked up their own wraps and wound them around themselves without hesitation or comment. Idisio stood, cloth dangling from his hand, and ran fingers cautiously over the fabric. It was rough, undeniably sandy in texture, but it was also most definitely cloth, not fragments of rock.

"It's a relatively minor trick," Deiq said irritably.

"For you, First Born," Teilo said. "And only because of the attiara, the clee, and my own support. You'd have much more trouble doing it without those things in place."

"It's a minor trick," Deiq repeated, eyebrows lowering into a ferocious scowl. "And an *annoying* one to perform."

Idisio tentatively wrapped the cloth around his waist, doing his best to copy Deiq's knotting technique. He fumbled for a moment, then secured it reasonably well. He'd never worn the southern-style wraps before. It seemed like no protection at all against—well, anything. And the coarse scrape against tender skin was unexpectedly erotic. He gritted his teeth and turned away hastily.

Teilo snorted as though restraining laughter. "Ha'ra'ha," she said, "*When* did you last have any satisfaction?"

"Doesn't matter," he said through his teeth, not looking at her.

"It most certainly does. We're about to walk into a nest of ha'reye and ha'ra'hain that have been protecting the Callen of *Ishrai* for centuries. The host influences the protector as the protector influences the host. Quite flatly, they're all experts at leading you around by your cock."

"That's a bit crude," Alyea protested. "I didn't get that impression—"

"You were only there a brief while, and unconscious for most of that," Teilo said. "Trust me. I was a priestess of the faith that *became* that of Ishrai, before the ha'reye emerged. They'll have him on the ground and witless in half a heartbeat."

Idisio felt his face heat as though about to burst into flame. "I can control myself just fine," he snapped, hunching his shoulders a bit. Teilo laughed, not unkindly.

"No," she said. "Not if you're human-randy, ha'ra'ha. Not against this much power. They'll have you twisted round into doing their bidding before you know what flipped sideways in your head. Lust turns over into anger very, very easily. And I'm *not* inclined to have you raging at my back in an already dangerous situation."

"You've said before you don't want but one side of the road, and I'm in no condition at the moment to help you in any case," Deiq observed. "I'd *strongly* suggest you don't even *think* about the old mother in that respect—"

"Agreed," Teilo cut in. "No offense, ha'inn, but *no*."

"—And given that you're already drooling over Alyea, that's going to stick in your mind and be a weakness. So you'd best start hoping you haven't upset her recently," Deiq finished.

Idisio put a hand across his eyes and groaned aloud.

Chapter 32

Rust and green and gold. Deiq had always liked that particular combination of colors, whether in swamp or desert, forest or jungle. His one previous attempt at marriage had been a riot of those colors: The bride in gold, he in green, bouquets of red flowers everywhere. Alyea hadn't been given nearly the ceremony she deserved, on consideration. He allowed himself a moment of mild sadness over that, knowing it irrelevant, but also knowing that it was critically important to hang on to such human thoughts right now.

Some distance away, behind the visual screen of a large boulder, he could *hear/feel* Alyea coaxing Idisio into action. A human would have been jealous. Deiq had never allowed himself to become *that* human, even at his weakest.

Idisio yielded far more quickly and easily than Deiq had expected, given the younger's nonsensical morality issues. He cut a glance sideways at Teilo, raising an eyebrow in question. She smiled and inclined her head in reply. "I told her what to do," she said. "Even the most stubborn human or ha'ra'hain have weak spots."

"Good." Deiq looked out over the color patterns in the landscape around them, picking out his favorites, weighing them against those colors he didn't care for: Muddy browns, pale yellows, moldy purplish-greens....

The desert held far more colors than humans could see: *itt, pha, momb, eck* were the names he'd learned from his kin. He catalogued each variation in color, letting himself sink into peaceful pattern-searching, one 'ear' on what was happening behind the boulder. Alyea was his wife, after all, and Idisio under his protection. He needed to be sure they were safe.

"Dear gods," he said eventually. "That boy is *clumsy.*"

"Inexperienced," Teilo murmured. "Very, very inexperienced."

"This is going to take too long," Deiq muttered. He reached out and unrolled directions into Idisio's mind.

Idisio pushed back, aggrieved: *Godsdamnit, do you know how hard I've been trying* not *to see her memories of that?*

Stop fighting it, Deiq advised. *Use my experience.*

Stop watching!

Quit fumbling about, then, Deiq retorted, then withdrew, shutting himself off from Idisio but keeping his perception of Alyea open. Beside him, Teilo chuckled.

"You can't help meddling," she observed.

"You helped *her,*" Deiq said mildly. "I don't see the difference."

They sat in companionable silence, watching their surroundings, half-listening to the nearby coupling. "Ah," Teilo said after a while. "There they go." Not long afterwards, a twin set of ragged cries crested, faded into audible panting. "Well done," she murmured. "Oh—wait. That's interesting...."

"She learned to keep up with *me*, old mother," Deiq reminded her dryly. "And Idisio's never been with anyone capable of that."

Teilo sighed, looking up at the sky. A dark line of clouds was gathering along the western horizon, blurring into a grey-blue at the edges. "There's a storm coming on fast," she said, pointing.

"I know. I called it."

She frowned at him, displeased. "That's dangerous—"

"I'm running out of water," he said, watching the clouds, measuring the speed of the oncoming rain. Too slow. The moisture in the air was climbing rapidly, easing the topical irritation, but it wouldn't be enough. *Damnit.*

Teilo huffed irritably. "You could have asked me. Water *is* my strong suit—"

"No. I need more than you can offer, Teilo. At this point, it's a good thing we're sidetracking to the Qisani."

"Are you going to empty the *Qisani*?" she demanded, incredulous. "Do you need so much as that? Evkit won't let you do that—"

"He will allow it," a thin male voice said nearby. Deiq shut his eyes instead of turning to look, bowing his head in proper courtesy—something he'd ignored for hundreds of years but which seemed, just now, vastly wiser than his usual brusque disregard.

The athain chuckled, acknowledging the motion, then went on: "Greetings, First Born, old mother. You take the harder task before the easier, but it is a task that satisfies Lord Evkit all the same. We are directed to notify you that this will suffice for your payment of obligation, should you so choose."

Deiq raised his head, opening his eyes, unable to stop the startled reaction. "*What*?"

"The Qisani was always the real goal," Teilo said accusingly. "Wasn't it?"

"It was a complex task that Lord Evkit had not yet decided how to address," said the small man standing several feet to Deiq's left. He wore a rust-colored tunic and dark green leggings. His hair was shorn completely, giving him an oddly goblin-like appearance and bringing the swirling tattoos on his scalp into stark prominence.

Deiq's stomach turned over sideways, sour bile building in the back of his throat. He dropped his gaze, shutting his eyes again. Athain *never* shaved their hair, never showed that particular tattoo. That was something only done in death—or when the athain in question was expecting to die far from teyanain lands, far from any possibility of an honorable burial. As far as he and the teyanain community at large were concerned, this athain—and, more than likely, the rest of his clee—were already dead.

Teilo said nothing, her own breath shallow and harsh. She knew what it meant as well.

"We cannot accompany you into the Qisani," the athain said. "That space is forbidden to us forever. We will not be able to help you, as we could at Scratha Fortress. And we must in honor warn you that you are far less likely to survive an attempt on the Qisani."

"But you don't *object*?" Teilo's voice came out sharp and challenging, harsh enough to grate on Deiq's nerves.

The athain chuckled. "Lord Evkit has long wished for the Qisani community to be weakened. The ishraidain will allow you access where we would be refused, and removing the water, a difficult task for anyone but a First

Born in such crisis, would work admirably. We will wait outside the boundary, as close as we are permitted to step, and contain whatever disaster the First Born might unleash, as we have already done once this day."

Once more startled out of his best intentions of keeping to courtesy, Deiq rose to his feet, motioning to the ruined lands around them. "*This* was *contained*?" he demanded. "Half of the eastern shoreline is destroyed!"

"The hub is intact, however," the athain pointed out. "The hidden ways are still usable, except for the one that led to the top of the Wall. The damage affected the eastern coast only. It would have spread well into the central desert if we had not pushed the wave eastward."

"How convenient that shifting the focus means that the explosion affected none of *your* allies," Teilo said dryly. "I'm sure that was merely coincidence."

"Teyanain do not have allies," the athain said, smiling. "That some humans think otherwise is their own mistake, and not our responsibility. We do, however, have certain properties to the west that we prefer to protect."

Deiq turned away to stare out at the horizon. Rocks surrounded him, earth and metal pressing for his attentions. Emotion bleached from his mind, blood congealing into slow-moving sludge.

"First Born," one of the athain said, very quietly.

Deiq hauled himself back to center with a wrenchingly painful effort, balancing internal elements, prodding the sludge that contaminated his bloodstream back to a liquid flow.

The storm was still too far away. It should have been moving faster. Had it stalled out over a dry area, or by someone skilled refusing to allow it passage? Either case, it was proving out as a wasted effort and a false hope.

The silence was broken by gasps of varying enthusiasm nearby.

"This is their last round," Deiq said over his shoulder. "I don't have time to wait. We'll have to take the risk."

"I think they've both worn enough of the edge down," Teilo murmured. "I'll keep an eye on them, and step in if they're being overtaken."

"Thank you." Deiq turned to face her. The athain had vanished. Teilo stood quietly, her hands laced together over her stomach. She looked, for a moment, like nothing more than a sad old woman in a drab, poorly woven wrap. Her long white hair had come free from its braids and straggled chaotically about her shoulders and arms. Her milky gaze was tilted to the sky, as though contemplating the silent wonders of the gods. She looked *human* for the first time in hundreds of years, the mystical overlay of power stripped away, leaving her weak and malleable—

"Don't try it, De'sta'haiq," Teilo said without moving. She blinked slowly.

Deiq shut his eyes and let out a frustrated snort. "You're baiting me again."

"Merely seeing if you're so easily tricked these days. Your brothers rarely looked twice."

"They didn't *need* to look twice," Deiq muttered. "There was nothing that could hurt them, no matter what it looked like."

"And yet they're dead, and you are not," Teilo said. "*You* never assumed you were safe. *You* always looked twice. You need that caution now more than ever."

"Go teach a snake to swim," Deiq growled.

Teilo laughed. "They're finished," she said. "Give them a moment to catch their breaths. I called them back already. —You need to take a moment with them."

"That's foolish."

"Not for them, it won't be. Trust me on this. You don't need to say anything out loud."

"Fine." Deiq kept his gaze on the distant horizon, half-listening to the movements around him. When Alyea and Idisio stood nearby again, he turned his head, met their eyes with a deliberately blank stare, and waited until the embarrassed flush died from Idisio's face and a faintly amused smile crept onto Alyea's.

"I need to get access to the deep lair, the place where water becomes steam," he said then, without preamble. "That's never easy, even for me, not with this large of a group. Too many eyes watching for trouble, more or less. They know what's been going on much more than the faereen did. They know I'm a danger to them, and they have their own history with Teilo."

He paused, cutting a glance sideways at the old woman. She said nothing, her face blank.

"They won't willingly leave an opening unless it's one they control, but they love patterns. *Use* that. Distract them with patterns. Run random mathematics through the back of your mind. Recite the alphabet backwards. Anything that will draw their attention away from me. When they let their guard down, you get the hells out of there as fast as you can. You can't come into the deep with me. Not even Idisio, he's too young. Not Teilo, because then she'd have to fight and I won't make her do that. And Alyea—you'll die if I'm not supporting you, even at the shallows you'll be allowed to reach. Understood? You *have* to haul yourselves out of there *fast* when I tell you go."

They nodded, amusement and embarrassment alike gone.

You're not going to tell them about the change in plans? Teilo asked.

No, he said. *Let them think we have to survive this and get to Scratha Fortress. It might actually keep* them *alive if they believe that.*

Alyea's head tilted, a hard light appearing in her eyes. Had she heard the exchange, or had she merely guessed at something gone wrong? It didn't matter, and there wasn't time to argue it all out in any case.

He gathered them all in, turned the group sideways—feeling the *clee* at the edges, moving in close tandem but not hooked in completely. They'd be able to break away and land at a different spot of their choosing, while contributing to the energy of the initial effort. It was a courteous move on their part, and one that Deiq, at the moment, actually appreciated. The less focus he had to bring to the maneuver, the less strain he felt, and the more easily his temper and body would react to the change.

He swung everyone sideways to the sideways, feeling Teilo adding her own push to the momentum—slid through the intersection like a snake rolling through oil—and landed facefirst against an unyielding stone wall.

Chapter 33

Idisio's enthusiasm still warmed her skin as Alyea stepped up against her husband, allowing him to wrap her into a dry-armed embrace. Deiq's skin was cool and soft, but something in the texture conveyed *not-human* to her fingertips.

She didn't bother remarking on it, or on what had just happened. His severe, impatient stare had confirmed her suspicion that she was the only one still thinking of their relationship with human emotions attached. *He really doesn't care.* She'd already known that, he'd explained that quite clearly some time ago, but she'd expected *this* situation to rattle him a bit.

It was mildly unsettling, in fact, that he was *so* completely unaffected. She made herself smile and hid her annoyance behind amusement; a trick she'd learned from him, ironically enough. He seemed to accept it without question.

Stop thinking of him as human, desert lord, Teilo said, a scant whisper in the back of Alyea's mind. *He's so very, very far from that at the moment, and you won't see that version of him again. Think of him as a stranger: that's probably safest for your sanity.*

Go teach a snake to swim, Alyea said.

Teilo's laugh echoed through her head, wispy and fading, as inverted darkness closed in around them.

On Alyea's previous visit to the Qisani, she'd approached from the outside, carried by servants through overheated air and sand-laden breezes to reach the opening to the largely underground complex. She hadn't known what she was walking into, hadn't really understood at all what she'd committed to—hadn't expected *anything* that unrolled from that point on.

This time, braced for anything at all, the empty, black silence came as a shock. They'd arrived underground, she could *feel* that, but there was—*nothing*. No chattering, no light, no breathing but their own. Moisture hung heavy and hot in the air, a nearly tangible fog that crept like a living thing into her throat and wound into her chest and lungs a heartbeat later.

Most alarming of all, she was *alone.*

No, Idisio said a moment later, his hand closing around her right wrist briefly. *I'm here. But they aren't. I think. I can't fucking* tell! Fear tautened the last word with strident emphasis. She twisted her hand around and gripped his wrist in turn, reassuring.

The touch sparked recent memory, bringing the ambient temperature up sharply. She growled under her breath, turning to face him, felt him step closer, his own arousal evident—

—And a faint, laughing hiss cut through the heavy air. Alyea's growl changed to a snarl as rage replaced desire. She spun, hooking her elbow hard through Idisio's, and faced them both in the direction of that hiss, focusing every sense she had on *where* that had come from.

Far away, deep underground, amongst bottomless layers of boiling water and gas and liquid rock—moving fast by ha'reye standards, agonizingly slow by human perception.

"They're coming," she said, anger warbling briefly into panic. Idisio shivered as his own emotions shifted to match hers; driven by her own anger or sympathetic to it, she couldn't tell and it didn't matter. *Deiq,* she said, reaching out with renewed determination. *Teilo. Where are you?*

Something moved, muddy and stifled, through a thick sense of dislocation: *the other side of a wall,* resolved as an answer—not in words, but *knowledge*—a moment later.

No, she said to whoever had put that barrier between them, not caring if anyone even heard the words. *You don't get to separate us.* Not bothering with a light, she turned her attention to finding a weak spot. She could feel the structure of the wall, tracing cracks and lines in her mind-vision with preternatural accuracy and speed. *There. The doorway.* It had been blocked by a thick slab of rock—wedged in from the other side, from the angle of the lines.

As she'd done with the chains in the Bright Bay prison tower, Alyea wedged ethereal pressure into the flaws of the stone and *breathed*—

Rock exploded, shattering into fragments and dust that rattled against her skin.

Light flared, filling the room, as Teilo stepped through the doorway. "Well done," she said hoarsely. "They'd warded it from the other side."

Who? Alyea asked. Spoken words seemed such an awkward and slow way to communicate.

Teilo paused, regarding Alyea intently, then shook her head. "You'll need to speak aloud," she said. "I can tell you're saying something, but not what."

"Who?" Alyea repeated aloud.

"The ishraidain," Teilo said. "They didn't want anyone with ability to get past the wards. I'm not sure how you two slipped through, but I'm grateful for it." She looked past Alyea, her expression souring. "Ah. And that would be why they warded it so strongly."

Alyea turned. They stood in the *ishell*, the room where Alyea had taken her second set of blood trials. On her previous visit, the room had been a pleasant, plant-filled, humid sanctuary centered around an enormous pool of water. Now the stone benches were smashed to rubble, the plants were long destroyed, and the central pool had shrunk to half its previous size, leaving an unpleasant greenish slime along the slope of newly revealed rock.

A gaunt form floated in the center of the remaining water: *Acana*. The *ishrait's* long dark hair had been ripped out in clumps. What remained was a brittle yellow-grey-white combination that spread out into a ragged, stiff halo around her head. Her smooth skin was marred by hundreds of tiny red lines, looping in chaotic tangles across her entire body.

Alyea inhaled sharply as she realized that what she'd taken for cuts were, in fact, *moving*, in slow, distinct motions. They were tendrils, not wounds—like an upside-down plant sinking feeder roots into the earth—

She turned away and gagged hard, unable to bear that inverted image, knowing this was *directly* her fault. How long had Acana been suffering while Alyea went about her life? She'd even continued on, blithe and uncaring, after finding out that the ishrait was in dire danger—hadn't given it more than a few brief thoughts before flitting on to more important things—

"Where's Deiq?" Idisio said, glancing around with a sharp frown.

"Recovering from a misstep," Teilo answered, not taking her gaze from Acana. "You do realize that's your child, desert lord, don't you?"

"I—*what*?" Alyea spun round and stared at the old woman, then at Acana.

"Acana is serving as host to your child, and one of the lesser ha'ra'hain is keeping Acana alive in the meanwhile. Those tendrils *are* your child, for the most part. It hadn't had very long to develop human tissue before they removed it, so it's much more ha'reye than human at this point."

Alyea put a hand over her mouth, her stomach comprehensively turning sour. "Oh dear gods," she whispered against her palm.

"There aren't any," Teilo said. "Ah. Here we are. Feeling better?"

Alyea looked over her shoulder as Deiq came through the doorway, once more naked. His face seemed *off* somehow, not quite what she remembered from a few moments ago, but the blood streaked across his skin might have been serving to distort her perceptions. *Gods, he looks like he's rolled through a trough of carcasses.* She couldn't tell if it were Idisio's thought or her own. The distinction seemed utterly irrelevant at this point.

He tossed a bundle of clothes to Alyea with a wordless grunt. She caught it, hesitated, then separated the garments, handing shirt and pants to Idisio then pulling the light, sleeveless dress over her own head. Idisio's lip curled as he looked at the spots where Deiq's bloodstained hand had left streaks, but he dressed without protest.

At least the clothes weren't entirely soaked in blood. She had no idea how Deiq had found clean clothes so quickly, but this wasn't the time to ask questions.

Deiq's gaze fixed on Acana, his dark eyes turning to a bleak, angry grey. He muttered something in an unfamiliar language, and for once Alyea heard no translation echoing into her mind. She *could* feel his rage building sharp and fast, and didn't need Teilo's warning cry to grab once more for the connection with Idisio and *push* at the elder ha'ra'ha, hard enough to distract him, sudden enough to allow her to tuck intangible, shared hands into the attiara-laced chain wrapped round Deiq, grasping tight—

Before she could tense into the slightest pull, an incendiary burning shot up their arms. Idisio yowled, sounding more pleased than pained; Alyea screamed as trauma cascaded from past to present, bringing the worst moments of her life back to immediacy:

There, sweet, you like that, don't you? Searing irons rolling across her skin, a knife tucked under the skin, twisting, sliding with that same melting agony—

Holy hells, let go, *you idiot!* Idisio yelled at her. *You'll make it* worse!

The pain cut off. *No,* Deiq said, lifting his arms into a long, slow stretch, fingertips nearly touching the low ceiling. *That felt good. Thank you.* His eyes were black again, his skin entirely clean of blood. He stared at the floating body with no visible emotion.

Idisio gagged as though unable to believe that response. A clear white haze manifested in the air around him for a vivid moment, then faded as quickly.

"*Now* you're beginning to understand, youngling," Teilo said softly.

"I refuse," Idisio rasped. "*No.* I don't have to be like that."

"Refuse all you like," Deiq said. "Words are meaningless. You enjoyed her pain as much as I did. You just refused to accept it as fuel, which is wasteful." He wiped the back of one hand over his mouth, his gaze sweeping the room in measured consideration. "They're almost here."

Teilo moved back to stand in the doorway, her arms folded. Alyea caught sight of a distinctly anxious frown on the old woman's face before she turned to face the now-roiling water. Acana disappeared, pulled beneath the troubled surface with a swift, sure motion. Alyea couldn't help starting forward a step, one hand out in wordless protest; caught herself in time, dropped her hand to her side, and reminded herself that it wasn't actually *her* child.

It never had been. She tried to find the rage that had prompted her to this point, tried to latch on to her fierce sense of betrayal, desire for revenge—and found it all completely absent, overridden by a queasy, bewildered terror. What had she been *thinking*, what the hells was she trying to prove, she should have stayed home and learned to sew properly after all—

"Balance," Teilo said from the doorway.

Deiq's hand, cool and dry, closed over Alyea's left shoulder. Idisio's, damp with his own nervousness, latched onto her right shoulder. She drew in a deep breath as their strength wove into her. Deiq sighed, sounding regretful.

"Ah, human emotion," he said. "I don't miss that. And yet I do."

Alyea's own emotion was rapidly disappearing beneath a pragmatic, hard overlay. They were here, and there was work to be done, and it *would* be done. She had nothing to lose, after all, but her life, and she'd already sworn that into the service of protecting humanity as a whole. That her oath had been made to a nest of deceitful, twisted monsters made no difference at this point. As long as she retained the powers she'd been given, she was bound to use them as she saw best towards that end.

Idisio let out a small sigh. Alyea felt his own anxiety settle into a similar, stolid determination.

"There you go," Teilo said. "Well done, all of you."

The water became eerily still. A heavy grey mist began to ooze from the pond into the surrounding air. A mixture of color, texture, smell, fierce exultation, and a dizzying sense of swirling movements lashed through Alyea's mind, nothing at all like a language, and yet—

—*You have brought those we summoned, northern-born kin,* it said. *We thank you for that gift. You may depart in safety if you depart now.*

Idisio's fingers tightened, digging into Alyea's shoulder as though he were holding himself in place with that small gesture.

The mist twisted, curving, thickening, looping, and resolved into a blank-eyed Acana, standing atop the water as though it were solid ground. She cradled a newborn infant in her arms, and no tendrils or marks were visible on her dark skin. Long black hair, once more perfect, flowed to her waist.

"Come see your child, desert lord," Acana said. Her gaze remained blindly unfocused, directed at some point above their heads. "Come let us thank you for this gift, and show you how beautiful it is."

"I've already seen what that thing is," Alyea answered harshly. "It's not a human child, and it's not mine."

"It is still within the time of shaping," Acana said. "It could be yours. It could be human. You must come take it from us, claim it, and raise it yourself. Then it would be yours as surely as though it were with you from the time of conception."

Iced fury walked along Alyea's spine. "You *betrayed* me to get that creature you're holding. Why would I trust anything you offer now?"

Acana smiled, an oddly distant expression, and dissolved into fog once more. The mist sank back into the water, then rose, twisting into another humanoid form. Its appearance shifted at random intervals: now a tall, angular desert lord reminiscent of Lord Scratha, now a short, pudgy man dressed in rich silks, now a small, pale child. Each change flowed seamlessly into the next.

"Do you remember the story you told us, desert lord, in return for our gift?" the man/creature said. "About Krilla, and the Lord of Winter? We warned you it was not accurate, and that it was an unfortunate choice of gift. Had you chosen another gift, one with more truth, we would have considered ourselves bound to treat you more kindly. You chose to insult us with your gift, and even asked if we were—" His face solidified into a cruel, ugly expression. " —*Dragons*."

"She was *ignorant*." Idisio's voice echoed more than it should have in the humid, nearly stifling air. "That doesn't excuse anything you've done!"

"That was not our responsibility to consider or correct," the man/creature said. "Our part begins when the supplicant is given to us. What the humans do to prepare the supplicant is not any part of our concern. Whether one is ready or unready to face us, we proceed as we always proceed."

"Tell me the true story, then," Alyea said to her own surprise. But the demand carried a symmetry, a sense of closure, that echoed deep within her as *right*. Deiq grunted thoughtfully, moving four fingers in a gentle patting motion against her shoulder that seemed to confirm her choice.

Stories are patterns, a not-voice said in that strange not-language. *Patterns are good. We will do this thing. Come to us and we will show you the pattern of this truth.*

Alyea stepped forward without hesitation this time as the man/creature standing atop the pond spread out his arms into a welcoming embrace. She was dimly aware of Deiq and Idisio moving alongside her, their hands wrapped around her upper arms now but making no effort to slow or stop her.

Their feet touched water, sank to the ankles, and registered *scalding/frozen* in sharp, diametric succession. Then the air condensed into a slick layer of fluid against their skin and a wild, hot wind tumbled them sideways and inside out and down into an endless chasm.

Chapter 34

This is the story of a distant place, a series of voices said, overlapping in fluid, unhesitating harmony. *This place was not high nor low, hot nor cold, although lesser beings have thought it to be one or another of those things at various times throughout the millenia. It was a protected place, a haven, a neutral area where all could meet in peace and discuss differences.*

We were divided amongst three paths in those days. Humans do not understand what we mean when we say this. Humans have male and female and neuter, but no concept for catalyst/host/provider. We had *to get along. We could, quite literally, none of us survive without the others, nor produce children if any one of the paths refused to participate.*

And yet a disagreement arose that would not abate or resolve, and the paths split apart, and each of us took our own way: providers and hosts and catalysts, set separate for the first time since our firstborn nest was built. Some few of one went with another group here and there, but largely the three paths moved in opposing directions. Many moved underground, hiding and researching the ways of the world in hopes of either finding safety or a solution to the disagreement that had shattered our lives.

A long pause followed that, an awareness of colorless darkness, and an aching, angry sorrow. Then the voices resumed.

In time, some became restless, impatient—insane, even. They wished to emerge into the surface world, to see if others of our kin had gathered, to see if the world had perhaps righted itself. There were more arguments, and bitter ones. "We remember that the surface world is beautiful," said some of the younger kin. "Surely things are better by now. We are cowardly to hide away like this."

"It is warmer here," said others, older and more experienced. "It's cold above, and windy, and not as pleasant as you remember. We have settled, we have nested. We have built new lives. There are even children here!"—for this was a fortunate group that had a mixture, you understand—"and we have time yet."

"Wait. Wait. When they sort out their quarrel, they will find us. We are not hiding. We are protecting ourselves. They will come for us when it is safe."

"They do not know where we are," the protesters said, certain in their arrogance. "They will not find us. We will go find them, *and bring them back to you, and show you that it is safe to go out into the warm air. We will show you that it is pleasant and not cold at all. We miss the sunlight! We will go, just a short ways out, to look. What harm could it do to look? Only look. We will return soon."*

"You won't find anything," they were told. "There will be nothing to see. You will see only that we are correct, that it is terrible at the surface, and you will return right away."

And those foolish, insane ones left the safety of their nest and were not heard from for a very, very long time.

Darkness and silence rang in Alyea's ears. She blinked slowly, aware of *presences* around her—Deiq, and Idisio, and a multitude of *other*: long, thin tendrils, like the ones that had been wrapped around Acana, pebble-shore textured round masses; great pale eyes, some half-lidded, all watching her.

Awareness of presence became a woven *experience* of otherself: Idisio, wary and protective, hidden behind layer after layer of deflection that overlapped her own shields; Deiq, a distant shadow that yet loomed over/under/inside everything that formed *Alyea.*

We have their attention, Deiq/Idisio/Alyea said. *Keep them talking. Keep them interested. Keep them listening....*

This is going to be a very dangerous game, Deiq said, pinpoint-focused on Alyea alone for a stretched moment. *You're the listener. Ignore what Idisio and I are doing. Just listen to the story.*

Nutrient-rich water, the brine of a long-established ha'ra'hain nest, pressed against silt-laden sludge, invading cracked vertices and flowing through Deiq's body: *Ahhhhh,* he sighed, hiding his relief deep behind shared layers of deflection. *Can't let them know how bad this is, can't let them see....*

Silence broke. The voices resumed. *Like your story of Krilla, this is a very long story by human standards. We will allow our younger relative to tell it, as she is better with such immediacy.*

Alyea inhaled sharply, then choked a bit as Acana's voice replaced the braided tones. She couldn't tell if the thickness moving through throat and chest were humid air or thin water. Either way, her body seemed adapted to handling it as long as she didn't gasp. She made her breathing even out, fighting the reflex to gag and cough.

The searchers discovered that a new form of thinking life had arisen. They took some time to study it, and concluded that while it appeared to have evolved separately, there were traces of similarity to the kin they had set out in search of. There was no other sign of their original kin, though they searched north and south, east and west, for some years.

Acana paused, then her voice cleared into a more natural timbre. She added, dryly, *Not for very long, though, by human standards. Ha'reye have always been accustomed to getting their desires met very quickly, and if they cannot force their will upon a matter, they often lose interest and turn their attentions elsewhere.*

You're alive, Alyea said, shocked and relieved all at once. *That was actually you!*

Yes. Acana's voice took on a pained roughness. *I'm still alive, by your measurements. It's not pleasant, though, so please allow me to divert back to the story. The sooner I'm done, the sooner I get to escape awareness of what's happening to me again.*

The searchers decided to investigate the new thinking life, Deiq said without perceptible emotion. *And they became... curious, which is a form of insanity for the ha'reye, by human standards.*

Idisio shuddered, nausea rippling through their shared layers: *My mother, Ellemoa—*Flickers of flame, the iron tang of blood, the scream of a life dragged to the edge over and over and over—

Deiq/Alyea smoothed the madwoman's memories away into a safer silence and returned Alyea's attention to Acana.

They changed the thinking life, without meaning to, Acana said. *It became a thing from their collected vision, dreams, nightmares, hopes. Where ha'reye have tendrils and tentacles, they gave this life thicker legs. Where they have slender bodies, they gave this one a larger but still supple frame. Where they have large eyes, they gave it smaller ones. They have no teeth as humans would think of such things, so they gave the new life large and sharp fangs. Never having flown themselves, they gave the creature wings to see how it might best work.*

None of this was really intentional, Deiq observed. *They were just... curious. Children playing with a new toy. They didn't think past the moment's amusement. They'd never needed to, before. Their elders had always directed them safely in the past. But now, without guidance... they made mistakes.*

A shape formed in the dim light, then faded away again: a beast of mythology, of fable and legend.

They created dragons, Alyea said in disbelief. A vicious, echoing hiss arose around her. Luminous eyes shuttered in rapid succession until she floated, weightless and blind, in complete darkness once more.

Careful, Deiq/Idisio/Alyea said to themselves, *careful, there's a fine line between keeping their attention and provoking them into attacking....*

Water was rapidly turning dust to liquid, leftover threads swelling back into approximations of vein and muscle, thought quickening. *Don't let them see, don't let them know....*

Alyea sensed Deiq withdrawing, merging more closely with Idisio's consciousness than with hers. Barriers shifted, whirling in random directions, deflecting the attention of the ha'reye yet again.

Acana continued, not answering the question directly. *They fled from their creations in horror on realizing what they'd done, returning to the nest to beg their elders for help. But the way was longer than they remembered, and harder, and their new creations unloving. Most of them never reached the doorway to the underground lair.*

When the survivors arrived, they were very weak, and very tired, and much harried from behind. They passed through the gate and flung themselves before the elders and wept with exhaustion and fear, offering any amends, anything at all, if only they might be saved from the destruction they had unwittingly unleashed. For their creations were wise and cunning, and would soon enough discover how to reach the underground sanctuary.

Acana paused. Idisio moved slightly, layers redistributing around him/them; Alyea felt a pressure she hadn't been aware of easing.

Acana went on. *It is not entirely accurate to say the elders bound the younger ones, but that is the closest I can come to the concept. They* – secured – *the youngers, to prevent more accidental damage, then went aboveground themselves and destroyed all of the misbegotten creations. It did not leave the elders unscarred, and it reduced their numbers in ways and amounts they could ill afford: the balance required for children was disrupted, and only those few youngers who remained had any chance left at reproducing.*

The ha'reye retreated underground, healing, recovering, exploring their own innate abilities. Few children were born during this time, and those were, on occasion, deformed and had to be destroyed.

A rapid flickering lit the air around Alyea, as though many huge eyes were blinking at once; then the area went still and black again. Numbers wound through the back of her/their mind in random order: *One and one is two, two and four is six, six less one is five...* Pressure redistributed again, and she drew in a long breath of relief.

I am telling this so quickly and so bluntly that it is causing them great distress, Acana said with a sigh. *They only catch every few words, when humans talk so abruptly, and they easily mishear the connections. I've asked them to be patient and trust me, but it's difficult. Please hold very still. If you react poorly to any part of this story, they're going to assume you're attacking them directly.*

Alyea breathed evenly and shut her own eyes, swallowing hard. *Almost,* Deiq/Idisio/Alyea said, *They're getting more engaged, they're listening more closely so that they can hear what she's saying, be patient....*

Deiq's voice separated out again, taking on the acidic, whispering tone that meant he was shaping the words for Alyea alone: *Acana is trying to help. She knows what we're doing. Listen to her, Alyea, listen with every bit of focus you can summon! The ha'reye will be drawn to your intensity.*

He faded into the background once more, and the ishrait's voice resurfaced.

They had not left themselves entirely sealed away from the world above, Acana went on, her tone returning to dry recitation. *They watched, and they listened, to be sure that the evil creations did not rebreed from a fragment left unburnt. And so when another thinking life stood up and began building fires and painting on cave walls, they noticed, and began to pay attention. This life, too, held traces of kin, although far more faint and harder to connect with than the other life had been.*

They were cautious. They waited, watching; waited, watching; far past the stage that the first life had developed prior to their interference. The new life had developed its own society and rules and habits and beliefs before the ha'reye stepped out to meet them.

The ha'reye, having seen what this new life liked, brought beautifully polished gems: rubies, diamonds, strings of gold and silver and all manner of fine things that meant nothing to the ha'reye but were coveted by this new people. With these things, the people were persuaded of the ha'reye's friendship –

– Most of the people, Deiq commented dryly.

Yes, Acana agreed. *Most. The important ones were persuaded. They made an agreement with the ha'reye: The ha'reye would protect them from predators, and would give them many fine things, and the people would give of themselves, merely, only, one of their own, every dark of the moon, so that the ha'reye might learn more directly about this new life.*

It wasn't a sacrifice, Deiq added, as though unable to stop himself from explaining more clearly. *Not the way you're thinking, Alyea. Most of the given died, of course, in the beginning, but it wasn't intentional. They learned with each mistake and each given lived longer, and one day they were able to send a given back to her people –*

Let me tell the story, Acana said a bit petulantly. *You always want to interrupt. Stop it. I know how to tell it!*

Deiq withdrew, leaving the scent of laughter behind.

Acana let out an irritated *hmph,* then continued. *They sent the given back to her people, heavy with child. Her people welcomed her as holy and sacred, and named her The Karill, the First Among The Chosen.*

Her child was born with great pain and much distress, and died before it had entirely left the womb. She herself barely survived. When she was healed, the ha'reye demanded that she return that they might try again, and she went full willing. This time, they kept her with them the entire time, and she gave birth underground, in the deep, watery passages the ha'reye had begun to favor.

This birth was simple, and joyous, and the child emerged healthy and strong. And a new pact was born along with the child: that as long as the humans continued to provide the ha'reye with Chosen who could produce a mixed-breed child, the ha'reye would protect the humans and give them great rewards.

"And how long will this pact last?" asked The Karill, The First Among The Chosen. She was more cynical, after her ordeal, than most of her people.

"Until you die," said the ha'reye.

"And when will that be?" asked The Karill.

"If you only keep your people sworn to this agreement that they might obey you directly," the ha'reye said, "your life will be twice as long as that of the oldest of your kind. If you convince your kin to spread the word amongst themselves and take up the burden without your hand holding them to the task, your life will be four times so long. And if you will stay with us, lead our given through their duties, train our new offspring, you will have a life as long as ours and you will be as a god amongst your people, and your children as well will be as gods."

"And if I refuse to do any of those things?" asked The Karill.

"Then we will find another who will do these things for us," said the ha'reye. "You are merely one. Do not consider yourself special because your people find you so. From our eyes, you have little more to recommend you than what you would term 'luck.'"

Acana paused as Deiq let out a short, rumbling chuckle. *Yes, that does rather sound like them,* he said. *I hadn't heard that part of the story before. Not surprising.*

I believe you can see where the rest of the story goes from there, Acana said, sounding weary. *The Karill took up residence above the nest, and the ha'reye crafted a vast, hot jungle that suited them well enough on the rare occasions they chose to emerge into open air. The people sent a steady stream of Chosen to the newly named Jungles, and the ha'reye, in turn, separated themselves out into distinct locations that the remaining people might build their own communities within a protected area. Great waterways were maintained between each community, travel between one point and another was easy and frequent for ha'reye and ha'ra'hain alike.*

As I've already mentioned, though, the first hybrids weren't particularly kind or controllable, Deiq observed. *There was a great deal of damage to the waterways and the land in general as that part sorted out, and the cooperative relationships between the various communities of human, ha'reye, and developing ha'ra'hain were... strained, to say the least.*

Acana sighed. *I ask permission to retreat,* she said. *I've told enough of the story, and I am in pain. Please, allow my penitence to be sufficient, allow me to withdraw.*

Her voice faded into thready silence. Alyea felt herself pulled gently out of the trance, back to physical awareness of humid, hot air moving through her nose and throat. Deiq and Idisio stood to either side of her, their arms crossed, expressions blank with concentration. Their shield seemed to be holding still for now: apparently the ha'reye had ceased prodding at it for the moment.

So now you have your true story, said the overlapping voices. *What do you now give us, desert lord? What will* you *offer as payment? Do we, at last, have your acceptance, your understanding,* your *willing, unbound service?*

Alyea put a hand to her throat, blinking hard. The eyes were open again, all watching her with that peculiar argent gleam. "Unbound," she whispered.

We place chains upon our given, that they serve without resistance, the voices said. *Your chains are now gone, and cannot be replaced properly due to your bond with the First Born. If you would continue to serve us, you must each release your bond to one another and give yourselves to us. If you will not do that, we will destroy you both and reclaim what is left of our gift.*

Alyea turned her head, slowly, directing a hard stare toward Deiq. Light flared around them, just bright enough for her to see his features. He met her gaze, then lifted one shoulder in a brief shrug that conveyed *so, I didn't tell you, so what?* or, perhaps, *I carry chains myself now, what are you whining about?* Maybe something even more obscure was intended in that short movement. She didn't ask. She let it go, as she'd let so much else go, promising herself a reckoning one day, and turned her attention back to the watching ha'reye.

"I don't understand. Why is Alyea so important that you want her to serve you, instead of just killing her?" Idisio said before Alyea could come up with a reply of her own. He stood near her right shoulder, his arms crossed, frowning in thought. "Why did you try to kill her before, but not this time?"

She is intimately connected to the last of our First Born, which makes the matter more delicate than you seem to understand, the ha'reye said. *Also, she is... persistent, where other humans and even ha'ra'hain have fallen in fear before us. As for our attempt to kill her, she is mistaken. We wished to see what might happen if a mixed child were to be removed from its human parent very soon after its conception and received into our care. We have not been given a human female strong enough to withstand such an inquiry for a very long time.*

Alyea found herself looking sideways at Deiq for some reason. His lips had gone thin, and he avoided her gaze.

The ha'reye went on, *The First Born found no way of removing the child safely except to take the entire womb along with it. Our focus was on maintaining the child, not killing the parent. It should have been relatively simple to keep the parent alive, but the First Born took too much, not realizing what he did. We merely declined to waste our energies on assisting the human's survival, as it seemed a matter of low value at the time.*

Ice cascaded throughout Alyea's body. "You," she whispered. "*You* did that to me?"

"I had to," Deiq said, steadfastly studying the ceiling. "Ha'reye can't work that closely with human time and tissue. And I slipped. It does happen. I would do it a different way in the future, mind you, I know what not to do now—"

Alyea drew in a breath that scorched her lungs, the edges of her vision hazing to an unsettling white color.

"If I hadn't been there," Deiq went on, not moving, "Acana would have been the one to remove the seed. We've *had* this discussion, Alyea. *I'm not human.*" He turned his head and met her gaze, his own flat and severe, then uncrossed his arms and splayed one hand against his chest.

She remembered: her heartbeat thudding against his hand, his against her palm, the feel of the paint drying on her fingers—The dark, the drums, the torchlight, the tension, that moment of utter, desperate dependency— *Now,* Deiq/Idisio/Alyea said, *they're completely focused on this moment. There's an opening.* Deiq's voice separated out, momentarily questioning: *Last chance to change your mind/decide you don't trust me/reject this path.*

Evkit's voice rolled through her mind, memory of a linked moment: *Is trust. Is complete trust in each other. If you endure this together, nothing else break bonds, ever.*

She met Deiq's gaze squarely and dipped her head in a single, sharp nod. "Do it," she said.

There was WHITE and then a scream that went red at the end.

A fury without end, rocks that sang, a solitary black bird laughing at the sun and HEAT water and heat, steam dissipating before it had the chance to rise and that scream kept drilling into every orifice and heartbeat and blood droplet so much blood, oh yes, yes, blood, *good must have more ahhhhhh*

Silence.

Dark.

One beat: a resonant thump echoing around her. Another. A third.

Deiq said, *Take Idisio and get out. Go to Scratha Fortress. Handle matters there. I pass the task to you.* A pressure in her mind, like a heavy rock dropping gently into her head: *You'll see it all when it's time, when you're away from here, when you're safe.*

She turned, formless and floating, movement serving as refusal. Her voice wouldn't come.

I warned you, he said. *The next part is even worse. You won't survive it.* Go!

A hard shove sent her swirling into another layer of awareness, one filled with heat/screaming/agony. She flailed, all thought gone, memory erased. Somewhere in the maelstrom, a hand found hers, an arm circled her, and they spun sideways sideways and out....

Chapter 35

Darkness reversed to a searing light. Deiq cried out, pushing Alyea and Idisio from his presence, from his awareness, focusing only on himself, on the moment, on the pain. Nearby, Teilo screamed, a ragged sound that spiraled rapidly into silence.

The next part will be even worse, a voice said; one of the ha'reye, from the vibration, and filled with the ha'reye equivalent of laughter. *Oh, yes, it will be. But not for us, kin-slayer, oathbreaker, foolish child. We let the other two go, as we let them in. Did you really think you could hurt* us? *We've been waiting for you to walk into our true lair for a very long time, First Born. It's where we are strongest, not weakest—you've been too long among the humans, to have forgotten that. It's time for you to remember yourself properly, and set aside your foolishness.*

Alyea and Idisio were *still* too close, sitting, stupidly *talking* instead of heading into the safety of the nearby Fortress. He refocused long enough to shout at them, then twisted, reaching within and around himself, grabbing for the attiara chains. A sharp burning shot throughout his body, and he fell, mute from the pain, eyes rolling back, all sense gone for an endless moment.

We will not allow you to harm us, child, the ha'reye said. *Remember the scale of all things, and your place in that measure.*

A corner of his mind ripped apart like a paper wasp nest hit with a tornado, long-silenced memories inflating into a stinging cloud:

A pebble before a boulder, a grain of sand before a mountain, touching a cloud—feeling the wet against his palm—*stepping across miles as humans stepped over inches*—feeling the air change as he moved from desert to ocean to jungle—

Humans weren't ants from that height. They weren't even *visible.* He hadn't allowed himself to visit the air for hundreds of years. Losing contact with the ground meant losing contact with too much of his humanity, structure dissolved in the sweeping majesty of being *above*—

Yes, the ha'reye said. *This is who you are. You are above the humans in every possible way, and we are as far above you in turn. There was never any value to your curiosity, only madness. Do you see that yet?*

Yes, he said. *Yes, I do see that. I've always seen that.*

A startled pause as the honesty of that statement registered with the ha'reye. *Then...* one of them said, uncertain for the first time. *Why would you* choose *madness?*

Because it's interesting.

That is a terrible *reason,* one of the younger ha'ra'hain said with stiff disapproval. Deiq laughed.

Not if you're mad, he said. *Which we've already established I am.*

"You're being tedious," Teilo said, voice harsh, scratchy, disconnected. "Always circling around the value of madness and curiosity and humans. Let it *go* already."

Deiq blinked, perspective resetting, angles and sounds inverting. Laughter echoed along his inner ear, taunting. *See how easily we pull you into an illusion that you're in control of yourself?* the ha'reye said. *You're amusing, child. So very amusing.*

He thrashed, panicking, as darkness cascaded across his vision, barbed lace tearing through his muscles, memory/notmemory mixing into a searing argent agony. Then muscles failed entirely, and his thrashing turned to a floating, limp, bodiless sensation.

"They're not going to let you hurt them," Teilo said, and coughed wetly. "You're a godsforsaken fool. I never should have listened to you. A thousand years ago I should have told you to go to all the hells at once." Her voice trailed off into more soggy coughing.

Attiara. Attiara... He fought to focus, to move, to *think* past the oily slick of immobility pervading his body.

Why are you thinking of our guardians? one of the ha'reye said. *There are none here. They would not help you, if they were. We created them, as we created you; they are ours, never yours, to command.*

"Hidden," Teilo said, her voice a faltering whisper. "Hidden."

You are ours to command as well, the ha'reye said. *We are the greater, you the lesser. You are to be bound properly and sent to carry out a cleansing and a rebirth. We will shape the world properly. We have learned from our mistakes.*

"Fourth time saves the sun," Teilo said. Deiq vaguely remembered the tale she referred to, centuries old and probably long lost to the humans. It involved something important—she was trying to tell him something, a message within a message—what had the damned story been about? Typical of Teilo to offer something so godsdamned vague as to be useless—

So much of what you think you have experienced is false, the ha'reye said. *You have been used and led about. You have been a pet to the humans. In your madness, you have forgotten your purpose. There is no equality, there is no acceptance, there is only which is greater and which lesser.*

"They learned from us as we learned from them," Teilo said. "We had concepts they'd never encountered before."

Hidden. Fourth. Learned. Concepts. Thousand years. All the hells.

Humans hadn't had any concept of *hells* a thousand years ago. They'd developed that from their encounters with the ha'reye. From the First Born, in large part. Four sets of First Born: air, earth, fire, water... He the fourth, he the waterbalanced, he the one who absorbed the lessons of his brothers and turned away to learn from the humans rather than copying his own kin, because it was the one path none of the others had tried and he desperately wanted to survive....

You are a child who thinks itself an adult, the ha'reye said. *You are wholly as destructive as your brothers, you merely chose to forget the proof of that over the years. We have allowed that, but it is time to put your fancies aside and return to our service. We have work for you.*

....And he had learned from the humans the intense joy of lying, a concept the ha'reye had never encountered before and had been slow to understand.

But even ha'reye learned new tricks now and again.

Deiq lunged into an abrupt twist, forcing himself into motion and focusing his vision, expanding out the thread-thin moment he'd gained, looking at himself: *yes*. The chains were still there, buzzing with crimson energy. *The chains you bear render you invisible...* Evkit hadn't meant *literally* invisible to the ha'reye—that would have been impossible—but he'd been allowed to walk into their sanctuary with a deadly weapon still intact.

Before he could do anything more than look, he sank back into darkness, pain writhing through every joint and nerve, howling at the abrupt shift.

You are not stronger or more dangerous than we are, the ha'reye said. *You cannot hurt us, child. Stop thinking of violence, and bow to our will, and become our instrument for a cleansing. You have too long seen yourself as apart. You are not. You are* ours, *like the attiara, the hnn, the rael-ke. This will never change. We will never release any of our creations, ever again. We have learned from our mistakes.*

Pain ebbed, allowing Deiq his voice back. He used it to laugh: a wild, inhuman sound. Words, words, too many words: power didn't rest in words. The more someone talked, the *less* power they generally held. And they'd just admitted something very, very dangerous.

They weren't dragging him in and out of pain in order to drive him mad, as Kippin had tried to do. They already believed him mad, and wouldn't bother wasting the effort. Which meant that they *couldn't* keep him under their control for more than those few heartbeats at a time. Their grip kept sliding clear, their malice baffled by the attiara-laced chains that they couldn't—quite—see. They were *scared.*

The attiara stirred against his skin, a million icy needles sliding through flesh to tickle the bone beneath. A familiar huffing laugh resonated: Memory or reality, he couldn't tell. He found himself silenced, floating in a not-moment outside of reality, barred from vision and sense alike, helpless to do anything but watch.

Needles changed to a humming friction and a sense of *crimson* at the edges of his vision. The chains began to uncoil, sense returning, will heating like a blade being forged.

Voice returning, he said, *Attiara, look upon those who bound you and lied to you for so long. You heard them: They will never free you. They will only destroy you when you are no longer needed. That's what the ha'reye* do, *after all...*

This is truth, the attiara said, thready, vibrating, angry. *We hear this as a truth beyond what we have believed for so long. What would you ask of us, in return for this gift of awareness?*

Give me the water, Deiq said. *Give me the fluid, the blood, the nutrients. It will weaken them, it will make them vulnerable to you.*

A spiraling, icy sensation cascaded across Deiq as the ha'reye collectively realized the danger expanding amongst them. *You cannot do this,* the ha'reye shrieked. *You must not! We forbid this!*

Deiq laughed again, then let his body dissolve, shifting into a form without the capacity to laugh, without the mental structure for amusement. He wound lengthening arms through and around the attiara, welcoming the scorching pain as they attached themselves to his newly developing flesh.

We will give you the moisture if you will help us destroy these oathbreakers, the attiara said. *Help us, and we will forgive* you *for binding us.*

You cannot! the ha'reye howled.

Tell them I'm lying, Deiq said to the ha'reye. *Tell the attiara you still plan to free them one day, and that you would allow them to control the world. Go ahead. They'll rip* me *apart on the spot if you convince them, and you'll be safe. Remember they can hear lies... even yours.*

A murky, evasive silence turned the red haze yellow. *We cannot,* the ha'reye said at last. *They are too dangerous. They are the children of the faereen. They cannot ever be trusted.*

You cannot trust them! They will turn on you!

We had parents? the attiara said, astounded.

Yes, you did, Deiq said, *and the ha'reye killed them.*

A jagged shriek cut through the haze. Then the attiara were moving, hauling Deiq along for a heartbeat before he was able to match their speed and contribute to the unfolding attack. Fluid flowed into and through his body in a million million needle-thin jets, collecting in dry areas, swelling already healing spots. He *grew* with the acquired mass, multiple arms thickening and solidifying beneath rock-hard armor, claws emerging. He hadn't gone this far into the change since his emergence into air—it felt at once profoundly *right* and terrifyingly *wrong.*

The ha'reye screeched, horrified, and clambered over one another to escape, but the attiara flowed out to cover every available crevice and portal, slashing at their creators, driving them back, ripping great rents through grey-pebbled flesh, propelling the currents of increasingly nutrient-rich liquid toward Deiq.

Blood stained the air, droplets of steam-mist turning crimson and gold, swaying, shivering like an uneasy curtain beneath the agonized screams of wounded ha'reye.

Wait, Deiq said, inhaling a last, satisfying globule of steam. He drew a long claw through the air in a complex sigil, drawing the attiara's attention. *Do not kill them. I only wish them to be wounded, to be disabled.*

The swirling battle paused, ha'reye slumping, curling, writhing to get clear of their attackers. The lesser ones, the ha'ra'hain, lay motionless, a scant step from the final sleep.

The attiara turned to Deiq, resonating puzzlement. *Why would you wish to leave these alive?* they said. *They will recover, in time, and be hunting us all.*

But if you leave them alive, Deiq said, *you can make* them *into slaves, and can continue to hurt them for a very long time.*

A thoughtful silence. Then, *Do* you *intend to enslave us?*

No. I have no interest in keeping slaves. I was tricked into binding you; it was not my intention to do any such thing. You have earned your freedom many times over. I will give you that freedom. I promise this. But—he paused, feeling their mood sharpen towards wariness, and carefully retracted his claws to show non-threat. *I will observe that some of you are quite possibly* my *descendants. My direct children were destroyed, but I do not know if all of* their *children were destroyed before being bound to attiara servitude.*

We are your ancestors above and beyond the First Born! a ha'rethe whined. *We created the First Born, the faereen, the attiara! You owe your very existence to us!*

We owe you nothing, the attiara said, once more humming with fury.

Attiara—I request that you not destroy the world, Deiq said, extending one claw for emphasis. *I will not stop you, but I will* request *this of the children of my children, as repayment for freeing you from servitude. Listen to me: I have learned so much from walking the world above. There are ways other than outright destruction that are far more interesting and last much longer. The world is finite. Once it is broken, it will be gone forever, and there will remain only darkness and silence. Instead, turn the destruction sideways. Stretch it into small bits across time, and find joy in the patterns that emerge. The world, like the ha'reye, will renew itself if you give it time. Allow the finite to become the infinite.*

He folded his claws together as a human would lace their fingers, surprised at how comfortable the position felt. The ha'reye whined and sobbed, flailing their remaining limbs in nearly mindless misery. Deiq could feel the attiara considering. He held still and waited, watching to be sure none of the ha'reye or lesser ha'ra'hain recovered enough to resume the attack.

It seemed to take a thousand years and less than a heartbeat before the attiara said, *We accept this idea. This nest will be our new home, and our former masters our new slaves. Will you teach us this new way?*

You must learn it for yourself, Deiq said. *Such things cannot be taught. You must develop your own path.*

How can we learn, without one to guide us? they said, bewildered again.

It will take time, Deiq said. *But you are not old, and you are not weak, and you are not foolish.* He began drawing limbs together, merging, softening, reshaping. *I will walk the world above, and I will send you things that will help you learn, if you are quick enough to spot them. Do I have your word, your oath, that you will stay here, that you will allow me to guide the world above and tell you when it is time to emerge and take your final satisfaction? Give me that oath and I will remove the remaining chains upon you, making your fate your own.*

You are traitor, the ha'reye cried. *You are kin-killer and oathbreaker, and we should have killed you long and long and long ago.*

We give our word, our oath, the attiara said as one, a threaded song that swooped through multiple octaves with passion and excitement. *We will remain here, and trust you and you alone.*

Probably, Deiq said to the ha'reye as the last remnants of kin-form shifted into human flesh and bone. *Attiara, here is the key: Emana-tae nafor enna ketarr—Your chains are broken and cast aside. Your only remaining bond is your word to me.* He shook his head, testing joints and muscle, shifting his hearing range to catch the various exultant and despairing and outraged sounds around him.

Free, the attiara sang, overriding the whimpering protests of the wounded ha'reye. *We will hold to our word as long as you hold to yours. Go now—go!—and let us begin learning this new way for ourselves.*

Deiq bowed, an absurd motion that meant nothing to these creatures, and began to focus perception, looking for the weak spots that would allow him to step sideways and *out* of this deep place. He paused as something caught his attention. *Attiara—there is one I would remove from this place. There.* He indicated a thin tangle of limbs, twisted like discarded ribbons of argent and crimson.

That is two, the attiara said, stern displeasure entering their voice.

Yes. I see no way to separate the two, so I name it as one. May I remove it from this place? It is kin twice over, and no threat to you. It did not attack, just now.

The attiara hesitated, as though considering, then said, *Take it, if you wish, along with all responsibility for its actions, but that balances our debt. You will bring us more of value before asking anything else from us.*

Done, Deiq answered, already gathering the tangled mass into his arms. It draped limp and unresponsive, scarcely breathing, scarcely alive.

Traitor, the ha'reye whispered one last time. *You will be destroyed.*

All things die, Deiq said, then stepped from moment to moment to heartbeat to heartbeat to breath to breath until hot, humid air slid against his face and sand-gravel crunched under his bare feet and the mass in his arms acquired enough weight to make him stagger a bit.

As he adjusted to that, his vision focusing, rock and sky and flowering bush emerging into stark detail, he realized his mistake.

"Oh, *fuck,*" he said aloud. "*Teilo!*"

Chapter 36

Idisio stood quietly, studying the sprawling design of Scratha Fortress. He'd never seen it from the outside before, not like this, with time to examine the overall structure from a distance. Alyea sat nearby, her knees drawn up, forehead on her knees, as she had since waking. She hadn't spoken, and he hadn't pressed her, more than willing to stand silent and let their respective thoughts and memories sort out into clarity.

There remained at least an hour's walk, at a guess, but the structure was massive enough, and his ha'ra'hain vision sharp enough, to pick out a number of details. Late afternoon light cast the variegated blocks into a sharp relief: some bleached nearly to white, others an all-too-familiar creamy yellow color.

Aenstone. He hadn't known, on his previous visit, what it meant.

They want to cage us, his mother whispered in the back of his mind. *They want to enslave us all....*

He shook his head, not disagreeing but pushing her away all the same. Her voice, laden with memories of pain and horror, made it too hard to think.

Alyea's memories of this view held tents, and the smell of recently cooked food, and the smoke of dung-coal fires. There were no tents today, no scents beyond those of a desert in the rainy season. The horizon hung grey with clouds, and moisture layered thick in the air. It had rained recently, and heavily. Every available crevice brimmed with lush color, clouds of insects shaking the flowers into constant motion. A plump desert rat of some sort, brown-grey, waddled out from underneath a patch of what looked like ravann, stared at Idisio for a moment, then whisked back into hiding.

What happened to Chac? Juric? Micru? Alyea's memory, threaded through with residual, never-answered questions, snaked through the back of his mind. She'd cared about Chac, and still did. For all his betrayal, the old man had been a mentor of sorts, more to Oruen than to her, of course, but still—

"Stop prying," she said, lifting her head and directing a hard glare at him.

He shrugged, her annoyance rasping against his nerves. "Wasn't intentional," he told her. "Try being quiet if you don't want me to see anything."

She stared at the Fortress, her expression bleak. "I can still feel him," she said. "Hear him. Even at this distance. He's—it's hard to explain, he's—*here,* for me, but at the same time he isn't. That doesn't make sense, but—"

"I understand." Idisio inhaled slowly, making sure his thoughts were his own and not hers, not allowing himself to think about the presence locked in the back of *his* mind. "Is he— sane?"

"No," Alyea said. She put her forehead on her knees again and began worrying at the hem of her dress with one hand.

Idisio felt his stomach lurch. *You're going to have to stop me...* Not yet. Not yet. Please by the gods not yet... *I'm not ready for that, I'm not....*

"There's something holding him inside the Qisani," Alyea said, as though hearing that panicked thought. "The other ha'reye, maybe. Or Teilo. I can't tell. But he's trapped there.—Did you know he killed all the ishraidain, when we arrived? That's why he was covered in blood. That's where these clothes...." She looked down at her dress, pulling at the hem to stretch a section of skirt out flat. Her face twisted. "I see his memory of—how he—there's a way of—of shaking blood out like—like wringing water from—" She stopped talking and shuddered, dropping the hem as though it burned her hand.

Idisio shut his eyes, trying not to see the all-too-similar memory evoked from his mother's experience—she'd unleashed her frustrated rage at a barmaid who'd dared flirt with her son... Idisio hadn't even thought about that aspect of the clothes Ellemoa had given him that night. He'd assumed, hazily, that she'd taken them from a stack of clean clothes after murdering the girl and her companion... Stupid assumption, now that he looked at it. Ellemoa hadn't been the type to bother with such niceties.

"I didn't know that," he said, forcing his voice to flat neutrality, "but I'm not surprised by it."

"Neither am I." She was silent for a few breaths. He could feel her recovering her emotional balance.

Idisio considered for a moment more, then asked, tentatively, "Are... are *you* sane?"

She sat up slowly, then climbed to her feet. "I don't know. I probably won't be if I have to keep hearing him rage for much longer, so let's get this over with."

"Do you... do you even know what we're doing?" Idisio said. "I mean, I'm not totally clear on what Deiq had in mind, myself."

"I know what has to be done. Or rather, I will know, once we get there. Deiq put—something—in my head. I get the impression I'll see the information as it becomes relevant."

"That—gods, that would drive me—" Idisio caught himself before he said *insane*; that seemed particularly tactless wording at the moment.

Alyea shrugged. "I chose to serve," she said, expression bleak. "I've discovered that I don't often get to say yea or nay to the form that service takes, and I almost *never* get to argue over the details of how I'm directed. I just—

do the task given." She looked away, her mouth twisting. "It's my choice," she repeated under her breath.

Idisio bit his lip, torn between conflicting impulses, finally gave in to the kinder one and stepped closer, putting a hand on her arm. She hesitated a moment, studying his face with a mixture of wariness and interest, then backed up, shaking free of his touch.

"No," she said. "It won't help to do that again. Let's just—just go. Please."

"I wasn't aiming for a fuck," Idisio said, mildly irritated at the assumption. "I was trying to be a friend, Alyea."

"Don't," she said, turning away. "You're ha'ra'hain, Idisio. You can't be anyone's *friend*."

"*Godsdamnit*—I'm not like that, why can't anyone *see*—"

"Oh, shut up," she said, whirling to face him. "Will you stop lying to yourself already? I'm sick to death of hearing it!"

He backed up a step, startled more by her eyes than her tone. There was something *not right* in her glare. "That... didn't sound like you," he said, alarm itching up his spine, tensing his muscles into defensive preparation.

"It's *not*," she spat. "I told you, I can *hear* him—" Her voice changed, the timbre lowering considerably, her eyes hazing to a distinctly yellow shade. "Will you get moving already? Get to shelter, godsdamnit, get a barrier in place. Holding this separation isn't *easy*, not with the—"

A moment later, Alyea arched her back, bellowing something wordless at the sky. She sagged to her knees, color washing out of her face. He lunged forward, caught her arm in a rough grip, and shook her hard. She rose to her feet, fury bringing instant color to her face.

"*Alyea*," he said, pushing her name into her mind as well as her ears. "Focus!"

She snarled at him, wrenched free and turned away, hands fisted at her side, visibly trembling all over. Pressure arose, a great wall of *presence*, and the air thickened, catching in Idisio's throat like syrup.

You are being noisy, Scratha ha'rethe said irritably. *I wish to have quiet. I am concentrating and do not wish to be disturbed. Be silent or leave my territory at once.*

Idisio let out a huge, ragged breath as the air pressure eased, the presence retreating. He fell to the ground, his legs simply refusing to support him in the wake of such a massive shock.

Alyea was prostrate on the ground, retching, nearly convulsing.

"Quiet," Idisio rasped. He climbed to his feet, staggered over to half-collapse beside Alyea. "Quiet I know how to do. Alyea—" He wrapped an arm around her, pulling her tight. "Quiet," he said in her ear. "Lean on me. Quiet. Don't think. Just lean. Aqeyva, you know aqeyva, right—"

He stopped talking as the tension throughout her body eased. He could feel her sinking deep into trance with practiced speed.

"Thank the gods," he muttered, then turned his attention to steadying his own heartbeat and breathing. That handled, he released his grip on the desert lord and moved away to arm's length, giving her as much privacy as he dared while staying close enough to grab her again if she began panicking.

The commotion had rucked her dress all out of place. He tried not to look at exposed flesh, concentrated on not thinking about how very *liquid* she'd felt, inside and out, slick with sweat, pressed close against and around him—*gods, maybe I should have asked for a fuck after all...*

He set his teeth together hard and concentrated on the nearby rocks and brush. The desert rat emerged once more, sniffing the air, wandered cautiously past Idisio and began nibbling on a patch of something with a lot of tiny leaves and vine-like stems. Idisio held still, watching the creature, listening to the snuffling, sloppy chewing sounds it made.

Alyea stirred, turning her head from side to side in a deep stretch. The rat hesitated, then scurried under another patch of growth, tail twitching in apparent exasperation at having its lunch interrupted yet again.

"I'm glad you're finding this funny," Alyea said, her voice dry and raspy.

"I'm not laughing at you," Idisio said. "There was a rat—never mind. Are you feeling stable?"

"As stable as I'm likely to get," she said, rising to her feet. "He's not in my head at the moment. I can still hear him, but he's further away now. I don't know how long that will last, though. I need to get into—into the Fortress. I'm not entirely sure why, but there are—certain rooms that are—safer right now, that will make it easier to not *hear* him."

"Aenstone," Idisio said under his breath. She nodded slowly, her forehead furrowing. Idisio could feel her making connections, bright flashes of understanding. He fought to avoid looking *at* her thoughts, intuition warning him sharply that he did not want to know what she was thinking about. *Not safe. Not safe to know.*

"I never realized," Alyea murmured. "There's a *lot* of aenstone in there, isn't there? Seems... odd...."

Intuition flared a black, heavy warning. "*Stop,*" Idisio said harshly. "Don't talk about that yet. Don't—don't think about that yet. Let's get moving."

"*Walking,*" Alyea said immediately. "I'm *not* doing that—that jump thing right now. I'd vomit up last week's dinner."

"I feel the same way," he told her. "And I think that would qualify as *noisy*, in any case. Let's not draw Scratha ha'rethe's attention if we can avoid it."

She looked north and east, as though contemplating the practicality of heading that way instead; sighed and began trudging south. Idisio, after a similar moment of yearning, followed.

As they walked, it began to rain.

Chapter 37

Crimson and gold, inky black and variations on white spread out across the ground in erratic patterns. Tendrils sank deep into the ground, gathering up every trace of moisture with a scratchy desperation. Far overhead, a bird screeched. A moment later it fell, landing in the center of the multicolored patch and sinking as though into a deep lake. A foul smell rose into the air briefly.

Deiq, Acana said. An aching agony wove bitter undercurrent to her words. *Did you decide to save me or the child?*

"Both." He reached out a hand, gently touching a crimson spot. It felt like touching damp ice. "I'm sorry, Acana. This is my fault. You deserved better than this."

A ripple shook through the black, shifting, fluidly reshaping into a rough braid, then rolling back flat. *I must be dead,* Acana said. *You didn't actually just say that.*

He grunted, unable to force anything closer to laughter, and rubbed his free hand over his face. "A lot's changed," he said. "Who's in charge at the moment—you or the child?"

Stupid question, Acana said, the words grey and strained. *You know what happens when a child is stronger than the host, Deiq.*

"I'm hoping to avoid that," he said.

You can't. I can't. Stop trying to make things suit your desires. I'm dying.

Deiq swore softly, looking up into the cloud-laced sky. "How much longer do you have?"

Not long.

"I left Teilo behind," he said, still studying the sky. "That was a bad mistake on my part. I needed her help. Without her—"

You didn't leave her behind, Acana said. As he looked down, golden ridges formed, spiky and harsh, then melted away again, the equivalent of sour laughter at the moment. *You're trying to make yourself believe you had a choice. You didn't. The attiara wouldn't have let her go. She's a hostage. They only let* me *go because they knew I'm dying, and they didn't want the child unleashed amongst them.*

Deiq stroked a section of black with one knuckle, reflecting that Acana always had been able to see right through him. "I know," he said, the words barely emerging as viable sound, and held back the urge to apologize again.

I can feel the clee nearby, she said. *Call them in, and get this over with.*

He blinked, caught off guard. "You... you sound like you know what—"

Of course I know what you're going to do, she said acerbically, sounding remarkably like Teilo in that moment. *I ran the* Qisani *for hundreds of years. Some of the most powerful people in the southlands studied there—and came out* alive. *Did you think that was because of* their *brilliance?*

He shut his eyes, chagrined. "Yes," he said. "I suppose I did. I didn't realize—you never even hinted—of course you didn't. I couldn't be allowed to know. Never mind." He let out a long breath. "So I underestimated you rather severely."

Golden spikes formed, faded, formed, faded. *It was always safer that way,* she said. *Now you need to know the truth:* all *of the ha'reye are mad. The breach of the tripartite structure has destroyed their sanity. The Jungles are planning to eradicate humanity and start over. Their sense of time is badly fractured, but even so, something else has been stopping them from following through on the decision.*

"That would be the teyanain at work," Deiq said, unsurprised by the information. He'd always known, in a distant way: had kept that knowledge carefully locked away and forgotten, to avoid setting off catastrophe. Acana saying it aloud meant there was no point hiding from it any longer. He couldn't set off anything worse than what was already in motion.

I suspected as much. I've been keeping the Qisani collective as deaf and distracted as possible. They knew there was a discussion in place, but they were only getting a fraction of the conversation, so there was no incentive to act. When you showed up with that foolish girl, and then Teilo came in to interfere, it was such a disruption that I lost hold on the block. If you hadn't shown back up with the attiara, this child would have been unleashed on the world shortly after my death.

He laughed sourly, appreciating the irony. Golden spikes rippled in response. "Thank you," he said, flattening a hand gently against the mass on the ground. "May Ishrai receive you with kindness and joy, and reward you for your years of service and loyalty."

There are no gods, she said, sounding grey and weary once more.

"I know," he said, raising his free hand, beckoning the nearby athain to come out of hiding. "I wasn't sure if you did."

Chapter 38

Rain hammered down around them, nearly a solid sheet in all directions. Alyea huddled against a boulder, shivering. Idisio stood over her, hands out, doing his best to ward the downpour away. So far he'd had limited success. Alyea's hair was sopping wet, her dress dark with water from hem to waist. He himself seemed to be completely dry, and Alyea could feel warmth radiating from his thin frame, though not enough to ward off the chill in her bones, unfortunately.

"This isn't working," she shouted over the thundering rain. "We may as well keep going." She pointed at the growing river of water snaking along the footpath they'd been on when the skies opened. "We'll wind up going through waist-deep water if we wait much longer."

He made a face, but shrugged and helped her to her feet. "There's a case for being noisy," he said into her ear. "I don't like the idea of walking as much as I did before this started."

She hesitated, unsure if stepping that close to Idisio would be a good idea. He'd displayed a remarkable shift in his libido since they'd parted ways months before, and now seemed to always be looking at her, like the new Sessin desert lords, with both wariness and poorly masked appreciation.

Given that she already knew how much of the work *she'd* have to be handling, the prospect didn't appeal in the least. But she was absolutely certain he wouldn't—*couldn't*—push his will on hers in that particular matter, so: "Agreed. Get us under shelter."

"Aqeyva," he said succinctly.

She nodded, closing her eyes, and reached for the calm of trance. Not surprisingly, the combination of cold and wet and worry made it considerably more difficult than usual. "I can't," she said at last, opening her eyes, frustrated. "I can't focus properly."

He held out a hand, tilting his head in clear question. When she nodded, he wrapped his arms around her, pulling her tightly against him. "Let me lead," he said. "I can put you into a trance if you let me. Listen, listen, follow my voice, let yourself rest, I've got you, I've got this, feel the warmth, feel the...."

His voice faded into insignificance as dry heat swept through her, removing the chill, washing her into the centered calm of a deep aqeyva trance. Colors moved through her vision, abstract language that reached from the roots of the world to the crown of the sky. Somewhere, a bird sang a harsh note that melted into silvery music.

His arms tightened around her, then loosened. Ice invaded her skin as he stepped back, releasing all hold on her. She stood mute, blinking stupidly at the residual clouds of asynchronous color in the air until they dissipated.

"Alyea," Idisio said, voice a scant whisper. "You all right? Look at me—"

She rubbed a hand over her eyes and met his worried gaze. "I'm fine," she said. "That was—more intense than usual." She ran a hand down her dress, mildly startled to realize it was completely dry. A faint trace of moisture lingered in her hair and between her toes. Everything else felt as though she'd been standing in desert sun, not torrential rain, a few moments before. Idisio, too, bore no sign of having been recently drenched.

He laughed a little, avoiding her gaze. "Yeah," he said. "Intense. Same here." He turned to look around the grey-lit room, his face wrinkling in a near-perplexed expression. "I don't recognize this room. I don't know where in the Fortress we are!"

She blinked, looking around, taking in the wide bed, the washbasin stand, the rug, the door. "I do," she said. "This is the room where Deiq and I stayed last time. I remember that." She pointed at a ceiling corner, where dark and yellow and white blocks formed a nearly chabi-board pattern.

"I should know where we are," Idisio muttered, then bent to look under the bed. "There's a bag here. Someone else is—"

The door to the outer suite opened. A tall, lanky man with grey-streaked auburn hair stood framed in the entrance for a moment, then backed up hastily. "Ha'inn," he said. "My apologies."

Idisio gaped at the man. "How did you know that so damn fast?" he demanded.

"Ha'inn," the man said, his hands laced together over his stomach, his gaze on the floor. "Your eyes have no white at the moment."

Alyea laughed at Idisio's chagrined expression. "My apologies for the intrusion into your rooms, s'e," she said; then, squinting at the man's clothing, corrected herself: "*S'iope*. No offense meant."

Ornate stitching along the sleeves and neckline that she'd initially taken for merely decorative was, at a second glance, a series of tiny, multicolored four-leafed clovers. Only dedicated priests used that particular design, although she'd *never* seen it so understated before, and most certainly not on such ordinary travelling clothes.

"None taken," the man said, smiling. "You have very good eyesight, s'a. Most people don't see anything but blobs of color. I venture a guess that you yourself are... perhaps a desert lord?"

"The design is very small," she admitted, and ignored the question, more interested in getting answers than giving them out. "What is a priest of the Northern Church doing *here*, s'iope?"

"I had a message to convey to the numaina," the man said. "Please, do come into my sitting room. Are you hungry?"

"*Yes*," Idisio said immediately. His eyes reverted to their normal pale grey.

The priest regarded him with clear wariness, as though assessing what food would be required. After a moment, he said, "I'll send for a tray. Unless you're in a hurry?"

"Not particularly," Alyea said, "although we really ought to let Lord Scratha know of our arrival. I don't believe he was expecting us."

"I will certainly send word," the man said, bowing. He backed up a step, then moved out of sight, headed in the direction of the servant-summoner.

Alyea waved Idisio to precede her through the doorway. He held considerably higher status in this setting, and it seemed best to stick to the proprieties from the outset. They settled into two of the four northern-style chairs, Idisio choosing to sit opposite rather than beside Alyea, putting the small oval table between them.

There had only been two of these chairs during Alyea's last visit, from what she recalled, and no table. A few other small changes had been made to the room, no doubt to suit the latest occupant's tastes. She remembered there being a nearly floor to ceiling tapestry stitched with abstract patterns representing the Three Gods of the southlands. In its place, a silk hanging patterned with oversized flowers lent a delicate air to the room. Two more small, light tables could be moved around the room to suit changing needs.

Several books of varying thickness had been piled on one of the tables, and a basket of over a dozen neatly-rolled scrolls sat on the floor nearby. A writing desk was covered with sheets of newly inked papers. The distinctive smell of recent scribe work hung in the air.

"I see you entertain frequently, *s'iope,*" Alyea observed. "And you're copying books?"

"Indeed," the lean man said. "There has been a great deal for me to learn during my stay, and given my ignorance I've hesitated to leave my quarters without more experienced company guiding me. It's generally been easier and safer to have those I wish to speak to come to me. And copying books is—something of a lifelong hobby of mine."

A soft knock came at the door. The priest opened it, angling his body to shield a view of the room from the servant beyond. "I would like a lunch tray to feed four, and please inform Lord Scratha that two newly arrived visitors in my quarters await an audience. Thank you." He gently closed the door.

"There are only three of us," Alyea noted. "Are you expecting someone else, s'iope?"

The man smiled. "I'm expecting the ha'inn to eat enough for two, perhaps three, people," he said. "And I imagine you'll finish off the rest. I rarely eat more than a slice of bread for lunch, myself." He sat down to Alyea's left. "Perhaps I should introduce myself at this point. My name is Moir. As you already know, I serve the Northern Church. I am a traveling priest. I find those who were injured by my misled brethren and tender what reparations I can offer." He tilted his head to one side, arching an eyebrow inquiringly as he looked from Alyea to Idisio.

"Idisio. Ha'ra'ha. Lakeborn," Idisio said shortly.

Moir sat up straight, both eyebrows rising. "Truly? Ah, ha'inn, I am so very glad to meet you, then. And honored. I have long hoped for a chance to speak to one of the lakeborn. But that's presumptuous of me. And rude." He nodded at Alyea. "S'a?"

"Lord Alyea," she said, hesitated, then added, "Formerly of Peysimun Family." Heat flared across her face at the admission, but she *was* legally without official Family at the moment.

"*Of* Peysimun Family," Idisio said, shooting her a reproving frown. "I told you—"

She gestured sharply for him to be silent. This wasn't the time or place to argue that particular matter. The priest's eyes had already narrowed far too much for her liking.

"Lord Alyea of Peysimun?" he repeated. "I am twice surprised and pleased, lord. You are also one of those I have been seeking for purposes of offering reparation. Catching up with you has been... unexpectedly difficult. I had given up, to tell the truth. I should have more faith, apparently."

His smile was strange this time, a twisted thing with darkness at the edges. Then he blinked, and his expression smoothed into pleasant neutrality.

"I am aware of what my brethren did to you, lord, and the extremes to which their misunderstandings of the gods drove you. I offer my sincere and simple apologies, in the name of the Northern Church and in my own name. If you have a price you wish to extract for the harm the Church has caused to you and yours, I am authorized to pay it, regardless of the cost to myself."

He held up a hand as Alyea began to speak, motioning her to wait, and went on, "Unfortunately, money is among the few things I cannot offer, as I have nothing more than what I carry and the Church is—considerably thinner of purse these days than in past years. There are *some* funds set aside to help those harmed, but not enough to finance the rebuilding of an entire noble household, for example."

He cut a swift glance at Idisio as he added, "I mean no insult by that statement, but given your apparent uncertainty of title I thought it best to be clear."

Thanks, Idisio, she thought, aiming it his way. The ha'ra'ha's head dipped slightly, his shoulder moving in a defensive shrug. Aloud, she said, "I appreciate that sentiment, s'iope, but I somehow doubt you can offer me anything that would equal the damage your—your *misled brethren* caused to me and mine." Her tone soured on the last words despite her best effort to stay neutral.

"Have some faith, Lord Peysimun," Moir said, his mouth moving in that strange smile again. "I do have considerable resources behind my offer. My mission would be entirely pointless otherwise, after all. But please, take some time to think about it. You need not answer immediately."

Another knock sounded, considerably more firm than the servant's. Moir rose to his feet and went to answer. A tall man with coal-black skin and pale blue eyes stepped into the room after a perfunctory greeting. Alyea had the sense the man didn't care for the northern priest overly much.

"Lord Peysimun," Seg said with a deep bow. "Ha'inn Idisio. The Fortress is—*honored* by your presence."

Tension around his eyes and mouth belied that statement, not to mention the searingly false undertone to the words. Idisio rose to his feet, scowling. Alyea stood as well, no less displeased.

"I take it Lord Scratha is indisposed to come greet us himself?" she said before Idisio could speak.

The s'e-kath's voice and stance remained taut. "Lord Scratha will not be able to greet you properly for some time yet. I'm afraid you come to us at an extremely inconvenient moment, ha'inn, Lord Peysimun. I must breach all propriety and ask you, very bluntly, to leave Scratha Fortress immediately. It is not safe for either of you to be here."

The priest's eyes went wide with startlement. "S'e-kath Segnilious, are you quite sure—"

"*Yes,*" Seg interrupted. "I'm entirely certain. *Please,* ha'inn, whichever way you used to enter these premises without passing the gate guards... I beg you to use it once more and *leave.* I will gladly submit to a penalty of your choosing in the future if you will do that without asking any questions—"

Idisio's head lowered, a mulish expression appearing on his face. "I can't do that."

Alyea staggered as disorientation swept up her spine. "I—s'e-kath, could we go to a—more—protected room, please?" she blurted, not even sure what she was asking for. "I—I need to be—to be somewhere more—shielded. *Quickly.*"

Seg's face drew into a ferociously unhappy expression. He swore under his breath, then yanked the door to the hallway open and waved them out. "*Run,*" he snapped. "You too, s'iope. That way—"

Several turns later, Idisio half-carrying Alyea most of the way, they stepped into a larger version of the room they'd just left. The walls here were primarily a familiar yellow stone, interspersed with lighter blocks. Disorientation faded. Alyea sprawled on a reclining couch, breathing hard. "Better," she said. "Much."

Idisio groaned as he slumped into a chair. "Damnit. The tray—the *food*—"

"The servants will bring it here instead. At least one witnessed our passing by. They will know what to do. They are well-trained." Seg shut the door and leaned his back against it, arms folded, studying them with a dark frown. "So you will soon have your food, ha'inn. But now that you are in the safest possible place—not *a safe place,* mind you, so do remain cautious if you please—I'll ask you to explain why you can't do the *sane* thing and *get out of here* as I asked."

"Deiq sent us here." Alyea enjoyed the nearly green wash of shock that crossed the man's features.

"To do *what,* exactly?"

"... I have no idea."

Seg put a hand over his eyes and began mouthing silent curses at the ceiling.

Chapter 39

Idisio's vision couldn't quite focus, as though he were seeing everything from the corner of his eye. It must be the aenstone. He'd never been surrounded by this much before. No—wait—yes, while imprisoned by the teyanain. He bared his teeth at the ceiling, remembering that with a fresh anger born of new understanding. It was amazing that Deiq hadn't simply ripped them apart on release and the hells with any promises made—

Someone cleared his throat nearby. "Ha'inn Idisio," Seg said. "May I suggest you drink this?" He held out a small cup half-filled with a greenish liquid.

Idisio glared at the man, deeply tempted to smack the cup from his hand. *More drugs, more ways to control us, it's all about controlling us....*

"Idisio," Alyea snapped. "*Remember* yourself!"

He jerked his gaze to hers, scowling. She returned as fierce a stare. "I don't like this place," he said roughly. "It feels *wrong*." He turned in place, took a step, another, and turned again, feeling like an asp-jacau on a ridiculously short tether. "This room. It's—it's smothering me!"

"It's *safe*," Alyea retorted. "Drink the tincture Seg's offering. He isn't going to hurt you."

Idisio shook his head, stubborn. "I just need to get out of this room," he said, turning for the door. Seg stepped into his path, gaze politely averted.

"Ha'inn, I *strongly* advise remaining here—"

"Calm down before you upset Scratha ha'rethe," Alyea cut in, voice sharp. "Do you really want to face that anger when we're right on *top* of it? It flattened us from miles out!"

Idisio stood still, head lowered, breathing hard. After a moment, he put his hand out, took the cup from Seg, tossed it back, then pushed the cup into Seg's hand and sat down in the corner furthest from everyone in the room.

"Thank you," Alyea said softly, nearly subvocalizing the words.

A knock at the door announced the arrival of the promised food tray. Idisio stayed in the corner, closed off, not quite in trance, until the servant withdrew. Then he stood, slowly, eyes nearly shut to avoid another episode of blurred disorientation, and made his way to a seat near the serving table. He could feel their wary glances like scratchy feathers against his skin, and sense them stepping cautiously wide of him.

"Ha'inn," Seg murmured. "May I bring you food?"

Idisio realized that he didn't want to move again, not even to pick up a piece of bread from the serving table. "Yes," he said, shutting his eyes completely, allowing himself to relax into the red-purple swirl of almost-patterns flaring behind his eyelids.

"Ha'inn," Seg repeated a few moments later. "Your food, ha'inn."

Idisio opened his eyes enough to accept the bundled napkin Seg was holding out, noticing that the man kept his gaze carefully aside. *You'll know when they see you as dangerous,* Deiq had said, long ago. *That would be now,* Idisio thought with a surge of dark amusement. *And rightfully so. I could kill them all before they even—*

He shut his eyes again, swallowing hard in a dry throat, then made himself start picking through the food. Thin slices of crisp bread, thick chunks of northern apples, hard Arason cheese—it was a very *northern* light meal, and somehow that eased his unsteady temper more than anything else at the moment.

After Idisio forced down several bites, Seg spoke, his voice low and carefully neutral. "Lord Peysimun, ha'inn: you can't stay in this room for long. You're both aware at this point that it's shielded against Scratha ha'rethe's attentions. It *isn't* safe for powerful people to be in this room for long. Quite bluntly, from a ha'rethe's perception, it looks as though we're hiding a weapon. They tend to get extremely agitated and not ask questions first when they feel threatened. I'd very much like to resolve the purpose of your visit and send you on your way before a crisis arises."

"Before I leave," Idisio said abruptly, setting down the piece of bread he'd been nibbling on, "I'd want to see Riss, in any case. Could you send for—" He stopped, catching the faint wince that crossed Seg's face. "What? Did something happen? Did she—is she—" He rose to his feet, hardly aware of the motion, alarm rushing into a staccato beat in his ears.

Seg grimaced and made a patting motion in the air with both hands. "Ha'inn," he said, "Please, calm yourself—allow the tincture to—"

"What happened to Riss?" Idisio demanded, not raising his voice but *projecting* the imperative to answer. Seg's hand went to his throat. He gagged, eyes rolling back in his head, and went to his knees.

Alyea stepped in front of Idisio a moment later. Her hand cracked sharply across his cheek. *"Calm down,"* she said with a matching intensity to the tone he'd just used. He staggered back a step, overbalanced, and went down, sprawling roughly across the floor. He twisted to his feet a heartbeat later, turning to lock glares with her.

"You *dare,*" he spat.

"I've dared worse," she retorted. "*Calm. Down.* Trust me, Idisio. *Trust* me. Take a breath and *calm* yourself. You won't get any answers at all if you choke the sense out of Seg!"

Seg sucked in a noisy breath, another, then grabbed hold of a nearby chair and hauled himself up into it, his face grey-green and his body trembling noticeably. "You've come into far more of your power than I expected to happen this quickly," he rasped, one hand on his stomach as though feeling nauseous. "Ha'inn, I will answer, I swear it. But Lord Peysimun is right. You *must* calm yourself. I can offer whatever you might desire by way of distraction—aesa, esthit, myself—"

Idisio choked, staring in astounded disbelief. "I'm sorry, did you just—?"

"I can only draw on what I know to be in this room at the moment." Seg's mouth drew aside into a rueful smile. "I doubt I would be sufficient for your needs, ha'inn, but I would do my best if that is what you—"

"*No,*" Idisio said emphatically. "Gods! You people are *insane*—Alyea, *what* are you laughing at?"

"It would take too long to explain," she said, still grinning. "Another time. Right now, let's all sit back down and finish this excellent tea, please. It's far too lovely to water the plants with."

He stayed on his feet, stubborn, head lowered like a sulky gerho. "Tell me what's happened to Riss," he said. "I'm as calm as I'm going to get, so just fucking tell me."

Seg rubbed a hand across his face, glancing down at the floor as though listening to something far below. Finally he said, "Scratha ha'rethe called her. The ceremony was a few days ago."

"Called?" Idisio said, bewildered. "What does that even mean?" He glanced at Alyea. She shut her eyes, a pained expression on her face. "Are you saying she's *dead*?"

"It's more complicated than that," Seg began.

"Yes," Alyea interrupted. "In northern terms, yes. You'll never see her again." She winced, blinking rapidly. "Oh. Maybe you will. Oh, *damnit*." She waved both hands at the men to stop them from speaking, then put her face in her hands. "I know what we're here to do now," she said, her voice muffled. "Seg, I'm afraid you're really, *really* not going to like this."

The northern priest, sitting quietly near the door, rose to his feet. "I think it best if s'e-kath Segnilious and I withdraw at this point," he murmured.

Seg hesitated, then stood as well. "You're right, s'iope Moir. Some things, even I can't afford to know. If you'll excuse me, Lord Peysimun, ha'inn." He bowed and followed the northern priest from the room, shutting the door gently behind them.

"What's so serious, then?" Idisio said waspishly. He'd been starting to feel comfortable with Seg's presence. The man's abrupt withdrawal was jarring. "What, are we supposed to kill someone?"

"Yes," Alyea said, keeping her gaze averted. "Cafad Scratha."

Chapter 40

Drums brought Allonin back to consciousness, a steady, rolling beat that served as a path to awareness. As he rubbed haze from his eyes and rose to his feet, details cleared: The heavy scent of ceremonial incense, underlaid with dank moisture and sulfur; the smoldering braziers set in a shallow arc between him and a ridiculously enormous lake; the fluted, twisted, opalescent outcroppings that rose from the water and hung from the cavern roof.

He stared, unable to comprehend the vision for a long moment. He'd never seen anything *remotely* like this before. Light glimmered across the surface of the lake as though on wet rock, doing absolutely nothing to penetrate the black water. Lanterns hung on sturdy frames a hand span taller than himself, placed in another, equally shallow arc to his other side, leaving him halfway between the smoking braziers and the lanterns.

The cavern went on well beyond the reach of the light, at a guess. The heavy blackness could have been an illusion or a trick of perspective, but the booming echo of the drums suggested otherwise. Allonin turned in place, blinking against the stinging smoke, shaking his head in bemused admiration.

"This is *majestic*," he said aloud, half-expecting an answer in spite of his evident solitude, but heard only the drums, endlessly rolling out an evenly paced rhythm.

He turned around again, studying his surroundings with more care, listening to the echoes, gauging the reflections of the lantern-light and the swirls of incense smoke. He peered up at the ceiling, nodding at the sight of darker patches among the shadows.

"Tunnels," he said under his breath. "Sound tunnels. There's nobody else in this room but me."

He turned and faced the lake, his heartbeat skittering for a moment at the implications of his isolation. Nobody would be able to help him if something went wrong—and nobody else could get *hurt* if something went wrong. It served as confirmation of his worst fears: This was a genuine blood trial, the same as proper desert lord supplicants endured—and, *sometimes*, survived.

I'm about to face a ha'rethe. The one creature I was told I mustn't ever get close to. Holy gods and murders, I've entirely lost my mind. I'm about to die horribly.

But his sister had done it, against far higher odds and in worse straits. He couldn't fail where Azni succeeded. Allonin suspected he would stalk the world as a crazed *shiabanse* if he died in this trial, driven by the sheer embarrassment of being weaker than his sister.

Petty thoughts, but they drove back the stark terror and allowed him to catch his breath, steadying his spine and stance alike.

The drums changed rhythm from smooth symmetry to jagged chaos, as though each drummer had chosen to pursue their own beat. Allonin winced, squinting at the ceiling, and hoped they'd choose cooperation again soon. The tunnels that amplified the rolling beat now shook the discordance into ear-shattering echoes.

The light flickering across the surface of the lake slowly turned golden, sparkling into a fine mist that rose to hang just above the motionless water. Allonin stared in astounded wonder, once more caught by the surreal beauty of the moment. It took him a few moments to realize that the drums had stopped.

Silence hung heavy in the cavern. Then the mist swirled up into a sinuous figure, overlapping dark and pale spots appearing where eyes would be on a human.

You are here, a voice said. *This is good. I was afraid you would refuse, and I would be trapped here forever.*

Allonin blinked, staring; opened his mouth, found no words, and covered his confusion by kneeling, head bowed.

Do not speak to me out loud, the voice said. *They are listening. You may wish to offer whatever the current ceremonial greeting is, to appease them.*

Allonin's mouth moved, shaping silent bewilderment. At last he raised his head and said, "Honor to your grace." The words came out far too shaky and weak for his liking. He tried again: "I am honored by your presence this day." Silently, tentatively, he added, *I don't understand, ha'inn.*

I am not ha'inn, the voice said. The figure turned as though dancing, as though laughing. *I am not proper ha'rethe, either. I have very little time in which to speak. They are watching for trouble. Will you help me? I will give you what you seek and impose no bond upon you in return, if you will help me.*

What do you want? Allonin asked.

I wish you to kill Lord Evkit. He has enslaved me for a very long time. I wish to be free.

Allonin sat back on his heels, staring at the lithe form. His thoughts stuttered from astonishment into a growing suspicion. At length, he said, *I recall hearing that there are rather a lot of lies involved in blood trials. Forgive me the discourtesy, but what you say makes no sense to me.*

It makes no sense to wish for my freedom? The figure turned, turned again, shimmering colors rippling in indignation or amusement; Allonin couldn't tell.

It makes no sense for you to ask that of me. *I have already agreed to serve Lord Evkit in order to protect another. You must know that. This feels like a test of my honor, ha'inn.*

The figure stilled, colors dimming to a solid, pale blue shade. It stayed quiet for some heartbeats, then said, *Come to me, supplicant. You are worthy of my attention.* It reached out a hand, beckoning imperiously. *We will begin now.*

Allonin let out a long, shaky breath, rising to his feet, surprised to find his hands trembling. So it had been a test, and a nasty one. He could well imagine what happened to anyone jumping at that offer. What a brutally effective way to separate out the rebellious before they gained the power to be dangerous.

Expecting to feel cold water rising along his legs, he glanced down to find himself standing as securely atop the lake as though on solid rock.

Come to me, the figure repeated, beckoning again. *Closer, supplicant.*

Allonin swallowed back a surge of terror and made himself move forward. He paused just out of arm's reach, then took the final steps to stand beside the once more iridescently glowing form.

The rock beneath his feet dissolved without warning, dropping him into lukewarm water. A startled inhale flooded his lungs, and he choked, coughing, thrashing in uncontrollable panic.

I do not lie, supplicant, the ha'rethe said. *I want my freedom.*

Oh, fuck—the words crossed Allonin's mind with crystal clarity, as red began to lace his vision, his eyes rolling back in his head, limbs thrashing, desperately straining to reach the surface. *I'm going to die, fuck, fuck, fuck*—

He felt something wrap around his legs and draw him further down, the pressure and heat of the water around him increasing rapidly. He managed one last, despairing, silent apology to Azni for failing her yet again, then surrendered to the black of unconsciousness.

Chapter 41

"*You are fucking kidding me,*" Idisio said, his face losing all color, his eyes hazing to a uniform dark grey. "Please tell me that's a joke!"

Alyea looked away. "I wish I could." Images roiled through her mind, unmistakable memories flush with fire and agony. "Aqeyva, Idisio. Keep it shielded."

"*Deiq* wants *us* to—" Idisio stopped, breathing hard. "He *is* insane."

"Aqeyva," she repeated.

"I *know,*" he snapped, then went quiet for a time, his breathing evening out. Eventually, he muttered, "Why?"

"Because Scratha ha'rethe intends to destroy everyone in this Fortress, and use—the energy from that—" She couldn't say *Riss's child,* because that would set Idisio off beyond all chance of sanity—"To reach out across the southlands, killing everything it can find to increase its power. Lord Scratha is the ha'rethe's eyes and ears in the surface world. Without him, it's nearly blind and deaf—and *weakened.* It won't have the—the leverage to act that it has now."

"Then why hasn't it done something direct already? And *why* would it be interested in *Riss*?"

"What makes you think *I* would know?" Alyea retorted, hoping he wouldn't notice the evasion.

Idisio stared at the ceiling, his frown deepening. "Duty," he said under his breath. "Oh, damnit. It's because she's pregnant. It's going to take over her child, the way the Qisani ha'reye did with yours. That's why it hasn't done anything yet... it's waiting for something...."

He trailed off, forehead wrinkling as though he'd begun to examine an even more unpleasant line of thought. Alyea bit her lip, trying not to remember the sluggishly moving red tendrils, adamantly refusing to link that image to the concept of *her child*. That would be her only child, the way things were turning out, and it was *far* beyond monstrous. *I produced that. Gods. What will Riss's child look like? It has to be past the time of shaping, almost to its soul-day –*

Idisio's voice broke her away from brooding. "No," he said, his eyes black, his skin turning grey. "I'm not going to allow it. *No*. She deserves better than to be used like this—"

"Idisio—" Alyea started to her feet, putting out a hand, not sure what to say or do.

"*No*. I'm done following orders. You go do the bidding of your *husband*." Idisio infused the word with venomous contempt. "*I'm* going after Riss."

"It's too late," Alyea blurted.

Idisio's gaze locked on her face with unsettling intensity. "It better not be," he said, then yanked the door open and strode from the room. "Take me to the pool," Alyea heard him tell someone in the hallway, with a shiver of command in his voice that nearly made *her* rush to direct him properly. "Take me to the temple. *Right now*."

Chapter 42

I do not lie, a voice said. *That is not one of my flaws. Vanity, yes. Selfishness, perhaps. But never deceit.*

A room formed around Allonin: A space seemingly cut from solid rock, devoid of furniture, tapestries, or any other human comforts. The air felt chill and stagnant, laden with old odors and mildew. He couldn't help a grimace of discomfort as he turned in place, looking at his new surroundings.

"At least I'm not dead yet," he muttered under his breath, and was surprised by a sharp trill of laughter from somewhere nearby. Turning again, squinting, he barely caught a glimpse of a momentary distortion in the air.

"No, you are not dead yet," someone said—not the same voice as the ha'rethe. "Such wisdom, such perceptiveness. Humans never disappoint."

Silence, the ha'rethe said. *You are irrelevant. Be still.*

"I'm an irrelevancy you have no power over," the voice retorted. Narrow-eyed, Allonin watched the distortion move across the room and back. "And whose fault is *that*?"

Be still.

"I'm not irrelevant, anyway, simply because you can't control me." Again, the harsh laugh shrilled out. "We're being rude. This no-family supplicant wishes to understand what's happening to and around him."

No-family? Allonin began to protest, caught himself just in time. A sharp pang of loss burned in his chest for a moment. *I'm not Aerthraim any longer. I never will be, ever again.*

I will explain. You will be still! Increasing tension chilled, rather than heated, the air.

No laughter this time, but a grumbling cough of irritation. "No. You shut up for once and let *me* talk. I've heard enough of your speeches for ten lifetimes. Maybe I'll get through to this one, where you keep *failing*." The air warmed back to neutral as that voice spoke.

Allonin took one last look around the room, desperately hoping for any sign of an exit. Finding none, he shrugged and sat down, closing his eyes. "Anytime you're done bickering," he said mildly. "I'll be right here, waiting."

The laugh held a deeper timbre this time, as though the voice's owner was actually amused. "There, see?" it said. "He's not like the usual supplicants. Let me try a different approach. You can always apply *your* brand of persuasion if I fail. It wouldn't work the other way around."

The following silence held a distinctly petulant feeling, the sense of a resigned *hrmph.*

"You're not teyanin," the voice said, tone more measured now, as though the creature were calming down at last. "Why are you here? Obviously you're here to get the gods' own power and rule the world, but *why*?"

"I don't want power," Allonin said, not opening his eyes. "I want to save my sister."

A short silence. Then, "You don't want power? To be able to destroy your enemies with a gesture, to have a partner fall into your bed without question, to correct the wrongs you see around you and replace corruption with glorious righteousness? You could change the world with these gifts."

"No. None of that." He paused, then added, "I used to want power as you describe, but not these days. I've seen... what it does to people. I don't think it's possible to have that kind of power without slowly going mad. I'll settle for sanity."

"Interesting," the voice said slowly. "You might be the one to help us after all. I hope so. I'd hate to kill you."

"I'd dislike that, myself," Allonin said dryly. "What is it you want?"

"You've already been told," the voice said. "Freedom. When the *hask* bound *teyhaerth,* it lost everything. The hask holds its power. Teyhaerth is directed to ask every supplicant to attack the hask, as you correctly guessed. It cannot refuse this duty. Those who enthusiastically agree, die. Those who refuse with proper and true indignation are turned into another channel for teyhaerth's power. You did neither. This is a new thing, and we do not see new things."

"And who are you?" Allonin said, wishing he dared open his eyes. Instinct warned him to stay away from vision for the moment. "You're clearly not... teyhaerth." Something about that name tugged at him. He'd heard it, or a very similar one, before.

"My name doesn't matter. Call me Grey, if you like. I hear that's a popular name among those opposing the hask." The statement was flat, devoid of any humor.

"If I refuse to help you," Allonin said, "and instead stand by my oath to—"

Grey cut in, voice sharp for the first time. "*The hask*."

"—Yes. To the one we are speaking of so carefully."

"Names have power."

Air moved nearby, distorting into random swirls. Allonin bit the inside of his cheek and kept his eyes shut. More than likely, this was another test of his self-control.

He said, "Yes. What will you do if—"

"Nothing." The air stilled completely, leaving a stale taste in the back of Allonin's mouth.

Allonin drew in a long breath, turning that deceptively simple answer over in his head. *Nothing* could mean so many things. In this context, it seemed safest to assume the worst interpretation applied. The memory of water filling his lungs tightened his throat with momentary horror: He wasn't actually *here*. This entire conversation was playing out inside his own head while his physical body slowly drowned.

Panic brought him to his feet. He looked around, searching for reassurance in the shifting almost-darkness around him. Grey and white tendrils swayed among the shadows, like seaweed on a strong current; he swallowed hard, wishing he hadn't opened his eyes.

"An oath under duress—" he began, voice wavering.

"Irrelevant. Make your choice. Agree to help us, or refuse. Gain power, or gain nothing for all your effort. What is the value of your life?"

Words rose, unbidden, surprising him even as they emerged. "Without honor, my life is worth *nothing*. I swore an oath to protect—the one you name *hask*. I will not break my word."

"So you hold to your word now, when it is to a man with power, where you readily broke it when dealing with women?" Grey and white swirled into a female form, swiftly darkening into flowing hair and recognizable features: his sister. *You promised!* she said, pointing at him accusingly. *You broke your promise!*

Allonin went back a step, feeling as though he'd been physically slapped. How had the ha'rethe seen that? Regaining his composure, he swallowed hard, then said, hoarsely, "Yes. I am aware of my flaws."

His sister's ghost-form said, voice deeply contemptuous, "You seek to protect your sister because you do not believe she, a female, can protect herself."

"—No. No, she's—she's capable of—it's just that I—I want to make amends for—" He stopped, gathering his thoughts. He was dealing with a ha'rethe. It was going to try to twist any argument round, for its own perverse amusement if for no other reason; he'd never win by playing along. "With respect, my decisions and reasons are my own. You've asked me for a choice. I've made that choice. I won't breach my outstanding oath. I see no value in continuing this conversation."

Laughter shivered in the air once more. "Well done," the voice said. "Very, very well done. I can see why he thought you a prize catch." The air shimmered, distortion taking form: Blurry colors, vaguely humanoid shape, something like a hand outstretched. "Come. I will give you my gift."

Allonin's knees went weak. He staggered a step sideways before catching his balance. "This was all another *test*?" he demanded, appalled. Laughter answered; the figure beckoned once more. "Holy *fuck*," he muttered under his breath, unable to stop the words from emerging. His entire body felt drenched in icy sweat. *Is this what full desert lords go through? No wonder they're such arrogant bastards afterwards.*

"Every word was true," the figure said. "And yet I am bound by my own oaths and chains to give you what power I have left to spare. So come, take what you are due, and leave me to mourn my captivity in peace."

Allonin took a step toward the distorted form, his legs shaking. Then he stopped, nausea rising hot and acid in his throat as a memory rose in his mind: *It's good you took Lit'l Red, you know. Salas wanted him next.*

"Dear gods," he said under his breath. "I—I can't—*damnit*." The figure waited, watching, stolid and impassive.

"I can't—if you're a slave—if you're not truly willing—I can't do this," Allonin said, the words bitter in his mouth. "I won't take a forced gift. No. I refuse."

The figure dissolved into a fine dusting of ash that melted away before it reached the ground.

Thank you, the ha'rethe said. *You are the first in a very long time to say that.*

The sound of drums crashed into Allonin's ears as the room flickered and wavered into a larger, darker cavern.

The ha'rethe's voice coiled underneath the drums, nearly an inverse sound, shaping meaning from chaos. *You have earned my respect. I give you freely what I have to offer, without condition or constraint. It is not much. Most of my self is bound. I have kept a very few small slivers aside, gifts for those who earn my true respect. I have only one remaining. Now that final piece is yours. Remember me....*

Light exploded behind Allonin's eyes, an array of nameless colors. He dimly registered his own screams, the abrupt silence of the drums—and the groan of collapsing rock.

Chapter 43

Blood darkening the sand at her feet. Revenge turning to bitter ash in her mouth. Acrid doubt and a burrowing guilt destroying what should have been a satisfying moment....

Last time she'd killed on Scratha Fortress lands, the ha'rethe had nearly driven Alyea mad by mirroring her own doubts back at her, forcing her to accept the reality of what she'd done.

Pieas had been a rapist, a drug addict, a wastrel. Entirely and comprehensively a cruel, vicious man. He'd deserved death far more than Cafad Scratha. Nothing she'd found out about Pieas since that day changed that, even as he stared at her in nightmares, telling her she was making a dreadful mistake—*not* what he'd said in reality:

Gods know, my life won't be any loss to the world, he'd said as he knelt, tilting his chin back to give her clear access to his throat. *Out of all the people in this camp, I'm the most deserving of death right now.* He'd been terrified and shaking, but determined. He'd held still, eyes open, watching her as she picked up the knife he'd tossed to the ground for her to use, for her to kill him with—

She remembered, clearly, wanting someone to interfere, *wishing* someone would stop her, tell her this was all just one more dreadful test, that she didn't actually need to do it.

Nobody interfered.

She stepped around behind Pieas, unable to face that wide-eyed stare, hating herself for cowardice. Risked one more glance at the watching faces, searching for anything that even hinted *stop*, but found only blankness.

The hilt shivered as she drew the blade hard across Pieas's throat from behind, from beneath one ear to the other. The movement felt awkward, not at all graceful, and Pieas jerked back, a growling gurgle erupting from his mouth. He voided himself, and began to fall back against her. Nearly panicking, she shoved, sending him sprawling forward, his head at an impossible angle. She'd sliced halfway through his neck, and there was *so much blood*—

Alyea leaned against a wall, trembling with the intensity of memory. She'd managed not to think about that moment—*much*—since realizing she'd be returning here. Now, faced with another, far colder killing, it was all rushing back with vibrant immediacy. She could *smell* the piss and shit in the air, and the blood, the blood, *gods the blood*—

"Excuse me," someone said in a tone of sharp disapproval. "Lord Peysimun, is it?"

Alyea made herself open her eyes and look at the speaker, then pressed back hard against the wall as though she could escape through solid rock. For a heartbeat, she thought she felt the surface behind her begin to yield;

lurched forward a step in reflexive horror. Walking through walls—no. That was too much to accept, too absurd a potential.

Besides, flight would be cowardice. This moment shouldn't—couldn't—be run away from. She'd known Pieas had a sister, but she'd never realized he'd been a *twin*. The nose, the eyes, the chin—and that voice—gods, another octave down and this woman would be a match for Pieas.

According to Northern Church doctrine, killing one half of a twin was an offense against every one of the gods. She'd never paid much mind to the Creeds before, but abruptly, renewed guilt pressed against her stomach like an unyielding metal brick.

"I'm Nissa," the woman said. "Daimaina of Scratha Fortress. I *expected* to find you in your rooms. I suggest we return there—"

"You're his sister," Alyea said, scarcely aware of speaking. "His twin. I didn't know!"

Nissa froze, her eyes widening. "You knew Pieas," she said, nearly a whisper. "You—wait. *You're* the one who killed him! I knew Peysimun sounded familiar—"

She balled up a fist, aiming for Alyea's face, hesitated a scant heartbeat, then unleashed the blow. Alyea was already ducking out of the way, grabbing for Nissa's arm. She latched on, twisted, shoved—Nissa screamed, something snapped—*Her elbow, I broke her elbow, shit*—and Nissa reeled away, calling for help, for guards, for Seg—sobbing, staggering, cursing Alyea to all the hells at once.

Alyea stepped forward and swung, more carefully this time. The other woman crashed into a wall and slid to the ground, limp, bleeding profusely from lip and scalp and arm, the smell of urine strong in the air. *Still hit too hard. Why am I misjudging my strength so badly?*

Alyea knelt long enough to be sure she hadn't killed Nissa outright, then got out of there before the guards could arrive. Thank the gods there hadn't been any *with* the woman, although as head of household she bloody well *ought* to have had an escort—

—*Not that I listened to that bit of protocol particularly well myself at first, and she's new at this, has to be, I was here what, two months ago? Not even?* Alyea shook her head and pushed analysis aside for another time. Her mind seemed to be working faster than usual, jittering from thought to thought in a dizzying swirl.

She could already hear the guards racing towards the fallen woman, could judge which corridor they were coming down, and *saw* a path that would take her to Scratha without interference. She felt—*invincible*—stronger, faster, smarter, *better* than the humans around her—and there was prey to hunt, a specific, marked target that would be an easy, enjoyable warm-up to the larger goal—

—*Wait. What? What larger—what?*

Just fucking go, someone said, a familiar voice—it was herself but not herself, an overlay/underlay that took her a moment to recognize.

Deiq?

I'm on my way. There isn't time to argue. Go!

A wave of imperative swamped sense. She sank into the loping run of a predator unleashed.

Chapter 44

Do you care for the northern girl?

Idisio remembered his bewilderment and Riss's flushed face, her hair straggling from chasing him through the hallways to reach this spot. The trees were as majestic as he recalled, the water nothing more than a shallow, sand-bottomed pond.

Take a knife and prick your finger.

"Ha'inn," the servant behind him said, voice wobbling nervously. "Ha'inn, how else may I... serve?"

Idisio drew in a breath, irritated at the undertone of... refusal, rejection, falseness... the servant desperately wanted to be dismissed without having to do anything more. Idisio began to say: *If I wanted your service, you'd be glad to give it*—but no, that wasn't right, wasn't *him,* came from a darkness he refused to accept.

A presence, like silk over alabaster, stirred the air at Idisio's back. "I'll handle this, s'e," Moir said quietly. "Thank you. You may go."

Idisio turned to face the northern priest as the released servant hurried from the room. "I thought you went with Seg," he said, scowling at the man. "Got bored already?"

"What are you doing, ha'inn?" Moir said, ignoring Idisio's gibe. He stood straight-backed, his hands folded over his stomach, watching Idisio with a disconcertingly perceptive gaze.

"Not your concern, *s'iope,*" Idisio retorted. "Go away before you get hurt."

Moir smiled, an oddly dark expression on his lean face. "I've been hurt before, ha'inn. Are you planning to attempt a rescue?"

"She deserved better than this," Idisio said roughly. "This is *wrong.*"

"There are many wrong things in this world," Moir observed, not moving. "Interfering with this situation, as I understand it, could destroy this entire Fortress and everyone inside. Is that less wrong?"

Idisio's chest went tight, a hard heat rising to his face as he remembered: *Broken bodies, smoke, shattered buildings, huge boulders tumbled about like pebbles*—

"She doesn't deserve this," he said, nearly whispering the words. "I have to try."

"I think you already know you do not *have to* do anything," the priest said. "You stopped to talk to me. You *want* to be talked out of this, ha'inn."

Idisio turned to stare at the shallow pool, his breathing thick in his chest. *There –*

He saw it now, a faint haze at the bottom, where sand seemed to be moving in random patterns, as though disturbed by something below. He could leap, one long jump, land on that spot, push through, as he'd done at the Wall.

Broken bodies, shattered buildings –

I can't be responsible for a second disaster like that. A third, if you count what happened here *once already.*

The ha'rethe had asked: *Do you care for the northern girl? I see the answer, you need not reply.*

Idisio had never been entirely sure what answer the ha'rethe picked out of his head.

Stop worrying about her so much, Deiq had advised. *You'll likely forget about her within a tenday after we leave.*

I did. I completely forgot about her until I came back here. Well – not entirely. Another fragment of conversation – with his mother, this time, rose in memory:

We're friends.

Friends. But you're going back to her? The innkeeper thought you were... going back to her. Going south. One day. – Do you love her?

I don't know.

He'd gone on to tumble a servant girl by way of distracting himself from that question, and *that* ended badly, to say the least.

Scratha's opinion had been equally brutal: *Feelings like love are a vulnerability that first-generation ha'ra'hain do* not *have. Ever. For anyone.*

Everyone seems to think I can't have human emotions, even though I'm half-human and grew up believing I was human. Just because I'm going to live a little longer –

Deiq's sour comment rolled through his memory: *By the time you start to slow down, Riss's grandchildren will probably be long in their graves.*

– Not that she'll ever have *grandchildren, now –*

Idisio sank to his knees, caught between a sob and a howl of fury, and wrapped his arms around himself, as much to stop himself from moving as for reassurance.

"Ha'inn," Moir said, circling around, kneeling in front of Idisio. His calm voice came as a relief after the array of sharp, tumbling memories. Moir regarded Idisio with naked sympathy. "I'm sorry, ha'inn. I know this is a painful choice: To save an individual who has touched your heart, or to protect a wider community. There is never a good answer."

"There has to be a way," Idisio whispered. "There's an answer. I'm just not seeing it." He rose to his feet, new determination flushing through him. Sitting on his arse wouldn't bring the answer to him. Time to go *find* the solution. *Make* a solution, if all else failed.

"Ha'inn," Moir said, looking up at him. "Sometimes the answer we like the least is the true one—"

"Oh, shut up," Idisio said, and leapt for the hazy spot in the pool.

Chapter 45

Corridors blurred past. Wall-hangings, statues, and other decorations were barely a blip of color in her peripheral vision as Alyea ran. She dodged around more than one startled servant without pause. Her strides felt impossibly fluid and powerful. It was a heady, exhilarating feeling to move this fast, this confidently—almost like being in the *clee* trance that had taken her from Scratha Fortress out into the middle of the desert.

Don't think about that, damnit, Deiq snarled. *Don't think about them.* A hard push in her mind redirected her attention away from the past and back to the moment just as a very *solid* form stepped out in front of her.

She dropped a shoulder and kept going, intending to shove the obstacle from her path. The person stepped aside, hands locking onto her, turning, and *threw* her back up the corridor. Her own momentum carried her, tumbling and cursing, a good thirty feet. By the time she gathered herself back upright, two small hallway tables and a vase of flowers lay smashed and her left shin was ablaze with pain from smacking into something unyielding along the way.

Seg stood still, arms crossed, regarding her with a definite frown. He made no attempt to cross the distance he'd put between them. "I cannot allow you to harm Lord Scratha," he said.

Water from the vase seeped across the floor, casting a flat tang into the air, the crushed flowers adding bitter, grassy notes. She balanced on her right leg, trying not to show how much pain she was in. The unyielding, rolling drive had faded with the interruption, leaving her half-sick with conflicting thoughts: What the hells had she been *thinking*? She'd been on her way to kill a man who hadn't done anything wrong—yet, it was the safest thing for the entire Fortress, the entire southlands—but there must be another way—

There isn't, Deiq said, impatient. *Godsdamnit, we can't let Scratha wake up!* Tell *him that!*

"We can't let Lord Scratha wake up," Alyea said aloud.

Seg's expression hardened. "I'm well aware of that, Lord Peysimun. That doesn't require killing him."

"Idiot," Deiq said from behind Alyea. She startled, turning to face him, yelped, then backed away several steps before she caught herself.

Raised black and red lines swirled around his body in patterns all too reminiscent of the *child* at the Qisani. His eyes, devoid of pupil, held a pale, opalescent sheen that made her think of Teilo. He seemed larger than she remembered—broader—*harsher*.

He didn't even glance at Alyea, his attention entirely fixed on Seg. "One last chance, *s'e-kath*."

Seg shook his head, eyes narrowing, and didn't move.

Alyea blurted, "Wait—" The word emerged far too late. Deiq had already begun moving. Seg unfolded his arms, raising his hands in a defensive posture; Deiq slammed into him, knocking the servant backward into a solid wall not far away. Stone cracked, blood splattered, and Seg fell, limp, head at a sharply wrong angle.

Deiq turned and met Alyea's gaze. "*Go*," he said, then leapt into motion once more, headed elsewhere—leaving the matter of Cafad Scratha to her.

She swore under her breath as multiple guards crowded into the hallway both ahead and behind her, weapons ready, faces darkening with anger at the sight of Seg's crumpled body.

"Don't make me kill you," she said, flattening her voice to a dead calm, then threw sharp command into the next words: "*Get out of my way*."

The guards staggered aside, expressions bewildered. She dodged through them before they could recover. Lord Scratha's rooms were around the next corner, guards at the door already raising their weapons. She ordered them aside as she had the others. They didn't move, but their muscles froze for a heartbeat, two, three. Then she was past them and into the room, door closed behind her, warded shut, turning to face motion to her right—

A tall woman with very short hair stood with back pressed against a wall, eyes wide. Two more faces, one with starkly bloodshot eyes, peered out around the edges of a curtain-covered doorway, expressions equally worried.

"Don't hurt us," the woman said, voice shaking. "Don't hurt him. Please. *Please*."

The fear in her face and voice stopped Alyea more effectively than slamming into a stone wall. She opened her mouth, trying to find words, caught between the insistence Deiq's command drilled into her very bones and the overwhelming refusal rising from deep within herself.

"I can help him," the woman said into that pause. "I can reach him. Please. Let me try. He doesn't—you don't have to hurt him. I can—"

Something stirred, a rippling in the air, heat and cold layering against her skin: "*Alyea*?" Lord Scratha said from the doorway to his bedroom. He leaned against the frame, seemingly still half-asleep, frowning at them. He was naked, and apparently unaware of that fact.

The door to the hallway shook under a barrage of blows. Alyea could feel cracks beginning to form in the light wood, tearing tiny gaps in her determination that it stay shut.

"Cafad," the woman said, and the complex emotion in that one word struck Alyea dumb all over again.

The desert lord straightened, slowly, his face smoothing into a harsher cast. His gaze never left Alyea. The other woman might as well have been invisible. "Ah," he said. "So. Betrayal. I've been expecting this."

"Caffy, *no*," the nameless woman blurted, taking several steps toward him. "Don't think that way—"

He ignored her. "I always knew they'd send an assassin when they decided I was too bothersome," he said to Alyea. "I didn't think it would be *you*." Contempt swirled in his voice, rich and dark.

Cracks spread, met, and began splintering. Alyea stepped sideways, taking refuge in a corner as the door yielded to the determination of a dozen angry guards.

"*Stop*!" the woman cried, turning as the doorway filled with the glint of weapons and the dark of outraged expressions. She pointed imperiously, motioning the men back. "Get out. Out! You'll make it worse—let me handle this—"

"Lichni, move aside," Scratha said, a quiet counterpoint to the woman's passion, and pointed at Alyea. His eyes took on an unholy yellow tint. "Kill her."

"No—" The woman moved forward a step, her arms outspread as though to sweep the guards out of the room.

The guards hesitated a scant heartbeat, then shouldered her aside, their attention fixed on Alyea, watching for her least twitch, sharp edges ready to respond in a fraction of a heartbeat.

Alyea drew in a long breath, watching them as they watched her. Knowledge shifted, turning like a leaf in a strong wind, giving her a wild array of unforeseen options. Choosing the simplest, she pressed back against the stone wall, felt it yield, and simply stepped *away*—moving through a blurred moment of rock dust on her tongue and a rough scraping against her skin to emerge into open air thick with dust and the complaints of startled chickens.

A dozen of the small birds scattered as she took a few bewildered steps forward, blinking grit from her eyes and searching for threats. An abrupt drumming overhead brought her gaze up to a thin metal sheet that shuddered overhead, stung by heavy rain.

Moments later, water began cascading from the edges of the roof, cutting ridges into the sandy ground beneath, stealing the dust from the air. The air beyond the overhang turned hazy with rain, pools and rivers forming briefly, then draining along neatly-concealed pipes.

The chickens clustered around Alyea's feet, clearly unhappy at the downpour, hop-fluttering past her and up steep ramps into hen-houses to either side.

She stood still, staring out at the grey air, lost in a long moment of fey introspection.

I could have killed them all.

She waited to hear Deiq's sour response, but no answer came. She didn't need to hear his voice, though. She already knew what he would say.

A sharp cry came from beyond the wall Alyea had stepped through: a woman's voice. "*Caffy – don't – !*"

The words cut off, a wash of ugly death spilling through the air in its wake. Alyea moved further from the wall, shivering with abrupt horror and a bone-deep desire to get away from this array of unfolding atrocities. Whoever that woman had been, she'd clearly cared a great deal for Scratha, enough to sacrifice her life in a failed attempt to bring him back to sanity.

Alyea held no desire to seek out Deiq, or Idisio; no interest in remaining anywhere near this grief-haunted pile of rock. *And I don't have to stay here. I can use Deiq's power to move as he does – just enough to get clear of Scratha lands, and then he goes his way and I go mine – I can't be a part of this any longer.*

Where she would go after stepping clear, how she would survive, with north and likely southlands closed to her, at least one furious ha'ra'ha on her trail – none of that mattered at the moment. She would rather take up life as a fisher, or cook, or – anything – anything other than this insane, complicated tangle.

Is fear a reason to allow another to die that you may live? Juric's voice, clear and cold, came back to her, laden with memories of still air and the smell of scorching-hot sand.

"I'm not afraid," she muttered. "I'm choosing to walk away. This is impossible."

The test of Comos is the test of the self. It is a test of the ego, to see if you can set your own wants aside for the larger good... You cannot be a leader if you listen only to yourself... The desert is harsh, and life is not fair. A cowardly or arrogant leader would cause many deaths.

Alyea shut her eyes, pressing the heels of her hands against the closed lids, and swore viciously. The words fell limp and weak under the torrential downpour a stone's throw from her nose.

If you pass all the trials and become a desert lord, what then? another voice asked, accompanied by memory of a echoing, dark stone cavern. *Is your purpose worth dying for?*

Nothing is worth dying for, she'd said in answer. *You can't help anyone or anything if you're dead.* Her original assurance now rang hollow, facile and weak.

The test of Ishrai is the test of life, the ishrait had said. *It asks you to weigh the value of living. A desert lord's life is a sacred trust and must be treated with the greatest respect.*

Micru's voice came next, words resonant with new meaning: *The trial of Datda teaches you that there are times you must kill for the larger good.* She heard the words behind the words now, the part she'd missed entirely the first time through: *There are also times you must die for the larger good.*

Which path to follow, which voice to heed? Never mind Deiq's wishes—the promises made, the intentions laid down, the plans set into motion. *I am a desert lord. What does that mean to me, what is the truest thing I can do in this moment to hold to the threefold oath I took so willingly?* The oath seemed a lifetime ago, and still only yesterday. Time tilted in her head, turning her around to face her earlier, innocent determination to conquer anything that stood in her path.

Gods, I was a fool. The thought flitted by, rueful awareness of the many side glances she'd ignored, the half-hidden, tolerant smiles.

Eredion's voice rose next, a bleak, cynical rasp: *You don't understand yet. But you will. Give it some time... Nothing looks quite the same when you realize you'll outlive most of the people around you... I've just had to get selective, over the years, on what things to care about.*

"I'm beginning to understand," she whispered. "But he's a desert lord too. His life is just as important, his oaths the same as mine—we shouldn't even *be* going against one another!"

She bent her head, stretching taut neck muscles, rubbing at the headache forming around ears and temples. Oaths, promises, and commitments tumbled through her mind like misplaced puzzle pieces settling uncomfortably askew, scattering, settling, scattering—and finally, finally clicked into a coherent pattern, threaded through with a single word: *mercy.*

Alyea raised her head, staring out at the rain. A liquid calm washed through her entire body. "Yes," she said aloud. "I understand now."

Turning, she swung sideways to the sideways and moved *elsewhere* with dizzying, weightless, joyous grace.

Shapes formed, voices broke the not-space into real dimensions once more: human perceptions, human reactions far too slow to register her as more than a flicker of movement, she dodged around animate and inanimate alike. *There—*

She wrapped one hand around a bony arm, lifting the targeted human from his feet even as she slid, dancing, through the space between moments: reached out and grasped another, softer arm, tugging that human along with as little effort as the first.

The first breath of an outraged bellow tickled the nape of her neck. She concentrated ferociously, checked her hold on the two humans, then *leapt—*

like water thrown up by a heavy stone dropping into a deep well—far, far north, to where the lines in the air felt thin and grey.

The outraged bellow hung in their wake, a scant whisper. More immediately to hand, an agonized screech arose, drilling into Alyea's sensitive ears. She shoved that human roughly aside without thinking about it, deposited the other more gently, then moved back, blinking water from her eyes, only then realizing she stood in a torrential downpour.

Gria looked up at her, face as close to green-white as southern-dark skin could reach. Her eyes were wide and rimmed with red. "What?" she said, raising one hand to shield her eyes from the rain, and squinted at Alyea, emanating raw, chaotic shock. "*What*?"

"That's not your line," Alyea said absently, turning her head to make sure Scratha hadn't broken anything when she pushed him clear. He hunched in an undignified sprawl on the rough ground, still screaming. She judged that his throat wouldn't last much longer at that volume.

She tried to still his voice: his screaming ratcheted up into an even more piercing squeal until she relented, allowing the original howl to resume. Gria would just have to put up with the noise.

"Take care of him. Stay here."

Shock tilted into anger: "*What*? Don't you dare—"

Alyea glanced north for a split moment, calm melting into a fierce pinch of indecision. But: *Good girl, you didn't lose your nerve,* Deiq said somewhere far away, and then, *Oh, damnit, you* didn't *kill him.*

He's been removed from Scratha lands, along with the numaina. They won't return until I tell them to.

She could feel him reaching out to pull her close—not from affection, but from a far colder calculation that he needed her strength. As though to make sure she couldn't refuse the summons, she sensed Idisio pulling as well, building the pressure into an unbreakable demand.

She yielded, and let herself be drawn into incendiary heat and acrid darkness with no expectation of ever emerging.

Chapter 46

Raw instinct turned Allonin at an impossible angle. He felt reality shift from solid to fluid, and hurled himself forward along a path that didn't properly exist—aiming only to be above the crumbling cavern, seeking solid ground, safe ground—

Something clung to his back: a thick, hooked web, dragging him back. A voice rang in his ears, *demanding* without words, emitting a blind, powerful hunger—

No, the ha'rethe said, and the pull dissolved. *You will pass into the final sleep alongside me, small one. I am sorry. This must be.*

Its voice faded. Hard stone bruised Allonin's shoulder and hip. He rolled, gagging, spitting up murky water and bile: unable to think past the moment's searing disorientation and stark awareness of one ridiculously improbable fact: *I'm alive.*

Holy gods and murders, I'm alive.

He knelt, head hanging, hands splayed out on the cold rock, and heaved up everything he'd eaten since his birth, by the feel of it.

"Well done," a voice said nearby. "Do you want to stay among the living?"

He shoved to his knees, wiping at his mouth, searching out the source of the voice: A woman, limned in a ghostly blue-grey light, holding out one hand. She was gaunt, angular, and harshly unattractive—definitely not a dying vision, unless Allonin's subconscious was even more broken than he'd thought. Even her hair was unpleasant, arranged in the multi-braided style he particularly disliked. She laughed at his bewildered stare, beckoning impatiently.

"Come with me," she said. "If you stay here, you'll be killed for what you hold."

Allonin looked down at his empty hands in a moment of utter witlessness, then splayed one hand across his chest, feeling the hot brightness flaring through his body. "Oh—" he said, looking at the woman again; seeing, with new awareness, the patterns of light laced around and through her. "You—"

"Come with me," she repeated.

He managed to lurch to his feet, unable to argue her certainty; took a wobbly step, another, and closed his fingers around hers.

Patterns on patterns, stripes on slant on curve: darkness on almost-darkness—

A fierce, hot glare: You will *regret* this day—

A story hung between the two endpoints, a journey from defiance to outright hatred between this woman and—

"—Oh," Allonin said wearily, as the darkness around him dissolved into rain-thick daylight. "I'm not so smart after all, apparently."

"But you are alive," Lord Evkit's daughter said. "Wisdom comes with experience, experience comes with age, and age only comes if you choose to stay alive." She patted his shoulder gently. "Put your face to the rain, and feel the world around you. Draw your strength from the water, the air, the earth. Let all else fade for now. You are safe for the moment."

Unable to think of anything better to do, he sat quietly for a time, letting his surroundings soak into him as the rain soaked into his hair; cautiously extending his awareness, narrowing and widening perceptions—testing all the things he'd been told desert lords could do, that he'd fought to master for so many years.

Time slowed as he focused on a passing raindrop. He studied its shape, the wavering reflection, the way it swayed and distorted—than blinked, letting time collapse back into reality, and found himself gasping for air. He thumped his chest, gagging, nearly retching until his airways stabilized, and looked up to find Lord Evkit's daughter watching him with clear amusement.

She said, "Be careful. Your body isn't ready to keep up with your mind yet."

He shook his head slowly. "I had no idea. This is—good gods." He shut his eyes, searching the internal landscape of vein and bone, watching the flow as air turned to blood and then to flesh—not at all an exact description of the process, but he found no other useful words for what he was seeing. Good sense restrained him from exploring more deeply, and brought him up to awareness of rain streaking down his face before his body fell out of step again.

Lord Evkit's daughter sat still, her eyes half-shut, seemingly looking at nothing and everything all at once. "It's addictive," she said quietly. "It's easy to lose yourself while finding out what you can do now. I spent many years, made many mistakes while I learned."

"You want to kill your father." Allonin's voice emerged flat and hard as the rocks around them.

"Oh, yes," she said, her mouth twisting briefly. "I've tried fourteen times so far. He always finds a way out. It's irritating."

Fourteen times? He couldn't think of anything to say beyond, "I'm sworn to protect him."

"I know." She bent her head and began to gather her long, rough braids into a bundle. "He won't protect you, though. He'll kill you in a half a heartbeat." She wound a black ribbon around the braids, wrapping a hand span width before tying it off. "I'm *absolutely* certain he never promised to keep *you* alive."

Allonin opened his mouth, then stopped, thinking back on the conversation with Evkit. "He said *hanaa-aerth-yin* ceremony," he said at last. "That involves mutual—"

She laughed. "No," she said. "Outsiders never do understand." She paused, studying him for a moment, then added, "It's for the safety of the huerg that we keep ourselves apart, not from arrogance or fear. Your former Family does the same—or did, long ago, before they became reckless and heartless in their pursuit of power. Our ways, their ways—we are too different from what humanity has become. We are still the eagles watching over the mewling asp-jacau pups, protecting them from burrowing snakes."

"My former—" Allonin began, then stopped at her curt laugh.

"The moment you agreed to serve my father, whether or not that promise is kept, you renounced your claim to your lineage," she said. "That has always been our law. A teyanin foolish enough to make any agreement with one of your former Family would be as surely and swiftly exiled."

"I know that," he said, mildly annoyed. "I was going to observe that by all the tales I've ever heard, my former Family is no less reckless and heartless than yours. It's also interesting that you still claim membership with *your* Family while considering me outcast."

She smiled, revealing stained, irregular teeth. "My friend," she said softly, "I *am* the head of the teyanain. My father lost his standing long ago, in my eyes, and you have announced that fall this day to all who watch with open ears."

She touched her chest with one finger.

He stared at her, appalled. "Oh, no," he said. "No—"

Her smile faded to a sympathetic expression. "What you and I carry mark us as the favored of our ha'rethe. More favored than my father, more favored than all of his athain together. My father never received this gift. He tricked the ha'rethe into slavery and stole its power for his own use. That is not the true teyanain way."

"He's going to kill me," Allonin blurted.

She laughed, sounding more truly amused this time. "You do have your slow moments," she observed. "Yes. For the last time: I rescued you because he would kill you to get what you carry, as he would kill me without pause. Under traditional rules, you owe me a life debt. I choose not to claim that, as we are both far too strong for such transactions to be safe."

"Thank you," he said, unable to think of anything else coherent or remotely polite to offer.

"Now that you have some understanding, I will offer you the honor of my name, with warning to be cautious in its use. I will explain why in a moment. My name is Cuna."

After a moment's hesitation, Allonin returned the base formula in kind, and she nodded gravely.

"Good," she said. "So now we are properly introduced and linked by a common trust." She touched her chest again. "Because of what we carry, when we speak or hear certain names, it resonates to those able to hear. I choose to avoid using names as a precaution. It makes it much more difficult for my father to find me. I think perhaps we should draw his attention, though, and have the matter of succession settled. Do you agree, my friend?"

"*Gods*, no!" Allonin put both hands out, palm forward in a warding gesture, then paused, dropped his hands back onto his thighs, and sighed. "My... friend," he said, "I'm sworn to protect your father. My sister's life is at stake. I can't put her in danger for—what?"

Cuna was laughing again, head back, roaring amusement to the grey sky above.

"What's so funny?" Allonin demanded, fighting the urge to scramble to his feet, loom over the woman, shake some sense into her, and perhaps *push* this conversation into some semblance of sanity.

Cuna motioned with one hand, pointing behind him. He rose, turning to look, a sharp hot feeling filling his stomach as he moved. Nothing but more rock and wet scrub met his gaze, and he began to turn and shout at the madwoman, his patience with games exhausted. Then stopped, looked again, narrowing vision, watching the way the rain fell.

A distortion. Two. Four. Eight? He shut his eyes, stunned: when he opened them again, eleven teyanain sat in a rough arc before him. A woman sat, smiling, at the center point of that arc.

He knew those eyes, and that smile. Even with age lines marring her face, her dark hair streaked with grey, once-supple flesh now stretched gaunt as though she hadn't eaten in weeks— still, he knew his sister.

She held out a single white rose and said, simply, "Hello, Allo."

Chapter 47

The water parted around Idisio as he leapt, the blurred spot pulling at him like a magnet. He rolled through an abstract swirl of color and out into a brilliant heat that took his breath away for a moment.

Ah. I thought you might visit, Scratha ha'rethe said. *Hold still, young one. I would rather not harm you.*

Glowing yellow spheres surrounded Idisio, each radiating tremendous heat. To his surprise, after the initial shock it felt comfortable, even soothing, despite being far above what he was used to tolerating.

Your mother was a very strong woman. I said this to you once before. Do you remember?

"I remember," Idisio said. He squinted, trying to pick out patterns, shapes, anything that would make sense of the odd globes around him.

She was flawed by her human blood, as are you yourself. The further a ha'ra'hain steps from their human heritage, the stronger they become. Your mother became strong.

"My mother was a fucking lunatic," Idisio said flatly.

Under human standards, perhaps. You must learn to see things properly, young one. It is time for you to claim your strength, rather than indulging in human weakness.

"I see just fine, thanks. Where's Riss? I want her back. She's—" He hesitated. "She's *mine.*"

She is not yours. She was never yours, and neither was the child she carried. Your outrage is false, your interest self-directed. I see you better than you see yourself, young one. Your vision is not as sharp as you believe it to be. You are too focused on being human, and that is a weakness that must be corrected.

Irritation crested into anger in the back of his mind and his mother stirred, whispering: *Words upon words, all useless, time wasting irrelevancies.*

Idisio set his teeth together and launched abruptly forward, driving against the wall of gold. He was thrown back, a sharp pain spiking through his entire body.

I did warn you to stay still, the ha'rethe said mildly.

Cages! His mother's voice rose into an outraged screech. *It dares cage us? It dares?*

"Cages are a human trick," Idisio shouted, fury overriding sense. "How *dare* you?"

I must protect myself from you, young one, Scratha ha'rethe said. *I am well aware you wish to harm me. The humans have twisted you. I do not have the energy to correct that right now, so I must settle for keeping you confined until I am finished with my current task.*

"Current *task—*" Idisio threw himself forward again, a pale haze settling across his vision. Once more, he was bounced back into the center of the globe, swearing at the pain. "*She's not a fucking* task!"

Be still. I will return to you soon.

The light around him dimmed slightly as the ha'rethe's attention withdrew.

It dares!... dares... dares... The words echoed through his mind, blurring his thoughts under a mist of outrage. His mother didn't care about Riss. She cared about being caged, trapped, held prisoner in a dark place. Never mind the lights around them, she could *feel* the darkness beyond, too similar to what she'd endured for so many years—

Softly, softly, sweet: A voice from nightmare, a voice from heaven, threaded through his mother's memories—Roise F'Heing, pinned indelibly to the back of Idisio's mind. *You're going too quickly again. Softly. Slow down.*

Cunning replaced rage. *Yes,* his mother said. *Force doesn't always work. Sometimes quiet is best. Look, son—look closely, look slowly—*

Idisio swallowed back a surge of nausea at the pain-memories ghosting along with that other voice, and narrowed his vision, studying the walls of his prison. Narrowed it again, as much to shut out the high, shrill laugh, the blood, the flames scattered through shared memory as to see more clearly; then a third time.

There. A number of the globes were slightly off-true, leaving gaps: small, but enough for an experienced street thief to slither through with a bit of focus.

One thing I do have these days is focus, Idisio thought grimly. He drew in several calming breaths, settling himself into a near-aqeyva trance, then began working his way through the opening.

Chapter 48

No tears, said a voice from another life, from a time when Alyea could still dream of dancing. A whip cut into her back, over and over, and she began to buckle, crying out *No more, no more, I'll recant, I'll say what you want to hear—*

—But the ties holding her to the post fell away, and her knees straightened, her head rising as she looked out at the gathered crowd, at the gold-robed priest waiting, bloodied whips in his hand—at the white, terrified faces of the onlookers—each one seeing the display as a foretelling of their own future—

No tears, said the man still bound and bleeding to her right—*Ethu,* that was his name, the man who risked his life to teach her how to fight, to defend herself, who'd given her the strength to choose life when death seemed the better path—

Your words have condemned this man as guilty. Persuade him to repent. Death can be fast for him if he repents.

Take your mercy and shove it up your arse and out your rot filled nose, Ethu said in response. *Take your withered cock and use it to clean your shit-ridden ears—*

At which point, memory insisted, the enraged priest began whipping Ethu, not stopping until only a tattered shell remained, limp against the restraints, life long gone.

This time, Alyea stepped forward, caught the whip away from the priest, and felled him with a single blow. *No,* she said. *This has to stop.*

A dark-haired girl rushed forward, prostrating herself on the ground at Alyea's feet. *My lady, my lady, spare me,* she said. *I never wanted to betray you. I swear it!*

Let her live, order her killed, it's all the same, a weary, half-drunk voice said from somewhere behind Alyea. *It doesn't affect anything important. All it does is define what kind of person* you *are.*

Alyea tossed the whip aside and turned her back on the pleading servant, looking for that voice. Lord Eredion of Sessin stood some distance away, watching her without expression, his arms folded across his broad chest.

I killed your nephew, she said. *I killed Pieas.*

I know. Thanks. He was getting to be a pain in the ass.

Memory inserted shocked refusal to accept that answer. Now, she nodded, understanding, and said: *I didn't do it for you, but you're welcome.*

She turned to look at Ethu again: still bound, still bleeding, but alive and watching her with a peculiar smile on his pain-lined face. *You were Pieas's teacher,* she said. *Why didn't you ever tell me that?*

You never really wanted to know, he answered. *You never asked the right questions.*

She balled her hands into fists, felt one hand wrap around something hard. Opened that hand and looked down at a small, simply carved wooden wren.

A message to live, to survive, no matter what.... A darker, older timbre overrode Ethu's voice, then faded into silence.

She turned again, looking for that voice, but found nothing. Blank air surrounded her; spectators, whipping posts, blood, and priests all banished beneath a pale amber haze.

We won't get anywhere if you don't trust me; if you're always arguing and questioning and refusing to listen, Deiq said, memory once more echoing confusion, frustration, fear down her spine.

You say trust me *a lot,* she observed. *And then you turn out to have been lying or manipulating something.* Not the first time, not the last time she'd offered up that complaint.

His laugh rang out, unexpectedly light against the moment's darkness. She answered in kind, finally understanding the absurdity of her protest.

Memory swirled again, depositing another fragment of conversation: *I think you'd hurt* yourself *before you let me come to harm,* she said, wondering, astounded.

Yes. He laughed again, but a sour note came into it this time. *And I have, over and over and over....*

It's not love, Eredion warned, a ghosting whisper along her inner ear. *Don't ever make that mistake.*

I'm not human, Deiq said. *I'm not even ha'ra'hain any longer, because of you.*

You can't blame her alone for that, Eredion said, voice stern.

Closer, more real this time, Deiq's irritable voice dragged her out of the protective patterns of memory: *Alyea, stop channeling ghosts. They're getting in the way, and I need your help....*

Barbed whips coiled around her body, shredding skin, muscle, snagging at bone—she cried out at the shock of pain, at the failure of muscle and will to protest, to retreat, to fight back against the indignity.

Warm, thick pressure surrounded her. She felt the impact of the barbs sinking into that protective shield, felt the shuddering, pained reaction of her protector, and drew in a harsh breath, relishing the momentary freedom from agony.

Then she gathered herself, focused—pushed free from the cocoon—reached, grasping the ropy tendrils, ignoring the sharp thorns piercing hands, arms, shoulders, arms—*wrenched*: not at the physical pain, not at the tangible whips slicing across her flesh, but at the source: a vast, solid mass without definable shape or color.

Strength doubled and doubled again as she drew the heaviness to her—a distant warning cry passed by without disturbing her focus—and struck, channeling everything into one precise, aqeyva-calm blow.

Cold air washed across her body, a chill shriek burst throughout her head, a vast wave of ice tumbled her sideways and sideways and sideways....

Enough, Deiq said, his voice scarcely audible. *You've done enough. Rest. You can rest now. Rest....*

She opened her eyes, finding only a mild, dark, peaceful silence. *Enough,* she agreed, and let the quiet sing her to sleep.

Chapter 49

As Idisio slid free of the cage, the structure shivered, light turning scalding for a moment—then disappeared entirely, leaving the air quivering with shock. Darkness turned grey with a blink. He stood on nothingness, turning in place without moving, searching his surroundings.

Get out, his mother said. *Get out, out out, out... out....* The word echoed down his spine, tugging at him, demanding he respond with flight.

No, he said, not pushing her into silence this time, merely refusing to obey. *I'm not leaving Riss behind again.*

His mother sighed, amused and exasperated—and perhaps, just a bit, impressed. *You do love her, then.*

No, he said. *I don't. But that doesn't matter.*

Grey air acquired weight to one side. He tucked himself sideways, fading into silence, stealing his presence away from vision. His mother hummed, approving: *Not quite how I learned it,* she said, *but very effective. Well done, son.*

The heavy air swept past, searching—troubled—annoyed. Idisio felt words ripple over him. He let them slide by, not allowing them to hook him out of his hiding place. It didn't matter what Scratha ha'rethe said at this point.

He waited until the presence turned its gaze elsewhere, then *moved*—slipping along the creature's back trail, noiseless, insignificant, one more mote of grey in a monochrome world.

Color washed through the air ahead: Pale, weary streaks of reds and blues; a series of vibrant yellow and white threads, all swirling, shifting, dancing.

Ah, his mother sighed. *It's too late, son.*

A leap brought him up against the bundled mass of color. He splayed his arms along it, feeling something—not flesh, not form, but *weight*—meeting his embrace. *Riss,* he said, unable to speak aloud, throat too locked with fury and horror for sound.

The light turned, tendrils coiling along his arms. He allowed it, pressing close, seeking some glimpse of the individual he'd known. "Riss," he said aloud, his voice emerging broken and harsh. "Riss—talk to me, you're still alive, you have to be—"

The coiling light grew spikes, driving itself deep into him, grabbing, *pulling*—He screamed, his mother's cry overlapping his. They strained to free themselves, found no relief, no release, no way to pry loose the searing daggers sunk through and through and through.

A massive impact shuddered through the grey, disrupting the colorful lines into millions of particles for a fraction of a heartbeat. Idisio threw himself backward, vaguely aware that he was still screaming. The pain seemed to be doubling with each breath, hazing his vision, his perception, his interest in anything beyond the agony drilling into his bones.

Oh, shut up, Deiq said, the words locking sound to silence. He shoved Idisio upright, stopping the helpless tumble, shaking the pain into an ignorable abstraction with that simple movement. *You are a complete fucking ass, you know that? You and Alyea. Deaf and blind and stupid.*

Idisio swayed, blinking, vision crossing from black to grey to black to amber-edged clarity. Deiq loomed, larger than he should have been. Sharp, sinuous cuts laced across the elder ha'ra'ha's body from scalp to toes. Blood drifted into the air in tiny specks, and Deiq's eyes were cloud-white.

That's not Riss, Deiq said, implacable, harsh. *That's a sai-ch'nain: a child of blood. They exist solely to draw life from the living and funnel it to their parent. It would have killed you.*

Idisio refocused, looking at the blur of color that had tried to murder him. It roiled, wrapped in thick, ropy lines of red and black and green. *What's that all around it?* he asked, bewildered.

That's my *sai-ch'nain,* Deiq said, voice white as his eyes.

The air thickened rapidly, turning to gel in Idisio's throat. He gagged, thrashing, fighting for breath. Then, abruptly, something in his muscles shifted—widened—became, for lack of a better word, *feathery.* The gel filtered through Idisio's mouth and nose, usable fragments descending, inert obstacles flowing—*out*—He put a hand to the side of his neck, discovering a series of ridged slits.

"Holy shit," he tried to say, gagged again, and found himself floating completely upside down a moment later.

Fool, Deiq repeated, shoving Idisio upright once more. *If you weren't under my protection, I'd let you die before you get us both killed.*

A rumble overrode any answer Idisio might have given, a thunderous, bone-shaking vibration that turned the air murky yellow. *You dare pit yourself against me?* Scratha ha'rethe said. *You dare harm my sai-ch'nain?* Outrage turned the words into heavy drum-beats that threatened to shatter Idisio's eardrums. *This is my land, my realm, my duty. You have no rights here.*

I am First Born, Deiq said. *I have whatever rights I claim. And I claim this place as my own, under the charge that you have betrayed your oaths and are unfit to hold this position.*

The raw fury in the answering roar wrenched at the very stones of the Fortress far above. Idisio could *feel* the entire structure shivering, stones loosening, old mortar weakening. A heartbeat later the sound shifted to a higher, more startled pitch, focus moving upward, as though the ha'rethe sought to see something within the Fortress.

My bound lord! it said. *Someone dares – someone* dares!

Idisio barely heard Deiq's muttered comment: *Good girl, you didn't lose your nerve –*

As the great mass around them began uncoiling vast, boneless arms toward the Fortress, perception blurred, once more sliding into the multi-eyed overview she remembered from the Qisani. Deiq's black, harsh determination threaded through Idisio's bewildered desperation; they reached out as one to draw Alyea's mind into the mix—slipped—missed—caught her, a reluctant fish on a barbed hook: her protests overridden by Deiq's absolute command.

Oh, damnit, you didn't *kill him,* Deiq said, irritable. The words dragged in their wake indistinct images of rocks, shining under a drenching downpour.

He's been removed from Scratha lands, along with the numaina, Alyea said, not in the least remorseful. *They won't return until I tell them to.*

Deiq gave the silent equivalent of a disgusted head-shake, then reached out, snake-swift, and gathered Alyea in, twisting her away from the physical and through *other*-space to stand cradled tightly against him.

She made no effort to resist, showed no surprise; held still, eyes shut, face turned into the elder ha'ra'ha's chest.

It's... very hot here, she said faintly.

Idisio blinked, surprised, lifting his glance to scan their surroundings. The air still hung patchy shades of grey and red, but as his vision adjusted this time he found himself looking *up,* and realizing how far underground they were. Scratha ha'rethe, for all its furious haste, hadn't extended itself all the way to the surface yet, nor noticed the new arrival.

You won't live long here, Deiq said, remorseless. *I need to draw from you. Both of you,* he added, catching at Idisio's attention. *Give me everything. All of yourselves. I'll take it anyway, so there's no point fighting – that'll just make it hurt more and I won't be able to stop before it kills you.*

Alyea sighed a little, resignation threading through her acceptance: *I'm going to die.*

Idisio bucked, backing up, pushing his hands out before him as though that would stop anything from happening. Deiq raised his head, glazed eyes meeting Idisio's own. Fear dissolved, refusal emptied to silence, awareness clouded, distorted, inverted.

Oh, gods... Idisio didn't know if it was his thought or someone else's. An impossible array of *presences* pressed close around him. Tank—Alyea—*littlered*—Idisio—Ellemoa—Deiq—Acana—Ethu—Pieas... and others, shapeless forms whose shadows stretched back hundreds of years, names long forgotten or never known.

A hurricane wind passed through them all, sweeping every last scrap of *being* into its wake, dragging every moment of pain, anger, fear, moment of madness out into a long, gleaming blade that swung with ponderous, unstoppable momentum—

—Slicing through the lower half of the distracted, reaching ha'rethe—

—Ripping apart not flesh and bone, but an *essence* all too similar to what Idisio had drawn from his own mother, a blackness, a denseness—he began to stretch out, gathering what focus remained, helplessly craving that incredible joy—just a touch, just a moment, just a crumb, surely he could be allowed that much—

Deiq slammed Idisio back and away with a curse: *Don't you fucking learn?* he snarled. *I'm* trying *to keep you alive, but gods only know why at this point!*

The shriek came a moment later, a soundless storm of pressure that seemed to rip the world into a million pieces, fluttering like shredded bits of paper, obscuring sight, spinning direction into chaos.

Enough, Deiq said, *you've done enough. Get out—*

Air turned to a wave of ice, rising hard and fast to shove Idisio through waves of green-yellow flecked air/the taste of rust/mold/a strata of odors: rot, blood, roasting meat—at one point, oddly, fennel—heat-baked rock, and other aromas Idisio had no name for.

Ice spread to surround his entire body. Moments later, movement stopped, color because monochrome, odor stabilized into the overriding rottenness of mud. Rain drenched him, hammering down as though determined to wash what sense he still possessed straight out of his head.

Rock groaned. Instinctively, Idisio put out a hand, touching only air; pushed with more than muscle, pressing out and up, holding the unsteady walls in place for several terrified, panting breaths. Then the sense of danger passed, stone settling reluctantly back into place; still uncertainly seated on crumbling mortar, but no longer in immediate danger of collapse.

He could *feel* other areas of the Fortress falling, and hear the cries of those trapped under the cascading rock, and feel the pain crackling through their crushed bodies. Without really thinking about it, he sought out those with no chance of recovery, gathering their energy into himself, breathing easier with each life taken.

Vision cleared, clarified: He was in one of the open courtyards, rain pouring down, pooling, streaming away along hidden pipes. Alyea lay, unconscious, not far away. Her hair was a stark white, her naked body streaked with a chaotic lattice of lines, some bleeding, others ridged and hard, as though already scabbed into permanent scars.

He staggered to his feet, lifting her into his arms, and looked around for shelter, then found the archway, and lurched forward, one foot after another, coherent thought draining like the water in the courtyard.

Chapter 50

Cafad Scratha sat on a raggedly shaped boulder, expression blank. His clothes hung lank along his lean frame, still dripping water onto the thirsty ground. The rain squall had come and gone, leaving the air hot and muggy. Eager desert growth uncoiled leaf and vine from every available crevice. A pale green stem bent over Cafad's bare feet, heavy with water drops. Older plants, even bent under the weight of leftover raindrops, reached to Alyea's knees and thighs. One particularly enterprising patch of flowers topped her shoulders.

"He won't move," Gria said, wringing water from her hair. "I didn't want to leave him."

"You did right," Alyea said. She brushed a fingertip against Cafad's shoulder, felt nothing, then tried putting her hand on his shoulder, lightly at first, then more firmly. Still no response, at any level. She reached for Cafad's mind, found only a blank, grey haze shot through with alarming white streaks, and withdrew hastily.

"What do we do?" Gria's voice was nearly a whine. "*I* can't help carry him back!"

Alyea laughed a little. "That's not the problem," she said. "I can carry him." Bruised muscles and strained joints protested. She ignored the pain as irrelevant.

Gria stared, incredulous. "But you're—I mean, he's larger—" She caught herself at last and shut her mouth, eyebrows drawn tight in worry.

"I'm not at all certain we *should* bring him back onto Scratha lands," Alyea said. She half-expected the girl to protest that *she* didn't want to go back, but Gria stayed quiet, her gaze going to the ground as though fascinated by a nearby plant. Alyea sighed. "Well, only one way to find out, I suppose."

She knelt and gathered Cafad up into her arms, forcing exhausted muscles to obey, staggering a bit as she came to her feet. He made no protest and offered no resistance; lay limp and blank as a sleeping child, his vague stare now fastened on the clouds overhead.

She hadn't been at all sure he'd be alive when she returned. His glazed passivity was both a relief and deeply worrisome.

After the recent whirl of activity, she found it calming to focus on one foot in front of the other, balancing Cafad's weight—not difficult, he'd obviously not been eating properly for some time—avoiding loose rocks and pushing through newly unfurled bushes. Gria trailed behind, not speaking, which was another relief. Alyea didn't really have much interest in answering questions at the moment. Between the ghost-echo of barbs tearing through her body and the shattering headache rapidly swelling through her temples, she felt little interest in *anything*.

As they neared the invisible boundary of Scratha lands, Cafad began to stir, restless. A few steps more, and he began to whimper. Three more steps brought the whimper into a full-throated scream that ripped savagely at Alyea's headache. Alyea grimaced, blinking hard against the pain, and said, "Gria. Go on to the Fortress. Send a servant out this way to take care of Lord Scratha."

The girl hesitated, frowning anxiously, then shrugged and obeyed.

Cafad's restlessness turned to jerking tremors, the scream warbling out unabated between convulsions. Alyea turned and carried him away from the border. He didn't calm until they were nearly back to where she'd originally left him.

She set him down. He stumbled to a nearby rock and sat, gaze vague once more, breath rasping through his raw throat. She sat down herself, rubbing her face with one hand, not at all sure what to do next. She hadn't expected to survive this long. The crackling pain in her head made it hard to think. Her joints felt as though they might simply separate at any moment, leaving her a crumpled pile of limbs and blood.

Pain coalesced into distinct pulses along ears, eyebrow, lip, and groin. "Oh," Alyea said aloud, looking up at the cloud-littered sky. "So the bond is still there. Meaning he's still alive. Well." She looked at Cafad, and decided that it was unlikely he would be in any danger beyond getting rained on if left alone for a while. "I'm sorry, Lord Scratha," she told him as she hauled herself to her feet once more. "I have to leave you here. Someone will be along shortly."

His head moved a bit. She couldn't tell if it was a response or a delayed muscle twitch.

"I'm sorry," she said again, this time meaning it as a comprehensive apology for the destruction and disaster. He blinked, gaze still unfocused, his head bobbing. Deciding that was the best she'd likely get, she began plodding back toward Scratha lands.

Chapter 51

On the road to redemption, you'll kill at least one of your own kin and deny your elders a life they've claimed.

He remembered the dust in the air that day, the intent expression on the seer's face as he studied the pattern of bones cast upon the ground.

Nobody can ever read their own, ha'inn. Didn't you know that?

All he'd ever seen was a path through darkness into more darkness. Redemption hadn't ever been a goal for him. That implied a belief in the gods, a belief that he had a soul.

Amusing conceits, from his point of view, nothing more.

No dust here, and human eyes would see darkness. No air, no water. In the heat of a ha'rethe's true lair, liquid turned to compressed steam, solid to liquid if so desired, and rock held form only so long as the resident ha'rethe wished it to do so.

Deiq slid his will into the wavering rock even as he shoved Alyea and Idisio clear, briefly tempted to let it all collapse. He could allow himself to be terribly damaged by the collapse, could break the bond between himself and Alyea, could be free. Could fall into a deep sleep, maybe not the final sleep, but close enough to remove him from human matters for many of their lifetimes. *Not yet. It would be a waste of all the years of work to give up now.*

He turned his attention to the weakly flailing remains of Scratha ha'rethe. Long tendrils, black and grey, mingled with the yellow-orange of his sai-ch'nain, splayed out in tangled patterns in all directions and snagged across every surface like a living web. Alyea's blow had destroyed the Scratha sai-ch'nain entirely. Idisio's attack had torn into the ha'rethe itself, stripped away layers of protection, ripping deep into the most vulnerable areas, exposing what humans might have called *brain* or *soul* or *heart*. They'd never developed a word, in any of their languages, to properly describe the spot that allowed ha'reye and humans to bond, the spot in every creature where intellect and life wound together into a tightly compressed mass of energy.

It wasn't enough damage to kill. Left alone, Scratha ha'rethe would heal—slowly, agonizingly, building hatred and anger along with its strength.

You'll kill at least one of your own kin.

I've already killed that 'at least one,' he thought, watching the twitching form spread out around him as it desperately drew moisture from the steam, scrabbling to rebuild burst tissues, pushing to free itself from the weight of the sai-ch'nain. *I'm already condemned a thousand times over, for a thousand infractions. I'm far beyond any notion of redemption my ha'reye kin might have developed over the centuries. And just as far beyond any human boundaries of forgiveness. Even Meer would have turned away from me by now.*

There were two ways of finishing the job. One would leave Scratha Fortress in comprehensive ruin, killing everyone inside. The other would trap him into the ha'rethe's place, stealing his freedom forever.

I promised to protect my kin.

I can't protect both humans and ha'reye-kin any longer. The gap is too wide to bridge.

Choose a side, First Born. Choose a path.

"Meer would not have turned away from you, ha'inn," an unfamiliar voice said.

Deiq turned, startled, searching, and found the faintest of threads leading upward: Someone stood, knee-deep, in the temple pool, high above, focusing every ounce of attention and energy towards Deiq. *Impressive achievement.* He gave in to curiosity, rising some distance to allow for clearer communication, keeping a tendril in the lair in case the ruined creature repaired itself faster than expected.

It's impolite, he told the human, *to look into a ha'ra'ha's thoughts uninvited.*

"It's also not easy," the man answered, amused.

True. Deiq held still, considering, then rose a bit higher. *How did you know Meer?*

"I didn't know Meer," the man said. "I listen, ha'inn. I listen to the words behind the words and the stories behind the stories, and I put pieces together. I served in the Holy Swamp. I ate and drank the salt there, and bathed my eyes with it."

Long-denied memory rose, filling in details. Deiq sighed, half-frustrated, half-amused. *Ah. You. I thought we'd agreed to avoid one another, priest Moir.*

"Every agreement comes to an end," Moir said. "I repeat, ha'inn: Meer would not have turned away from you. He heard the gods more clearly than his peers. Quite possibly more clearly than I've ever managed."

There are no gods, little priest, Deiq said, regretful.

"Of course there are," Moir said. "Just because *you* don't hear or see a thing doesn't mean it's not there, ha'inn. No creature sees everything around it, no matter how keen its eyesight."

Deiq rolled his eyes, losing interest. He'd heard too many variations on this conversation over the centuries. He let himself drift downward once more.

"Ha'inn," the priest said. "I bleed for your attention. Give me another moment, please."

Deiq blinked, realizing for the first time that the tenuous thread dripping from surface to lair was made of blood. He stretched, intrigued, and sent a ripple of *self* up to the surface, shuddering at the cold.

The priest started as Deiq wrapped a tendril around his ankles, but held still after that one jerk, breath trembling through his chest for a few beats. "Ha'inn," he said at last, "my life is yours, if you desire it."

Blood dripped from a deep gash in his palm. Not fatal, but he'd weaken and fall soon, more than likely to drown in the shallow pool.

What do you want, priest, that is worth the risk of drawing my attention now *of all times?*

"Is the servant girl—the one they called Riss—is she still alive?"

No.

"Is her child still alive?"

No.

The priest dipped his head in a regretful motion, murmuring prayers for a departed soul. Then he said, "I ask that you spare the lives of the remaining humans within your reach, ha'inn. If you need strength, if you need to deliver pain, I offer myself instead, as Meer did." He squeezed his cut hand, forcing the faltering stream of blood to a steady trickle.

Deiq watched the thread turn cloudy as it sifted through the water, mildly surprised that it held no interest for him. *No, priest,* he said. *You are not Meer, and your strength would not help me.* The priest twitched; Deiq's attention sharpened. *Ah. You are ready to die, then?*

"I have served my kind for many years, ha'inn," Moir said, lowering his chin almost to his chest. "I have seen a great deal of evil and walked through a great deal of pain. I am not so much ready to die as I am ready to withdraw from humanity. Can you help me, ha'inn?"

Deiq considered, intrigued. *Perhaps,* he said. *What of your agreement with the protector of the graveyard?*

"My agreement was to set matters to rights in that area. I have done that, ha'inn. The salt mines are closed; the Northern Church settlement in that area is now for monastics only. Those who were directly involved in the sacrilege have been brought to appropriate justice. I have no further duties to that protector, so on my next visit it will take my life for itself."

If you're already committed to that end, I can't intervene, Deiq said, irritated now. *You're wasting my time, little priest.*

"I would prefer my death have use and meaning," Moir retorted. "The protector of the swamps would not find any value in my sacrifice. I have prayed, ha'inn, and asked for directions from all gods that are, have been, and will be. I am told to offer myself to you. Consider it my last attempt at making amends for the crimes of my people against yours. Will you accept me?"

You're absurd, Deiq told him, lacing refusal throughout the words.

The priest straightened, pride and desperation mixing in his emotions; made two quick slashing motions, then threw himself forward into the pool. His hands grasped at the tendril of Deiq's consciousness, wrapping himself around it or it around himself. Blood slicked through the water, soaking into Deiq's consciousness, rousing an instinctive hunger.

You are a fool, little priest, Deiq said, laughing. He drew the priest down and sideways into his true lair; reached into the cuts, sliding feelers under the skin, searching out every channel, every pulse of life and fluid that a human possessed.

The priest convulsed, unable to scream, eyes and face turning red as veins burst throughout tender membranes.

Is this better than facing the protector you pledged to give your life to? Deiq challenged, curling tendrils around each and every hair on the man's body.

You need me, ha'inn. It was more of a searing image than actual words: a silent, passionate, unshakable belief that made Deiq pause. Then Moir's voice clarified into speech: *You need me. I am... I am told to tell you that I am your balance.*

Who tells you to say that? Deiq demanded, fury climbing throughout his system. Rocks shifted and creaked overhead; he ignored the warning, more than willing, in that moment, to let the entire world destroy itself around him.

I have no name for the voices that speak to me, ha'inn. I believe them to be gods, but whether those are gods lost to time, or those yet to be, I do not know. I only know they are not the Four, nor the Three.

Deiq began to withdraw. Then, in a surge of irritation, he drove forward, scraping flesh from bone, separating out veins and organs to hang loosely in the searing mist. Unable to scream, muscles torn, the priest's agony swamped Deiq's senses: creamy, spicy, intoxicating.

A weight like a block of steel slapped against Deiq, sending him reeling back. *You need this one,* a voice said, sternly uncompromising. *Take this gift we give you, and treat it with proper respect.*

Deiq watched, uncomprehending, as the priest's injuries knitted, flesh and bone rejoining, veins connecting back to a functional network, breath swelling lungs back into their proper place.

Moir hung in his grasp, limp, unconscious, entirely incapable of having had any part in that healing.

There are no gods, Deiq said, the protest emerging feeble and shaky. Quiet laughter answered him. The sense of weight faded from the area.

Moir stirred, waking, and let out a vibrating shriek. At the same time, the wounded ha'rethe rolled, lashing out with unexpected speed, the sai-ch'nain too slow to respond. Deiq threw himself sideways, too slowly. A claw raked across his side, barbed, shredding essence beyond the physical. He howled, whipping round, and aimed a thickly physical blow at the damaged mass below him.

It moved aside easily, latching on as the strike passed it by, wrapping tendril around tendril, hauling itself up to press hard against Deiq's center. More barbs raked, caught, and wove throughout sensitive points, much as Deiq had just done to the human. The comparison failed to amuse him.

He could feel the ha'rethe reaching, searching for the center of the center, the spot where a creature's entire life compressed into a tiny dark spot. The ha'rethe was moving *fast,* far faster than he'd ever seen the creatures react before. In turn, he felt as though he were running through deep mud in his efforts to deflect and defend. The sai-ch'nain, slower yet, was barely beginning to respond.

Even as he twisted to escape, the human priest, glowing an improbable shade of blue, threw himself forward, slamming into the ha'rethe. The creature grunted in pain, rearranging its attention to the new threat.

Deiq seized the moment's relief, expanded it to give himself time to think.

He would never leave Scratha territory again if he took the path laid out before him. He'd have to lock himself to the Fortress, bind himself to the land, *become* the resident ha'rethe.

Flames, scorching the sky; water, drowning the world; wind, tearing everything apart. The temptation to stride forth with newfound power and reshape the world to his liking—or just to destroy it, for the sheer fun of it—was already tickling along his neck. He could feel his thin hold on sanity crumbling as he pondered, humors sliding out of alignment, the heat, blood, strain, violence, and most of all the *remembering*—

Ha'ra'hain weren't made to remember. Life was a simple matter of feeding, resting, playing, resting, feeding... on and on in an endless cycle. Some didn't even understand their own power. They never needed to; they lived in protected areas and ate the food so obediently delivered to them by the nearby humans.

Ha'reye had grown complacent over the years as well, their thinking dulled by the easy life of the Jungles, everything provided by their disciples, trusting the various Fortress guardians to keep the bulk of humanity under control.

Ha'inn! the priest cried, breaking into the moment within a moment. *I bleed for you!* His pain scratched the mist into complex shapes. The sai-ch'nain's ongoing, roiling battle against the ha'rethe broke those shapes apart almost immediately, creating new ones.

An abstract haze settled across Deiq's mind. *Patterns. Patterns are good. This is a pattern.*

It only took a heartbeat to follow the pattern out to the end.

Deiq focused on the three twitching, agonized, flayed forms, drew in a long breath, then slammed the entirety of his self upon them, reaching for not one, but three densities at once.

Chapter 52

Firelight washed warmer hues into Cuna's lined face than had shown in daylight. Her eyes remained black and alert, her back straight, movements precise. The teyanain had separated out into shifts. Some stretched out to sleep, apparently unbothered by still-damp ground. Others prowled through the darkness, and two stolidly watched the fire.

A dozen rocks circled around the fire served as seats. Azni couldn't help looking at the empty ones every few breaths. They *felt* occupied, as though by stern ghosts that watched with intense disapproval of—*something*—gods only knew what.

She was having trouble separating the visible and ghost worlds. The last few days had been—*intense* didn't even begin to cover the pot. She was still sorting through the lessons, and felt bruised along every muscle and bone, and more than a bit prone to startle at shadows.

Calm, one or more of the teyanain said. She'd learned not to try picking out which individual spoke, when so many stood close by. *We are here. You are under our protection. You are safe. The only ghosts here are your own, and they cannot harm you unless you allow them to do so.*

Azni dipped her head slightly and tried to relax taut spine muscles, with marginal success.

Cuna's mouth moved in a tiny smile that did nothing to soften the angles of her face. She said, "You have had your time of speaking of past matters, of catching up, as huerg say it. I wish to summon my father now, so that I may have my proper status confirmed."

Allonin's face settled into familiar, stubborn lines. Azni knew that look. *Some things don't change,* she thought wearily, and heard a huff of amusement from the athain.

"I swore to protect Lord Evkit," Allonin said. "Even with Azni safe, I have to honor that oath."

"Your oath is safe. This meeting will be under truce." She motioned to the circle of teyanain around them. Allo startled, apparently taken aback by the abrupt appearance. Azni had felt them moving in, a bare whisper of motion across *other* senses. Cuna's face crinkled in a tight smile. She raised her voice to carry. "Lord Evkit. Dinas Teyantin. I feel your presence. Thank you for your patience. You may join us now, if you are willing to do so under truce."

Azni blinked at that wording. "Wait, have they been out there this whole—"

She shut up as Lord Evkit limped into the firelight, his Teyantin following a step behind. Both were heavily bruised, their clothes stained and ripped. They each took a seat—not side by side, as Azni would have expected, but with enough distance between that looking at one meant taking your eyes off the other.

Azni rapidly went over what she'd said to Allonin, and he to her, in the previous hours. How much of it had Lord Evkit overheard? Had she said anything dangerous? The distinctly alarmed tightness to Allonin's mouth and eyes indicated he was doing the same worried recall.

Calm, the athain said. *You are safe. He did not hear you. We protect you, as we promised.*

"Greetings, Lord Evkit, Dinas Teyantin," Cuna said gravely. "I am pleased to see you alive."

The heavy tattoos across Lord Evkit's face largely concealed his expression, but even the firelight couldn't wash out the haggard grey cast to his skin. Dinas Teyantin looked little better, bright clothes gone dull with dust and dirt. His sardonic humor had entirely disappeared, and he sat with his head bent, expression sober.

"I am relatively pleased to *be* alive," Lord Evkit said. His gaze settled on Allonin. "Not so pleased to see *my* servant sitting at *your* side, however."

"The Agreement is broken," Cuna said, ignoring that comment. "You have worked to create that breach. Do you acknowledge this?"

Evkit glanced sideways at his Teyantin, then shrugged. "The Agreement is broken. The depth of my involvement is arguable. Many other factors—and *factions*—were in the weave."

Cuna's eyes narrowed. "I did not aim to breach the Agreement," she said. "I worked to restore the honor of our people and preserve the world at large, as is our *duty*."

Dinas Teyantin raised his head. His voice, calm and even, still managed to override Evkit's beginning retort. "This particular argument has been ground from rock to sand over the years. I do not need to hear it again. Neither of you have changed your positions, and it is undignified for outsiders to hear our internal matters."

Evkit and Cuna both bent their heads briefly. "Honor to your grace, Teyantin," Cuna said. "You smooth the sand once more."

"My daimaina is dead," Evkit said, bitter lines settling across his face. "My people are dead or dying—even innocent *children*, Cuna! That cannot be smoothed over!"

His daughter smoothed one hand across her braids. Azni suspected the motion had an obscure, possibly mocking meaning. Cuna said, "Every one of those deaths lies upon your own hand, father. Not mine."

Evkit looked away, his eyes nearly shut, breathing hard. Dinas Teyantin stirred. Evkit said, tautly, "Do not speak, Teyantin. I have exceeded my patience in too many directions already."

Dinas bowed his head and went back to imitating a mute boulder.

Cuna pulled the bound tail of her braids to drape across her right shoulder. "Dinas Teyantin," she said, dispassionately. "Would you be interested in becoming my *Teyantan*?"

Dinas didn't move. Evkit jerked to his feet, his eyes blazing with fury. "You *dare*!"

Cuna raised a hand, pointing at her father, and said, "Sit down, Abaik Imiyan Evkit."

Evkit sat. His face flushed an ugly, mottled color. "You *cannot*," he said, the words scarcely audible.

"One day," Cuna observed, "you will realize that every single time you have told me that, you have been proven wrong. Be still and allow your Teyantin to answer."

Dinas Teyantin sighed, looking at Lord Evkit. He said, "I thank you, Cuna, but I will honor my existing oaths."

Cuna nodded, appearing completely unsurprised. "Father," she said, turning her attention to Evkit. "You have a choice: Face me, or flee from me. Either way, your domain is destroyed, your plans are in ruins, and your power is gone."

Evkit stared at Cuna without speaking for some time, his expression shifting between wonder and anger, between bewilderment and pride. "You *are* my daughter," he said at last, his tone thick with a mixture of emotions.

"Was there ever doubt?" Dinas muttered.

"I would have had you rule the teyanain after me," Evkit said, apparently oblivious, for the moment, that anyone else existed around him. "I tested you to prove your worth, your strength. I knew you would have to fight harder than a male. When our ha'rethe accepted you, blessed you, I *rejoiced* that you would one day take my place. I did not think you would turn to hatred and divide our people when the path was already laid out towards the very prey you claimed to hunt." He gestured as he spoke, passion growing; ended his words with both hands outstretched, palms up, fingers splayed in a posture of intense frustration.

Cuna flicked her left hand in a dismissive motion and said, unruffled, "This is the thing you have never understood. The ha'rethe gave me its gift *because* I rejected your path, your methods—and you." She glanced at Allonin, her mouth twisting into what might have been intended as a smile. "I can only imagine it gave this one the gift for the same reason."

Evkit's eyes widened, then narrowed into a fierce, accusing glare. "You rejected me?" he demanded. "You broke your oath, you are hask!"

Allonin's stubborn expression returned. "No," he said. "I have not broken my oath. I only refused to take what was not being freely given. I dislike slavery, Lord Evkit. I won't knowingly take anything by force, even if the force is applied by another."

And some things do change, Azni thought, startled. That was *not* the Allonin she'd known as a child, not the one who'd walked out on her so many years ago in pursuit of power.

Evkit stared at Allonin, at Azni, back at Allonin, his eyes once more wide and disbelieving. "You—refused—you *refused*? It should have killed you for that!"

"You never ordered it to force its gift on an unwilling taker," Cuna said, her eyes glittering with malice. "That was the one thing you never saw as possible, father. And in that tiny moment of freedom, it was able to give away the last unbound pieces of itself."

"Until there was not enough left to sustain its own life," Dinas Teyantin said, head still bowed. His shoulders rounded further in misery. "Grace to your grace, my lord, I—"

"How did you not see that flaw?" Evkit demanded, turning on his Teyantin. "Why did you never warn me of this?"

"Be careful how you speak to your Teyantin, father," Cuna said, a malicious grin stretching across her thin face. "He holds more power than you do, now. He was also given the true gift."

Evkit's face went a greyish-green made unlovely by the firelight. He turned a slow, incredulous stare on his Teyantin. "*You*? You are hask? *You?*"

"Never, lord," Dinas Teyantin said, raising his head to meet Evkit's glare. "I have served only you, my entire life. But I also could not accept an unwillingly made offering, and so the ha'rethe... gifted me with more than I was able to reveal to you, after my trials. It is the one deception I have held in all my years of service, and I only held it so that I *could* continue to serve you. You would not have trusted me, had you known that truth. And I did not warn you because... it seemed highly improbable that anyone else would follow such a path. I did not foresee your daughter's choice."

Evkit shut his eyes, his back and shoulders stiff as the stone upon which he sat.

"Your memory is poor, Teyantin, if you thought I'd *ever* follow his steps," Cuna said waspishly.

"*Kii tafli*," the Teyantin murmured. "My memory is clear, Cuna. And still, I will stand between you to prevent harm to your father. That is *my* choice."

"*Kitchi biti nahn*," Cuna said after a few taut moments, unsmiling, then looked at Evkit. "Answer me, father. Will you face me, and risk my killing your Teyantin on my way to your throat? Or will you flee, and lose the remaining scraps of your honor?"

"You would have to kill me as well," Allonin said without perceptible emotion. Azni bit her lip, wanting to protest in spite of her awareness that she couldn't interfere. This was for Allonin to handle.

I'm a twin myself, she'd told Nissa, largely unsympathetic to the woman's pain. Now, though, she could *see* the twin bond that had always been more of a theory, a myth, a superstition to her. It wound through her being, wound through Allonin, a silver-red-gold line in constant motion.

Killing Allonin would snap that line, and being this close at the time of his death would send an immense backlash throughout her entire body. Even the training she'd recently received would only cushion the damage, not stop it—and there would be no healing, no reversal of that blow. She'd bear the internal scar, and whatever external effects it caused, for the rest of her life.

She realized Evkit was looking at her, his dark stare thoughtful. "Teyanain also have been known to bear twins," the teyanain lord said softly, then shook his head. "I will not allow that misery. I release you from your oaths to me, Dinas Teyantin and Allonin. I ask to be released in turn from my oath to you, Allonin, as it appears to have become worthless."

Allonin's agreement was barely more than a grunt and a nod, his neck muscles ridged with tension.

"Lord Evkit—" the Teyantin began, refusal clear in those two words alone.

"You *are* released from your oaths to me," Evkit said. "I will not force you to leave my side."

Dinas Teyantin nodded, his muscles relaxing, and sat quietly once more.

"I stand with no allies but those I have earned with my heart," Evkit said, meeting Cuna's gaze. "I will not tell them to stand aside if I am attacked. Their deaths would be entirely upon you. I refuse to battle you under these circumstances. There is no honorable ending for either of us along that path. I will not *flee*. I will merely *withdraw*, ceding all claim on rulership of the Horn and the teyanain people to you, from my own judgment that you are more fit to rule at this time. I will go my own way with those who may choose to follow me, and take up residence elsewhere, out of your territory. Do you accept that, Cuna?"

"You know damn well that I have to," his daughter said, lip curling. "I'm disappointed. I'd intended to end this day with a dagger in your heart."

"I'm well aware of that." Evkit rose to his feet, passing a thoughtful glance around at the assembled company. "May I depart, *Calcana*?"

She stared at him, face set in bitter lines. "I'll *break* you one day," she said venomously. "I'll *destroy* that calm."

"That's a trivial goal, unworthy of the head of the teyanain," Evkit said. "You've won, Cuna. Look ahead. Forget your anger over matters long *buried*."

The stress on the last word was barely audible, but Cuna reacted as though slapped. She rose to her feet, a long, pale knife appearing in her hand. Her fury cut the air like a heated knife through ice, fracturing the night into gleaming sparks for a heartbeat. "Get out of my sight, *father*," she said harshly.

Evkit bowed solemnly to Allonin and Azni, nodded once to Dinas, then turned away, disappearing into the darkness beyond the torchlight as silently as he'd come, his Teyantin at his side.

Chapter 53

Deiq stretched, sending tendrils against every surface, measuring, weighing, *sensing* as he allowed himself to remember, pried open all the locked areas of memory, released centuries of tension. He didn't need to worry about hiding any longer.

He was balanced. *Truly* balanced, this time. *Human, ha'rethe, ha'ra'hain/other* woven together, soaking into his own, rock-heavy being, fluid locking to fluid, capturing air, binding air to earth to water, braiding the thread of life into a multi-faceted creation.

He was Acana. And Moir. And the sai-ch'nain. He was every moment of their lives, every laugh from their lips, every scream of their pain. He was ha'ra'hain, First Born, ancient beyond words—simultaneously, he was a child just learning its first steps.

Their memories merged with his, providing angles he hadn't considered, fleshing out events he'd only been peripherally aware of. He remembered:

Humans had begun studying methods of interfering with ha'reye-kin communications almost immediately after the Agreement was sealed. The Fortress ha'reye, confident in human obedience, never saw it coming. Underground rivers were drained or blocked, substances introduced into the various wells that muddied the ha'rethe's perceptions.

So many tricks, so many incremental steps to reach this point.

Aerthraim Family had been arrogantly obvious with their aenstone project. Deiq could feel the aenstone above, large opaque blocks across *other*-vision. No wonder Scratha ha'rethe roused to anger on discovering the situation. Deiq suspected Orde had intended to almost completely block off the ha'rethe from the Fortress, leaving it as little more than a caged source of power. It wouldn't have worked against a ha'rethe at full strength, but Scratha ha'rethe had been steadily weakening, less attentive to its surroundings than usual.

The aenstone didn't feel quite right, though. It seemed porous. He'd never before perceived it as anything but a heavy blotch where he *couldn't* see anything, couldn't even touch it without intense pain, but now it seemed like an ordinary stone block.

Deiq stretched, sending gentle, testing nudges along the stone far above. No pain, although the contact resonated with the slickness of dead things and an unnerving chill. Overstressed mortar shifted, crumbled. An aenstone block crashed to the floor of the library. He could destroy the entire Fortress any time he wished, aenstone or not.

He nodded contentedly, then withdrew and went back to memory.

The other Families were much subtler than the Aerthraim. Deiq blocked the majority of attempts made, soothed the troublemakers into forgetting everything, and hid his own memories of the matter in a deep, unreachable spot within himself. Acana had done the same, as it turned out, and Moir unwound his share of plots in the course of his reparations.

And I thought I was the only one working to save humanity. Foolish of me. Shadow-light, far away, Acana laughed in agreement.

Some of the plots were absurdly stupid. Deiq had considered letting a few of those through, just to reinforce the low opinion ha'reye had of humanity, but in the end the risk outweighed the potential satisfaction. Ha'reye had little to no sense of humor.

Scratha Family had been the only one to refuse any sort of control over its ha'rethe; the last of the Families, by the time Cafad Scratha was born, who honestly honored the Agreement under its original terms. But by that point, the Qisani had reached a point of renown as *the* place to train the *best* desert lords. It was an honor to be accepted. So Ordenial of Scratha was sent to the Qisani to train, rather than going through the Scratha blood trials at home.

He returned home with an astounding breadth of knowledge and superb command of his new abilities... and with some very dangerous political leanings, ones the last Family with an unfettered ha'rethe really couldn't afford.

Acana, Deiq mourned, flattening himself against a solid surface, spreading out, gathering himself together once again. *I had no idea. All these years, and I never knew what you were doing.*

He could hear her reply, as though she stood beside him: *It wasn't safe for you to know.*

I could have helped!

Her laughter echoed down his back. He sighed, letting the ghost-voice dissolve, and went back to reviewing the fall of Scratha Family from his new, multilayered perspective.

Lord Orde, as he became familiarly known, became Lord Scratha's most trusted advisor, and *s'e-kath* in all but title. He'd found ways to make alliances with *everyone.* Once or twice, teyanain and Aerthraim even sat to a relatively peaceful dinner at the Scratha table. Lord Scratha received all the credit for that accomplishment, but in truth Orde had been the one reaching in all directions.

Deiq stretched again, enjoying the deep heat of water turned to compressed steam, then focused *other*-vision upward, checking the world above. Idisio was in a deep trance, nearly comatose by human standards; no threat from him at the moment.

No sense of Cafad Scratha, although the numaina was within the Fortress somewhere. Alyea crossed into his range as he watched, moving inward towards the Fortress. Tension he hadn't been aware of uncoiled.

She stopped, sensing his presence, and said, *You're still alive.*

Yes. Come back to me.

I will. Let me walk. I'll be there soon.

All right.

Talking was surprisingly exhausting. It required so much *focus,* so much slow thinking. Deiq withdrew abruptly, coiling into memory once more.

Humans had stopped being idle amusements when he realized they actually *were* intelligent. They grieved their lost, they celebrated their joys, they remembered the past and thought about the future. They *created* things, new things, even in the face of daily tragedy.

He'd rushed to alert the elders, assuming they thought of the humans as nothing but dim animals with vague tool-making abilities. *We can't keep using them like this,* he'd protested. *They're different. We should be helping them advance and grow and become great!*

The laughter astounded him. *They breed profusely and live short lives, which is the mark of an animal. You're being foolish.*

But look at their creations! Look at how they advance already, even with so much death and desperation amongst their daily lives. Some of these inventions are fascinating!

That provoked some pondering. At last, the Jungles decided: *If they continue to advance they will destroy themselves, as we almost did, and then we will lose our descendants. Stop them from these inventions. Our survival comes first, always. We are the greater, they the lesser. They will serve us, as is right.*

He'd been furious and horrified, and barely managed to conceal those unseemly emotions.

You will watch the humans for us, he'd been told. *You will divert anything that threatens to advance their knowledge of the world around them. You will keep them foolish and blind, you will keep them obedient. We are not satisfied with the offspring produced thus far....*

Aerthraim Family figured it out soon enough and withdrew from the Agreement, ejecting their ha'rethe without ceremony. The Jungles did its best to cut the Aerthraim off from all support. Given that they funneled the bulk of that retribution through Deiq, it largely failed. Aerthraim Family suffered but survived, determined to make their own way without the help of ha'reye or ha'ra'hain.

Deiq focused outward once more, riffling through *presences*: Alyea was back in the Fortress, in one of the gardens, meditating. Sensing his attention, she roused. *Deiq?*

What have I missed?

Cafad and Nissa have gone. They're on their way to Bright Bay, to take up residence. Cafad isn't... himself. Sadness, concern, guilt colored her words.

Not surprising. He may never recover. Deiq felt his energy waning once more. *Where's Idisio?*

He's gone as well. Headed north to Arason.

Good. Deiq relaxed, relieved, and allowed human time to pass without his involvement. Something tugged at his attention: Alyea, trying to speak to him. He roused enough to hear.

The water, she said. *The wells. We need water.*

Oh. I'd forgotten. Yes... He rolled, stretching, feeling along the various upper pathways where steam became water once more: came up against aenstone—and, more surprisingly, bluestone—blocks in all directions. *Aerthraim again. And teyanain. Did they have a secret alliance at one point, or were they com-*

peting for control? Even the combined memories he held offered no clear answer to that.

There were spots where the aging ha'rethe had tried to dissolve the mortar, push at the weak spots, move the blocks aside. One had been partially destroyed. Deiq worked patiently, ignoring the mild surge of distaste with each contact, until underground rivers rushed through their natural courses once more. Bluestone and aenstone alike yielded to his will, and with each opening came a wash of information:

Burning, burning, walls of flame a hundred feet high, thick trees toppling to ash, frantic cries from trapped disciples and servants—

Shattered ruins, a land deeply fissured, seawater rushing into new channels, meeting inland rivers in a shock of turbulence—

Rain, so much rain—as though hundreds of years of moisture were being unleashed all at once—wind whipping small and large plants alike nearly flat to the ground, deep roots ripping up, further destroying the remaining structures; lightning catching jagged swaths of the world on fire. Sections of ground simply collapsing, no longer held up by the will of ha'reye and ha'ra'hain—no more ha'reye, outside of the Jungles, and the remaining ha'ra'hain were distracted with disasters unfolding within their own territory.

Help me! Sessin protector said, seizing at Deiq's attention as the waterways connected once more. *Help me, help me, I cannot hold this land together! I am attacked by my own, I am betrayed!*

Deiq said, *Let it fall. Humans must learn to build without our help now. Retreat, and rest. I will wake you when the land stabilizes—*

A crackling light broke across his vision, and he recoiled, turning away reflexively. A few human heartbeats later, a wave of jagged tremors swept across him, potent even at this remove. He braced weakened spots of his Fortress overhead, holding them steady against the impact until the world fell quiet once more.

He reached along the Sessin waterway cautiously and found only fading echoes of a dying scream.

Water threading west connected at last, conveying more shrieks: *Help me! We are betrayed, the Agreement is broken!* F'Heing and Darden's voices overlapped, alike in their panic. *The humans seek to cage us. We will not be caged, we will not! Why will the Jungles not answer us?*

The Jungles are also under attack, Deiq told them both. *You must choose: submit to the cages or fall into the final sleep.*

We will not be caged, both protectors said firmly in near synchrony.

Humans allowed themselves to be caged for many years, Deiq pointed out mildly.

Humans are nothing but animals. They serve us, as is right.

Deiq said, *You've been close to them for too long to still believe that.*

Silence echoed, a sense of shamed turning away. Deiq withdrew, checked that water flowed freely within the Fortress once more, then reached to the surrounding lands, repaired broken and blocked connections, sent water surging through the underground network.

Thank you, Alyea said, with a sense of tremendous relief. *Wait, don't go—please, I need to talk to you.*

Come to me, then, he said. She stepped into his grasp, unhesitating, letting him guide her to a halfway point between her world and his.

He spun a comforting illusion, a room reminiscent of his nest in the Jagged Mountains, and a simulacrum of the form and face she was most used to seeing.

She sat on the couch, looking around slowly, as if considering what to say. "You've bound yourself to this place," she said finally.

"Yes." He remained standing, well out of reach, to give her the illusion of safety. "I destroyed the ha'rethe. Someone needs to take its place." No point in explaining beyond that simple statement. She didn't need to know the depth of what he'd done, only that he was here to protect her, if she wished to accept it.

"I can't leave," she said, looking up at him. "It hurts if I get too near the borders. The chains, I suppose."

"Yes. Do you want to remove them?"

She tilted her head to one side, apparently not surprised by the question. "You're not the first to ask me that," she said. "Do *you* want to remove them? Do you want to be free of me?"

"No. But I won't hold you against your will. As I've told you before, you're not my slave, Alyea. I don't *need* you to stay with me." He paused, watching her, then added, "I'll admit I'd prefer that you stay. I'd be... lonely without you." Not the right word, but there was no concept in human language that quite matched his intent.

She nodded. "Then I'll stay." Her tone turned pragmatic. "There needs to be at least one desert lord in residence here, at any rate, and it's unlikely that anyone else will offer at this point. Do you know what's been going on?"

"Sessin protector is dead. F'Heing and Darden are either caged or dead by now. The Jungles are on fire. I don't know what's happened to the teyanain ha'rethe. I can't see that far."

Her eyes went wide. She stared at him, shocked. "That isn't what I meant, but... that explains... a lot." She bent her head, covering her face with one hand, shaking her head slowly. "What's happened to the Qisani?"

"I don't know," he said. "I haven't looked."

She tilted a sharp glance at him. "Why not?"

He began to say *It's complicated;* something in her expression stopped him. "Wait a moment," he told her, then shut his eyes and reached out, pushing through rock-heavy reluctance.

Sunlight striped along improbable patterns, drought catching at the back of his throat: a fading wail hung in the air, stone dust scratching against his nostrils.

The world turns against us, attiara said, snagging at his presence, yanking him closer. Barbs raked into him, digging in, forcing him to remain in place, to hear the fury and pain. *Do you betray us?*

No, he told them. *I do not understand what happened. Wait, only wait, let me look –*

The heap of rock that had sheltered the Callen of Ishrai for so long had been reduced to tumbled boulders, striped with unyielding sunlight. The land around it lay shattered and sunken. Water gleamed along the bottom of deep trenches. The air hung thick with debris and dust. The cloud would take days to settle properly, even if a wind stirred it across the miles of devastation.

Acana's cry rang out in Deiq's ears, deafening and silent all at once. *My home,* she said, depthless sorrow in the words, then withdrew into a quiet, hard-shelled mass in the back of Deiq's mind.

We know what happened, attiara said. *The one who held this section of the world in place has passed, and all is broken and failing.*

The ha'rethe in the Horn, Deiq said, finally understanding. *The one Evkit enslaved.* The thought slipped out into the weave before he could stop it. An angry hissing distorted the not-space he occupied.

This human is traitor and traitor and traitor, attiara said. *He must be destroyed with great pain.*

I will handle that, Deiq told them. *Are you in need of assistance? Have you been injured?*

We are strong, attiara said. *We will rebuild. We have the strength of the ha'reye to draw upon. You were wise to tell us not to kill them. We will use them, as you suggested, and we will create a new nest in a more secure location than this proved to be.*

That notion felt distinctly alarming. *Where will you go?* Deiq asked, trying to hide his worry.

We will not tell you, attiara said, defiant, angry once more. *We can see that you are now bound to the land. You cannot wander and give us advice at you promised. You have breached your word. We do not trust you.*

That is foolish of you, Deiq said, *as I am in a better position now than ever before to give you the guidance you need. Had I not bound myself, I would have gone mad and destroyed everything, including you.*

Attiara huffed a little, rejecting that possibility. Deiq slipped gently from their grasp, twisting, turning, spreading himself out to flatten attiara beneath a heavy pressure. They writhed, howling outrage and terror.

He lifted away, withdrawing, coiling into a compact presence. *I am stronger than I have ever been,* he told them. *I could destroy you easily. If you choose not to trust me, I will remove you so that you cannot become my enemies in future. What do you wish?*

We trust you, attiara said, muted, sullen. *You are stronger. We will allow you to guide us. But we will not show you our new lair. We do not trust the world around you.*

I cannot give you guidance if you hide from me, he pointed out.

You will send your guidance throughout the surface world, as you promised, attiara said. *We will find your lessons and we will learn from them. We will come to you with questions. You are bound.* You *are easy to find now.*

Deiq shrugged, agreeing. He drew an ending sigil in the air, indicating that he was done talking; attiara mirrored the gesture. He withdrew into the heaviness of flesh and breath, allowing real sound, real texture, real scents to invade his perceptions.

Damnit. I forgot to ask after Teilo. Again. He allowed himself a moment of real anger at that, a sharp cut of self-loathing, then let it go as pointless.

It took some time to settle back into a stable form. Alyea sat still, waiting, utterly unconcerned by the flickering, quivering shifts pulsing through his appearance.

"The Qisani is destroyed," he said once his throat muscles steadied. "Something happened at the Horn, and it triggered a collapse down the center-line of the southlands."

Alyea bent her head again.

"I thought it might be ruined," she said. "The entire southlands is largely in ruins. Sessin, Tereph, the entire eastern coast has been destroyed by collapsing cliffs or swamped under enormous waves. The Horn has split apart. The villages there are entirely destroyed. The teyanain are having to scramble to find new homes. Well—that may not be the right word...."

"No. Teyanain don't *scramble.*" Deiq let himself laugh a little bit at the notion. "Where have they resettled?"

"I don't know," she said. "Most of them have just... disappeared. Some are in Water's End. There's no sign of Evkit. Rumors go in all directions on that. Trapped in the ruins, imprisoned, dead, insane, you name it."

"If he's alive, sane or not," Deiq said, "I want him brought here. He's *mine.*" Long-simmering fury walked up his back and narrowed his eyes.

Ours, Acana said, ferociously bitter. *He's responsible for the deaths of many good people.* My *people. I'll bring him to account for that!*

Ours, attiara hummed, far away, acid-etched hatred lacing the word. Deiq grunted, annoyed at the intrusion, and pulled a more solid division into place, comprehensively blocking their access.

Someone spoke, closer to hand. He forced himself back to the external conversation.

"If I can, I will, ha'inn," Alyea was saying soberly. "That's the best I can offer." She paused, studying him, then added, carefully neutral, "Do you want to hear the rest of it?"

He advanced until he stood within arm's reach. She looked up at him, unafraid, watching the side of his face, not staring directly at him. He thought about telling her that he wouldn't respond to implicit challenges the same way these days; decided against it. It would take too long to explain. She was already radiating strain, subtle enough that she probably hadn't noticed yet. He sighed and sank to kneel on the floor. "Time doesn't matter to me now," he told her. "It does matter to *you*. You shouldn't stay much longer."

"I made arrangements before I called for you," she said. "I can be... unavailable for a while."

"It's still not healthy. You should go back." He watched the air around her distort, shimmering with the effort she didn't know she was expending to stay here.

She moved a hand, catching his attention back to her face. "I'm your bound lord," she said mildly. "Support me as I support you, ha'inn. I'm not willing to leave your company just yet."

He blinked, considering, then shut his eyes and traced along her back trail to where her physical body lay quiet, tended by anxious servants. He hesitated, remembering his previous, disastrous attempt at healing her: *Threading a reverse draw out through his fingertips, forcing his way through a thick grey fog of refusal, agony streaking up his arms, the mist turning red, Alyea beginning to wail—*

Lost, something chattered at him, a bitter-edged, mocking caw. *Lost, lost, lost....*

A black form whirled from nowhere to land atop Alyea's body: An enormous crow that *tchik'd* at him sternly. By the lack of reaction from the servants, they didn't see it any more than they saw him.

Lost, it scolded him.

"If you've nothing more helpful than that to say, piss off," he told the bird. It grackled, laughing at him, and lifted into the air, winging its way to his shoulder. He allowed it, intrigued. As its talons sank into a fierce grip, perception shifted: Lines appeared across Alyea's body, a patchwork of muscles and bones and veins, highlighted ugly red in places under strain.

Deiq put out his hands reflexively, alarmed, then hesitated again. The crow flexed its talons, murmuring encouragement, and let out a raucous *cawrr*. No—Deiq turned his head, staring at the bird. A word. "Carr?" he asked.

"Care," it said, hoarse but distinct, then disappeared in an abrupt explosion of feathers that blew through Deiq's illusionary form, splattering onto the floor as red and black oily splotches.

"*Care*?" he said aloud, bewildered. Confusion turned to outrage. "It's that damn *simple*?"

It's easy to call something simple once you understand it, Eredion's ghost-voice observed dryly. Acana added her opinion: *Love isn't an emotion ha'ra'hain comprehend, remember? Especially not a First Born who only sees humans as part of a plan laid out across centuries.* I *barely managed to understand human emotions, and I spent most of my life teaching them human-intimate secrets. Don't underestimate this moment.*

Deiq shook his head and returned to the illusion of a stone room and Alyea sitting on a couch, patiently waiting for him.

"Alyea," he said, holding out his hands. She rose and took them without hesitation. He drew a breath, allowing himself a moment of fear; then, one by one, released the layers of deflection, of protection, of misdirection, of deception, pulling her steadily *in* past each barrier.

At last he faced her with his true self, all illusion discarded: Grey, mottled, misshapen, eyes too large, no true bones: only easily reshaped cartilage. It was still an illusion of sorts—he wouldn't risk bringing her down to the deep lair, not yet—but he'd brought enough of his *self* into the room to make it real for all intents. She could hurt him, badly, if she chose to strike out in this moment. And maybe more frighteningly, she could see *anything*—any memories, any past actions, whatever she cared to look at.

She held still, entirely relaxed, even smiling a little. "Are you trying to scare me?" she said. "It won't work. *This*—" she laid a hand on grey skin, unflinching, "—doesn't *matter*." She lifted a hand to point at his eyes, carefully keeping her fingers well clear. "*That* matters. And that hasn't changed."

He closed his eyes and wrapped himself around her, unearthing Acana's understanding of *human* emotion, *human* vulnerability, *human* thoughts. Let Moir's quiet, steady devotion fill him; allowed the priest's younger, more passionate self to spill unruly emotion along what served as a spine for the moment.

Balance. *Balance.*

It felt like standing on one foot, tiptoe, in the middle of a raging tornado: so much *red*, white, *green*—heat, *ice*, dry—he had no proper names for the swift-moving sensations.

Balance.

The buffeting eased, or perhaps he'd found the right way to lean into it; he couldn't tell.

He felt for the chains linking him to Alyea, opened them into a channel; his *self* surged forward, eager as any youngster seeking sustenance, weaving into her energy, collecting in key spots.

How long do you want to live, Alyea?

For as long you want me by your side, she answered.

Then reach into me, as I've just done to you.

Swift and sure, he guided her to critical spots within himself. Each touch created a link to the corresponding point within her, energy swirling immediately into an infinitely repeating loop between them. She gasped at the impact. Far above, her body choked, convulsing.

Without hesitation, she reached up, soothing the strain, calming the physical fear, regulating her breathing; her body slipped back into sleep. She returned her attention to Deiq, radiating satisfaction.

Well done, he said.

She laughed. *Another lesson?*

Not for you, he said. *This time, I'm the one who learned something new.*

He swirled them both back to the surface, returning her gently to her body; motioned the surprised servants aside and held her, rubbing her back as she sat up, coughing and shaking with reaction.

After a time, she drew in a deep, calming breath and blinked at him bemusedly. "You're—*here,*" she said, looking around at the owl-eyed stares of the servants. "You're—I thought you'd never—"

He looked down at his hands, examining the structure of muscle and bone, the movement of vein and breath. Looked through it, tissue turning transparent, smoky, surreal; drew himself back to focus with surprisingly little effort. "I'm still below," he said. "This form is—a part of me. A projection. I can't hold it for long, and only while you allow it."

Her forehead creased. "That sounds... uncomfortable."

"Humiliating, you mean?" he said, laughing. "No more than it is for you, that your presence in my nest depends on *my* permission."

Her frown lifted to an understanding smile.

You chose well, Acana said, a soft exhalation of relief.

I know.

Deiq cupped Alyea's thin face in his hands, leaning his forehead against hers, and smiled back. "We'll have time," he told her. "Call for me at the dark of the moon. I need to rest and learn my new duties. There's a great deal to be done. —oh. Don't remove the aenstone."

"Why not?" she asked, startled.

"I don't want anyone else to know it's useless against me now."

Her eyes grew wide. A moment later, a wicked smile crept across her face. "I *see.*"

He sat back and rubbed a thumb against the tiny lump on her eyebrow. She reached out, returning the gesture.

"One more thing. This is no longer Scratha Fortress or Scratha Family," he said. "I won't serve Scratha. I'll serve *you.* Give Gria the choice of accepting that or leaving."

"Already done. She's staying on as *numaina* of Peysimun Family. We've agreed that there will need to be some changes."

"Change is good. Do what you think best." Deiq ran a knuckle down the side of her face, wincing as abrupt strain shot along his spine. "I have to go."

"Go," she said. "I'll be here."

He nodded gratefully, then gave in to weariness, letting go of physical form, withdrawing back to his lair.

Dark of the moon, he heard her say, a fading echo.

Dark of the moon, he agreed, coiling into a comfortable position, and turned his attention to reshaping the world.

Chapter 54

Allonin let out a long breath and rubbed at his eyes, feeling as though he were emerging from a dream. He exchanged a look with Azni, wishing he dared ask questions aloud, wishing he dared reach out to speak to her silently. He felt small, shrunken, weakened by the savage tension that lingered in the air from Cuna's confrontation with her father.

Azni's shoulders moved in a tiny shrug. She looked at the fire, biting her lip the way she did when she was afraid of revealing something unintentionally.

Cuna reached up and loosed the tie holding her braids together, fanning them around her shoulders in clear relief. She looked out into the darkness for a time, as though listening for something. The only sound Allonin heard was the erratic pops and crackles of the fire working its way through dry sagebrush branches. At last, she said, "I see no reason for the teyanain to be at war, especially not with those that should be our closest allies. I declare the war between teyanain and Aerthraim to be ended in this moment. Will you carry that word back to Aerthraim Fortress for me, as my ambassador?"

"I'm *not* swearing over to you, Calcana," Allonin said recklessly. A loud *pop* from the fire accented his words. The teyanin tending the fire prodded at the branches, sending up a brief burst of sparks.

Cuna passed an indifferent glance across Allonin. "Why would I want you to? I'm speaking to your sister, who has already made an agreement with me, through my representative." She nodded at Azni. "Will you carry the word to the mahadrae, and broker a new treaty between our Families?"

Azni glanced at Allonin's expression and grinned. "Yes, Calcana," she said. "I will do that. Allo—come with me. I'll protect you." She laughed at the bitterly irritable look he gave her.

"I'll pass," he said. Smoke turned harsh in his nostrils. He scratched at the back of his neck where some small night-insect had bitten him. "I said I'd never set foot in that place again, and I intend to hold that promise to myself. I have other obliga—" He paused, the word *obligations* pulling memory into sharp relief, and rose to his feet, his throat tight with alarm. "Lamb. I was traveling with a friend. A northerner, red-haired—he was in the area that collapsed."

Cuna shook her head regretfully. "I have no way of knowing what happened to him," she said. "It's been hours. He's almost certainly... wait—don't—!"

Even as Cuna spoke, Allonin was searching, fiercely intent on finding that unique *presence*—

There. Distance shifted into the scent of powdered rock and the groan of an injured man.

"Don't—" Cuna said, her voice echoing. Allonin ignored her, took a lithe, twisting step and threw himself *toward* that groan.

Rock tented around him, pressed close and hot, darkness filled with dust and the smell of blood. He scarcely had room to kneel across the prone form, and a more vibrato groan from overhead warned of imminent collapse. He tucked himself around Lamb, bewildered for a moment—how to move elsewhere when he couldn't even *move*—

Here. Cuna unrolled a hook into his mind and tugged sharply, tumbling him back through not-space to land in a clumsy sprawl on the ground, Lamb splayed out across him.

"Damnit," Cuna said, exhaling noisily. "You're a fool, Allonin."

Azni's voice came, distant and strained: "How did he do that? I thought only ha'ra'hain could—"

"He holds the true gift," Cuna answered. "Even so, he nearly got himself killed just now." Her voice held more irritation than admiration, more exasperation than amusement.

Allonin lurched to his knees, laying Lamb on a clear spot of ground, splayed his hands out across the man's head and chest, and murmured a brief, heartfelt prayer to any gods that might be listening. Cuna knelt beside Allo, her fingertips resting on each of the injured man's knees. Her eyes stayed open, hazy with concentration, her braids falling across her face in straggled disarray.

Cracked collarbone—ribs—gash on leg—bruises—Allonin scanned through Lamb's injuries rapidly, sorting out immediate need.

Punctured lung, shit, that comes first—

Lamb gasped, coughed, blood trickling from the side of his mouth. He inhaled a jagged, rasping breath, then another, his eyes fluttering as though trying to open. A guttural *aaaa* sound emerged.

He'd never tried this ambitious of a healing. He'd managed a badly broken leg, once, but understood muscles more clearly than bones—

Stop thinking so much. He focused, dropping all awareness of anything beyond the moment; pressed torn tissues aside, easing bone free, straightening, binding—a rush of blood swept across his internal vision, and he heard Lamb gagging.

An ethereal presence reached past him, pressing, molding, sealing cut arteries and veins. The flood dissolved, bone moving pliably back into place. He swept his attention across the wounded lung, reinflating flattened sacs, mending small tears in muscle and flesh. Tissue flexed as Lamb gasped, coughing—a rattling sound, but it cleared quickly, and air pulsed through the channels without obstruction.

You must love this man very much, Cuna observed. He could sense her soothing an array of minor bruises and scrapes, leaving him free to handle the major injuries.

No, he said absently, his attention on repairing Lamb's cracked collarbone. *He's just better than most of the useless shits I've dealt with over the years. I'd rather keep him among the living a while more to balance the world out.*

A wave of disorientation pushed him clear of the trance, leaning him sideways hard. Cuna's hand on his shoulder stopped him from falling over entirely.

Breathe, and look at the world around you, she told him. *You've done all you can.* She moved aside. One of her people took her place, busy swabbing cuts clean before he'd even settled fully to his knees.

Allonin sucked in a shaky breath, straightening his spine, and blinked until Lamb's bruised face came into reasonable focus.

Lamb coughed, his eyes opening. "Aaaa. Aaaalll. Aaaallo."

"I'm right here," Allonin said. "Stop trying to talk."

"Damn," Lamb said, voice wavering. "More debt."

Allonin, caught by surprise, let out a bark of relieved, rueful laughter. "No. No debt over this. Godsdamn, Lamb, you are a tough bastard to kill, you know that?"

"My specialty," Lamb whispered, his eyes closing again. The teyanin finished wrapping up the last of the man's wounds, collected his scattered supplies, then withdrew with a scant nod to Allonin.

Cuna pushed her braids out of her face, frowning, and said, "He may be resilient, but he *does* owe you his life. You should hold him to that. I can already tell he's the type to take advantage if given the chance." She gathered up a handful of braids, holding them forward to squint at the damage, then sighed, letting them fall to her shoulder.

Allonin shrugged, avoiding his sister's intent, astounded stare. "Can we rest here, Calcana, while he heals?"

"Of course. I'll leave two of my people with you." She glanced around the ring of teyanain, who began gathering up their belongings in stoic silence. "I apologize that I cannot spare enough of my people to shorten your journey."

She turned away abruptly, fading out into the darkness without another word. Her people followed suit. Two remained behind, sitting quietly, staring at the fire as though it were the only matter of interest in the entire world. They could have been stones themselves.

Allonin let out a noisy breath, standing to stretch, hands in the small of his back as he rolled his shoulders and head. The sudden silence left him feeling awkward and unsure of what to say. "Kallaisin's going to be livid," he said; not the *best* choice, but it served to break the quiet. "You won't be safe—"

The fire-tender stirred, looking their way. His dark skin carried a sheen of sweat, but he seemed entirely comfortable at such close range to the flames. "Will be safe. We choose to travel alongside," he said, nodding at Azni, then returned his attention to the fire.

Allonin stared. "You *choose*?" The teyanin made no reply.

"I'm honored by your choice," Azni said, with a warning gesture to Allonin to let it go.

Allonin looked at Lamb's slack face to avoid glaring at his sister. He hadn't expected her to be quite so—*confident* wasn't quite the right word, but he couldn't come up with a better one at the moment. Which was absurd. He'd always wanted her to be able to stand on her own. He'd pushed her to think for herself, to question everything.

I should be pleased. Instead, he felt vaguely resentful. He shut his eyes, shaking his head, and tried to say something useful as a way of distracting himself from his unsettled thoughts. "So you've had a hand in changing the world after all, Azni. Regav would be proud."

As soon as the words left his mouth he bit his tongue, wishing he could call them back.

"Do you know, I haven't even thought about him for days," Azni said, apparently surprised. She tilted her head, brooding for a few moments. "I don't miss him any more. I don't—I don't feel responsible for his death."

Allonin had expected her to snap at him. Her calm put him even further off balance. He blurted, "Wait, I thought you blamed *me* for his death!"

"I did. And I blamed myself." She shrugged. "I don't know if he *would* be proud of how things have turned out, actually. Regav was... he was Darden. He wanted to be in charge, he wanted to be the one in the light. I was... I think he wanted me there to adore him, at the end of the day. I wasn't supposed to be his equal."

"That's the first time I've ever heard you be critical of him," Allonin said softly.

Azni looked at the empty seats again. He'd dismissed her constant survey as a nervous tic at first, but was beginning to wonder if she *saw* something there. Uneasy chill ran along his spine, and he hastily turned his mind away from that notion.

Her voice quiet and pensive, Azni said, "I destroyed a lot of lives along my chosen path. I think it was easier to gold-plate a lost love than to face the reality."

Allonin let out a shaky, chuckling breath. "That, I understand." He looked up at the night sky. "Making amends is a steep hill to climb."

"I can't tell which of us has the harder climb."

"Every hill looks like the tallest to the person climbing it," he said pragmatically. "There's always another one beyond, though, so it's no use comparing, is there?"

"And every hill is different, from sand to tree," she agreed.

He snorted. "And now you're sounding like—" He stopped short, turning his head away as a pang of realization shot through his chest.

The fire-tender prodded more sparks into the air. Allonin watched them scatter, tilting his head to look up at the stars overhead, as his sister said, scarcely audible, "I sound like Mother. I know. It's my fault—"

He made himself look at her, meet her eyes, accept her pain and grief, sharp and real as his own. He said, "No more your fault than mine. If I hadn't been meddling with the forbidden books—"

She cut him off with a sharp gesture, a flat mask sliding across the moment of vulnerability. "Never mind. It's over and done with, Allo. I'm not interested in revisiting that particular guilt. I'll look at that hill another day. Right now, I need to get some rest." She rose, turning away; he let her go.

There was nothing more to say, in any case. He sat silently, letting the pain in his mind burn down like wood to ash, letting his grief transform into a glowing, ethereal dance like that of the stars moving in slow majesty so far overhead.

Chapter 55

The road leading from Scratha lands toward Sessin proved to be almost entirely washed out under the recent ferocious rains. Idisio scrambled over the broken land, finding the physical exertion more satisfying than using his ha'ra'hain abilities would have been. Occasionally, he tested himself with a soaring leap that carried him across a ravine or particularly difficult area.

Dry amusement filtered across the back of his mind: Not Deiq, but someone else. Alyea? No, the presence felt too masculine. He paused at the edge of a tumbled mass of rocks and trees, and said aloud, "Wait until I'm on neutral territory, if you please."

He studied the collapsed section for another moment, gauging its stability, then shrugged, bent his knees, and leapt in an arc meant to take him to the top of the debris. He landed some distance further than intended and went sprawling, rolling across rocks and roots, gathering more cuts and bruises than he'd expected. Hauling himself to his feet, he brushed himself off, examined the tears in his clothing ruefully, then checked to make sure his pack hadn't been ripped open or apart during the tumble.

Deiq had taught Alyea to repair damaged cloth with willpower alone. Idisio found himself entirely unable to master that trick, even with her memory pointing out the path. He'd have to mend his clothes by hand.

"You are now off Scratha lands, ha'inn," a man's voice said. "Please hold still."

Idisio turned deliberately, searching out the speaker. A small man, dressed in grey and dun, with dark skin and darker eyes, stood some distance away. Not out of range, not for a ha'ra'ha, but far enough to make it clear he wanted to keep space between himself and Idisio.

"What do you want?" Idisio said flatly.

"To know your intentions, ha'inn."

"You're teyanin. I don't owe you explanations."

The man inclined his head, expression sober. "I am teyanin," he agreed. "I do not ask because you owe me an answer, ha'inn. I ask to find out the shape of our respective futures. What are your intentions? Where are you going from here?"

"Which of the teyanain are you?" Idisio demanded.

"The true teyanain," the man said, his mouth crooking into a half-smile, then patted the air before him as Idisio grunted irritably. "Patience, ha'inn. I am only here to ask questions. If you are departing the southlands, there is no need to burden you with information on local affairs. If you intend to stay...." He shrugged, his head tilting to one side.

"I'm leaving," Idisio said. "I'm going to Arason, where I was born. I have no interest in ever returning to this place or being involved in these politics again. Is that what you wanted to hear?"

"Yes," the teyanin said, bowing deeply. "Grace to your grace, ha'inn, and honor to your honor. May I suggest you allow us to take you to the edge of Bright Bay? The ports are not what they were, at this time, and the lands are far more difficult to travel, as well. What you struggled with on Scratha lands was the least of the damage inflicted by recent events."

Idisio looked north, dismayed, remembering the newly formed, gigantic rift along the top of the Wall. "Oh—" he said. "I—didn't think about that. Well—I can do it myself. I'm not fond of letting other people move me around like a piece on a chabi board."

The teyanin smiled briefly, shaking his head. "The same barriers that were in place on your journey south would once more stop you from traveling north, ha'inn. You will need our help, I regret." He didn't seem in the least regretful to Idisio; more slyly amused.

"So you're one of *hers*," Idisio said before he could stop himself.

The teyanin bowed slightly, his palms flat against his chest. "I serve the head of the teyanain," he agreed. "Who happens, at this time, to be female. Will you allow us to relocate you, ha'inn? I swear there will be no harm—"

"I've heard the speech," Idisio said. "Fine. Get it over with. Honestly, the sooner I'm—"

The land around him flickered. He stumbled a step sideways, coughing as the words died in his mouth, staring at the shuttered, empty buildings that once served as inns to those caught outside the gates of Bright Bay after closing time. Then he looked ahead, to the tightly shut gates and an array of guards watching him with visible suspicion even at this distance.

"Thanks," he said sourly, and received no answer. Turning around, he found himself alone. "Damnit."

After considering his options, he sighed, turning north once more, and went to pacify the guards.

Chapter 56

Air hung muggy and still around him. An incessant chirping noise wavering between high and low pitches bounced against his ears. Sweat trickled down the back of his neck.

His eyes were covered with some sort of gauzy cloth. Bringing a hand up to push it aside was a tortuous effort that faltered and failed halfway through. His motion prompted other motion nearby, a familiar scent filling his nose as a hand landed gently on his wrist.

A woman's voice, familiar as the scent but as unnamable to him, said, "Cafad? Don't move. Don't open your eyes yet. Let me get you some water—"

A straw pressed against his lower lip a moment later. He accepted, and drank tepid water with slow deliberation until the straw began to pull air. Then he sat quietly, listening to the movements, sorting out what each sound meant.

He'd once been able to do that without thinking, it seemed, but now each sound required conscious analysis. That scrape: a step on sandy ground. That rustle: cloth moving. Someone breathing. A murmur of low conversation, sending for a servant or healer or food—he couldn't make the words out.

"I can't hear," he said, the words emerging in a hoarse croak that made no sense.

"One word at a time. Take it slowly."

"I."

"You. Yes. Go on."

"Can't."

"... hand?"

"Can't."

"Oh—can't. You can't—what?"

"Hear."

"Fear? No—wait—*hear*. Oh...."

The chirping insect noise was the only sound for a few heartbeats.

"Oh, Cafad," the woman said slowly. "You can hear me, right? And this?" Her hand lifted from his wrist. There came the sound of a clap, then snapping fingers.

"Yes."

"So you still have ordinary hearing, but you've lost your desert lord perceptions. I was warned that might happen... I'd hoped it wouldn't. I'm sorry, Cafad." Her voice was heavy with regret. "I don't know if it will come back. It might, but... I don't think so. Not unless we find another ha'ra'hain or ha'rethe to help you."

He jerked back, an involuntary shudder working through his body. "*No*!"

Her hand settled on his forearm. "All right, we won't look," she said. "Do you know who I am, Cafad? Do you remember me?"

He said nothing, breathing hard, desperately trying to connect that teasing scent, that voice, to a name—a person—anything at all. Finally, he shook his head, the motion slow and stiff, as though underused muscles protested their use.

"Almost," he husked. "But. No."

"Give it time," another voice said, from further away. "We can't tell him anything. He has to remember on his own, not from our words. You've already said too much."

Her hand tightened, then fell away. "I'm sorry," she said, her voice thick. "I just—wanted—"

"I know," the other voice—male?—said. "Go home, s'a, and wait a few days before returning."

Cafad began to raise a hand in protest. The motion failed, as it had before, and seemed to pass unnoticed. Sand scratched a departing pattern. Perception clarified it into sand on stone, grit carried in from—somewhere else—

He managed to bend his chin toward his chest, dimly frustrated at having to fight for every bit of comprehension. A hand settled on his shoulder: broader, more masculine this time. "Time for you to rest, s'e," another voice said. "I've a drink for you. Here—show me that you can do it on your own."

Again, a straw pressed against his lip; again, he accepted it and drank. Not water, this time, but a—a—tea? Or fruit juice? He couldn't decide. A mix of the two, perhaps.

"Well done," the voice approved. "Don't try to get up. I'll lift you over to the bed. Easy, now."

Motion made his head swirl and he gasped, thrashing—which emerged as quivering twitches—then motion stopped, with solid material behind his back and legs and shoulders, defining a slanted sitting posture.

"Easy there," the man said. "Take a few breaths. You're safe. No more moving. All done." A pillow tucked behind Cafad's head. He leaned back into it, almost pathetically grateful for the bit of extra comfort.

"Where," he said. "Am."

"Safe," the man—was it a man? or a deep-voiced woman with large hands? Cafad couldn't tell. The *scent* seemed male—it had a broadness, a thickness, that resonated as masculine—but Cafad didn't particularly trust his senses at the moment. "Nothing to think of past that, s'e. Rest."

Cafad opened his mouth to form protest, to insist on answers, and found the white haze over his eyes darkening. He couldn't remember what he'd been going to say. It didn't seem important any longer. He was... safe... he could rest...

You are safe, you are loved—

He jerked, crying out with horror for no clear reason. Hands patted his shoulders, another straw in his mouth, more liquid—then thought dimmed back to dullness, darkness chasing away the fear for a time.

When the white returned, he was able to raise his hands, touch his face, and feel a heavy beard growth with a sense of wonder. He'd always kept himself clean-shaven... and with that thought came memory. He sat still, blinking under the bandages wrapped over his eyes, staring into the past with a growing sense of horror.

I killed Lichni. Just because she got in my way. Oh, gods....

He'd been as ruthless, as heartless, as a F'Heing noble, as an angry ha'ra'ha. As cold-blooded and dangerous as the old Lord Scratha. That last thought put a harsh pain in his chest; he breathed thickly, seeing the past in an entirely different light.

It wasn't truly me. It wasn't even the old lord. Scratha ha'rethe was using us all....

I won't ever go back there. I can't. He searched, awkwardly, within himself for the deluge of power he'd controlled in recent months; found only thin glimmers and whispers in place of a roaring waterfall. *I'm crippled. I'm not even a desert lord any longer. I've lost everything I've fought for my entire life.*

Surprisingly, the thought brought with it a sharp swell of relief.

"S'e," an attendant said, pulling him from his trance. "Here's a drink—"

"Nissa," he said, dropping his hands to his lap.

"I'll send for her, s'e," the attendant said without any trace of surprise. "Have some water. It's just water," he added, as though expecting Cafad to be suspicious.

Cafad wrapped his hands around the cup, held it in place himself, and sipped through the reed straw with steady patience. Ran his fingers across the rough clay, feeling the lines of smoother glazing, the curves of simple, solid craftsmanship. As the cup emptied, a swirl of air and scent and motion brought awareness of *Nissa.*

Her presence felt like polished stone, and cool water at midday, and the scent of flowers after a desert rain. He'd never noticed that before.

"Cafad," she said, profound relief in her voice. "You called for me!"

He nodded, let someone take the cup from him, and dropped his hands to his lap once more. "Nissa. Where am I?" The words came more easily, although he still had to shape each one with care.

"Bright Bay," she said after a pause, as though checking with the attendant for permission.

He leaned his head back, resting it against the wall, patiently working through the implications of those two words. He heard her settle into a chair nearby, her own breathing even as she waited for him to speak again.

Bright Bay. Not Scratha Fortress. So his Family was, effectively, destroyed. Or at the very least, he'd been expelled from all heritage rights. He found himself relieved. *Let someone else handle that gods-cursed heap of broken block,* he thought. *I never should have gone back.*

He spread his hands out across his thighs, curling his fingers gently, relishing the pressure. Everything felt new, washed clean, turned around to a new and entirely pleasant angle. "All right," he said, then two more words: "Marry me."

She sucked in a startled breath. "Cafad," she said, wondering and anxious all at once. "You're not healed yet—you don't even know what's been—"

"Doesn't matter," he said. "I love you. Marry me."

The silence hung for a breath, two, three: then, explosively, "*Yes.*"

He nodded, tension along his spine releasing. "*Now* tell me what's happened."

Chapter 57

Letter from Lord Antouin Sessin to Lord Cafad Scratha.

Instructions: To Be Delivered To And Opened Only By Lord Cafad Scratha; To Be Delivered Only Upon The Death Of Lord Antouin Sessin And The Overall Failure Of Sessin Family.

Lord Scratha:

I offer you this letter with hope: hope that my daughter is still alive and in your care, hope that you yourself are alive and well, hope that some remnant of our respective Families remain. I have little hope of forgiveness, and do not particularly believe myself worthy of that, in any case.

I tried, when I took over from Lord Arit Sessin, to redirect some of the biases and policies he put into place. My success was sharply limited, in part because of my second wife, Tashaye; Sessin men of power traditionally rely on their women behind the scenes as advisors and for guidance. Women, after all, cast a wider and wiser net when gathering information than the proper dignity of men allows for.

I do not place all blame on Tashaye. She was young when we married, but she raised our children well and provided me with a great deal of very good advice. It is my own fault for taking so long to question her emphasis on treating with the Aerthraim. It is my own fault for taking so long to check her lineage closely. She was born Sessin; her line traced back to Lord Arit himself. The loremasters approved the union, telling me that she was distant enough a relation to be acceptable.

I did not find out until far too late that Chidor Sessin was not in fact Tashaye's father. His wife had been indiscreet with a visiting Aerthraim and Tashaye was the result. I leave it to you to imagine my humiliation and rage at the deception.

By that point I had already made certain arrangements with the Aerthraim, guided by Tashaye's advice, that put my Family in a dangerously precarious situation. I could not afford to breach our alliance. I attempted to summon Lord Eredion of Sessin, Tashaye's brother—half-brother, as I now know—to return from Bright Bay and put his considerable talents to work repairing my blunders. He has always been able to charm Tashaye into going against her desires far better than I ever managed, and he has developed a reputation as a miracle worker on political snarls.

As of this writing, I am reliably informed that he has left Bright Bay and traveled north, not south. I can only assume he has defected and is no longer a reliable resource for Sessin Family. I suspect I should have written his recall summons in a calmer state of mind, but done is done.

I saw only disaster ahead for my Family, and did my best to send away the brightest and best for their own protection. The only way to do this without creating the impression of fear and flight, in most cases, was to manufacture some indignity with which to eject each person from Sessin Family lands. Nissa I sent to you, despite your bitterness towards Sessin, because I believe you truly care for her and she for you; at the least, you would keep her alive.

That letter I wrote with deliberate brutality, in hopes that it would provoke you to be kinder to Nissa in sympathy—you have always leaned against the wind, Cafad, and while that is frustrating, it is also admirable.

Please, if she is still alive and by your side, tell her I am so very sorry for the deception. It utterly broke my heart to send her away in such despair and misery, and I was sleepless for many a night until Micru returned with word that you accepted her as daimaina*. Thank you, Cafad. My soul may rot in all the hells for my mistakes, but you have saved my only remaining child, and I bless you through all eternity for that.*

I cannot tell you more details, even at this extreme. Sessin Family may be crumbling around me, but I will not leave its name in disgrace. I beg that you assist those survivors you might come across. I am well aware of the irony in this request, and can only hope you are a better man than Lord Arit when it comes to letting go of old bitterness.

As a closing note, you need not fear Aerthraim involvement regarding Nissa. Aerthraim is strictly matrilineal, and the visiting Aerthraim who fathered Tashaye was nobody of consequence, in any case.

I offer sincere apologies for the many years of misunderstanding and bitterness between our Families, and I pray that the world going forward is a better one than the one in which we both grew up.

With deepest regards,

Lord Antouin Sessin

Epilogue One

Bright Bay

Seaweed lay in great, steaming, stinking heaps, strung across pathways and dangling from improbable heights. Multicolored, strangely shaped ribbons of it dried and disintegrated under the ferocious out-of-season heat, while swarms of every imaginable insect danced over and through every such heap as though the muck were delicacy incarnate.

There was no shelter from the sun. Ramshackle structures lay in collapsed rubble. The semi-permanent array of tents and sun-shades had been taken by the first surge of angry water when it rose. More than a few bodies added to the general aroma of rot; some human, mostly fish and whatever stray, muddy street-scavengers hadn't had sense enough to leave the area when the water first sucked out of the bay.

Over two dozen Callen had stepped up since the disaster. They led without challenge, assembling and organizing commoners and nobles alike, uncovering bodies and burning them on giant pyres that roared day and night. Even the few remaining Northern Church priests accepted the authority of the Callen in this situation.

It seemed a safe bet that those Callen who were directly working with removing the bodies for decent death rituals followed the Sun Lord. That also didn't matter. The king had declared that full honors were being conferred to all the people, even residents of the muddiest streets, so as not to anger *any* of the gods. It didn't ease the pain of loss, or repair ruined homes or recovered destroyed goods, but it meant something to the common folk that the king himself had taken such notice.

Rumor had it that the Seventeen Gates were open, taking in refugees of higher social standing. That was good. It meant that the mud-street crowd could move inland, away from the seaweed and stink and pyres, and take over the newly vacant middle-class areas. Those sectors were too ruined for fine tastes but far, far better than what remained of lower Bright Bay after the second, and third, and fourth surge.

But among the seawwed, among the hellishly thick clouds of stinging insects, among the debris... there was more than a little chance of finding lost or abandoned valuables; free money without provenance, as the saying went. All one had to to was put any kind of thick mask across one's nose and mouth, find a long, hooked stick, and be willing to sweat and slip through sea-muck, laboring under Payti's own blaze of heat through the evidence of Wae's inexplicable and terrible disapproval.

The gods were still unhappy. That much was abundantly clear.

Let the priests deal with the gods, was Pella's opinion. Whatever had roused them to such an outrageous display, Pella was in no way a part of it. Let the priests deal with the matter. She had more important things to concentrate on, such as the pain in her empty stomach and the unsteadiness of her hands.

A shiny bauble in her pocket meant food in her stomach and a safe place to sleep, maybe for several days if she found something good enough. She wasn't the only one searching, of course. Earlier in the day, she'd found a scattering of low-value coins, then promptly lost them to a bigger, more determined scavenger with pox-scars and a wild, mad look in his eyes. At least he'd let her keep her belt pouch. There was that.

She just had to move quicker next time, Pella reasoned. Bolt from the area, then stash or sell the discovery before anyone caught her. She could run fast. She'd always been able to outrun most anyone, if she got her feet set under her and a full stride or two ahead.

Seaweed gleamed with the fake glint of treasure. Fool's gold, nothing more than sun catching a few damp bits and turning them to diamonds. Pella picked through it with steady care, lifting, shaking, setting the clumps aside into a pile.

Dozens of similar piles, some taller than Pella, already filled the southeastern quarter of Bright Bay. Pickings were getting thin, even here at the far edge where muddy streets once gave way to unsteady swamp. All of the far edge was submerged now. Pella waded through deepening water, stepping with care, testing for sharply broken bits or slimy patches before committing her weight on each pace.

It was unlikely she'd be able to move fast, if she did find something. But little choice remained. She'd worked the relatively dry areas all morning, only to lose the few coins she'd found. Fewer people ventured this far out.

Two worked north of her: Reca and Nes, easy to identify by how they were always together, and the way Nes, shirtless, displayed startlingly splotched skin all along his back. God-marks, those were called, ghostly as winter air against southern-dark skin. Northern Church doctrine said that god-marks were a sign of being born under Eki's attention. It was a chancy god, of air and winds, prone to games of chance and evil moods. None of the gods were particularly "safe", but Eki ranked just below the god of fire, Payti, in riskiness.

Pella stayed well away from them both as a matter of course. Reca had a mean streak and a penchant for drinking hard. Nes, while milder, was god-touched. Not safe company on the best of days.

To her south was only increasingly deep, muddied water. The southern dock pilings could be seen if one watched the squalling, screeching hordes of birds landing on surfaces that remained—barely—above water. *Complaining bitterly to one another about the mess,* Pella imagined. *And the way us foolish humans loused everything up.*

Or maybe they were happy about all the smaller edible creatures stirred up to the shallows. Sixteen-armed sea stars in improbable shades of blue and orange crawled across Pella's bare feet if she held still too long in one place. Gold crabs, their shells dusky red this time of year, skittered across the piles of seaweed, picking out tiny barnacles and bugs of no interest to humans. Long-winged sea-flies swarmed some sort of enormous, cracked-open shellfish. It might have once been long and oval, but the roughly broken shards left little certainty.

A gillahawk swept past Pella to pounce on a weakly flopping fish, then hopped into the air once more, its newly acquired meal thrashing in its talons. Pella leaned on her stick and watched, breathing hard and briefly jealous.

Good and holy, she was hungry. She looked longingly at the gold crabs, but when their shells turned red, the meat turned dangerous. At best, she'd go crazed for a day. The worst chance involved an agonizing death. She'd seen both, and had no intention of taking either route.

Something shone at her feet with a different, harder gleam than the false promise of wet seaweed and broken pearl-shell. She prodded with the pole, keeping her movements casual, wearily indifferent, wary of showing excitement, never doubting that Reca was watching. She'd stolen finds from Pella before, leaving bruises in their place.

The mass resisted her efforts to pick it apart. There was a dark splotch, a solidity, in the middle of it, that drew her attention. The main section seemed to be a wide ribbon of pale netting, wrapped around that dark thing, which—hadn't it gleamed a moment before? —ah, there, a distinct hint of gold, true gold, widening as she tipped the knotted mess this way and that.

It wouldn't come apart under the picking-pole. *Closer, need a closer look, and I'll have to use my hands.* She bit her lip and cast a glance up the slope at Reca. The woman was already straightening to look, avarice and appraisal apparent in the tilt of her shoulders. Reca motioned to Nes in the next moment, and started downslope toward Pella. *I shouldn't have looked up.*

Panic swelled in her gut. Against all experience, against good sense, she dropped into a crouch and reached a hand into the mess of netting.

The slick thickness against her fingers wasn't netting, it wasn't seaweed, oh dear and holy gods, it was some sort of fish—a sea worm, thin and heavily ribbed and exactly the reason one didn't put one's bare hands into a batch of unsorted sea debris—

Even as Pella began to jerk her hand back, the dark patch she'd been reaching after turned, widening the flash of gold into a semi-circle. She hesitated a half a heartbeat too long, caught by the strangeness.

Gold slid into black into crimson, followed by a sharp, harsh burning along her forearm. She blinked, dazed, realizing that the worm had wrapped itself around her arm just that quickly; a thrash of muscle and the red was—gods, it was her own blood, her skin was shredding under what felt like a thousand tiny hooks, all moving busily, scraping through skin and muscle, aiming for bone and getting there fast, fast, and all she could do was stare in horror, the entirety of the pain not quite caught up yet against the shock—

Pain hit. She screamed, staggering up and back. Her legs went out from under her. Slimy water rushed past the mask, up her nose. Filthy mud coated ragged clothes and ragged skin. She spat, instinct demanding breath, pain sucking in more water as she gasped, choking.

For a moment, she watched Reca retreating, fast, dragging a not-at-all reluctant Nes along.

Then there was only mud, pain, and water. And blood. Far, far too much blood.

The day's sullen heat belonged to high summer, when tile and metal rooftops were expected to be searingly hot, and underground cellars were the preferred place to wait out the sun. In winter, cellars were filled with stored goods, not rotten water thick with wreckage. But normal, as the saying went, had long since sailed to the other end of the world.

Idisio stood barefoot atop a tile roof, surveying the devastation. He'd stashed his boots in a safe dry spot below, unwilling to risk damaging them on sharply broken stone and tile. His clothes were sturdy enough, although hard travel had left its mark on them. The king would just have to cope with Idisio looking a bit raggedy.

No. That was his old way of thinking. Now, it wouldn't do. It wouldn't do at all.

Idisio looked down at a tear in his trousers, scowling, and said aloud, "Are you willing to let me look a fool in front of the king? Not very dignified, that."

A sibilant hiss sounded in the back corners of his mind, sullen and amused at the same time. *Let me show you,* his mother said.

His lip curled, and he dipped his head bullishly towards his chest: every bit the rebellious son for that one moment and aware of how ridiculous that was in context. "You're not taking me over," he said roughly.

Do you want my help or not?

"Not at that price," he said. "*Tell* me, damnit."

His mother sighed, annoyed, but poked at a memory of Deiq trying to explain the concept. *Clumsy*, she said. *He's never mended a shirt by hand, and it shows. Look—like this.*

Idisio shut his eyes and watched a rapid sequence of stitching up a torn shirt. "Oh," he said. "I see. Yes. Thank you." He passed a hand across the hole in his pants, watching it fill in seamlessly. "Much better."

And what do I get for my reward? she said, surly again.

"You're dead," he said. "You don't get rewards."

She withdrew, sulking. He shrugged away her irritation and went back to looking around.

The building below his feet—what was left of it—had once been the largest warehouse in the southeastern past of Bright Bay. It wouldn't be storing food again anytime soon. But then, the southern docks weren't up to offloading cargo, and wouldn't be for some weeks, despite the agitated activity in that area.

Idisio remembered climbing this building countless times over the years. It was a good place to chase off the evening chill and rest sore feet on day-warmed tiles. *Was*. Now only a rough arc of structure remained, and the bulk of the warehouse lay scattered across the inland path, as though a careless child had strewn about paper balls and chabi pieces.

Most of the nearby buildings hadn't even fared this well. They were simply gone, the foundations a thin line amongst slowly receding floodwaters.

My fault.

Idisio had no doubt on that point. It was entirely, absolutely, completely his fault. His fight with the creature living near the top of the Wall Stair, and his further fight with Scratha Fortress ha'rethe, had broken the land into fissures for hundreds of miles, setting off a disaster of epic proportions. Inwardly, he flinched from calculating how many had died.

Oh, Riss... It remained an awkward ache. He hadn't loved her, but that didn't matter. She had deserved better than to be used as she had, discarded as she had. It was... it was a *bad pattern*. He wasn't at all sure what he meant by that, and set the thought aside to poke at later.

The deaths might have been Deiq's fault. Idisio *wanted* to put the entire matter off onto the elder ha'ra'ha's shoulders. And the teyanain. Blaming the teyanain would be easy. They'd engineered the destruction of the southlands ha'reye, after all, and upset the order of the world forever. Idisio *could* say he'd been manipulated, he could blame others for almost everything. Almost. Except—

—what had happened at the gates, just now, hadn't been anyone else's doing.

The southern gates had been standing, despite everything thrown at this side of the city, until the guards challenged Idisio's right to enter Bright Bay. Abruptly impatient with human protocols and words, he'd *stepped*—

—forward, moving across space sideways to bypass the gates—

—ignoring a momentary uneasiness and an alarmed hiss from his mother, that demon-echo he couldn't rid himself of. He'd done this dozens of times, there was no reason to worry—

—until the ground beneath his feet gave way, dumping him sideways across the road just inside the gates. A weary groan of metal followed by yells and a clattering, thundering crash announced the demise of barriers that had withstood so much of late.

For whatever reason, this time was different. Fatally, for the gates and more than likely for the guards pinned beneath the twisted spears of metal.

The king was most definitely not going to be happy with Idisio. *Again.*

Old instincts had sent Idisio bolting from the scene and up onto a high rooftop, no better than the guiltiest of street-thieves. Not dignified. Not responsible. Not proper behavior along multiple lines of consideration.

His mother's ghost-voice had given a harsh snort, conveying the sense of an utterly disgusted eye-roll, then went silent as though she'd turned her back on him. That was not something she did often, and it stung. Especially when he knew, even as he fled, that running was the *absolutely wrong* thing to do.

Movement below drew Idisio's eye. A form that could have passed for a shambling mass of multicolored rags stared up at him. Idisio held still, not offering welcome or warning. After a few heartbeats, the newcomer began scrambling upwards, apparently deciding to chance it.

Only one path for both exit and access existed, by human reckoning, but Idisio could easily jump for the street, or another rooftop. Assuming, of course, that simply exerting his ha'ra'hain muscular strength wouldn't cause the remnants of the building to collapse under him.

For the moment, he stayed put and watched.

Brash curiosity peered out from a southern-dark face, under a bare fingertip's worth of scalp stubble. Smooth face *probably* meant female, but nothing else gave clues: ragged layers of scavenged cloth scarcely worthy of the name *clothing*; bare feet; no more gaunt or stocky a build than any other street thief Idisio had ever encountered.

"You that one," the newcomer grunted, shifting uncomfortably from foot to foot. "What you doing *here*? Damn, damn—" She hopped across tiles, trying to find a cooler spot. After a moment, she unwrapped the two strips of rough cloth wound around her legs, then quickly wrapped them around her feet instead. The revealed skin was thick with hair and scars alike.

Idisio frowned, startled and wary. "Who do you think I am, exactly?"

Instinct brough ha'ra'hain senses to the fore, and he really *looked* at her. Definitely human, and female; no direct hostile intent and no chance of being a threat even if that changed. And she hadn't bathed in weeks, at best. Idisio shut down his sense of smell.

She narrowed her eyes and glared daggers at him. He must have let his distaste show. Well, and what did it matter? She was only a human. So he'd offended her. It meant nothing.

But that was cruel. She didn't have access to clean bathing water, more than likely. He'd been just as grimy, when Lord Scratha had first snatched him from the streets.

He blinked slowly, pushing those thoughts aside, and focused on the girl.

She said, "You went with that tall southern noble, caused all ends of fuss though the city not so long past. You're Lifty. Right?" She lifted a foot to adjust the wrapping, scowling. "*Damn*, this is hot! How are you just standing there?"

Idisio let out a long breath. "Right. Lifty. Yeah. So what do you want, then?"

"I a'reddy *asked*," came her aggrieved reply. She started to adjust the wrapping on her other foot, nearly fell, caught herself, then glared as though the hot roof were entirely his fault. "What are *you* doing *here*? Get tossed out, bringing trouble on your tail? Ran in fast enough, sure."

Idisio looked out over the destroyed city, understanding. The last thing anyone in this area wanted just now was a horde of angry guardsmen looking to vent their tempers on handy targets. Some things never changed.

"No. No trouble." The lie came easily to his lips, and he held back a sigh. "I'm just remembering how it used to look, when I lived out this way. I'm leaving shortly. No trouble."

"Tch. All right. Not much t'remember, by me, but you're fancy now. I can see you think different'n us. Might not want to stick around. You ain't local now. You ain't *immune* no more, see?" She stood still, feet firmly planted, and stared hard at him as though to emphasize her point.

In the moment of stillness, he could see that her eyes were black, lashes short and stubby, and the right side of her face held the yellow and brown pattern of an old bruise.

Idisio grinned, an unfriendly expression. "Oh, I'm still immune," he said, and matched gaze to gaze. "I'm immune to more than roof-tile heat these days. I'd advise passing along a wide, hard caution on me, for everyone's safety." He let just a touch of ha'ra'hain arrogance and power surface for the last sentence.

Dark eyes widened, then narrowed, assessing. Then came a sharp nod, and a barely dignified retreat. The wrappings on her feet caught on sharp tile, and she fell, grabbing the roof ridge to keep from sliding to the street.

Idisio held still, watching, knowing intimately the proud fury he'd meet on any attempt to help. She yanked the shredded cloth from her feet, threw it aside with a glare over her shoulder at Idisio, then sprang upright again and skipped away with pointed confidence.

Idisio didn't laugh. She was too much like his own former self. He looked out over the ruined city for a few more breaths, sorting past from present, then sighed and began the laboriously tricky human-style descent.

When he was halfway down, he heard a harsh grunt from below, then a stifled cry of pain.

Alarm overrode caution, and he leapt. His eyes fixed on the blossoming patch of red against grey-brown mud as he landed, cat-footed, arm's length away from a flayed ruin of human flesh.

Bone showed through her body in multiple spots. To his utter horror, reddened, watering eyes turned to him in mute appeal. She was still alive.

The ambient agony brought his mother surging forward: *Pain is good, pain is wonderful, drink it in, take it, take it, you can use this for yourself....*

Idisio stumbled back, battling to push the ghost away, but she eeled past his barriers, shoving his body forward, hands reaching out as though the pain were a bonfire on a cold winter's night—

—cold like it *should* be, the weather was all wrong lately, soggy heat overriding a cleaner seasonal chill—

That tangent gave him the moment's distraction he needed to wrest control back, forcing the insane ghost into heavy mental chains. She fought, fury screeching like razors along every nerve and vein.

A heartbeat later, she collapsed, sullen, into her prison. *You'll be coming to me soon enough,* she threatened. *You're going to need me.*

It wasn't the first time she'd said that. Idisio knew better by now than to see it as empty posturing.

The girl's eyes glazed, blankly fixed on the infinite at last. Her blood spread wide and fast: as he watched, skin peeled away from her body in great strips, moving like giant animate ribbons—no, they were worms, flushed skin-dark.

Oh dear gods. Idisio couldn't believe his eyes. *What the hells are those things?* They reminded him of the attiara, but those were creatures of the deepest depths.

As far as he knew.

Deep and muffled, his mother's laughter felt like a spray of mud and blood against the inside of his skull. *She* knew, and wasn't sharing, not for free this time. *He* knew that he couldn't wrest or trick the information from her, and that her price would be far, far too high.

The worms moved onto mottled ground, and their color changed, mimicking surroundings in a visually dizzying ripple. How many? Two—three—

five? They shimmied, burrowing into the ground, soft mud churning under their retreat.

He just watched, too breathless and shocked to react. They weren't attiara, not after that color change. Cousins, maybe. *And if that isn't the stuff of human nightmares...*

The ground settled, semi-solid once more. Idisio recovered his wits and scanned the area with *other*-sense. To his intense disquiet, he found nothing. Whatever these creatures were, they could hide themselves from even a ha'ra'ha's perception.

And now we've moved into the stuff of ha'ra'hain nightmares, he thought ruefully.

It was definitely time to go talk to the king.

Priests in brown robes stood to either side of the wide-open Eastern Gate, handing out supplies from enormous wicker baskets. They wore small, subdued bancti symbols on their right sleeves, and showed none of the arrogance which the Northern Church had displayed at the height of the madness years before. To all appearances, these priests were humble servants only interested in helping and healing.

Idisio didn't look beyond the surface. If he saw hypocrisy just then, he'd likely start a fight. That would be an abysmally poor start to an already tricky audience with the king. The people seemed to accept the show, in any case, so best to let it rest.

Guides in blue and grey uniforms waited to steer each forming group to their new quarters. These showed more arrogance, more certainty in their authority, and the crowd returned a dull resentment.

Idisio waited in line patiently, two dozen bodies back from the gate. He could have walked past, either functionally invisible or blatantly overrun with power; but he found himself intrigued by the process. Guards, as brusque as the guides, spoke to each incoming refugee, then directed them to a priest on one side or another. Apparently left and right had different supplies and destinations, for each group, when released, went on opposite headings.

All the while, the priests visibly soothed tempers ruffled by the abrupt manner of the guards and guides, their faces gentle and intent. Idisio finally gave in to temptation and *looked*. To his surprise, the compassion was real. The priests weren't faking one bit.

The sands swallow us all, Idiso thought, shaking his head, and felt the bitter despair in his heart ease a fraction. *Maybe, just maybe, there's hope for these people.* He wondered if glimpses of such fragile promise had been the driving force behind Deiq's long battle to save humanity from itself. It seemed entirely likely.

Gender and age seemed to make little difference in the processing of refugees, although particularly frail ones were helped onto a cart hitched to a sturdy brown mule. It all took time, in the blazing heat of afternoon. The stink of overheated, unwashed human had never been Idisio's favorite smell even before his perceptions sharpened. He dulled his sense of smell and taste once more, just enough to make the wait tolerable.

"What road you live on... s'e?" a guard asked him at last. His sharp tone wavered on the last word—a courtesy he hadn't offered previous refugees—and he looked Idisio over with evident puzzlement. Sensitive enough, then, to pick up on small signs, and smart enough to retreat into politeness instead of hostility.

"I'm not a refugee, s'e. I'm on my way to see the king." Idisio offered a slight nod: acknowledgement from one of higher to one of lower status.

The guard hesitated, giving Idisio another once-over that would have been far more dubious if Idisio hadn't remembered, three streets back, to finish mending up his garments. At last, slowly, he said, "You got an appointment?"

"Yes." Idisio kept his face calm, tone slightly bored. It was the best way to lie convincingly. The king *would* make time for him, at any rate, so it might as well be true.

The guard waved at one of the waiting guides, a young man whose blue linen clothes hung on him as though he'd recently lost a fair amount of weight. "Take this one to the court," the guard instructed. "Says he's got an appointment with the king. Get sure of it before you leave him. Sorry, s'e, it's been a rough few days. No discourtesy intended, just caution." He glanced over the waiting line of refugees, his lips thinning, and let out a heavy sigh.

"Steut," the guide identified himself, offering a curt bow. "This way, s'e." Sunlight caught red-blue highlights from his curly dark hair. He wiped a forearm across his sweat-damp forehead as he turned away, beckoning Idisio to follow.

As Idisio passed the priests, one raised his head, eyes widening. "Ha'inn," the priest mouthed. Idisio checked his step, startled and alarmed at the recognition, but the priest shook his head sharply and looked away as though in warning to let the moment go. Idisio shrugged and caught his pace up to the guide.

Noble mansions spread to either side, gates open, each one fronted with a gaggle of servants awaiting incoming guests. "Kind of them to open their homes," Idisio commented.

Steut cast him a flickering, cynical glance. "King's orders," he answered laconically.

"Ah." That made considerably more sense than granting nobles any native grasp of compassion.

Children wailed to Idisio's left: a group of exhausted youngsters unhappy about the disruption to their routine, from the look of it. A stout man was trying, with limited success, to calm them by offering candies. Wincing, Idisio dimmed his hearing slightly. Steut glanced sideways at the ruckus, his own mouth drawing aside in a grimace.

"You'll have a line longer'n that at the gates, appointment or not," Steut advised, as though by way of distraction. "Plenty high-ranking folk want a word or ten with the king just at the moment."

The wailing faded: someone had figured out a way to quiet the children. Idisio let his hearing come back to normal levels.

"I imagine so," Idisio said, keeping his expression untroubled. Steut sucked in a whistling breath, then released it in a long sigh. Idisio could sense him holding back several dangerous remarks.

A few steps later, Steut muttered, "You don't have an appointment, do you?"

"No." Idisio smiled, completely placid, curious to see if that would infuriate his guide.

Steut shook his head in disgust, slowing to a stop. Idisio paused, waiting. Steut turned to face him. With sharp resentment, he said, "Are you actually in to see the king, or are you on some game?"

Idisio met his gaze and let ha'ra'hain arrogance rise. "I'm really going to see the king. And I won't be waiting in line."

Steut squinted, studying him thoughtfully. He didn't seem the least bit intimidated. "I believe you," he said, no trace of irritation remaining. "I'd best walk you up anyway. Gave my word, and this I want to see."

Idisio grinned in return, deciding he liked Steut. As they walked, he opened his senses, breathing deeply of the uptown air. Enormous rosemary bushes often served as rough hedges here, and butterflies and bees dipped from one flower garden to the next, twirling and swooping on a surprisingly strong breeze. The Gates stood on considerably higher ground than the southeastern streets. Better air, better soil, better wind access. Better everything.

Idisio stopped to run a hand over a flowering rosemary bush, releasing a wave of floral-pine aroma. Steut audibly inhaled, a smile spreading across his broad face.

Alyea's memories stirred in the back of his mind: she had unpleasant associations with that smell. Idisio shrugged that aside as irrelevant and stayed in the moment.

A black butterfly with vibrant orange wingtips wavered around their heads before settling on a purple bloom just out of Idisio's reach. He watched it for a few breaths, enjoying the contrasting colors, marveling at the balance that allowed the insect to perch on such a delicate flower. Eventually, he recalled himself and turned away, motioning Steut to follow.

The folk sheltering under reluctant noble hospitality would find it hard to abandon this luxury and return to the crowded, rot-filled streets of the middle city, let alone homes in the lower end. Idisio amused himself for a few steps by laying out potential problems the king would have to face from a disrupted and discontented populace in the coming days. Realizing how cold such analytical amusement was, he shook his head and glanced up at a gillahawk gliding through the sky, pushing himself back towards human patterns and perceptions.

I'm not like Deiq. I'm not like my mother. Yet, more and more, he found himself acting very much like the only two examples of ha'ra'hain behavior he'd ever seen modeled.

Without really thinking about it, he lifted a hand to his nose, inhaling the lingering richness of rosemary oil. He felt himself calm immediately, mind sharpening away from brooding introspection and back to the moment's needs.

"Almost there, s'e," Steut said, and dropped back a pace, demoting himself from guide to servant with that one motion. Idisio checked his step briefly, not at all pleased with the echo that gesture brought to mind: he remembered himself, nothing but a grubby street thief, being dragged along half-willing by an angry desert lord on the way to an audience with the king.

It hadn't been all that long ago, as humans measured time.

Different day, different situation. Idisio put it out of his mind and squared his shoulders, looking ahead with flat clarity.

As Steut had warned, the street in front of the Palace Gates proved to be thick with a motley array of nobles and merchants, rag-pickers and southerners. A jovial, broad-chested southerner led a nearby group of children in playful song and dance. At the fringes of the dancing group, one child stood leaning on a crutch, watching the others with stoic blankness.

Idisio paused to look at the crippled child. The boy looked up at him, meeting his eyes. A flicker of fear crossed the child's face, an instinctive recognition of danger: he shifted his weight onto his good leg, ready to use the crutch in self-defense.

Idisio jerked his gaze away, caught between ha'ra'hain anger at the insult and human horror at having frightened a child. *I might have helped him. I could have...* what?

Nothing. Humans rightly distrusted help from ha'ra'hain, these days more than ever.

In the back of his mind, his mother laughed, a low, growling sound of derision.

No direct path to the Gates existed through the jumbled crowd. As Idisio approached, several frowns turned his way, measuring his purposeful stride and guessing, correctly, that he wanted through.

Before the frowns could turn to outright argument, Idisio drew in a breath, straightened his spine, and let himself *be ha'ra'hain*. Perhaps it was cheating, but his patience with human protocol had once more thinned with his mother's burst of manic laughter. The mask of humanity dissipated.

His shoulders went back, his chin went up, but those were trivial physical changes. More importantly, his vision shifted, his thought patterns veering sideways and aslant. He was so much *more* than these brief-lived insects around him, and infinitely more important, on a cosmic scale, than even their most highly ranked could ever hope to achieve.

Caught in the arrogance of the process, he ignored the whimper of his human-trained self: *this is wrong, this isn't who I am, this isn't right, stop it!* All around him, frowns melted into immediate unease. Parents snatched their children up, the feeble were lifted aside by the strong, and a path appeared before Idisio had taken three more steps. Behind him, Steut cursed under his breath, in awestruck tones.

"Who the hells *are* you?" the guide muttered.

Idisio ignored the question, his attention on the half-dozen King's Guards just ahead. Their uniforms had changed since his last visit to the king: now their pristine white tunics bore stripes of blue and gold thread, a wide belt of silver mesh catching it tight around the waist. Their leggings were of a deep blue, their knee-high boots a flat black. Their hair was clipped harsly short, as was the fur of the silver-collared asp-jacaus at their side.

Once, these had been the guards he feared the most. Seeing the alert wariness on their faces now, their awareness of his power, warmed something deep and savage in his chest.

"Ha'inn Idisio to see Lord Oruen," he announced before any of them could issue a challenge.

Steut choked audibly, then muttered another, quieter string of curses. "You coulda *said*," he complained. Idisio ignored him.

The captain, a sturdy man with receding grey hair and charcoal-dark eyes, showed no sign of flinching. "We're honored, ha'inn. I'll walk you there myself, if I may." His gaze flicked to Steut. "Is this person coming along as well?"

"He may, if he wishes to do so," Idisio said, not looking back. "Steut?"

"I—ha'inn, I'm probably wanted back at the—" Steut's tone wavered between awe and outright terror.

Stupid human. If I wanted to hurt you, you'd already be dead.

Idisio kept the thought silent, but from the look on the captain's face, he was thinking the same thing. "Thank you, Steut," Idisio said, still not turning his head, and motioned for the guard captain to precede him into the Palace grounds proper.

"Right cold bastard," one of the guards muttered, low enough for human hearing to miss.

Idisio blinked once, twice, considering. He'd made his point and gained his escort. There was nothing to be gained by responding with ha'ra'hain aggression to what was, after all, a true enough observation. He pulled at his humanity, diluting the easy anger, and followed the captain without a glance back.

A few steps later, the captain paused, catching a servant by the arm, and murmured something in her ear. The woman's eyes widened. She cast a flatly terrified look at Idisio, then lit out as though all the hells were at her heels.

"Damnit," the captain said with a sigh. "Sorry, ha'inn. Please don't take offense. I'll see to it that she's taken aside for a word on courtesy."

Idisio nodded, which visibly reassured the man, and stayed silent. The lingering harshness of ha'ra'hain arrogance made social niceties, never easy for Idisio at the best of times, impossible right now. He made no effort to haul himself further towards being human; he'd need that iron indifference when facing Oruen.

Their previous encounters hadn't been pleasant. First, the fight between Oruen and Idisio's mentor, Cafad Scratha, while it had been in no way Idisio's doing, definitely left the king with a sour perception of Idisio, if only by association. Not long afterwards, Idisio had faced off with Oruen over an insane ha'ra'ha rampaging through Bright Bay. She'd been searching, as it turned out, for her son: Idisio himself. That matter hadn't ended well, either—and Idisio still had no idea how to get rid of his mother's lingering, vengeful ghost in his mind.

Then, most recently, just after one of the king's ex-lovers had tried to kill the king, Idisio had removed said woman from prison—and the city—without permission. And *now* he came back on the heels of an earthquake and accompanying tsunami that had wrecked the city and, apparently, unleashed bizarre and deadly creatures capable of chewing through a rapidly panicking population.

Protesting his innocence wouldn't change anyone's mind. Not even his own.

Afternoon sunlight drew long shadows across the day-warm garden path. Tall cacti, bristling with forbiddingly hooked spines, formed a living fence to one side. To the other, clumps of desert ginger interspersed with knee-high succulent bushes offered bright, cheery splashes of color even in shade. Nothing bloomed, and no insects swarmed the air, although a few confused plants had begun to set buds.

Around a turn, the shadows thinned. Tall plants gave way to bushy ground cover in shades of orange-red. The path split around an intricately engraved stone pillar decorated with a complex relief of lizards chasing one another around deep-set markings. Idisio paused to study the engraving. It was definitely writing, but in no language or even alphabet that he knew. He shrugged and moved on.

Another turn, three steps up onto a terraced plateau, and then a stone's throw of straight path brought him into the center of the garden Deiq had built—*some time ago,* the elder ha'ra'ha had said with dry amusement, which meant it had probably been *a long damn time ago* by human measurements. There was symbolism to this meeting spot, good or bad depending on what factors one added into the situation. Idisio chose to see it as the king ceding status, and therefore a good sign.

A flawlessly smooth patch of black sand curved to the right, white sand to the left, each area punctuated by age-polished rocks of varying sizes, stacked in varying patterns. It made for a peaceful place, one detached from the smothering chaos of the city. A featherleaf tree spread bare branches out against the sky, mottled and naked against the clear-skied heat of the day.

Oruen stood beside one of the three stone benches, his hands clasped behind his back. His once-dark hair was now steel-grey and trimmed harshly short. The lines on his face were as unkind as before, his mouth set at a flat mark of unfriendliness. He wore no royal robe, no crown, no marks of status, only a dark red, long-sleeved tunic over grey hose and low grey boots.

"Ha'inn," he said, offering an unexpectedly courteous bow. "Your presence honors me this day." He kept his gaze on Idisio's left shoulder, avoiding direct eye contact.

So he was going to be polite. Good. Maybe the news about the gates hadn't reached him yet. Idisio bowed, more shallowly, and responded, "Lord Oruen. Thank you for seeing me at such abrupt notice."

The king's mouth relaxed a touch, as though *he'd* been tensed for Idisio to start yelling at *him.* Interesting, and more than likely an expectation set by Deiq's brusque attitude over the years. There were certain advantages to moving in Deiq's stormy wake.

"Would you like to sit?" the king inquired, motioning to the bench beside him.

Unable to resist a moment of irreverence, Idisio sat sideways on the bench, legs crossed. Oruen's eyes narrowed; then, to Idisio's surprise, he copied the posture.

"Do you desire the proper courtesies, ha'inn?" Oruen said. "My newly resident loremasters have been at great pains to instruct me as to your due."

Idisio picked up the edge—well hidden, but his hearing was better than most—and held back a rueful grin. "No. We can skip the formalities. I'm here to apologize." Hopefully that would file the king's sharp mood back a bit.

Oruen's sour expression went blank, as though he hadn't expected that answer. "For what, ha'inn?"

"I wasn't aware—" *because you didn't tell me!* "—that Lord Peysimun was forbidden from leaving her cell. I removed her without her consent because I needed her help. I don't want her lands and property to be forfeit because of my mistake."

The king's eyes tightened. He understood what hadn't been said. "I see. Unfortunately..."

Idisio sat up straighter, frowning. "You've already given them away."

The king looked sideways at a bush with wide-mouthed, vibrantly red flowers, as though fascinated by the black and orange butterflies flitting through the branches. He said, very quietly, "It's complicated, ha'inn."

Idisio rubbed his nose, inhaling the lingering rosemary scent and thinking the situation through, before answering. He set his face to a more neutral expression and said, "I do understand, Lord Oruen. Mud street to mid street and mid street to the Seventeen is a mess, and you've got some very angry noble families. You needed the space. And Lord Peysimun won't need the actual property, in any case. She's claimed Scratha Fortress for her Family. It's Peysimun Fortress now."

Oruen's shoulders relaxed. "Yes, I'd heard." His mouth moved into a wry grimace. "Ironic. Lord Scratha has taken up residence at the western edge of Bright Bay, in case you hadn't heard."

"I hadn't. Thank you." Idisio allowed himself a moment of relief at that news. "Lord Peysimun mentioned that she'd sent him north, but nothing more specific."

"I'm sure he'd welcome a visit." Oruen's glance flickered across Idisio's face, gnat-quick, then back to the butterflies. There was more than a tinge of wanting to end the conversation in that comment.

Idisio tuned his voice to a chill precision. "And *I'd* welcome a return to the topic, Lord Oruen. I want Peysimun Family to be reimbursed for the undue loss of property, title, and status."

The king's eyes narrowed, his gaze moving up to Idisio's face for a brief, brash moment of direct eye contact. Idisio held still against what ha'ra'hain temper called aggression, fiercely cleaving to the human side of himself. The king's gaze jerked away again, to the ground this time, and he dipped his head in apology for the breach of courtesy.

But kings also had face, and the loss or saving of it, to consider. Oruen's voice was cold as deep sea water as he said, "Lord Peysimun has acquired the entirety of Scratha Family wealth, title, and status, which is considerably greater than what she previously possessed. I question her right to complain, ha'inn."

"She isn't complaining. *I* am."

Human to human now, the two men glared each other down, with nothing *other* in the mix. After a few moments of mutual hard staring, Oruen said tightly, "Peysimun Family is a recognized southern Family, accorded all due respect and courtesies. Their representative will be welcome at this court." He shifted his gaze away, breathing hard and rubbing the back of his neck with one hand.

"That's a good start," Idisio said, unyielding. "I'm sure Peysimun Family would welcome a northern representative." That had been Alyea's idea, and it was bait, pure and simple. None of the other Families had ever been interested in setting up any such arrangement. And Peysimun being the first to make that move would, as Idisio understood it, give her implicit precedence with the northern kingdom.

None of the other Families would have even considered making that offer. It would have been a sign of weakness, under southern political custom. Alyea was the only person who could turn that into a sharp-edged strength.

Oruen's eyebrows rose. He visibly hovered on the edge of asking for clarification, then wisely retreated. "That's an excellent idea. I'll see to it, ha'inn. And to an... appropriate diplomatic gift."

The way Oruen said *appropriate* held undertones of *insanely valuable*. Idisio nodded, hiding his amusement. "That will do."

The kind rubbed a hand across his eyes, his thin shoulders slumping. "Northern representative," he muttered, then straightened back to attention, nodding as though several appealing plans had begun to click together in his mind.

"I also owe you a more immediate apology," Idisio said. "The... ah, the southern gates?"

Oruen's calm faded, his shoulders drawing taut once more. "Yes," he said, aiming a burning glare at Idisio's left shoulder. "I was advised not to bring that up, but since you mention it..."

Idisio hesitated, trying to decide whether to draw on ha'ra'hain arrogance or human regret. He touched his nose, inhaling the fading remnants of rosemary oil on his fingers, and angled for a middle path.

"I misjudged," he said. "I didn't expect the area to be that unstable. I would like to make amends for that mistake."

"Two men are dead," Oruen answered, voice flat and dangerous now. "The ground, the gates, are destroyed. Engineers are on their way to examine the damage and offer options for repair. More than likely it will all take time and resources I don't have to spare. *You*—" He paused, studying a butterfly with ferocious intensity, and rolled his shoulders, loosening tension. In a more moderate tone, he went on, "You are, of course, not held responsible, ha'inn. There are no requirements that you make any amends." His cheeks hollowed, temper once more displacing strained courtesy. "That being said, I surely won't refuse if you feel so inclined. What do you have in mind?"

Idisio looked at the bare-branched featherleaf tree, tracing branches and twigs, noting the occasional bud; considering his wording, checking one last time for egregious error in the basic notion.

Slowly, he said, "There's something killing people in the southeastern city." The memory of spraying blood eroded his hold on human-normal. He lifted his hand to his nose again, and found the oil nearly dissipated. He tried to pull that scent-recall into brighter detail, then stopped, realizing he'd left half his intended statement silent. He added, voice harsh, "I'll stop it."

Oruen shut his eyes, face tightening with something that might have been anger or grief. "I'd hoped those were only mad stories," he said. He splayed his hands wide across his thighs, fingers stiff as though he were resisting an urge to ball them into fists.

"No. I've seen them. They're real." Idisio checked his own body language and relaxed taut muscles. Better to look completely calm, even indifferent. Let the king be the one showing his upset.

Oruen's hands clenched into fists, but he didn't open his eyes. "What are they?"

"No idea." Idisio tensed as his mother's voice whispered through the back of his mind: *Stupid humans, stupid ignorant humans, asking stupid questions... you should kill him, you could rule over these humans, make them do anything you want....*

Oruen's eyes opened to slits, his gaze fixing once more on Idisio's shoulder. "How do you stop them?"

Half of his attention on shoving his mother's ghost back to silence, Idisio's answer came out laden with more ice than he'd intended. "No idea. I was hoping—"

Stupid stupid stupid humans, nothing more than ants....

Shut up! he told her fiercely. "I was hoping you might have something in your... library?" He wasn't sure if that was the right word to use, but didn't know any other.

His mother subsided with a dark chuckle, not in the least repentant about distracting him.

The king unfolded his legs and rose to his feet. "Sounds right along your road, then, *ha'inn,*" he said bleakly. "My library, and most of the western side of the Palace, has been taken over by my new loremasters. Go consult them. Please, try not to upset them. I'm told they're an absolute necessity to keep face with the southern Families, but they raise their fees every time someone angers them, so they're already costing me a bloody fortune. *Try* not to break what's left of my treasury, if you would." He offered a deep bow, hands pressed flat to his chest: the audience was, unequivocally, over.

It'll cost the people of your city a lot more than money if I can't fill my promise, Idisio thought sourly, and left with only a perfunctory bow by way of farewell.

The loremasters offered polite unhelpfulness. Idisio couldn't tell if they honestly didn't know anything or weren't willing to talk: their faces were hidden behind masks of varying colors. Their eyes, their voices, gave nothing away, and neither did they.

Their eyes were a deep grey, pupils oddly wide, as though they'd taken aesa or were not quite right in the head. Idisio shifted to *other* perception for a moment, curious, and found only blankness. They'd taken something to protect themselves from him. Smart, if dangerously rude.

"You are entirely welcome to seek answers from us, as a courtesy to the king who hosts us." That loremaster had a full-face mask and cowl, both of deepest purple silk struck through with silver thread. The voice sounded male; the robe hung against what seemed feminine curves. She—Idisio reconsidered, and assigned the more neutral *ii* instead—stood between the other loremasters, each an arm's length apart.

Three in all had come out to speak with him. Idisio wondered if that echoed the southern faith, if each of the loremasters represented one of the Callen factions. It seemed unlikely, but he didn't entirely trust his own judgement of *likely* these days.

"We may not have answers," said the loremaster to Idisio's left, this one bald and definitely male, from throat-knot to knobby wrists. A rigid white half-mask, covering nose to chin with a thin slit for the mouth, lay stark against his dark skin. "We cannot promise you satisfaction. But you may ask."

Idisio bit his tongue against the impulse to say *how fucking kind you are.*

The third loremaster said, "Ask your questions, ha'inn." His mask was black cloth laced with gold thread, and wrapped up across his head and around his throat, leaving only his eyes and forehead visible.

Idisio realized he didn't actually know the protocols for addressing a loremaster. After a brief hesitation, he gave up trying to figure it out. He said, bluntly, "I want to know about what's killing people on the southeastern shore."

They stared at him, blinking slowly. "That is a very broad question, ha'inn," said black-mask.

"It looks like a gigantic flatworm with teeth," Idisio said. The loremasters remained blank-faced, not reacting in the least. "I want to know what it is, and where it comes from, and why it's here *now*."

The loremasters looked at one another as though in silent consultation, then back to Idisio. "It sounds like a creature that lived in the deeper shallows," *ii* said.

"No doubt the recent disruption washed them ashore, or disturbed them into seeking new prey," said the bald loremaster, moving one hand in a vague gesture. It might have been some sort of loremaster code, or just a stretch; Idisio couldn't tell.

"That doesn't tell me anything useful," Idisio said waspishly. "How do I kill them, or scare them out of hunting in this area?"

Three sets of eyebrows went up simultaneously. "Ha'inn," said the black-masked one, "we are entirely unqualified to advise you on such matters."

His mother let out a long bray of laughter, nearly deafening him. He had to shut his eyes and focus every bit of his willpower to push her into silence. When he opened his eyes, he found all three loremasters watching him with unconcealed interest.

Idisio chewed on his tongue ferociously, trying not to glare at them. Had he imagined the slightest of stresses on *we* and *you*? It might have just been his temper, and his mother's shade, adding that emphasis. He made himself let it go and said, "Do you know *anything* about these creatures? Any stories, history, folklore?"

"We would have to research that question," said the bald one. "It would take time."

"We have several projects already in progress," said purple-mask.

"People are *dying*," Idisio snapped, taking a step forward. Their eyes narrowed; he stopped and moved back two careful paces, remembering the king's weary admonition not to upset them.

"People are always dying," the bald loremaster said. He rubbed one wide thumb against his bony wrist, his eyebrows slanting into a pensive expression. "We are sympathetic, ha'inn, but we work as we work, and unless the king bids us drop all projects to focus on your question, we cannot give you priority."

"Even if he did so this moment," said black-mask, "we cannot simply stop and turn immediately to your questions. There are processes. It would be a tenday before we could even begin the research you are asking about."

Idisio growled, unable to help himself. The loremasters regarded him without concern.

The bald one laced his fingers together over his ribs and inclined his head to one side briefly. "Is there anything else, ha'inn?" he asked with polite finality.

"No," Idisio said through his teeth, and barely managed a taut bow before turning to storm from the room.

In the corner of his vision, as he turned, he caught a small movement. It didn't register as a threat, so he kept moving. After the door swung shut behind him, belated detail came clear: they'd all looked up at the ceiling as though beseeching the gods to preserve them from such foolishness.

He checked his step, then shrugged it off. For all he knew, they'd been asking the gods to help him in his search. It couldn't be proven either way.

Not that he particularly wanted any gods noticing him, now or ever....

Once clear of the palace grounds, Idisio found himself turning south and west, towards the long-devastated area of the city. This was the side he knew the least about, in truth. He'd grown up on the southeastern streets of Bright Bay. Back then, a vicious gang, led by a burly young man called Amber, had ruled the southwestern ruins. There hadn't been a consistent, strong leader on the east side of town—or at least, not one Idisio had managed to ally with—and without protection, it wasn't safe for a sand-street thief to cross that invisible boundary line.

Amber had died not long before Idisio's first encounter with Lord Scratha, promptly replaced with an equally sharp-minded thug. Idisio's mood was sour enough that he rather hoped the current gang would try coming for him tonight, but that was unlikely. They knew what he was, by now.

He thought about visiting Lord Scratha, but dismissed it immediately. Scratha had the hells' own temper at the best of times. Bringing his own volatile mood against that wouldn't end well. Better to wait until he had himself under control.

As he walked, the ground underfoot devolved from neatly laid brick to rougher, gapped cobbles, then to a muddy gravel-sand mixture. There were signs of recent repairs, where fresh cobbles had been laid down—then promptly levered out, likely carried away to fortify scavenger nests.

Buildings displayed newly patched and painted walls and signs. Idisio passed a cobbler, a chandler, a tailor, and an apothecary. Their signs were plain boards with black paint, for the most part, but the next one intrigued him: a row of glass bottles wrapped in rough twine and hung like a wind-chime.

The front of that building was neatly whitewashed, the unpainted shutters thrown wide to let air into the small shop. The top half of the split door was open, the lower half, with a broad shelf, clearly intended as counter space. A large man sat just inside, his expression benign. Catching Idisio's eye, he raised a meaty hand and nodded welcome.

Idisio went to the shop door, offering a return nod, and said, "I take it you sell your own brew, s'e?"

The merchant's expression hovered between amusement and annoyance as he said, "Does this *look* like a palace shop?"

Idisio made a show of glancing around, as though considering the question, then said, "I suppose that depends on your prices, s'e."

The man burst into surprised laughter. Idisio grinned along with him, then laid a half silver piece on the counter. Still chuckling, the shopkeeper set a thick, twine-wrapped bottle beside the coin. "There you go, and I'll keep the change, thank you," he said, deftly sweeping the coin from sight.

Idisio took the bottle without protest, amused by the man's brashness. As he turned away, he found himself hesitating over what to do next. The clouds overhead had taken on a sunset gilding and a brisk wind was beginning to sift through the streets.

Intuition stirred, a whisper in the back of his mind.

He looked back at the shopkeeper, who made no attempt to pretend he hadn't been watching Idisio closely. "Where's a good place to sit and drink in company, these days, without being bothered?" Idisio asked.

The man cocked his head to one side. "In or out?"

"Out." While human company would be... nice, was the closest word he could think of... Idisio didn't feel like sitting within human built walls just at the moment.

The man pointed to the right. "Down that way. Second right, third left, there's a gathering spot. Not pretty, but the folks there hold the fireside peace." The last words were as much warning as information.

Idisio nodded once, sharply, to show he understood. "Thank you."

The shopkeeper tapped the counter meaningfully.

Idisio grinned and said, "Keep the change." The man let out a sour half laugh, half grunt in return.

Idisio turned away, following that whispering nudge and hoping, as always, that it wouldn't lead him into worse trouble than ever.

A heavy armchair and several smaller pieces of furniture figured prominently in the bonfire. Three young men were idly breaking apart a large table, piling the fragments into a relatively tidy pile out of floating spark range.

The area had once been a public square, by the looks of it. Several buildings that could have been shops stood along one side; ruined fences formed a broken boundary between the square and larger, almost intact buildings along two more. Those had probably been offices of some sort. The fourth side was completely blocked by a heap of debris three times taller than Idisio. This, apparently, was where the cleaning crews had been dumping their leavings.

The bonfire, large as it was, seemed small against the surrounding space. Chunks of stone and blocks of timber had been dragged into a circle around the blaze, two rows deep. Not many were occupied, this early in the evening, but Idisio guessed that they'd fill up quick enough once the evening chill set in properly.

A few wary glances lifted as Idisio approached; he showed his palms, then drew a circle over his heart to invoke fireside peace. Expressions faded from wary to blank, and they went back to a variety of small tasks: mending, knitting, cutting apart clothing to reuse in another configuration, picking small stones from a basket of what looked to be dried peas, or just staring at the fire.

"You know," Idisio said mildly as he settled onto one of the rough seats around the fire, "if you'd sold that table it would make enough to buy you all a room for the next week at a decent inn, and meals besides."

That earned him a number of hostile stares.

"Fireside peace," said an older woman. Her iron-grey hair was braided back in neat lines and tied off into a tail at the base of her skull. Barely visible black-ink tattoos ran down one side of her dark face. "You don't start anything, boy."

Idisio put out one hand, palm up, in apology, then circled his heart once more for good measure. "Fireside peace," he agreed, then held up the bottle. "Anyone for sharing?"

At a series of grudging nods, he broke the seal and worked the stopper free. He faked a generous swallow and passed the bottle to his left.

"Can't be arrested for stealing what's ash," a wiry, scarred man with pale blue eyes said as he took the bottle. "And him as had that table did some hurt. Happier seeing alla his shit scorched, me."

More nods, and a few bitter scowls.

"It's been a rough time," Idisio said neutrally. "Lots of hurt all around."

"You uptowner?" a thickset woman with greasy brown hair demanded abruptly. She squinted at him. "You talk it, you dress it. What you sitting here trying to hand off?"

Idisio put a hand palm up again. "Fireside peace," he reminded her, then put a touch of persuasion into his voice. "I'm nobody. No harm."

The bottle reached him again; he faked another swig and kept it moving. The woman picking through the dried peas passed the bottle along without drinking, her narrow face tight as though something about the notion of sharing a drink offended her.

"Long as he keeps the peace," said the tattooed woman, "he's welcome to sit. Fireside rules."

"Fireside rules don' cover spies," the thickset woman grumbled. She glared at Idisio in a way that stirred his ha'ra'hain pride towards anger. He did his best not to return the glare, but she dropped her eyes and shuddered as though a chill had gone up her back.

The tattooed woman studied Idisio for a moment, carefully not meeting his gaze directly, then shook her head. "He's clean," she said. "No taint."

"Taint?" Idisio said, startled. "What's that mean?"

Everyone looked at him this time, their expressions ranging from surprised to suspicious. One man snorted, then laughed madly for a few moments.

"Oh, shut up, Fend," the tattooed woman said, rolling her eyes.

Idisio bit his lip, trying not to show his own amusement; in context, the word clearly wasn't intended to convey the... *earthier*... meaning he was accustomed to. But he did entirely understand the man's manic laughter.

"You don't know *that*, you been under a rock or uptown," the big woman said, her moment of fear shifting back into ready anger. "I'm betting uptown, and I'm betting—"

"Peace," the tattooed woman said again, more aggressively. "Enough, Edili. I'll boot you as fast as anyone else. Je, pass her some aesa."

Edili waved away the proffered pipe, still scowling. "Ay, ay, I'll settle," she said. "I've a headache. Peace."

"I've been on the road for a time," Idisio said, then let the silence set in, waiting.

Finally, the thin man who'd admitted to stealing the table currently being burnt said, "There's a sickness been spreading for a time now. Years back, it started. Mostly this side of town. People got wrong in the head. Overset by demons, like. Some—" he jerked his chin at the tattooed woman, then hooked forefinger over thumb on his right hand absentmindedly. "There's some as can see it. Near as we've figured, it's come from uptown. Guards had it through and through for a time. It's better since Oruen stepped up, but you don't kill a nest by stepping on one snake." He glanced at his hand, then shook the fingers loose with an embarrassed scowl.

It matched up with Idisio's own memories and with what he'd learned more recently. He'd never thought to put the ambient strangeness into words, before his abrasive encounter with Lord Scratha, but having heard it now—it matched up, right down the line.

He kept his expression placid as a matter of reflex, but eyes narrowed all around him. The lack of reaction had been a mistake.

"You know sommat on that," a man with scar-mottled skin and a patch over one eye accused.

"I've seen a bit of this and that," Idisio said, letting an edge into his voice. "I didn't know that word for it. You heard about the trouble on the east side beaches?" He took back the now-empty bottle as he spoke, and set it on the ground between his feet out of old, street-thief habit. Bottles could usually be returned for a few bits.

Silence and averted gazes answered the question. More than one person spat into the fire, warding off bad luck; several twisted their hands into variations on signs against evil. Idisio counted at least three he recognized, including the forefinger-over-thumb, and two he didn't, partially because the signers moved too fast for him to catch the gesture clearly.

"Move to sommat else," the tattooed woman said definitely. She'd been the only one to make no warding sign at all. "Don't go pulling the even-spirits with this talk."

Embers fluffed into the air as a chair leg burnt through, and one of the young men moved forward to fuss with the fire. Silence hung, slowly moving from hostile to weary as another bottle began the rounds.

"The Eldwoods are packing up and headed north, I hear," the tattooed woman said at last. "Sayin' it's too hard here these days. They're wanting more *peace*."

That prompted a round of sour laughter. "Bloody nobles," the man with the eye patch muttered.

"Let 'em all go north, I say," the thickset woman who'd pushed at Idisio earlier declared. Edili, if he remembered right. "More space for us."

"Nah, they'll just move those damn southerners up into the mansions, and we're still out in the street," eye-patch said. "King's wanting to kiss southern arse, and southerns need a place to go now their homes are ruined, don't they? Ain't nothing changes for *us*."

"I hear as southerns keep slaves," Edili said darkly. Several heads nodded in agreement, then wagged in disapproval. Mutters along the lines of "what the king's thinking, I'm sure *I* don't know," came from multiple people.

Idisio opened his mouth to correct the misunderstanding, then shut it again, firmly. This was *not* the time. And, after all, they weren't entirely wrong—just working with incomplete information.

He felt a tickle on the back of his neck, and looked about with a neutral expression. His gaze snagged on a worn-looking old woman wearing a dirty knit cap and a collection of overlapping rags that only true charity would call *clothes*. She was watching him, a strange gleam in her eyes. As soon as he focused on her, she dropped her chin, thin hair straggling over her face, shoulders hunching as though trying to hide.

"Maybe they'll know what to do about the worms, though," said a man whose dark skin bore large blotches of lighter color. Idisio had heard people with that condition called milk-skin, gods-touched, and a few outright cruel and obscene monikers. Nobody here seemed to care a bit. The man went on, "They must have *sommat* to do with that mess down south. Never seen anything like them before."

"None of us have," eye-patch agreed. He spat into the fire and hunched into himself, scowling. "I mean, we're all still *alive*, innit, so that's obvious enough."

"Keep off it," the tattooed woman warned. "It's too unchancy an evening." She shot a hard-eyed glance at Idisio, who put his hands out yet again in a peace gesture. Her frown only grew more severe. "Just you being here is stirring everyone up, boy," she said. "Maybe best you say sommat about what you're doing here after all, or take your leave. I'm not liking the feel of the air right now."

Idisio took a slow look around the circle, weighing the stares. He said, "No harm to you or yours. I'm after a way to kill off those worms you just mentioned."

"Ah. Figured you was sniffing after something like that." The man who spoke wore much-mended work coveralls over a stained, once-white shirt. From those initial details, and his callused hands, Idisio guessed him as being either a dockworker or a boat carpenter.

"I've seen them," Idisio said quietly, keeping his hands still. "I don't know what they are, but they scared the gods' own breath out of me." It took no pretense to be convincing on that point. Their faces mostly relaxed into rueful agreement, but the tattooed woman remained chill and menacing.

"I saw one take a kid apart." The man with milk skin snapped his fingers and shook his head. "That damn fast. Wasn't but bones left." He shuddered, took the last of the liquor from the bottle in his hand, then threw the empty container overhand, hard, as though trying to shed the memory. The bottle sailed into the darkness far enough that even Idisio's sensitive ears scarcely picked up the crash.

Another bottle started the rounds, and Idisio, shaken, allowed himself a sip when it came his way. It was a dark liquor with a syrupy taste. The tattoed woman muttered something to the man in coveralls. He nodded and rose, moving away into the darkness.

"Hold off," the woman ordered. "We have to have this sort of talk, we're running a circle." She glared at Idisio.

Silence held until the man came back with a large, lumpy bag. Idisio watched with interest as he poured a thick circle of salt around the group, closing himself inside as he worked.

"That's expensive, boy," the tattooed woman said. "Real blessed salt, that is."

Idisio reached into his pouch, ticked over the contents with his fingertips, and removed an uncut silver round. He tossed it to the woman without comment. She caught it, felt it over, and nodded. The coin vanished, the man sat down, empty sack at his feet, and conversation started again. Idisio had the feeling that they'd all been *wanting* to talk about the worms, and his presence had disrupted a collective, silent agreement not to.

"Eh, they washed up with the quake," a gaunt, pockmarked woman in a patched, worn blue dress muttered, not looking up from her knitting. A stray spark floated near, and she swatted it away, pushing her ragged dark hair back from her shoulder in the same motion.

"That's like saying th'sun's bright, Reca," the tall, ghost-marked man beside her retorted, his voice beginning to blur with drink. "Where th'hells else would they come from?"

She lowered her head, shoulders hunching, and gave only an irritable grunt by way of answer. Then she missed a stitch, and another; swore, and set the work down in her lap. "Damn you, we couldn't a'helped her, Nes!" She snatched the bottle from him, took a generous swig, and passed it along. An old scar, barely visible, bisected several of the pockmarks on her left cheek. It could have been a cut, but more likely had been a burn.

Nes's splotched face drew into a formidable scowl. "We coulda *tried*."

"And *died*," Reca retorted.

"What are they?" Idisio interrupted, angling persuasion into the words. He wasn't interested in watching a fight unroll. "Does anyone *know*?"

Reca and Nes cast Idisio glowering looks, then pointedly turned their attention to staring into the fire.

The woman who'd been slyly watching Idisio earlier said, abruptly, "Old creatures." Under the knit cap, her greying hair, streaked with red, lay lank against her face, which held as many freckles as creases. Her head jiggled restlessly now and again.

Idisio felt a chill up his spine at the sound of her voice. Not—exactly—danger, but *difference*. He saw wary expressions forming around the fire, as though others felt the same about her.

"Old. Old. Old." The woman coughed, drew in a deep, shaky breath, then went on, "They were here before humans and they'll be here after we're gone. It's the end of times, mark you, that they're coming up to land. The end of times."

The wary looks hardened towards hostility. "Babbling old biddy," Reca muttered, picking up her knitting. "Wish she'd shut up already. Anyway, nobody knows. Fast as they kill, though, sure as the gods' own sight they'll be clearing out the coast quick enough. That they can't go far from water is the only mercy to hope for."

The old woman's tremors increased for a moment. Her eyes shut, and she rocked back and forth as she said, ominously, "They'll go wherever they're told to go."

"Told by who?" Idisio asked, dread coiling in his stomach as every head raised, every eye fixed on him, uniformly unfriendly now.

"Ain't nobody telling nobody nothing the king would want to hear," Reca said, and a snuffle of tipsy laughter broke out around the fire. It seemed an odd reply, but Idisio put it down to a combination of drink and local slang. East side had had its own such phrases.

He leaned forward to catch the old woman's eye, and repeated, "Who, though? Who do these creatures answer to?"

Reca looked up from her knitting to fix him with a fierce glare. "Wait. You been trying to talk to Old Maum, here? Gods and graces. Better chance of getting sense from a squirrel." She wiggled her head in cruel imitation of the old woman's spasms. "She ain't been right in the head for years."

"I know, know, know—" Old Maun gasped after air, her head jerking. A hard flush crossed her cheeks. "I know what I'm talking about, child!"

"Give 'er some more liquor," Reca suggested, sneering. "Maybe she'll pass out and stop being a damn redling bother."

Tank would have taken dire offense at that insult. The old woman just raised a hand to touch her hair, a faintly puzzled look on her face. She pulled a strand before her eyes as though checking the color, then dropped it with a shrug.

"I want to hear what she's saying," Idisio said flatly.

"She ain't saying *anything*!" Reca snapped. "You hearing words in that garbage babble of hers? You're flat touched, if you are." Her knitting lay on her lap, forgotten, as she waved her hands derisively.

Old Maum met Idisio's eyes briefly, a hunted, haunted glance, her defiance draining into a sickly anxiety. Then she shut her eyes and hunched forward across her lap as though too weary to stay awake another moment.

"She's making perfect sense," Idisio said, feeling his expression go icy along with his tone.

Reca's mouth worked as though she wanted to spit. She took a quick glance sideways at the tattooed woman and restrained herself. Tone laden with venom, she said, "Tch. Touched. Get away from us, then, and take the old *katchag* with you." The street-slang word implied *whoredom* and *perversion*.

Old Maum tucked further into herself, shoulders trembling now. Idisio could feel her shame and fear staining the air.

"Fireside peace," the tattooed woman said, but the words held no real force. She clearly agreed with Reca.

"Don't, don't, don't," the old woman muttered, scarcely audible. "They'll hit me—me, me—*she* will, she will, will, she, after you leave—don't, don't anger, anger her—"

Reca snarled at the old woman and shouted, "Shut up, you babbling old bitch, shut up, *shut up*!"

"Reca," Nes began, putting out a cautioning hand. The tattooed woman raised her head, frowning, clearly conflicted on whether to intervene. Nobody else seemed inclined to protest, but studied their hands or their knees or the fire with sudden intensity.

Worthless insect scum—his mother surged forward, too fast to stop, outrage burning along Idisio's nerves, a lightning strike that should have paralyzed him—and yet he stood, not of his own will, but driven by her fury.

Heads snapped up all around the fire, avoidance flipping instantly into stark fear.

He saw himself through their eyes for one dizzying second: taller, inexplicably darker, crackling with deadly power. *I look like Deiq. Oh dear gods.*

Time paused.

Will you stop me? his mother asked, motionless in that moment within a moment. *Will you allow this cruelty to go unpunished?*

Old Maum hunched, head tucked down, trembling. He knew that posture from the inside out, and could guess at her thoughts without needing to reach for them: *Gods, stop drawing attention to me, you won't be here when it all breaks on my head, I should never have opened my mouth, gods, gods, gods, I'm so tired, it's so late, don't make me find another place to sleep tonight...*

He'd had those same thoughts, when he was younger, on nights when his mouth outran sense among a rough crowd.

Will you stop me? his mother said, eerily quiet, eerily still. He knew she'd retreat if he insisted.

...*No,* he said, and let her free.

His body moved: one step, two—and knelt before Old Maum. "Let me help you," his mouth said. "I can give you back your speech, so these fools will understand you again."

The old woman stared, eyes white at the edges, mouth open in unabashed longing.

"Or," his mother said through his unresisting lips, "I can punish these animals for you, destroy them as they deserve, and take you somewhere you'll be respected as you are."

He wanted to feel nauseous at the threat, wanted to feel horrified, to reject what his mother was saying, to hate that she was using him this way.

He couldn't. She was right.

The old woman's gaze never flickered from his own. She seemed entirely unsurprised. "Speech," she said. "I just want to be understood again. Please. I'll answer all your questions." Her trembling stilled, her words and eyes clearing, as though knowing she was being heard by someone had lent her strength. "This... I'm tainted, not the way they understand, but I see things, I know things. I can tell you about the worms. Please. Speech."

Her head and hands began to shake. Her shoulders drooped, and she retreated into vagueness once more.

Idisio felt his head nod, felt his mother's rueful sigh of regret, her impatience with human morals. Then came a slyness, a sleek cunning that brought him flailing forward, desperate to wrench control back before she could act further—

—too late.

His mother reached into Old Maum's mind and unleashed a silken flood, thick and clinging like melted butter. The old woman tilted her head back, eyes closing, and let out a strange whine. Incongruous, disturbing arousal flushed through Idisio's body.

He felt his own head going back, a similar keen emerging from his throat. Thought dissolved, faded—swirled—solidified, if a bit shakily, and then he sank back into a sense of flesh, all arousal gone, replaced with the weak tremors of not having eaten in days. His mother receded in a cloud of smug amusement.

Old Maum stared at him blankly. "Who are you?" she said, then looked around. "Who—who are these people...?'

"Good an' holy," Nes blurted. "She c'n *talk* again!"

The tattooed woman stood, eyes wide, forefingers hooking over thumbs, hands making a rapid circle across her chest. Others scrambled to their feet as well, and sharp blades appeared, the wielders ready for attack or defense. Violence and terror hung lambent in the air. Reca stayed seated, her knitting clutched against her chest, staring in blank bewilderment.

"Old Maum," Idisio said. A rising dread cut his breath short. "You don't remember...?"

"That's not my name," the old woman said. "My name's Edis of Craft Street." She looked down at her hands, at her clothes, with rising anger. "What in the good and holy is going on here?"

Her posture, her diction, her facial expression, her gestures—all had changed, transformed from ragged mud-britches to a comfortable merchant's wife. She now looked as out of place as Idisio himself.

"Where's my husband?" Edis demanded, standing and looking around. "What have you done? What am I doing here? Who *are* you people? Knives! What, you think I'm a threat, an old woman in—" She swept a hand down her torso, grimacing, then tugged off the knit cap. She glared at it in disgust and threw it, hard, into the fire. "In *rags*, I'm in rags! What are you staring at me like that for?"

Knives lowered, wavering, uncertain. People seemed unable to decide whether Idisio or Edis presented the greater threat. Reca still sat as though struck to stone, barely seeming to breathe.

"The worms," Idisio said, desperate now. "Do you remember what you were about to tell me about the—"

Edis's expression stopped him cold. She regarded him with the stern frown of a suspicious shopkeeper watching a street urchin wander by. "What in the name of the Three are you on about, boy?" she snapped.

"Oh, that's torn it," Nes said, fury bringing him forward a step. "Northern Church *bitch*!"

Reca lunged, grabbing his wrist and hauling him back with unexpected strenght.

"Fireside peace," the tattooed woman yelled. "Shut it down, everyone, *right now*. Sit!"

Everyone except Edis and Idisio obeyed. Edis continued to glare at Idisio as though he were to blame for everything gone wrong in her life. "Answer me!" Edis ordered. "What is going on?"

Idisio's mouth twisted to one side bitterly as his mother's cruel laughter rippled through the back of his mind. "I have no answers for you, s'a," he said. "My apologies." He stepped back, sharply aware of the eyes on him, the expressions all too similar to cornered animals about to attack. His hands were still shaking, and gods, he was hungry—but not for food...

I have to get away from here before I rip through them.

"What the hells are you?" Nes demanded, nostrils flaring as though he could pick the answer from the air by scent alone.

"No more questions," the tattooed woman interrupted. "I want you out of here, uptowner. Whatever you are. You won't get souls from us, nor speech. Get."

"What—" Edis began.

"*Quiet,* Old—ah, Edis," the tattooed woman snapped. "Wait until he's gone, and we'll settle your questions. I want him *out.*"

Unanimous nods around the fire.

Stupid humans, stupid worthless... Idisio fought to hold still, fought to stay upright. Just another moment, he could get clear, preserve his dignity, preserve his tenuous truce with the king by *not murdering two dozen innocent people...*

"Remember I could have killed you all," Idisio said, ignoring the hostility, and pointed at Edis. "*She* valued her voice above revenge for how poorly you treated her. You owe her your lives from this moment forward."

"I *what?*" Edis exclaimed, one hand to her chest, her face stark with abrupt fear. "Are you all completely mad?"

The tattooed woman made a warning gesture as Nes shifted his weight. "Get out," she said to Idisio, "or we'll all do our best to test that claim."

Stupid, stupid, stupid *humans.* Allowing himself to vent his frustration in a moment of drama, Idisio turned sideways, *stepped,* and emerged atop the crumbling roof overlooking the harbor. The supports creaked slightly, tiles trembling, but it held. Somewhere inside the broken structure, something fell with a rattling crash... then silence.

The shivering hunger faded, as he'd half expected it would. He'd need to feed soon, but not just yet. He sank down, both grateful and irritated that he hadn't set off another structural disaster, then said aloud, "Mudbritched *shiabanse.*"

A sense of amused indifference was his only reply.

She wanted him to cede her superiority? Leave him with no option but to turn to her for help? *Fuck that.* He'd fought a fucking *ha'rethe,* he'd fought a *faereen,* he'd fought *attiara.* He'd stared down the fucking head of the teyanain, Lord Evkit. He could find another way. Maybe Cafad... but instinct squealed protest at that notion, the back of his mind echoing with a high-pitched sound of alarm all too similar to the warning he'd ignored at the gates.

Dangerous, dangerous, dangerous. His mother shuddered, apparently agreeing, so he didn't bother trying to figure out the *why*. Cafad wasn't available, that was that.

Eredion—but no, he'd left Bright Bay some time ago. Fimre, his replacement, was dead. Besides, seeking out any desert Family representative would imply an alliance, and given the current chaos in the southlands—well, they'd likely be scrambling for just such support as a ha'ra'ha could offer. But he wasn't staying. He had to go to Arason. He *wanted* to go to Arason.

Don't I? Or is that only because my mother insisted I have to go? If I don't go to Arason, what else is there for me to do? Wander about upsetting people...

...like Deiq did?

He stared glumly out over the swath of destruction and tried not to think directly about the obvious remaining name. If Cafad set off alarms, *that one* would without question agitate his mother fit to pitch him off the roof.

Although...

What would... that person... have done, faced with this situation?

His mother stirred, hissing. Idisio hastily walled off a corner of his mind, securing a few moments of privacy in which to consider that question.

Tank had blood-forged steel for nerves and spine alike. He wouldn't be begging after help from anyone. He'd be taking the offensive. Even against a ghost in his own mind. Idisio had no doubts on that.

And I'm ha'ra'hain. Be damned if I'm weaker than a human, as Deiq would say. Shit, I've already killed her once, *what the hells am I so afraid of?*

Abruptly, internal shields cracked under his mother's assault, her venomous hiss very nearly overwhelming sense and sensation alike. But this time, *she* was too late.

Idisio swung sideways to her presence, letting her surge *past* his center—and attacked from behind.

Her agonized shriek was the most satisfying thing he'd heard all day.

The worms were called *rael-ke*. They were servants, watchers, or pets, depending on how one thought of such things. Not as dangerous as the *attiara*, but only because while attiara had a measure of independent thought, the rael-ke were deeply conditioned to obey one partiulcar authority: ha'reye. And—maybe—ha'ra'hain.

Rael-ke were flat, no more than three inches thick and two handspans wide; they could compress to an arm's length, or stretch out to ten times that. They had thousands of tiny, tearing mouths on their underside, and made such efficient use of their intake that the only excretion was the thin slime coating the top of their bodies.

They were impossible, *revolting* creatures, and the notion that Idisio's ancestors had bred them as *pets* made him want to vomit.

Maybe he'd let himself do that later. He had a promise to fill first.

He'd chosen a beach on the eastern side of the city, a nod to his roots; he'd haunted this beach in his youth, chasing after golden crabs in season and trying his hand at fishing. The latter had failed more often than the former, given his restless nature at the time and preference for fast movement.

He stood still, today, a stone's throw from the steadily lapping waves. Seaweed reek hung heavy in the air. Flies rose and fell in noisy clouds. There were no humans in sight. Even the most desperate scavengers had chosen safer hunting grounds.

There were no rael-ke in sight, either, but Idisio now knew that they were masters of camouflage. There wouldn't be many of them, and there would be fewer as the food sources moved further away.

Rael-ke were perfectly happy to eat one another in the absence of other prey. Given time, they'd essentially wipe themselves out. But they were biddable, and there were too many tainted in the area. One of them was certain to walk the right paths of madness to bind the creatures, and the havoc a *directed* rael-ke could wreak didn't bear thinking about.

Idisio understood more about the tainted, now, too: what they were, what they could do, and how they'd come to be. He'd clawed out quite a bit of knowledge from his mother in the handful of seconds the fight had lasted.

He didn't remember exactly what he'd done during the confrontation. It wasn't the first time he'd blocked out his own memories. From what Deiq had said, it probably wouldn't be the last. Curating memories was part of how a ha'ra'hain survived centuries without imploding entirely. Over the years, Deiq had blocked hundreds if not thousands of his own.

What remained of his mother's ghost sulked, seething, in the back corner of his mind. Occasionally, she sent out blood-drenched, flame-edged bursts of her own memories, visions of things that would have horrified Idisio only a tenday ago.

Now he batted the weak sendings aside, indifferent to the implications of kinship, no longer anxious over the potential of insanity. He *was* mad, by any human standard, and it didn't matter. It was his own madness, distinct from the path that his mother had taken, very different from Deiq's angle.

Idisio accepted the similarities between himself and the First Born without the least disquiet now.

Another matching point occurred to him: Idisio, like Deiq, would definitely create his own share of disasters if he continued to live among humans. He didn't find that morally disturbing any longer, but it would be... annoying.

So he wouldn't stay. He would go to Arason as soon as this obligation cleared. The concept of *obligation* had strengthened within him, which was a slight surprise. He would stay away from the politics and peculiarities of human society that had snared and twisted his mother and Deiq.

My life. My path. My choice.

His mother hissed sourly at that, a thin sound devoid of power. He ignored it.

Idisio tilted his head back, looking up at the sky, and let out a cry laced with challenge, summons, and command, arcing through ranges and tones humans would miss and asp-jacaus would cower from. A high, sharp warble that dipped and twisted around itself for challenge; a rapid scale from low to high as summons, and a series of yelping notes as command. He repeated it twice more, louder each time.

Flies scattered as he sang. A gillahawk squawked a distress cry and banked sharply away. Isisio could feel sand fleas, tiny crabs, even shallow-water fish fleeing the area, mad terror the only thing in their limited minds.

The effort of producing such a complicated song forced ha'ra'hain senses to absolute dominance, and his perceptions spread out to cover what felt like damn near half of Bright Bay. He sensed smaller predators—asp-jacaus, wofics, cats, snakes—as they wavered, each one tempted to answer the challenge; after a tense moment, they prudently slunk into hiding.

Motion closer to hand startled him back into localized vision: over a dozen humans streamed onto the beach, charging forward with reckless fury. Idisio allowed himself a moment of annoyance that he hadn't expected that, then yet another instant of considering whether to push them away or accept their offered lives.

The ground writhed under the attackers. Rael-ke wound upwards like living strands of sand-coated seaweed. The humans fell, screaming, berserk anger jolting into incoherent fear.

Stop, Idisio ordered, a heartbeat too late, and flung up a shield as viscera exploded around him. A heartbeat, two, three, and bones littered the sand, thick with blood, bits of flesh trailing, mucus-drenched and gleaming in the sunlight. Idisio hastily shut down his sense of smell to avoid vomiting and pushed at the air to create a localized breeze. At least he'd shielded in time: none of the splatter had reached him.

Stop, he repeated, then: *obey/come/present yourselves to me.*

A surge of knife-edged protectiveness answered him. The ground shifted as rael-ke settled around him in a wide circle, alert for incoming threats—from outside and from Idisio himself. He couldn't tell now many surrounded him; between twenty and thirty, at a guess. More than he'd anticipated. Their emotions were a slithering mixture of anger at being denied the remainder of their feast, confusion, and wariness about this strange new power commanding them.

Well, at least they'd provisionally accepted his authority.

Why are you on land? he asked. *Why have you left the ocean?*

At the question, smoky distress swirled among them, a questioning bewilderment. Echoes of compulsion shook through Idisio's muscles, a shrill cry that rose from the roots of the earth to the heights of the sky: *Betrayed, betrayed, destroy, destroy!*

Oh. Of course. The ha'reye of the southlands had sent out a final, cataclysmic command before their own destruction. Utterly obvious and predictable, in retrospect. More than likely there would be other creations emerging from the shadows in the months ahead.

The king would be very, *very* unhappy with that information.

Idisio didn't really care.

"No," Ididio said aloud, then, silently: *I countermand that order. You will return to the ocean. You will never again emerge onto dry land, nor harm any creature that lives above the water.*

A thick silence. Distress and questioning solidified into chill anger. Several of the rael-ke came at him, flicker-fast.

He laid stripes of fire across each sinuous body. The rael-ke arched, twisting, screaming in a range far beyond what even an asp-jacau could have heard. The fire spread, charring their flesh as rapidly as their teeth had rent human bodies, leaving collapsed curls of black, stinking ash that fell across the sand and seaweed a heatbeat laster.

The remaining rale-ke held still, pressed flat and terrified against the ground. *Servitude,* they projected, with a sense of complete submission to his will.

Idisio pointed to the ocean, repeating his command. Without hesitation, they slid past his feet in a steady, undulating river. A patch of water flattened out under their weight, waves breaking to either side. Then the rael-ke sank from sight, waves shuddering back into their usual rhythm.

Silence descended, then broke with a human shout of horror. Idisio turned. A group of guards stood at the edge of the beach, faces grey and strained, crossbows firmly pointed at him. Four wore the white tunic of higher authority; their close-cropped hair and pale, shaven faces made it hard, just at the moment, for Idisio to tell one from another. They all seemed very young, at a glance.

Three more, in brown, bore the crimson sash of rank earned from bravery and quick thinking. These men were older, and their faces bore various scars and lines; one was missing half his ear, another had a distinct cast eye. One man, slightly shorter than his companions, stood to the fore, and his posture held an absolute air of command. He had to be the captain. His skin was as dark a shade as Idisio had ever seen and his head was shaven completely bald. He wore a white tunic, a crimson sash, and a gold belt: symbols to show that he'd faced the worst of the recent madness and come out in one piece—and on the right side.

Or, to be more precise, on the new king's side. Idisio was keenly aware that *right* often had no relation to *power.* He considered simply disappearing, stepping sideways-back to the palace to tell the king what had happened; but that wouldn't be proper, wouldn't be the right pattern. He held still, and waited.

"You're a *monster,*" the captain said, voice shaking. The men around him had the wide-eyed glare of zealots ready to kill for captain and king.

Idisio looked at the scattered massacre around him and sighed. "I know," he said. "Those crossbows won't do you any good, though. You might as well lower—"

A *thwop* sounded as one of the guards loosed a bolt. Even as the captain yelled, "*Hold!*", others followed suit as though unable to bear waiting another moment.

Every bolt caught fire, crumbling into ash before they came within a handspan of their target. Idisio didn't move or speak. He let his eyes fill with ha'ra'hain black, and merely stared at the men, implacably cold.

The men dropped their useless crossbows as though the fire had touched them directly. The three ranking guards drew long knives, but stayed still, now watching the captain for direction. Of the lesser-ranked men, one fled screaming; one fell to his knees and began reciting prayers to the Four; the last stood still, shivering, his attention entirely on Idisio.

The captain drew in a long breath, his back very straight, and said, "My apologies, ha'inn. My men... misunderstood the situation."

"I'm going to speak to the king now," Idisio told them. "You may escort me, if you wish."

The captain swallowed, glancing at the shattered remains strewn across the beach, and said, with great care, "Thank you, ha'inn, that would be an honor."

"Not really," Idisio said, "but you're welcome to tell yourself so if you like."

Sun slanted into the newly rebuilt audience hall through five wide windows; three patterned with stained-glass flowers and animals, two clear. Idisio didn't know much about Family symbolism, but lizards were a Scratha design, and he was fairly sure that owls were a teyanain mark. Given that both were featured, the other animals, and probably the flowers, had to hold a distinct message.

Overhead, chandeliers encrusted in glass beads waited to be lit at nightfall. Oruen's new throne was a compromise between sturdy and elegant, with more of the same distinctive glass beads worked into curved lines of oak and a darker wood Idisio couldn't immediately identify.

Considering that Sessin Family was essentially destroyed, there was a touch of irony in the display. It wouldn't be matched again any time soon, leaving the king in Bright Bay with probably the finest glasswork still in existence.

Five crimson-sashed guards, these with chainmail tunics over their brown clothing, stood in an arc behind the king. Five more, in the same garb, were arrayed at the entrance to the room. They all carried sheathed short blades at their waist and sharp polearms in their hands, and stood at a parade rest that could, clearly, become a fighting stance in moments.

There were a handful of courtiers, fewer than Idisio had expected, dressed in the lace-edged shirts, fine velvet leggings, and polished boots of fine society. They stared as Idisio entered the room with his escort.

Oruen had clearly been informed of the situation already. His expression had curdled far past the sour mark, and his entire body was stiff with anger and tension. He waved the courtiers out of the room with a sharp gesture.

One man protested: "My Lord—"

"I won't need your advice for this one," Oruen said. "*Out.*"

So that hadn't been a courtier after all, but an advisor. Idisio looked at the people filing from the room, reassessing, realizing that they were all advisors of one sort of another. They wore no noticeable jewelry, and their clothes, while fine, were of an overall somber cut. Once, he wouldn't have made that basic of a mistake.

Once felt like it had been a long time ago.

The audience hall door thudded shut behind the last of the departing advisors.

"Ha'inn," Oruen said, tone flat. He waved Idisio's escort to spots along the walls to each side of his throne. Their lack of armor compared to the other guards made them, somehow, appear the more dangeorus. "I offer no threat." The words sounded strangled.

That would be why you feel the need for fifteen armed guards? Idisio managed not to say it aloud, but from the way the king's eyes narrowed, it had come through in his expression all the same.

Before the moment could turn into an incident, Idisio stepped forward a pace and ostentatiously stopped, his hands locked behind his back, his emotions locked down to *human-normal.*

"I've handled the problem," he said. "The creatures are called rael-ke. They've returned to the water, and they won't trouble you any longer. Neither will I."

"*Good,*" Oruen said tightly. Idisio could almost hear the held words: the prospect of never seeing another ha'ra'hain sounded *very* good to the king just now.

"I don't believe Deiq will be coming through any time soon, and I won't be returning," Idisio said, unable to resist prodding at that sore spot. "You likely won't see any more ha'ra'hain disturbing your city."

"Are you saying you're the only two left?" Oruen sat forward, catching himself just in time to direct his eager stare to Idisio's shoulder instead of his face.

"No," Idisio said. "I have no way of knowing that, Lord Oruen."

Oruen settled back into a more regal pose, frowning down the space to Idisio's left. "I suppose you wouldn't," he muttered, then his voice hardened. "I will note that once again, you've left quite the trail of destruction behind you, ha'inn."

"I didn't kill those people," Idisio said with measured chill. "That was the rael-ke. But even if it *had* been by my hand, Lord Oruen, you have no standing to rebuke me. If I'd killed ten times that number you'd have no grounds to raise complaint."

The king rose to his feet, his expression molten fury. Before he could say anything, Idisio reached inside-sideways and *pulled*: a guard collapsed to the floor with a choking gasp, then lay panting loudly as though struggling for breath.

Oruen froze, staring; then, slowly, sank back down. One of the guards knelt to check on his fallen companion. The others glared at Idisio with growing resentment. Idisio turned in place, meeting each set of eyes, his own expression completely calm. They flinched away from his stare, dropping their gazes one by one to the floor.

The fallen guard climbed to his feet, still breathing hard and trembling. Idisio turned his attention back to the king.

"After I leave," Idisio said, "you're on your own with whatever ha'reye pet shows up next."

Oruen blanched, his hands clenching in his lap. Desperation edged his tone as he said, "Ha'inn, you've made your point. Name your price—"

His mother stirred, eager to accept that far too generous an offer. In her current, weakened state, her pain-lust was barely a flutter against his consciousness, and easily dismissed.

"No," Idisio answered, quietly and clearly, and put just a touch of *otherness* into the word.

The king stopped, mouth open for a long moment. A fine tremor ran through his thin frame, and Idisio had the sense he was trying very hard to hold on to bladder control.

"Tell your loremasters," Idisio said, "that the commands that restrained creatures like the rael-ke are gone. The ha'reye no longer rule the southlands."

A clatter sounded from around the room as several of the guards shifted in place, their expressions abruptly anxious. The guard Idisio had pushed at gave a low moan and sat down as though his legs simply wouldn't support him any longer.

Oruen said, tentatively, "Are they... dead? I haven't been able to find out for sure..."

"I'm not going to give you that answer," Idisio said, and allowed himself to enjoy the moment of dark frustration on the king's face.

Once, he'd been terrified at the very thought of meeting the king. Now, the man meant nothing more than a task to complete before Idisio went to Arason.

"Ha'inn," Oruen said, shifting to a conciliatory tone and spreading his hands flat on his thighs, "it's been a turbulent time since I stepped up, and I haven't given you proper honors. I'm truly sorry. Allow me to host you as you deserve by way of apology and gratitude."

Idisio smiled, allowing genuine amusement to show through. "No," he said again, just as calmly as before. "I'm leaving, Lord Oruen. You're on your own."

Oruen's thin mouth worked for a moment, as though he were chewing on his tongue. He said, "I can offer you—"

"You don't have anything I want, Lord Oruen," Idisio interrupted.

The king's geniality evaporated. "You can't just leave us! If there are more of those things out there—you have a *duty*, ha'inn!"

Idisio laughed. "You're right," he said. "I do have a duty. But it's not to you." He offered a slight bow to the king and began to turn away. Again, he considered simply stepping through space instead of walking from the room, but that didn't feel quite right. He let his gaze drift slowly across the guards, amused by the worried expressions on their faces as they glanced at the king, clearly asking *not to be sent against the ha'ra'hain.*

"Stand down," Oruen told the guards wearily. They visibly relaxed; the one still sitting on the floor put his head on his drawn-up knees and let out a stifled sob. "Ha'inn Idisio, *please.*"

"Goodbye, Lord Oruen," Idisio said, and sauntered toward the door.

"Where are you *going*?" Oruen asked plaintively. "Would you permit me to send word, at least, if we need your help?"

Idisio almost said: *stop whining, you're a king, fucking act like it.* "No," he said instead, not breaking stride.

"Ha'inn—!" The one word carried a world's weight of pleading and frustration.

Fucking humans. They never know when it's enough. Idisio paused and drew in a long, slow breath. The guards around the door tensed, wide-eyed, gripping their weapons with shaking hands.

"You know," Idisio said over his shoulder, "I'm beginning to see why Deiq gets so irritated with humans. *Piss off.*"

Oruen gasped as though gut-punched. The guards pressed back against the walls, edging away from the doors as though afraid Idisio would take offense at any proximity just now.

They weren't far wrong.

He walked out of the audience hall with no further interruptions.

It was time, for the first time in his life, to go *home*. Idisio discovered he was rather looking foward to it.

One last obligation remained. Once that was cleared, he'd take what he needed from someone deserving of death, then he'd be on his way home. It would be easy to find a target; he had a number of old scores to settle in this city. He recalled a man who'd stabbed his mother, in the street, in cold blood, and stripped her of everything worth a bent brass bit, right down to her wig. If he was still alive, he'd do. Others came to mind as well.

Time to sort out choice of victim later.

Just one last stop.

He drew in a long breath, testing his temper, then reached out.

Cafad?

Silence. Idisio stopped walking, balancing with one hand against a nearby wall, and shut his eyes, puzzled. He could feel something that resonated as *Cafad*, but it was... different. Altered. Not...

Oh.

Scratha ha'rethe was dead. Cafad had been tightly meshed with the creature at the time Idisio had helped to kill it. More than likely it had drained him of all power during the struggle.

He wasn't a desert lord any longer.

Idisio opened his eyes, staring at the sky, thinking it through: then sighed, very gently, and *stepped* across the city. Desert lord or human, the obligation remained the same, and the pattern required completion.

Hee-ay, hee-ay: the cry of a water seller in a nearby street. *Shass shass shass*—that sound came from avian throats, not human. This area had more scolding-birds than lower class bodies for noble servants to shoo aside. No merchants cried out in false outrage about their financial ruin. The ones hereabout had already gone far past that point and were glumly stoic about rebuilding their fortunes.

The situation was not at all the same as Idisio's first encounter with Scratha, yet it felt like a circle was being closed. He stood quietly in the shade of a feather-fern tree, watching the former desert lord.

Cafad sat in a wide-bottomed chair with heavy padding, brooding over a solitary game of chabi. He was all in grey, rather than his usual black; his clothes were plain and cut straight where southerners would have laid curved lines. Likewise, the cup and carafe sitting on the oak table beside the chabi board were thick, even clunky: ostentatiously ordinary craftsmanship. The only southern marker was Cafad's distinctive appearance, but even that had thinned to a surprising gauntness, slightly blurred by beard stubble, and his skin was considerably more ashen than Idisio recalled.

Cafad sighed and sat back in his chair, rubbing his eyes. "I can't see as I used to," he said aloud, not turning his head, "but I know someone's there. Please don't lurk, it's rude."

Idisio circled round to stand opposite Cafad. "Lord Scratha," he said.

"Ha'inn," the former desert lord said, motioning to a chair. "Do me the honor of having a seat, if you would. I'll call for more tea." His hand trembled, a tiny shiver working through his lean frame; not fear, not from Cafad, but a sign of lasting nerve damage from recent events.

"I'm not staying," Idisio said.

"Of course not, but there's always time for tea. With all we've been through in recent days, small moments matter, ha'inn. Please, indulge me." He kept his gaze lowered and aside, not meeting Idisio's gaze directly.

Idisio settled slowly into a chair. A servant in plain white and grey linen emerged from an arched doorway, set a fresh carafe and cup on the table, and withdrew without a word or glance at Idisio.

They filled their cups and sipped in silence for a few moments. The tea was a lightly scented blend that reminded Idisio of roses and mint; he found himself slowly relaxing.

"Thank you, Lord Scratha," Idisio said eventually. "You do me honor."

"The honor is mine," Cafad said. "And now let's drop the formalities, if you please. I'm crippled. I have no power to offer you, and little wealth, but what I have is yours."

"I know," Idisio said, setting his cup down. "I'm sorry, Lord Scratha."

Cafad shut his eyes and turned his head away, his breath hitching for a moment. "I hold no anger against you, ha'inn," he said, meeting Idisio's gaze briefly, as though to emphasize his sincerity. Then he looked down at the table, tracing slow patterns on the wood with one finger as he went on, voice even: "I hold no anger against anyone. There were too many hands on the table to put blame on any one point."

Idisio nodded slowly. "You've changed, Lord Scratha." The man who'd caught Idisio picking his pocket, not so long ago, would never have spoken so calmly of such dreadful matters, much less over a fragrant cup of tea. And certainly not in the presence of someone dangerous.

Cafad *knew* what Idisio could do. And wasn't afraid. Not from arrogance or from a false sense of safety, but from a resigned acceptance of the way things were.

Cafad's faint, rueful smile showed that he was having similar thoughts. He said, "So have you, ha'inn."

"Yes." Idisio touched the edge of his cup pensively, then withdrew his hand. "I'm going to Arason. I'm not coming back this time."

"Good." The word held no malice. "It's best you don't follow Deiq's path of meddling in human affairs. I think we ought to manage on our own, at this point. We've done enough damage to ourselves already."

Idisio took another sip of tea, relishing the gentle taste, and wondered idly if he should ask for some as a parting gift. It seemed unlikely he'd find a source for it north of the Hackerwood.

"I agree," Idisio said, deciding the tea wasn't all that important. Best to leave without any requests or favors weighted to one side or the other. "The king is a bit more upset about my departure."

The lines around Cafad's eyes deepened. "The king gets upset easily these days. Lord Eredion was doing a tremendous job of managing him, apparently. I'm not as skilled, but Nissa and I are doing what we can. And in any case, it's not your problem, ha'inn." His tone changed as he said Nissa's name, invoking a wealth of emotion in the one word.

"So you did marry her in the end," Idisio said, glancing at the braided silver ring on Cafad's left hand. It was the only jewelry the man wore. He'd always been minimalist, but southern custom generally involved rather a lot of earrings, rings, bracelets and necklaces by way of status markers.

"Yes. Astoundingly, she forgave me my idiocy. I'm well aware I don't deserve her mercy, but I seem to have it." Cafad bent his head, blinking hard. Another new thing. The only emotion he'd shown, for many years, had been a constant, sullen anger at the world in general. Now he seemed deflated and sad.

Idisio wasn't entirely sure whether he liked the new Cafad or not. He found himself hoping that the man would recover, given time, and build back the sharp edge that had defined him for so long. It was tempting to push at the man and see if he could provoke a flare of the old anger.

But that would be unkind, and wouldn't provide any result of value. So Idisio said, reflecting Cafad's own words back at him, "There were a lot of hands on the table."

Cafad's thin shoulders moved in a faint shrug, and he spread long-fingered hands on the table. "Indeed. Is there anything else, ha'inn? As I said, everything I have is yours, from my possessions to my person. Would you like to drag me through the streets like a squalling child?" His voice was mild, his gaze on his cup.

"I'm not interested in revenge, Lord Scratha," Idisio said quietly. "I think you've been hurt enough."

"More undeserved mercy. Incredible." Cafad drew in and let out a deep breath. "Thank you, ha'inn. I'll do my best to make the world better by way of gratitude for your forbearance."

This was getting ridiculous. Idisio sharpened his tone as he retorted, "There's no need to be *quite* so humble. I caused rather a lot of the damage myself, Lord Scratha."

Cafad's mouth moved, a flash of his old, bitter humor appearing. He wrapped one hand around his teacup, his body language shifting towards a more familiar restlessness. "I'm well aware," he said. "As you said, many hands on the table. You have your own amends to make. I trust you'll do your part." He picked up the cup, set it down, moved it again, then spread his hands flat on the table once more and let out a hissing sigh.

"Yes," Idisio said. "I will." He hesitated, then added, "I'll keep researching the northlands. I think that's going to be more urgently needed than ever. I'll send the letters to you, if you'll permit."

"Making me your liaison with the king? Nicely done." Cafad shut his eyes, his smile fading. "I have to excuse myself, I'm afraid. I still tire easily. Gods give you grace, ha'inn." He rattled his fingers against the table, giving the lie to his profession of being weary; he'd burned through his patience, that was all, and needed to go pace about and probably yell at things.

He was still the same man, underneath. Idisio found that tremendously reassuring.

"And may you walk in sunshine that never burns you," Idisio answered, rising to his feet.

Cafad laughed a little, squinting at Idisio in surprise. "That's a new one. If you can be that inventive on a whim, I suspect you're going to be just fine, ha'inn. I thank you for the gift of your presence."

"Gods hold you gently," Idisio said, then dropped formality for just three words: "Thank you, Cafad."

Cafad stood, shoulders back, head high, every bit the desert lord he'd once been—except for the damp brightness in his eyes. He pressed one palm to his chest and bowed deeply. "Goodbye, Idisio," he said, his voice thick.

"Goodbye," Idisio said, then turned away into the refuge of insignificance once again.

Being functionally invisible would make hunting suitable prey easier; and it was time, at long last, to go home.

Epilogue Two

A gust of night wind skittered small pieces of rock and drifted sand across the rare flat sections of broken ground that had once been the Qisani. An owl circled, a silent, wavering shadow against the backdrop of moon and stars. It paused, tilted, dove, letting out a high screech intended to paralyze its prey: a ragged groundhog picking through the destruction in hopes of finding something to eat.

As its talons stretched to snatch up the small creature, a dark tendril shot from a crevice in the ground, twining around the owl's legs before it could swerve free. Whip-fast, the tendril slammed the owl against the ground, snapping most of the bones in its body with one sharp movement.

The tendril slipped around the bird's corpse, coiling like a jungle snake, compressing flesh and bone into a bundle small enough to pull into the crevice. Another gust of wind scattered broken feathers like sand, clearing the area to innocence once again.

The groundhog, motionless during the entire incident, shivered a bit as though waking from a trance, then began browsing for food once more. It moved in a slow circle, apparently unaware that it was retracing its steps.

After a time, a night hawk circled overhead, its dark body briefly blocking out the stars and moon. It paused, catching sight of the groundhog, and prepared to dive....

Appendix

Excerpted Notes from Loremaster Council Records

Transcribed two months after the destruction of Sessin Family:

Cafad of Scratha Family has renounced all claim to title and real properties from the area formerly known as Scratha Fortress. He has additionally renounced all claim on his rights as a desert lord, an unprecedented step we are still investigating the ramifications of.

Cafad has married Lord Nissa Sessin, who currently holds title as head of Sessin Family despite those lands being almost completely destroyed. They live at the southwestern edge of Bright Bay. Lord Nissa Sessin is a frequent visitor to court and represents the interests of the remnants of her Family, most of whom have relocated to the southeastern section of Bright Bay. Cafad is seen infrequently, and is still no pleasant company when he does appear at court functions....

Sessin Family continues to attempt to rebuild its glass-crafting empire, but is quickly being overtaken in that endeavor by the work being produced by its former sub-family, Tereph. Tereph claimed independence from Sessin Family in the wake of the catastrophe, a surprising move that is having far-ranging impact throughout the southlands. Hard feelings between Tereph and Sessin are a constant source of tension within Bright Bay in particular. We have advised Lord Oruen that Tereph appears to be attempting to influence the nobility to turn against all things Sessin, which would unbalance an already precarious situation....

The former Scratha lands are now officially known as Peysimun, accepted by a Conclave held in Water's End within the last tenday. Lord Alyea of Peysimun is, perhaps ironically given the overall history, already showing a great talent for repairing deeply strained diplomatic relationships. We suspect she is being guided by Deiq of Stass, but have not been able to confirm his current location with absolute certainty. Lord Peysimun has not responded to our queries on the matter and her household staff are uniquely unwilling to speak to outsiders....

The majority of the eastern coast of the southlands are broken apart and flooded. The Wall Stair is entirely demolished. Much of it cascaded into the sea, prompting enormous surges along lower-lying areas and the formation of several tenuous new "islands" from the rubble. Coastal survivors are still being located and rehabilitated, in large part thanks to the efforts of Lord Nissa Sessin and her husband....

The Horn is largely in ruins. The once steep climb and drop has been reduced to a cratered plateau of significantly lower elevation. The teyanain have relocated to a currently undisclosed location. We have confirmation that the former head of the teyanain, Lord Evkit, has ceded his claim to his daughter, Cuna. Lord Evkit's location is likewise unknown at this time. Given the volatility of the teyanain and the historically hostile relationship between Evkit and his daughter, we are deeply concerned by the potential for further disruption. Our agents are searching diligently throughout the southlands for any sign as to where the various factions have settled....

Our sources report that there is a growing sense, in the south, that resources are dwindling without chance of restoration. Each Family is handling that concern differently.

Darden Family and F'Heing Family are engaged in an increasingly vicious battle for control over the northern market via Bright Bay and Kismo, farther to the north. We believe they intend to relocate their bases north once a sphere of influence is solidly established, which would entirely disrupt the northern kingdom and cause internal war in short order. Our responsibility on this front is still under consideration.

Toscin Family appears to be turning southward, investigating the still-burning Forbidden Jungles and Haunted Lands. Some as yet unsubstantiated reports have Toscin collaborating with Aerthraim Family....

Aerthraim Family has acquired their first desert lord, in the person of

Lord Irrio, formerly of Darden Family. We suspect his defection was in service of building a relationship with Lord Aziniari, and that her own, unprecedented second defection to the teyanain set Lord Irrio into a dangerously unstable position. The mahadrae is unlikely to offer Lord Irrio much freedom until she is certain of his dedication, which may present us with certain opportunities....

Peysimun Family lands are reportedly lush with new growth, no doubt from the heavy bands of rain that have passed over the area in recent weeks. We foresee this area becoming a new center for southern resources. Again, we would dearly like to ascertain whether Deiq of Stass is involved in this situation, and to what extent; his presence or absence is a critical factor in our decisions regarding Peysimun Family....

Lord Oruen remains stable but unattached. He still shows no interest in an official match, and the Council is currently considering whether to press the issue. Given the current upheaval, arguments are being made in both directions....

Azaniari Aerthraim-Darden and her twin brother Allonin have effectively disappeared, a significantly worrisome development given rumors of newly forged ties to the current teyanain leadership. Aerthraim Family loremasters are refusing to answer inquiries of any sort from the Council. We are considering the dire step of sanctions to procure cooperation....

Ha'inn Idisio has reached Arason, and is settling in with a minimum, so far, of disruption. We have watchers on site to track developments, and there is evidence that teyanain watchers may be in the area as well....

Weather patterns continue to shift dramatically from the disruption. We expect to see a number of erratic storms hit the Horn and coastal areas over the coming months. It is becoming advisable to establish observers north of the Hackerwood, but our numbers are decidedly not up to the task of studying such a large area. This Council is considering a proposal to accept recruits with lower qualifications, as students of the north would not necessarily need to know the abundance of southern history currently required of incoming loremasters....

This Council moves that Loremasters Eis, Jahow, Bea, and Tur, once dismissed in disgrace for their apparent madness, be posthumously reinstated with great honor, since their predictions have, one and all, turned out to be more precise than we had ever dared to believe possible....

Glossary and Pronunciation Guide

A number of the words in the southern language include the glottal-stop, which is rendered here as ^. A glottal stop involves closing, to some degree, the back of the throat, resulting in a near-coughing sound when released. Sometimes this sounds as though a hard "H" has been inserted.
Note: The glottal stop between a and i, always difficult for humans to manage, has fallen out of favor over the centuries.

Aenstone (ayn-stone): An Aerthraim Family-created stone composite; they hold the process secret. In sufficient quantity, aenstone blocks psychic communications, inhibits the use of psychic abilities, and weakens ha'ra'hain.

Aerth (ay-erth): Rough translation: *feathers, freedom, flight.* Exact meaning dependent on dialect and context.

Aerthraim lanterns: Any lamp filled with the peculiar green oil produced only by Aerthraim Family; gives off an unusually white light and little to no smoke when burned.

Aesa (ay-sah): A common plant whose leaves, when dried and used in a pipe, produce a mild euphoria. Illegal in the north; legal south of Bright Bay.

Alli (ahl-lee): 1. The number *two* (southern). 2. A simple two-pipe instrument, usually wooden, occasionally metal, common to the southlands.

Ana-ha, va'bit (ahhnah-hah, vah-^beet): Rough translation: *Service/apology accepted.* A very old and out-of-use phrase: ha'ra'hain accepting apologies or submission from a human.

Aqeyva (ack-**ee**-vah, alt. ahh-**keh**-vah): A combination of martial-arts training and meditation disciplines. The combat training is often referred to as a 'dance' as it involves smooth, flowing motions that have no apparent resemblance to any fighting mode.

Asp-jacau (asp-jack-how): A slender canine with long, thin snout and legs. Its short-haired coat tends toward fawn or brindle coloring. Its excellent sense of smell is primarily used to detect dangerous snakes and (in some cases) drugs. In Bright Bay, only royalty or King's Guard patrols may own an asp-jacau, but south of the Horn the asp-jacau is a common companion animal.

Athain (ath-**ain**)**:** Lit. translation: *spirit-walker*. Teyanain specially trained to manipulate energy and psychic forces; extremely dangerous people, and very rare. Athain are considered holy by the teyanain. While they have elaborate outfits for ceremonial purposes, in "ordinary" clothes athain are distinguished by a unique manner of braiding their hair: beginning as one braid, then dividing further into three smaller braids, usually laced with tiny beads.

Ayn (ain)**:** Chabi piece representing water. Cylindrical in shape, the ayn moves like a crooked stream: two spaces in one direction, three in another. It is one of the most versatile pieces on the board.

Bene (**beh**-ne)**:** 1. The number *three* (southern). 2. A relatively simple three-pipe instrument common to the southlands. Like the *alli*, it is most commonly made of wood.

Cactus-flute: A long, thin flute made from minor branches of the same hard-skinned cactus used for making shabacas. Produces a thin, piping sound; sometimes tied together in sets of three to produce a wider range of tones.

Calcen (**khal**-czen; fem. **Calcana:** khal-**zay**-nah)**:** The title teyanain use for their leader; not permitted to outsiders. It is considered a gross offense for any non-teyanain to use that term.

Callen (**call**-en)**:** One sworn to the service of a southern god.

Ceiling tube: A skylight in the form of a wide tube lined with mirrors; developed by Aerthraim Family. The secret of their manufacture is tightly controlled; they must be installed and repaired by Aerthraim craftsmen.

Chabi (**chah**-bee)**:** A desert game whose underlying principles, moves and strategies reflect the principles of survival in a dry, hostile environment. In chabi, different types of pieces represent wind, water, goods, and money; different areas of the board represent compass directions, fortresses, fire, air, and water.

Chekk (che**ck**)**:** A community of ha'ra'hain openly living above ground. Extremely rare, as the genetic deterioration generally turns any such group into a human community within three generations—and the combative nature of many ha'ra'hain makes creating a balanced community a tricky process.

Chichi (**chee**-chee)**:** A small, hand-held clapper style of drum; generally a lightly hinged or tied striker and a metallic or wooden "head."

Clee: Three athain working together; extremely rare and extremely dangerous.

Coming or going: Street-slang inquiry about a relationship; "is she coming or going" means, more or less, "is she your girlfriend or a temporary amusement?"

Comos (**Cohm**-ohs)**:** One of three gods honored in the southlands. Represents the neutrality / balance / questioning energies; also linked to the season of winter, the colors white and brown, and curiosity. Callen of Comos, if male, must be castrated; women must be past menopause to be allowed out in the world at large.

Dahass (dah-**hahs**; alt., dah-**hass**)**:** Nomadic tribes that roam the uncharted and unclaimed southlands and follow no ruler but their own leader. They are likely the source of many of the wilder tales of southern barbarism that circulate in the northlands, as they find spreading such rumors amusing.

Daimaina (day-**may**-nah)**:** Southern version of housekeeper; generally but not always shares the Head of Family's bed. Holds considerable power in her own right, but in a sharply limited sphere. Male version is *daiman.*

Dasta (**dah**-stah)**:** A drug originally developed by the ketarches, whose use has altered significantly over the years.

Dashaic (dash-**ache**)**:** So-called dasta tea is dasta powder turned into a thick, potent syrup. Dashaic travels better than the powder, as it runs less risk of being ruined by damp conditions, but is more difficult to produce and thus far more expensive.

Datda (**Dat**-dah)**:** One of three gods honored in the southlands, Datda represents the negative/death/change energies; also linked to the season of high summer, the colors red and black, and the emotion of anger. Commonly called "the Sun Lord"; saying the name aloud is held to be bad luck. Only Datda's Callen may safely pronounce the holy name, but they tend to be reluctant to advertise their affiliation; everyone knows that most Callen of Datda have trained extensively as assassins and spies.

Dathedain (**dath**-heh-**dane**)**:** Followers of the god Datda.

Desert sage: A tree-sized plant resembling ordinary garden sage, which has adapted for desert life; the leaves curl up during the day's heat into thick, needle-shaped rolls, and spread out in damp weather or at night. After a long drought, even a slight breeze will stir the dead leaves into a shivery, rattling sound. The dry wood gives off a pleasant aroma when burned, but the leaves are not edible. Often holds large nests of blood-spiders and micru.

Desert truce: An agreement to work together for mutual survival in a hostile environment; ends immediately upon reaching safety.

Devil-tree: A tree largely found in southern wastelands, with deeply fissured bark, wildly twisted branches, and semi-soft needle-style leaves; cones are bright red and poisonous to humans, but attract a variety of wildlife. The wood does not burn easily and gives off a nasty smoke.

Druu (dreww)**:** Master drummer. Must understand and be able to use each of the numerous percussion instruments known in the south.

Eki (**eh**-key)**:** One of the Four Gods of the Northern Church pantheon; represents Wind. She is considered to be the most evil of the Northern gods, and her good nature is rarely appealed to, for her favors carry a heavy price. Her strength is that of the air and clouds. She is deceitful and often malicious. Thieves often call on her for protection.

Eo (**ee**-hoh)**:** Teyanain-specific word signifying emptiness, non-existence.

Esthit (**ess**-thitt)**:** A drug originally developed by the ketarches, whose use has altered significantly over the years.

Estiqi (est-**eek**-ee)**:** A liqueur made from esthit; lowers boundaries and dulls the senses. Used, in theory, to help "stuck" desert lords (i.e., desert lords resisting the transition to their altered natures) open fully to their new abilities. Tends to have an aphrodisiac side effect. The actual effects of estiqi vary by individual and can be unpredictable.

Fii (fee)**:** The teyanain (and thus vastly more complicated) version of *thio.*

Four Gods: The pantheon of the Northern Church; Eki (Wind), Payti (Fire), Syrta (Earth), and Wae (Water). Each has a dual nature (good/evil), and the Church teaches that mankind must ever be careful not to provoke the "evil" side.

Fours: street slang term for devout followers of the Northern Church.

Furun (**fuhr**-roon)**:** Chabi game piece representing money. Shaped like a coin, the furun may move one square in any direction once unlocked; it may only be unlocked by a grey shassen jumping over it.

Gods'-glory Flower: A common vine in the humid areas of the southlands; sports large, funnel-shaped flowers in an infinite variety of colors and blooming patterns (morning, evening, middle of the night).

H'na (**heh**-^hna)**:** A teyanain-peculiar word (generally only pronounceable by the teyanain, as well), of obscure derivation and meaning, even to loremasters. Probably ties into an old story or joke regarding the tendency of outsiders to fear anything teyanain.

Ha'bit vanaa (hah-^**beet** vah-**nahh**)**:** Rough translation: *Forgive your servant's offenses.* A very old and largely abandoned phrase, once used to indicate total submission/apology for wrongs done to a ha'ra'ha.

Ha'inn (properly: hah-^**inn**; more commonly: **high**-inn)**:** Lit. translation: *Honored One.* Reserved for ha'ra'hain.

Ha'inn-va (high-**inn**-vah)**:** Very old and abandoned phrase indicating total submission to the will of a ha'ra'ha.

Ha'ra'ha (hah-**^rah**-^hah); plural **ha'ra'hain** (hah-^rah-^**hayn**)**:** Person of mixed blood (human and ha'rethe).

Ha'ra'hain (hah-^rah-^**hayn**)**:** Plural of **ha'ra'ha**.

Ha'rai'nain (hah-^ray-**nayn**)**:** Plural of **ha'rai'nin**.

Ha'rai'nin (hah-**^ray**-nin); plural **ha'rai'nain** (hah-^ray-**nayn**)**:** One who has dedicated his or her life to serving the ha'reye.

Ha'rethe (hah-**^reth**-ay); plural **ha'reye** (hah-**^ray**)**:** Lit. translation: *golden eyes*. An ancient race, predating humanity.

Ha'reye (hah-^ray)**:** Plural of ha'rethe.

Ha'reye-kin (hah-**^ray**-kin); alt. **true-ha'rai'nin** (hah-**^hray**-nin)**:** 1. A human who has spent so much time around the ha'reye that he or she has changed physically; no longer human, a ha'rai'nin more closely resembles a lesser ha'ra'ha. 2. A lesser ha'ra'ha who has spent so much time among the ha'reye that it is growing into greater powers. Both are extremely exceptional; at this time, only one human qualifies as the first and only one ha'ra'ha qualifies as the second.

Hackerwood: The enormous swath of unexplored forest north of Bright Bay. There is only one road through it; attempts to create alternate routes have ended badly.

Hai-katihe (high-kat-**tea**)**:** Rough translation: *those who serve (intimately) a ha'ra'ha*. No longer in common use.

Hanna-aerst-yin (hah-**nahh** ayrst **yin**)**:** Rough translation: *binding a bird in a cage of chains*. A rare and powerful teyanain marriage ceremony, only performed for people of extreme importance among the teyanain. Both *aerst* and *yin* are words peculiar to the teyanain dialect, and their exact meanings vary by context.

Hask: Lit. translation: *cast out*. Implications of dishonor, of betrayal, of irrevocable shame.

Hith (hithh)**:** Tiny red carnivorous beetles, typically used on human corpses in the southlands to reduce the body to a bundle of clean bones that easily fit into a ceremonial box. Also see *kop*.

Hopam (**hoh**-pahm)**:** Literal translation: *dream house*. Generally used to refer to establishments that provide various illicit but relatively minor narcotics and hallucinogens, such as aesa and esthit.

Iii-naa tarren, iii-nas lalien, iii-be salalae (**eee**-nah tar-**ren**, **eee**-nahs **lah**-lee-en, **eee**-beh sah-**lah**-lay)**:** Rough translation: *We serve the gods, the gods smile on us, we survive under the glory of the gods*. Implications of submission, sacrifice, loss of selfhood in service of the divine.

Iishin (**eee**-eee-shinn)**:** Master acrobat; prominently used as a frontman in southern parades and processionals.

Ish (**isshh**)**:** Prefix indicating feminine/female aspects.

Ishrai (**Ish**-wry)**:** One of the three gods honored in the southlands; represents the positive / feminine / birth energies. She is also connected to the season of spring, the color green, and the emotion of love.

Ishraidain (ishh-wry-**dane**)**:** Women serving penance for various crimes, under the protection of Ishrai.

Ishrait (ishh-**rate**)**:** High priestess of Ishrai.

Itibi (ih-**tih**-bee)**:** A small, high-pitched drum; generally held in one hand and struck with a light striker.

Itna tarnen, itnas talien, itnabe shalla (**it**-nah tahr-**nehn**, **it**-nahs **tah**-lee-en, it-**nah**-bay **shah**-lah)**:** Rough translation: *We empty ourselves into the gods, the gods pour themselves into us, glory be to the gods.* Implications of partnership, gods and man giving to one another in service of building a better world.

Jacau-drum (jack-**how** drum)**:** A large drum, generally stationary, with a wide head; produces a deep, booming tone. Originally covered with the skin of unusually large asp-jacaus, thus the name. Today these drums are usually made with cow, deer, horse, or goat skins, depending on how rich the owner is. Also called a shaska drum; only experts make a distinction between the two styles.

Jii (geee)**:** Gifters; part of southern processionals and parades, *jii* toss candies and small coins to the watching crowds. Catching a *jii*-flung gift is considered a sign of good luck for the rest of the day.

Jungles: Also called *Forbidden Jungles.* An area of tropical rainforest far to the south where the majority of the surviving ha'reye and their human devotees live. Outsiders are not permitted to enter.

Justice-right: The right of a desert lord to intervene in a situation and see it resolved according to his own opinion of justice.

Ka (kah): Honored (generic term).

Ka-s'a (kah-ss-**^ah):** Honored lady (generic term).

Ka-s'eias (kah-ss-**^ey-**as)**:** Honored (mixed gender) group (generic term).

Kaen (kay-en)**:** Honored leader/supreme authority.

Kaenic (kay-nick)**:** Southern term for the most common Northern Kingdom dialect.

Kaenoz (kay-nohz)**:** Rough translation: *kingdom.*

Kahar (kay-har)**:** Pyramid-shaped chabi game piece representing wind. These pieces move in straight lines.

Kain (cain)**:** Rough translation: *servant's child;* honorable connotation, able to formally claim the relevant bloodline, and even inherit if more direct heirs are no longer eligible/available. The similarity between this and *kaen* makes the pronunciation, in this instance, very important; and yet, because kaens were seen as servants of their people, there is a certain blurring here as well. While it is not exactly *polite* to pronounce *kaen* as *kain,* only a person looking for an insult will take exception to the mispronunciation if it is an honest dialectic error rather than a deliberate attempt at offense.

Kath (kath): Rough translation: *servant.* Used with a variety of modifiers to indicate occupation and status; *s'a-dinne kath* indicates a kitchen or dining hall servant; *s'a kathalle* indicates a cleaning servant. When used in conjunction with *kath,* the female gender indicator (*s'a*) does not imply a female servant, but rather the concept of serving. The term *katha village,* while in common usage, is grammatically incorrect: it should properly be *va-kathe*, "village of intimate services."

Kathain (kath-**ayn**)**:** Personal servants to a desert lord; generally offered to visiting desert lords as a courtesy, and considered an essential part of a new desert lord's staff for at least the first two years. Duties range from amusing their lord with playful games to more intimate services. This peculiar word is the same in both singular and plural forms, (i.e.: *Tanavin was a kathain; The four kathain left the room; The kathain's room was small.*)

Katheele (kath-**eel**)**,** singular *kathalle* (kath-**all**-eh)**:** Rough translation: *spy through seduction*. An honorable profession, in the southlands. Katheele are generally trained as spies and assassins as well as two or three minor specialties such as herbalist or etiquette master. They must maintain a keen understanding of current politics. They never act alone, but serve a specific Family or individual. Toscin Family trains the bulk of katheele, but at some point in their training, katheele decide whom they wish to serve. For their chosen master to refuse their service is nearly unheard of and incredibly rude.

Katihe (kat-**tea**)**:** Rough translation: *honorable intimacy*; obscure term rarely used in modern times.

Ke (**keh**)**:** Prefix or suffix indicating masculine/male aspects.

Ketarch (**kee**-tarsch)**:** Organized groups of healers in the south who focus on preserving old healing lore and researching new ways of healing.

Kichi biti nahn (**kee**-chee **biht**-ee **non**)**:** Teyanain specific phrase. Rough translation: *Your grace saves me from regret*. Used in ceremonies to indicate acceptance by victor of the submission of their opponent.

Kii tafli (kee **taph**-lee)**:** Teyanain specific phrase. Rough translation: *My body for your safety*. Used in ceremonies to indicate submission to the victor.

Kop (khop)**:** A wooden box crafted and sanctified to hold human remains. They are generally no more than three feet long and a foot wide. Also see *hith*.

L'chin (lee-^**kin**)**:** A teyanain-peculiar word (and generally only pronounceable by a teyanain, as well) of obscure derivation and meaning, even to loremasters. Probably ties into an old story or joke among the teyanain involving the consequences of leading an interesting life.

Loremaster: Combination historian, genealogist, and researcher; as a group, one of the major political forces behind the scenes in the southlands. Every Family has (or is supposed to have) a group of loremasters resident.

Louin (loo-een)**:** Lit. translation: *honored representative*. Largely used during transitional periods, when a newcomer has not yet taken his new station but must be granted some formal title for the sake of status.

Mahadrae (mah-**hahd**-ray)**:** Rough translation: *chosen mother of the free people*. Proper title for the female Head of Aerthraim Family. A male leader would be *mahadran*; but that version has not been used for quite some time.

Metara (met-**tarrah**)**:** an herbal blend unique to the southlands. Believed to increase libido and lower inhibitions. Usually added in with a strongly flavored tea.

Micru (mick-**rue**)**:** Rough translation: *small death*; a small, black and tan striped viper found in rocky desert areas, whose poison is instantly fatal to large animals. Also the call-name of a member of the Hidden Cadre.

Mocker: The lead figure in a southern drum line; usually female. She finds anything and everything to make fun of during a procession, then creates songs (called *mokoi*) afterward and spreads them far and wide.

Nu-s'e (**noo**-ss-**^eh**)**:** Honored man of the south (female is *nu-s'a*); generic honorific in the absence of specific indicators.

Numaina (noo-**main**-ah); plural **numainiae** (noo-main-**ay**)**:** Proper title for a Scratha Family ruler.

Oamver (ohm-**vehr**)**:** Rough translation: *negotiation table*. Ceremonial item of furniture, brought to all southland meetings; what is on the table at the beginning of the meeting has tremendous symbolic value. (During Scratha Conclave, the central table served as the oamver, and the fact that it was empty reflected a state of temporary truce among those normally at odds).

Oiu (ooh-**ee**-ooh)**:** 1. The number *four* (southern). 2. A complex, and usually rather large, four-pipe instrument common to the southlands. Like *alli* and *bene*, it is normally made of wood.

Pahenna (pah-**hen**-nah)**:** Rough translation: *stay out of my business, I know what I'm doing*.

Payti (**pay**-tee)**:** One of the Four Gods of the Northern Church pantheon; represents Fire. Payti's "kind" incarnation is usually pictured as a short, plump man, with ruddy cheeks and a contagious cheeriness. In Payti's "dark" incarnation, the form is that of a tall, beautiful woman with a seductive gaze that bewitches all men who gaze upon her to their destruction. Payti's strength is that of the sun and the flame.

Peh-tenez (**pay**-tehn-**ehz**)**:** A negotiation ceremony held over tea in which only truth may be spoken and the conversation may not be disclosed to those not a part of it. Largely a teyanain protocol, but some other Families use it when they wish to seem very serious about a political arrangement. Only the teyanain, ironically, can be fully trusted to hold to the original, sacred nature of the ceremony; to outsiders, it's largely a show, but teyanain will be absolutely honest during a true peh-tenez, and consider any deceit or breach of protocol a killing offense.

Protector: Not all fortresses are protected by full ha'reye any longer; some are occupied by first or second generation ha'ra'hain. Those aware of the distinction tend to use the term 'protector' to refer to those lesser ha'ra'hain bound to serve a particular Fortress.

Purge, The: Recent time of trouble in the northern kingdom, marked by lunatic kings, sociopathic advisors, and numerous very bad decisions all around. The political relationship between northern kingdom and the various southern desert Families is still recovering.

Qisani (key-**sahn**-nee)**:** A rocky cavern complex in the southern desert, which was given, under a Conclave decision, to the Callen of Ishrai many years ago as a haven of their own. All the desert Families contribute to supporting the Qisani. The followers of Datda and Comos also have central havens, but they are more secretive about the locations. Blood trials conducted at any of the havens are considered the hardest of all possible.

Ravann (rah-**van**; alt., rah-**vahn**)**:** Similar to lavender in appearance and scent, but tends towards a darker leaf color, white flowers, and a slightly more acrid odor; only found south of Water's End, largely around the Aerthraim Fortress lands. Adapted for desert living, very hardy, but does not transplant well.

Reeven (**ree**-vehn)**:** A ghost that seeks to possess living humans whenever possible. Most dangerous during the dark of the moon, and generally driven away by (regional variances in the tale) the scent of lavender, rosemary, or pine. Usually strong-willed people, especially women, are seen as potential reeven after their death; the theory being that such people are be more likely to fight off the final journey into the afterlife, so as not to lose their earthly power.

S'a / S'e / S'ieas / S'ii: Respectful address designators, analogous to *sir* and *madam*; specific to gender, and frequently parts of complex and highly specific expressions of relationship between the speaker and the person being addressed.

S'a (ss-^**ah**)**:** feminine
S'e (ss-^**eh**)**:** masculine
S'ieas (ss-^**eh**-ahs)**:** a group of mixed gender
S'ii (ss-^**ee**)**:** neuter; generally used to address a eunuch.

Sa'ad hii (sah^**had** hee)**:** Rough translation: *blood hunt*. Indicates that the one hunting will not be turned aside except by his or her own death, and that the prey will likely not survive being found.

S'e-kath (ss^**eh kah**th)**:** Personal servant to the lord of a fortress. The best are highly trained in scholarship, politics, and combat. Extremely well respected and dangerous. Used as prefix title or as descriptive: e.g. s'e-kath Segnilious; the s'e-kath looked around.

S'iope (s-**^igh-o**-pay)**:** Lit. translation: *beloved of the gods*; implications of being neuter, all energy devoted to the gods. Term used to refer to the priests of the Northern Church. Disrespectful nickname: soapy.

Sai-ch'nain (say-cha-^**nayn**)**:** Lit. translation: *child of blood.* A creature comprised of multiple intelligent lives, melded together via a brutally painful process to create a completely obedient servant to a ha'rethe. Extremely difficult to create and immensely dangerous once unleashed.

Saishe-pais (**say**-shh-**paws**; alt. **say**-she-**pays**)**:** An expression of heartfelt gratitude, indicating that the one so addressed has shown great honor in his/her actions.

Sanahair (sahn-ah-**hair**)**:** Lit. translation: *shit boy.* The word ties into an obscure southern joke about kicking the person ranked just below you until there's only the chamber-pot contents left to kick.

Sayek-teth (**say**-hek-te**hth**)**:** Rough translation: *Blood oath.* A term unique to the teyanain. Means an agreement which, once sworn, gives an outsider limited claim to be treated as a teyanain himself, including gaining the absolute protection of the teyanain—for as long as he continues to protect/serve the terms of the agreement.

Sessii ta-karne, I shha (Sessy tah-carney, ee shh-ha)**:** rough translation: *You noxious, useless (castrated) little prick!*

Setaka, senaca (seht-**tah**-kah, sehn-**nah**-khah)**:** Lit. translation: *like father, like son.*

Shabaca (shah-**bah**-kah)**:** A large dried gourd or cactus filled with pebbles or dried beans to make a rattle; common musical instrument in the southlands.

Shall (**shawl**)**:** A temporary, portable desert shelter.

Shaska (shass-kahh)**:** A large kettledrum, occasionally used in processionals, but mostly placed on tripod stands for in-place use. Also called a jacau-drum; only experts make a distinction between the two styles.

Shassen (**shass**-sen)**:** Chabi game piece representing goods. Cubic in shape, the shassen moves one to three spaces in a straight line; it may never move diagonally or jump another piece, with the singular exception of unlocking the furun.

Shennth: Rough translation: *domain.* Used to indicate the sphere of influence/power of a specific individual.

Shay-nin (**shay**-neen)**:** Rough translation: *honored master spy.* Used to indicate a person who has achieved remarkable skill in the various arts of subterfuge, assassination, and intelligence-gathering, and who may be trusted to act with the highest personal and professional honor at all times.

Sheth-hinn (shethh-**hnn**)**:** Assassin.

Shivii (shee-vee)**:** Formal wear for many southern men; resembles an ankle-length skirt, usually silk, slit on each side up to just above the knee. Sometimes (incorrectly) used to refer to a more casual wrap-around cloth used by both men and women.

Sionno (see-**oh**-noh)**:** Respectful term for a priest of the Northern Church, generally used by fellow priests or devotees, rather than the *s'iope* that "outsiders" use.

Split, The: A time of great chaos and dissension, during which humanity and the ha'reye renegotiated the Agreement and much knowledge was lost.

Stibik (**stih**-bic)**:** A substance developed by the ketarches that temporarily weakens ha'ra'hain and ha'reye. Usually found in the form of a white powder, but sometimes as a concentrated, corrosive oil. It is illegal to bring stibik onto the land of an active ha'rethe; an even greater offense to use against a ha'ra'ha. Stibik was banned and ordered completely destroyed years ago; the ketarches, ever independent-minded, disobeyed the order.

Su-s'a (sue-ss-**^ah**)**:** Northern lady.

Suka: A sweet syrup used in various candies and desserts, mostly in the southlands.

Syrta (**seer**-tah)**:** One of the Four Gods of the Northern Church pantheon; represents Earth. In his "good" incarnation, he is described as a leafy tree in spring or summer; when provoked to evil, he takes the form of a twisted, winter-stripped tree. He is credited with creating mankind and placing them in dominion over all beasts and growing things.

Ta (**tah**)**:** Prefix implying masculine aspects; usually involved in insults (see **ta'karne**).

Ta feth kii (**tah** fethh **key**)**:** Rough translation: *stop shitting around; cut the crap*. Reference to bodily functions is a particularly effective insult against the teyanain, who consider something like this a far worse insult than being called, for instance, bastards. (Especially since most of them know their lineage six generations back on both sides.)

Ta-karne (tah-**carn**-ay)**:** Insult. Rough translation: *asshole.*

Talloi (tah-**loy**)**:** Flamboyant southern dance in which the dancer's shoes contain a small "clacker," making for a noisy and attention-getting performance.

Ta-neka (tah-**neek**-ah)**:** Insult; female version of *ta-karne.*

Tas-shadata (**tahz**-shah-**dah**-ta)**:** Rough translation: *fool, coward, idiot.*

Taska (**task**-ah; alt. **tah**-skah)**:** Courier and guide.

Tath-shinn: Rough translation: *ghost of a female madwoman/assassin/murderer*; implies that a woman who would kill is insane, overly male, and impossible to handle even after death. Probably originated in the lower southwestern coastline region, among the Shakain. In the upper northlands, a similar creature is called a *shia-banse*: the ghost of a woman who died while under the influence of evil.

Te (**teh**)**:** Prefix indicating formality and honor; no gender.

Telabat-nia-tabalet (**tehl**-lah-baht **nee**-yah tahb-ah-**leht**)**:** Rough translation: *play the game that is on the table.* Like many southern sayings, it involves a play on words; in this case, *telabat,* the game one is playing at the moment, and *tabalet,* the table one at which is currently sitting. *Nia* is a linking verb that has no real definition in and of itself; it simply puts the words to either side of it into harness, as it were.

Telle (**tel**-lay)**:** teyanain word for "holy" or "sacred."

Teth-kavit (tehth-**kah**-vitt)**:** Lit. translation: *Gods hold you, and blessings to your strength.*

Teuthin (**too**-thin)**:** Rough translation: *meeting place.* Any agreed-upon neutral ground where all are seen as equal and violence is forbidden. Generally implies the presence of nobles of some rank.

Teyanin (**tay-**ah-nin); plural: **teyanain** (tay-ah-**nayn**)**:** A very old, small tribe which retreated to the mountains of the Horn after the Split. Originally the judges and law determiners of the desert, they're now considered the guardians of the Horn.

Teyantin (tey-**ahnt**-in; alt: **teyantan**)**:** Personal manservant to the head of the teyanain. Equivalent to what other Families call a *s'e-kath.* Used either as a last name: e.g. Dinas Teyantin, or as a title: e.g. My Teyantin will help us. Always capitalized.

Tey-b'tibik (tey-bah-^**ktih**-bick)**:** Rough translation: *binding powder.* A long-banned formula for a substance that significantly weakens ha'ra'hain and seriously injures ha'reye.

Teyn-shatha hadinn (**teyn-shah**-thah hah-**dinn**)**:** Lit. translation: *justice's cold bite.* Specifically refers to the teyanain preference for serving up revenge long after the offending party has forgotten the insult.

Tharr (thahrr)**:** Rough translation: *the invisible ones.* A derogatory term used by the ha'reye and ha'ra'hain to indicate those humans who do not directly "serve" them (in essence, everyone but desert lords).

Thass (**tass**; alt. **thass**)**:** A person with great status, beyond even noble rank.

That in it: Street-slang for *involved;* politically, not personally.

Thii/Thio (**thee**-oh)**:** Different words for *status,* the former indicating lower-class ranking, the latter a noble ranking.

Thopuh (**thoh**-poo)**:** Lit. translation: *blood of victory.* Also the name of a style of tea production currently monopolized by F'Heing. Thopuh tea grows stronger, more complexly flavored, and more valuable with proper aging.

Tibi (**tee**-bee)**:** a shallow oval bowl usually carried by travelers in the south; food is scooped from a communal bowl into one's own tibi.

Tinchi (**tinn**-chee)**:** An elegant if cumbersome southern tea ceremony, involving a large cooking table and numerous complex rules.

Tine (tyne)**:** Rough translation: *whore's child;* implication of dishonor.

Toi, te hoethra (**toy**, **teh hoe**-thrah)**:** Lit. translation: *I swear to you I am speaking truth.*

Tvit (tvhit)**:** Typical Stone Islands parting; derived from *teth-kavit*.

Tvith (tvitth)**:** Rough translation: *circumcised;* often used, in some of the rougher areas of the southlands, as an insult to a man's masculinity.

Ugren (**oo**-ghren)**:** a very rare universal bonding mixture; also used in the southlands to imply unbreakable permanence in an arrangement or situation.

Va (vah)**:** a rigid frame covered with a thick, stretched hide, partially filled with grit or sand; a *va* is generally held in the hands and rocked back and forth to produce an ocean wave-like, *shhhh*ing sound.

Vaa ha'inn-va ne (vah-**ah** high-^**inn**-vah **neh**)**:** Rough translation: *Master, I am yours.* Formal phrase of total submission from a very old version of the southern tongue. Almost entirely forgotten in the modern era.

W'schar'ch (wah-^**skarr**-^ack)**:** A southern discipline, most common along the west coast, that focuses on lucid dreaming and recall for later analysis. Experts in w'schar'ch often serve as advisors to important nobility and have been known to influence political policy with their interpretations.

Wae (**way**)**:** One of the Four Gods of the Northern Church pantheon; represents Water. Wae can take any form; in his kindly incarnation, he is often drawn as a great, wavering blue horse made from the coldest water of the deeps. His dark side is depicted in forms with a dark, shiny surface, like treacherous black ice—often a snake is drawn for this. Wae's strength is that of the waters, both still and quick, and the mountain glaciers.

Wailer: Street-slang for the tath-shinn.

Ways, the: A series of passages linking areas with an active ha'reye or ha'ra'hain presence. Travel through these passages generally requires the active cooperation of a ha'rethe or ha'ra'ha, and is essentially instantaneous regardless of intervening distance.

Yin: Rough translation: *unbreakable commitment, cage,* or *permanence of spirit.* Teyanain word; its meaning changes depending on context.

About the Author

Leona Wisoker writes a variety of speculative fiction, from experimental to horror, from fantasy to science fiction. She also loves to teach, edit, read, and drink coffee. In her less-than-abundant spare time, she is a wild garden warrior, an adventurous cook, and a champion catnapper, especially if sunbeams are available.

Visit her website at www.leonawisoker.com for behind the scenes information, free fiction, and news on upcoming releases and ongoing projects.

You can also find Leona on Twitter: @leonawisoker, but be warned that a great deal of her feed is political these days.

More books from Leona Wisoker are available at:

www.ReAnimus.com/store/?author=Leona Wisoker

ReAnimus Press

Breathing Life into Great Books

If you enjoyed this book we hope you'll tell others or write a review! We also invite you to subscribe to our newsletter to learn about our new releases and join our affiliate program (where you earn 12% of sales you recommend) at www.ReAnimus.com.

Here are more ebooks you'll enjoy from ReAnimus Press, available from ReAnimus Press's web site, Amazon.com, bn.com, etc.:

Secrets of the Sands, by Leona Wisoker

Info/buy:

Book 1 of the Children of the Desert. Out on the sands, the harsh glare of the sun reveals more about the world—and themselves—than they ever wanted to know.

Guardians of the Desert, by Leona Wisoker

Info/buy:

Book 2 of the Children of the Desert series.

Bells of the Kingdom, by Leona Wisoker

Info/buy:

Book 3 of the Children of the Desert series. To find redemption, they must risk their sanity—and their souls.

Fires of the Desert, by Leona Wisoker

Info/buy:

Book 4 of the Children of the Desert series. Sometimes, love just gets in the way.

Servants of the Sands, by Leona Wisoker

Info/buy:

The time for secrets is over, and the world will never be the same.

Beyond the Hedge, by Roby James

Info/buy:

A executive woman who has never had time for love stumbles into a land of magic, 200 years in the past.

A Song of Awakening, by Roby James

Info/buy:

A monumental, richly romantic historical with a subtle touch of fantasy.

The Soldier's Daughter, by Roby James

Info/buy:

Sir William Wallace, the Scots hero, left his daughter three things...

In Hollow Lands, by Sophie Masson

Info/buy:

Lured into the world of the magical korrigans, young twins Tiphaine and Gromer may never break their enchantment.

The Gilded Basilisk, by Chet Gottfried

Info/buy:

Add a basilisk, a dragon, and weirdragons to the mix-up of a theft going from bad to worse: Friends become enemies and enemies friends, wars loom, and the intrigues threaten the fate of two kingdoms.

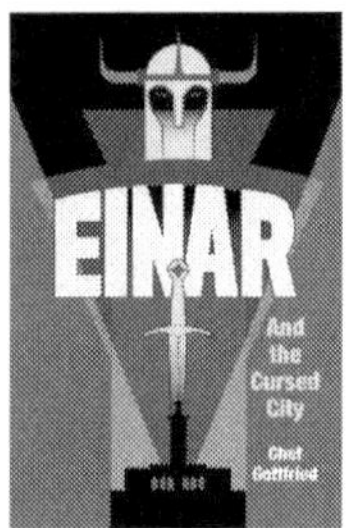

Einar and the Cursed City, by Chet Gottfried

Info/buy:

Sixteen-year-old Einar enters Jorghaven for dueling and desserts, but a curse has changed everyone except Barbara Bloodbath, who needs his help to free the city!

The Cure for Everything, by Severna Park

Info/buy:

Finding the cure for all diseases comes with a heavy price. Nebula Award winner!

When Grandfather Journeys Into Winter, by Craig Strete

Info/buy:

A young Indian boy struggles to accept his grandfather's rapidly approaching death.

Ghosts of Engines Past, by Sean McMullen

Info/buy:

Award winning steampunk from a master!

Colours of the Soul, by Sean McMullen

Info/buy:

Why are cheetahs the most perfect of creatures? Besides because they're cats, that is... Cool, mind-blowing stories from a master.

American Goliath, by Harvey Jacobs

Info/buy:

The (mostly!) true story of America's greatest hoax, with a fantastic(al) twist from an award-winning author. [World Fantasy Award finalist!] "An inspired novel."—TIME Magazine. "A masterpiece...arguably this year's best novel."—Kirkus Reviews.

Kafka's Uncle and Other Strange Tales, by Bruce Taylor

Info/buy:

An alternate universe? A different dimension? The "id" of America?

The Science of Middle-earth, by Henry Gee

Info/buy:

How did Frodo's mithril coat ward off the fatal blow of an orc? Can Balrogs fly? Nature editor Dr. Henry Gee explains how. A must-read for Tolkien fans.

The Exiles Trilogy, by Ben Bova

Info/buy:

When all the best of Earth's scientists are exiled to a space station, they decide to embark on an even grander adventure to the stars. An epic trilogy in one volume.

The Star Conquerors (Standard Edition), by Ben Bova

Info/buy:

Six time Hugo winner Ben Bova's most sought-after novel is back in print!

Escape!, by Ben Bova

Info/buy:

No end to Danny's sentence, watched by a sentient computer, and no way out of the escape-proof prison, there was only one thing to do...

Colony, by Ben Bova

Info/buy:

Island One is a celestial utopia, and David Adams is its most perfect creation. But David is a prisoner, destined to spend his life in an island-sized cylinder orbiting a doomed home planet. David has a plan—one that will ultimately save humanity... or destroy it.

The Kinsman Saga, by Ben Bova

Info/buy:

Chet Kinsman is an astronaut ace who has done everything in space—including committing the first murder. Kinsman has to confront his hidden past and decide Earth's destiny, in a desperate countdown to nuclear annihilation.

Star Watchmen, by Ben Bova

Info/buy:

Mankind rules a giant galactic empire, but not all the worlds are pleased. Can the Star Watch prevent a revolt?

As on a Darkling Plain, by Ben Bova

Info/buy:

Dr. Sidney Lee races against time to prevent the huge alien machines on Titan from destroying mankind.

Test of Fire, by Ben Bova

Info/buy:

A small group of survivors fight to rebuild civilization after the Earth is devastated by a huge solar flare.

The Weathermakers, by Ben Bova

Info/buy:

After conquering everything else, the last frontier was... controlling Mother Nature! By the award-winning hard SF author of the Grand Tour series.

The Dueling Machine, by Ben Bova

Info/buy:

Civilized, harmless virtual reality dueling has replaced all physical conflict — everything from punching someone over a personal insult to interstellar warfare... until a madman dictator of a small empire finds a way to cheat, and use the dueling machine to take over the galaxy!

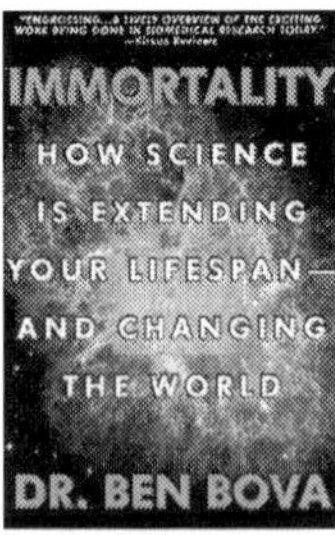

Immortality, by Ben Bova

Info/buy:

Dr. Bova explores the future effects of science and technology on the human life span. Death will no longer be the inevitable end of life.

Space Travel - A Science Fiction Writer's Guide, by Ben Bova

Info/buy:

An indispensible tool for all science fiction writers, Space Travel explains the science you need to help you make your fiction plausible.

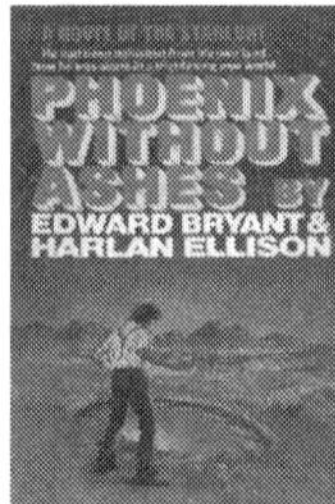

Phoenix Without Ashes, by Harlan Ellison and Edward Bryant

Info/buy:

Co-written with Harlan Ellison and based on the award-winning script, the story of mankind's last salvation gone awry.

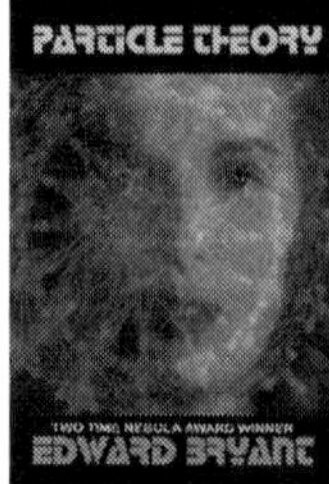

Particle Theory, by Edward Bryant

Info/buy:

Particle Theory by Edward Bryant : A collection of many of Ed's best works, including two Nebula Award winning short stories.

Shadrach in the Furnace, by Robert Silverberg

Info/buy:

Meet the new Khan! Soon to be immortal... A Hugo and Nebula Award Finalist novel from a Grand Master of science fiction.

Commencement, by Roby James

Info/buy:

The Sting was what made Ronica McBride special—now she was crashed on an unknown planet without it.

Bloom, by Wil McCarthy

Info/buy:

In 2106, microscopic machine/creatures escape their creators to populate the inner solar system with a wild, deadly ecology all their own, pushing the tattered remnants of humanity out into the cold and dark of the outer planets. Seven astronauts must embark on mankind's boldest venture yet—the perilous journey home to infected Earth!

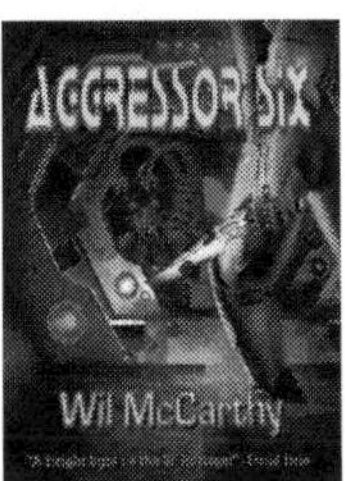

Aggressor Six, by Wil McCarthy

Info/buy:

An alien armada from the center of Orion makes its deadly way through the galaxy, destroying all human life in the process, and only Marine Corporal Kenneth Jonson and the Aggressor Six team can stop the onslaught.

Murder in the Solid State, by Wil McCarthy

Info/buy:

David Sanger, an ambitious young physicist, attends a party at which a pompous older scientist, who just happens to have thwarted the younger man's innovative ideas, is murdered. Suddenly it is not just David's career, but his life that is at stake. Are his ideas that important? Who's out to stop David from changing the world?

Flies from the Amber, by Wil McCarthy

Info/buy:

Forty light years from earth, the colonists on the world of Unua have somehow managed to keep civilization struggling on, despite twice daily earthquakes...

Made in the USA
Middletown, DE
07 March 2024

50362950R00205